Praise for Linda O. Johnston

"I_____ the
Alph_____ ikable
character, both sexy and strong, and Kristine's
clever moves in crisis show an intelligence
that will appeal to readers."
—*RT Book Reviews* on *Undercover Wolf*

"Ms. Johnston has a winner on her hands with
this installment of the Alpha Force series."
—*Fresh Fiction* on *Undercover Wolf*

"*Back to Life* is a crafty tale,
where the unseen paranormal element
packs a powerful punch. Ms. Johnston gives
readers a strong romantic suspense with life
or death situations, and adds a sizzling dose of
chemistry to heat up the pages."
—*Darque Reviews*

Praise for Alexis Morgan

"The spellbinding combination of passionate
desire, material consequences and the
supernatural make *Vampire Vendetta* totally
captivating throughout every enthralling scene."
—*Romance*

"This book was a quick, fun, steamy and
suspenseful read and I would ____ ___ __end it to
_____ption

"Savag_____ mantic
thriller..._____ onderful
job _____ and
I thoroughly enjoyed this book!"
—*Fresh Fiction*

LINDA O. JOHNSTON

loves to write. More than one genre at a time? That's part of the fun. While honing her writing skills, she started working in advertising and public relations, then became a lawyer…and still enjoys writing contracts. Linda's first published fiction novel appeared in *Ellery Queen's Mystery Magazine* and won a Robert L. Fish Memorial Award for Best First Mystery Short Story of the Year. It was the beginning of her versatile fiction-writing career. Linda now spends most of her time creating memorable tales of paranormal romance and mystery. Linda lives in the Hollywood Hills with her husband and two Cavalier King Charles spaniels. Visit her at her website, www.lindaojohnston.com.

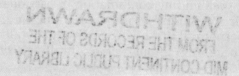

LINDA O. JOHNSTON

AND

USA TODAY Bestselling Author

ALEXIS MORGAN

Untamed Wolf

and

Immortal Cowboy

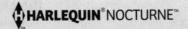

Recycling programs
for this product may
not exist in your area.

ISBN-13: 978-0-373-60638-2

UNTAMED WOLF AND IMMORTAL COWBOY

Copyright © 2014 by Harlequin Books S.A.

The publisher acknowledges the copyright holders
of the individual works as follows:

UNTAMED WOLF
Copyright © 2014 by Linda O. Johnston

IMMORTAL COWBOY
Copyright © 2014 by Patricia L. Pritchard

Printed in U.S.A.

CONTENTS

UNTAMED WOLF

Linda O. Johnston

Untamed Wolf is dedicated to wolves, real and shape-shifters. It's also dedicated to our military, covert and otherwise. It's dedicated to Maryland, including the Eastern Shore and the area south of Baltimore, where we visit often. Plus, it's dedicated to my friends and my readers…and, of course, to my husband, Fred.

And it's especially dedicated to Harlequin and the Nocturne series, its editors and most particularly my wonderful editor Allison Lyons. And last but definitely not least, it's dedicated to my excellent agent, Paige Wheeler of Folio Literary Management.

Chapter 1

Sara pulled her car up to the formidable black wrought-iron gate at Ft. Lukman. She had been driving her small hybrid for more than an hour from D.C. to this out-of-the-way military installation on Maryland's Eastern Shore.

Stopping at the security kiosk, she pulled her ID from the purse on the passenger seat. "Lieutenant Sara McLinder, reporting for duty," she told the guard, a tall man, wearing a standard camouflage uniform similar to the one Sara had on.

So far, nothing here looked different or surprising, no matter what Sara's superior officer, General Greg Yarrow, had suggested. Of course not.

Even so, maybe she should have waited until tomorrow, as the general had said. It was early evening already, and she wouldn't have much time to get settled.

On the other hand, it hadn't been an order, and Sara didn't like to delay. Facing new situations quickly and immediately was more to her liking than waiting.

"Is General Yarrow behind you, ma'am?" asked the soldier.

"The general will be here tomorrow," she said.

"Very good, ma'am." He looked over her identification and passed it back. "Everything looks in order. Welcome to Ft. Lukman, Lieutenant." The private saluted and the gate slid open, away from the car.

Sara saluted back. "Thank you," she said, then drove onto the base.

The general had provided her the layout in advance. She knew that the building comprising the Bachelor Officers' Quarters where she was to stay was to the right once she entered the base. That was where she headed. She was also aware that the cafeteria, not far from the living quarters, should be open late—a good thing. She hadn't stopped to eat on the way and was hungry.

Rather than pulling into the small enclosed garage, she parked in the open-air lot closest to the BOQ, finding a space at the far end, near a wall. She removed her suitcase on wheels from the trunk of her car. She had already been given a set of keys, so she had no problem either getting inside the functional-looking concrete building or into her apartment after taking the elevator up one floor.

Interestingly, or not, she didn't run into any other

people. Also a good thing, since she didn't really want to have a gabfest. Not now.

She didn't spend much time assessing the quarters where she would stay as long as the general kept them at this base. The place resembled a tiny one-bedroom apartment. That was good enough.

She was back outside in only a few minutes, walking in the remaining daylight along a sidewalk toward the cafeteria. As she neared it, she began to see people—others also in camo fatigues and thick-soled shoes similar to hers.

She wondered if she would be able to discern any differences between the two main units now present at Ft. Lukman. That was one of the reasons General Yarrow intended to station himself for a while at this base. He was in charge of Alpha Force, the special-ops unit that had been headquartered here for a few years. A new special-ops group, the Ultra Special Forces Team, had only been assigned here about a month ago to prepare for a highly classified and critically important team assignment with Alpha Force, and the general had heard about some friction between the two units.

He wanted to observe it—and, if necessary, make some changes.

Sara, as the primary aide assigned to General Yarrow, would be his eyes and ears and, if necessary, his mouth.

A group of four enlisted personnel—two men and two women—stood by the building's entrance. They stopped their conversation and saluted her, and she saluted back.

Interesting, since the general had said that things were fairly low-key and informal here at Ft. Lukman. These soldiers were therefore probably among the new arrivals.

The general had also hinted at a lot of other things about what went on at Ft. Lukman, none of which could be real. He liked to joke. His sense of humor was obviously quite different from hers. But she always admired how serious he appeared, even while jesting.

Inside an entry hall, Sara saw people going in and out through an open doorway in the middle—obviously the way into the cafeteria. The aroma of grilled meat grew stronger the closer she got, confirming her assumption.

The place was smaller than she'd anticipated for a base this size—a long room crowded with occupied tables. She headed toward the food line and picked out a hamburger and fries, then got a soft drink.

Once she paid, she looked around for an empty spot and saw none. She could get the meal to go, but for now was carrying a tray.

"Hi," said a female voice beside her. "You look lost." Sara turned and saw a woman in camo uniform with layered tawny hair and a big smile—another lieutenant, like her. "You wouldn't happen to be General Yarrow's aide, would you? We were told you'd be here tomorrow, but I don't think anyone else is expected right now."

Sara smiled. "Good guess. I'm Sara McLinder." She saw that her new companion's name tag read Hodell.

"I'm Colleen Hodell. Welcome. Here, we'll make room at our table for you." She gestured across the room where some other soldiers were seated around a table. "They're all Alpha Force members."

"Thanks," Sara said, and followed Colleen.

By the time they got there, someone had pulled an empty chair up to the table. Eight people were already seated around it. Sara smiled and nodded through the introductions. Interestingly, officers and enlisted personnel were all eating together.

Alpha Force protocol might be stronger around here than that of the regular military. Well, the general had warned her to expect things to be different from what she was used to, and some of it had to be real. If this fraternization made her uncomfortable, she wouldn't show it. Just being friendly wasn't prohibited under military regulations.

She placed her tray on the table and sat down.

"Welcome to Ft. Lukman," said the man seated beside her. According to his insignia, he was a sergeant. It wasn't the first time she'd heard a welcome, but this soldier's deep voice resonated with what sounded like irony. She looked at him, planning to maintain her rank and dignity.

"Thank you, Sergeant," she said brusquely, then looked away after noting what appeared to be sexual interest in his flashing golden eyes.

She must have imagined it. That would be the kind of fraternizing that was definitely forbidden under military regulations.

Although…well, she wasn't supposed to notice such things, but that sergeant was one handsome guy. He looked fairly young, maybe late twenties like her, but his short, black hair was flecked with silver. His features were sharp, his smile gorgeous and challenging— and she couldn't help noticing how broad his shoulders appeared beneath his camo shirt.

"Are you a new member of Alpha Force?" asked the sergeant, whose ID tag said his last name was Connell.

"Not exactly," she said. "I'm General Yarrow's aide, and I'll be here as long as he is. He is planning some exercises for Alpha Force while he's here."

"Then you're not—" The female sergeant across the table, whose name tag said Jessop, stopped speaking when Colleen elbowed her in the ribs.

"Has the general told you much about Alpha Force?" asked another man at the other side of the table. Sara nearly rose and saluted as she noticed his brass. He was a major. But the informality around here stopped her. Members of this unit might act all military elsewhere, but while eating dinner in this cafeteria they were all, apparently, just people.

"No, sir," Sara said. "Not really." Greg Yarrow had implied that things around here were quite different from the rest of the military without giving any credible explanation. He had even suggested that some of the members of Alpha Force went beyond any military skill she could ever imagine—because they were shapeshifters. Hah! She had worked with him long enough to anticipate and deal with that offbeat sense of humor of his. Despite his straight face, he knew better. He couldn't actually imagine she was a gullible subordinate who'd buy into that. Even so, he hadn't told her anything genuinely distinctive about the remote and covert unit. She figured she would learn the real differences here on the job.

She took a bite of her hamburger. Not bad for cafeteria food.

"Interesting," said the sergeant beside her. "Maybe I should show you around. Teach you what you need to know."

"Back off, Jason." That was the major. She squinted slightly to see his name tag.

It read Connell just like the sergeant's. Jason's.

Talk about interesting… Were the noncom and officer related?

That would be unusual—not that relatives had joined the military, but that both men would be in the same unit.

Was that somehow part of the reason that Alpha Force was considered different from other special-ops units?

Doubtful, but— Well, it made more sense than imagining that any of these very real-looking people could be shapeshifters, despite the general's teasing insinuations that they were. But just being related didn't make these soldiers distinctive, unless, perhaps, their family members had taught one another useful skills from youth that other people might not have. She couldn't think of a good example, though.

Maybe they really had taught one another how to shapeshift.

Not!

She took a sip of her drink and another bite of hamburger, then glanced back toward the sergeant to see whether he was, in fact, backing off.

The expression in his eyes was now filled with what looked like irony—even as he seemed to assess her from head to toe as she sat there. Oh, yes. He was a real man.

The gaze heated her insides. Made her sexually aware of the guy all over again.

Forget that, she cautioned herself. She was entirely military. Obeyed all orders and loved it.

No way would she allow herself even to notice if this soldier decided to play games with her.

Although, she realized, she already had noticed… and somehow liked it too much.

The rumors had been correct, Jason thought. Not that Major Drew Connell—no, not just major, but also Doctor Drew Connell, his cousin—told him much of anything around here.

Jason was just a peon. At least, because of his very special background that had led him to Alpha Force, he had been promoted to sergeant quickly and wasn't just a private.

In any event, Jason took a sip of soda water and continued to watch the gorgeous, hot—and unapproachable—lieutenant who had only arrived at Ft. Lukman that night. She obviously wasn't armed with the knowledge she needed to fit in here.

Those rumors said she was a very important aide to General Yarrow. So why hadn't her boss informed her about what she was in for at this base?

"So tell us something about yourself, Lieutenant," he said, addressing her. She was slender, with short, blond hair, a pale but perfect complexion, and high cheekbones that underscored eyes of an unusual blue-green shade. "Have you worked with General Yarrow long?" Those were nice, neutral, friendly questions, weren't they?

Jason was still on probation here. Probably would be for the rest of his life unless he figured out a workable way to resign.

On the other hand, he would be leaving behind some stuff he really liked along with the military regimen he despised. Some stuff he'd grown used to and didn't want to do without.

So he'd made his decision. He was staying—for the time being, at least.

He glanced at his cousin to make sure there was no angry scowl on his face, the result of every misstep Jason made in Drew's presence.

Fortunately, Drew just regarded the lovely lieutenant expectantly, as if awaiting her answer, too. So were all other Alpha Force members here—those who were like him, and those who weren't.

That was something damned special about this unit. They all worked together—and those who weren't like him were actually assigned to help those with the same characteristics as he had.

What would the lovely lieutenant think if she knew that half the members of Alpha Force were shapeshifters?

Oh, yeah, real dogs and other appropriate animals were kept on base as covers for them. Jason had even started helping to train the dogs in his spare time. But the reality was that Jason, and a lot of others, would be changing tonight under the full moon. By choice these days, which was especially cool.

"I've been in the army for nearly two years," the pretty officer was saying.

She was Lieutenant McLinder. Sara, she'd said during introductions. She didn't look as if she'd be thrilled for a mere sergeant to address her by her first name, even here.

"I've been an aide to General Yarrow for about five months," she continued.

Jason knew that the general had obligations in addition to being the commanding officer of Alpha Force. This lieutenant really could be as ignorant about the unit as she seemed.

Jason smiled. Wouldn't it be fun to see her expression when she finally realized the true nature of Alpha Force?

Maybe he could figure out a way to do that—although he would not be in a position, he was sure, to comfort the beautiful officer.

Not then, at least.

Would she run away screaming?

Somehow, he didn't think so. His first impression was that she was no-nonsense, all by the book. Her duty was to help the general, no matter what.

But Jason would bet she'd never anticipated this.

Perhaps he could help to educate her. Really educate her about what Alpha Force was about.

He would definitely try.

* * *

"Time for us all to go." That was the major talking, and clearly no one was about to contradict him.

Sara watched as everyone at the table rose almost in unison. She did the same.

So did the sergeant beside her. "Are you staying in the BOQ?" he asked.

Why? Did he want to accompany her there? Tear off her clothes the way his suggestive looks seemed to do, never mind the rules?

The idea made her private areas react in ways she hadn't felt in a long time—even as she shoved the very idea out of her mind.

"That's right. I assume you're not." She kept her tone brusque, not unfriendly but not anything but professional, either.

"Right. But…well, you'd better stay in your quarters tonight, Lieutenant."

Was he presuming to give her, a superior officer, orders? She glared—but at that moment his look wasn't sexy or suggestive… It seemed concerned.

Odd.

Although it was the night of a full moon. Maybe the general hadn't been playing her completely and this unit's members spread the word that they were shapeshifters to hide what they really did. But would anyone sane actually accept that?

"We'll walk you there." Colleen Hodell gestured toward a couple of other lieutenants who'd been sitting with them.

In a short while, Sara was walking toward the BOQ

with Colleen, and with Lieutenants Marshall Vincenzo and Jock Larabey. Marshall was the tallest of the group, with a shock of dark brown hair and thin but surprisingly sensual lips. Jock looked as if he might live up to his name. He seemed quite muscular, judging by the way his uniform hugged his arms and chest.

"So tell me something about Alpha Force," Sara said lightly as they trod the path toward their residence. Something real, she hoped.

"I think that's up to the general," Colleen said.

"In fact," Marshall added, "I think Jason—Sergeant Connell—was right. You should just stay in your quarters tonight. It's safer."

"The base is safe," Jock contradicted. "But if you're not familiar with it, you'd be better off not wandering around at night, and definitely not tonight."

Okay, they did seem to be playing the general's game. But did they all really want her to hide in her BOQ unit tonight, maybe put her head under a pillow and pretend she wasn't here? Were they going to put on some kind of act tonight? If so, she wanted to see it.

Or maybe this was completely a sham, so they could actually do something else under cover of darkness.

They all separated at the elevators. "Good night," Sara said, wondering what each of the others was thinking.

When she reached the second floor, she noticed a female captain and male lieutenant down the hall. She went to greet them.

Neither was part of Alpha Force, they told her. They were Captain Samantha Everly and Lieutenant

Cal Brown. Did she want to hang out in Samantha's unit with them?

Had they, too, been directed to stay indoors that night? If so, what story had they been told? But she didn't ask.

"Thanks," Sara said. "I just got here today and I'm really tired. I'll take a rain check, though."

She used her key to enter her apartment. There, she unpacked the scant clothing and other things she had brought, then sat down in front of the television.

She sat there for maybe an hour, but she was bored. And curious. She rose and walked to the window.

Lights illuminated the part of the base that she could see. So did a full moon that had just risen above the trees that surrounded the back portion of the base.

She saw no movement. No Alpha Force members or otherwise.

Hell, she was used to following orders, but the cautions she had been given didn't amount to orders, did they?

She wouldn't stay out long, and she would remain where the base was well lighted.

Would she need a weapon? Hardly. No matter what those Alpha Force members really did that night, they surely wouldn't hurt anyone, least of all the aide to the unit's officer in charge.

She stayed as quiet as she could, locking her apartment door behind her and taking the stairs rather than the elevator. She exited through the BOQ's front door.

The spring air was brisk but pleasant. She moved out

of the artificial lights toward the shadow of the nearest building, in case anyone was watching her.

Hell, she'd already determined that she wasn't disobeying orders. She was just outside for...for health purposes. The night air would help her sleep.

She walked around for twenty minutes, seeing nothing. Hearing—well, she wasn't sure what she heard. There were noises in the distance that she couldn't identify. Were there some kinds of wild animals living in the woods surrounding the base? Sometimes she thought she heard a howl.

Or was this all piped-in sound effects to make the gullible think there were werewolves out there? She wasn't about to buy that.

She drew closer to the edge of the woods, just to peek, not that she would get close. Had they really loosed some kind of wildlife, something feral, on the base?

Not likely. Not animals they couldn't control. Well, five more minutes out here and she would return to her quarters. It did feel a bit eerie after all, being alone at such a large facility.

What was that? She heard something—not howls, but a growl. There was no breeze that night, but she also heard crunching of leaves, as if something was walking in the woods.

Okay. Her imagination really was working overtime. Or maybe there were some kinds of animals out there. She'd better go back—

She stopped dead as something emerged from the woods. Not just one creature, but maybe half a dozen.

Wolves.

Should she freeze? Should she run?

An African-American man she hadn't met before suddenly appeared from behind them. He wore camos like her and didn't seem frightened by the wolves.

"What are you doing here?" he demanded. "Everyone was told to stay inside tonight. Go back to your quarters. Now."

"But are you safe with—?"

In unison, several of the wolves leaped toward Sara.

"Run!" called the man.

And Sara did.

Chapter 2

He wanted to chase after her, that foolish woman who hadn't listened to him or anyone else.

Didn't she know how dangerous it could be, wandering around on the night of a full moon in an area where shapeshifters prowled?

If he had been in his human form, he would have laughed.

But Jason was in his wolfen form, loving it. Especially because the time of his shift tonight had actually been his choice.

He stood in the midst of his also-shifted comrades. None chased Lieutenant Sara McLinder from where she had confronted them here, at the edge of the woods surrounding Ft. Lukman. Most of them had leaped in unison to scare her off.

Soon, though, since she was an aide to the general, she would be told, and shown, the truth.

Jason looked sideways. The wolf beside him was Drew, his cousin, who had coerced him to enlist in the military, to join Alpha Force, for his own good.

At this moment, despite his misgivings about the future, Jason couldn't thank Drew enough.

His cousin nodded his canine head and turned. He began walking into the woods. So did the other shifters.

They were followed by their single human aide for the night, Captain Jonas Truro, who was a medical doctor like Drew.

He was not, however, a shifter, but as a member of Alpha Force he was an expert at helping them, including assisting in perfecting the Alpha Force elixir.

All shifters here would continue to prowl until dawn. That was when they normally would change back on nights of the full moon anyway, even if they didn't have access to that very special Alpha Force elixir. His family had started to experiment with it, at least Drew had, and now, with the help of other Alpha Force members including Jonas Truro, he had developed some sophisticated and amazing formulas.

That elixir was one reason Jason's thoughts were so clear now, while he was shifted.

Why he could wonder, so precisely, exactly what lovely Lieutenant McLinder thought about her recent confrontation by an entire pack of wolves.

Oh, yes. He would laugh, if he could.

But since he couldn't for now, he would wait and look forward to a conversation, sometime soon, with pretty Sara.

Sara lay on her back in the dark, on the uncomfortable bed in her new apartment, willing herself to fall asleep.

She had closed the blinds, but a soft glow still penetrated between the slats. The light from the full moon.

Hell, she had trained her body as much as she had trained her mind. She never had trouble getting to sleep.

Except tonight.

Her thoughts kept returning to the pack of wolves she'd seen. They were wolves, weren't they? They didn't look like any breed of domesticated dog she knew of.

On the other hand, they had been so calm at first. Even when a few had moved quickly toward her, none had acted as if it intended to attack.

And then there'd been that soldier who shooed her away.

What was this?

Was the mysterious Alpha Force really composed of shapeshifters? Somehow, that didn't seem as nonsensical now as it had before.

Of course it could still all be some kind of ruse that the military was attempting to impose on enemy forces—couldn't it? That was the logical assumption. But if so, how had they tamed those wolves that way?

Sara turned over, trying to get comfortable. Maybe

she should pull up a training manual on her laptop. Read something, at least.

But she knew that if she did boot up her computer, she would instead search for something else entirely.

Werewolves.

She had gone to bed in her usual sleeping attire—a T-shirt and matching shorts. She was comfortable in them. She kept telling herself that the room's warm temperature was fine. So was what she was wearing. So was everything except for the outrageousness of her thoughts.

She needed sleep, but it wouldn't come.

What time was it, anyway? She turned over and pulled her smartphone from the nightstand beside the bed where it was charging.

Really? Was it actually almost five o'clock? The night was nearly over.

And she clearly wasn't going to sleep a wink.

Throwing the covers off, she flipped the light switch at the side of the bed.

She had an idea what to do next.

She was going to track down those damned wolves.

She had dressed in her camo fatigues. She once more used the stairs to get to the first floor of the BOQ, then slipped out the side door again.

This time, she was armed—with a camera. She had shoved it into her pocket.

Since this Alpha Force was supposed to be so covert, she suspected that if she took any pictures of the wolves she might be considered in breach of military protocol—at the least. She might even be doing something illegal. Certainly, it could be contrary to her security clearance.

But she didn't intend to show anything to the world. No, if she found those wolves again, she would take pictures only for herself.

Darkness still hovered over the base—the darkness before dawn, since the moon was setting behind the trees. Soon, the sun would rise.

For now, Sara kept in shadows as she crossed the paths toward the woods where the wolves had emerged from among the trees.

She stayed just outside the foliage. Canines, whatever their nature, had keen hearing. They'd hear her anyway, but she didn't want to make it any easier by tromping on dry, fallen leaves.

She found the base interesting in its layout. From where she was, most buildings—nearly all low and two- or three-story—were to the left, and the woods were to her right. It wasn't hard to stay in shadows, but that was changing with almost every minute.

Dawn was breaking.

She— What was that?

She heard a noise in the woods, as if someone else stepped on those dry leaves. Was it the man who had shooed her back inside before?

Or was it an animal?

A wolf?

Okay, if she was going to have any chance at all of seeing what she sought, of taking pictures, it was time to move. Slowly, so she didn't make any more noise than absolutely necessary, she slid between the trees.

It was darker here than in the open, but the fact that sunrise was beginning made it easier to see.

There. She heard something again.

A howl?

No…it sounded more like a moan. A human moan.

Was someone hurt? Had those damned wolves attacked someone?

Less inclined to be protective of herself when someone might need her help, she walked faster in the direction of the noise.

The moans sounded louder, accompanied by other noise, as if something thrashed in the underbrush. Was it a person being attacked?

Damn, she really should have brought a weapon. She had her phone in another pocket and could call for help if necessary, but the first minutes during an attack could be critical. She needed to find out fast exactly what was going on.

She started running in the direction of the sounds.

She emerged into a clearing among the trees where daylight was beginning to glimmer.

Sara blinked in confusion and disbelief as she looked at the source of the sound.

Only one being was present in the clearing. It definitely wasn't a fight but—what was it?

That wasn't one of the wolves. Or at least the furry being didn't look like one—not exactly. It was larger, more elongated, and as Sara watched, the hair on its body appeared to be sucked in until only flesh remained except on the head—and in certain private areas where humans also had hair.

Male humans—and hair wasn't all that was private that Sara observed.

This couldn't be. And yet, it was.

As she watched—and, fortunately, had the consciousness to start shooting pictures, including a video—the wolf-like creature disappeared, replaced by the form of a man.

Not just any man.

She realized quickly that it was Sergeant Jason Connell she watched, changing from a wolf back into a human.

She couldn't stop staring at him, and not just because of the incredible metamorphosis she had just observed.

Jason Connell stood there, breathing hard as if shedding final discomfort at what he had gone through. He flexed his body—his arms, his chest and yes, his most private areas, riveting Sara's gaze there as she, too, started breathing a bit harder. Lord, was he generously endowed there. Was that a factor of who, or what, he was?

She continued to shoot pictures, but only for a moment.

Jason grinned then and looked straight at her. He flexed once more, and she swallowed hard. How long had he recognized that she was there?

He certainly did now.

"Good morning, Sara…er, Lieutenant," he said.

"Like what you see? I'd be glad to demonstrate some more."

With a strangled cry, Sara turned and ran back the way she had come.

Jason considered just letting her go.

She wasn't supposed to be out here, anyway. But he didn't have any clothes here to slip on.

He had purposely separated from the rest of his pack a while ago. He had wondered if the lovely lieutenant would return to the area where she had found them to follow up on what she thought she had seen.

Sure enough, she had appeared where he had anticipated. Just by running into the pack last night, though, she really hadn't seen much of anything…then.

If he went after her now, he would only emphasize what she had seen this morning. Him.

Not that he minded. But even if he wanted to, he doubted he'd be able to slip into the BOQ nude to do—whatever.

He found the lieutenant hot. Presumably, she now found him hot, too. He hoped so. He hated to think all that moving and flexing, purposely giving her an eyeful, had been in vain. Not that either of them ever could, or would, act on it.

No, he would head back to his own quarters first. He would run into her casually on the base, anyway.

Hanging out with Alpha Force was why she was here.

"Hey, where've you been, Jason?" Jonas Truro slipped out of the woods. He held out a T-shirt and jeans toward him. "Not a good thing to wander around here like that, especially now." He nodded toward Jason's crotch.

At the moment, his private parts were at ease. He'd been alone there long enough, in the somewhat cool morning air, to chill out.

"Not with that new unit here," Jason agreed, taking the clothes and slipping them on. "Thanks." He wasn't about to mention that he'd been seen—especially considering who it had been.

Although it probably would have been worse had someone from the new special-ops group stationed here seen him. Though everyone was pretending cordiality, there'd been friction between Alpha Force members and the new unit, the Ultra Special Forces Team. They were here to engage, eventually, in some mutual training with Alpha Force for a so-far undisclosed covert assignment overseas. The team's unique skills still remained secret from Alpha Force. No one outside their group was supposed to ask questions about their nature.

And no one in the Ultra Special Forces Team was supposed to ask questions about Alpha Force.

"Everyone else back in their quarters?" Jason asked. All the other shifters were brass—officers, from lieutenants up through Major Connell. That was partly thanks to General Yarrow, he'd been told. Although their nature was revealed only on a need-to-know basis, the shifters in Alpha Force were regarded with esteem, and their special abilities were to be recognized by the military, at least by their ranks.

Everyone but him.

"They sure are. Drew said we should all get a couple of hours' sleep, then we'll meet up in the lab to compare notes about last night." Jonas yawned. "You okay on your own now?"

"Sure am." Jason gave him an exaggerated salute. "I'm off to my quarters. See you later, Captain."

Jason pivoted as if he felt like genuine, by-the-book military and headed in the growing light of dawn toward the better-than-barracks apartment building that housed a group of enlisted members of Alpha Force, not too far from the BOQ.

Jason was the only shifter in that building—the only Alpha Force shifter who wasn't a commissioned officer.

Most shifters in Alpha Force had individual aides to help them, primarily enlisted personnel quartered in the same building as Jason. For the exercises tonight, though, the decision had been that only one aide was needed, and Captain Jonas Truro had been it.

Jason didn't have his own personal aide, anyway. The only perk he'd been given was that he had been promoted to the rank of sergeant nearly immediately. Being a noncommissioned officer was better than just being a private, but he'd have liked the recognition given to the other shifters.

Of course he didn't have a college education—yet—like the rest of them.

And then there was the reason his cousin Drew had twisted some arms to get him accepted into the military, and Alpha Force, in the first place....

He still had a lot to overcome, damn it.

But having gotten a figurative taste of Alpha Force and how it worked, and a literal taste of the elixir that helped to make Alpha Force what it was...well, like it or not, he'd probably stay with this unit for a nice, long time.

Which meant that disobeying what Jonas Truro might consider to be an order wasn't in the cards. Not this morning, at least.

Instead of attempting to confront Lieutenant Sara McLinder after what they had—sort of—shared that night, Jason continued toward his small apartment.

The next time he'd see her would probably be at the upcoming meeting in the main building housing Alpha Force labs and offices.

There would be plenty of time then to embarrass even further the woman who'd watched him change that morning.

Chapter 3

Sara didn't even try to get more sleep.

Each time she sat down, or stood, or did nearly anything, her mind kept returning to that scene near the woods.

And so she spent the next hour sitting on the uncomfortable brown sofa in her quarters, trying to read a book on military history to distract her—and failing dismally.

She remained dressed in the camos she had donned earlier to go look for those damned wolves that had confronted her last night—and what a mistake that had been.

Had she imagined it? Was she nuts? She had, after all, performed some absurd research on her own earlier, about shapeshifters, after seeing the wolves. Had the general's strange attempt at humor and the innuendos about the unusual nature of Alpha Force left her susceptible to a really wild kind of joke?

But why would anyone here play a joke on her, especially Jason Connell? He didn't know her. No one here knew her.

Whatever Jason's reason, he'd at a minimum bared his very hot body to her. He had also somehow changed from a wolf to a man.

Impossible.

Yet… Her mind kept circling that impossible scenario over and over, which oddly gave it more credence.

She had never before hallucinated anything, let alone something so bizarre.

Yet somehow alluring…

She'd taken pictures. She looked at them again. Then put her digital camera away, hidden deeply in a drawer. It provided more questions than answers.

Once more she tried in vain to focus on the large volume she held on her lap. She barely got through the first ten pages.

At six-thirty, she headed for the cafeteria.

The temperature outside remained cool but comfortable. Once again, others in camo fatigues also strode across the base, a few heading in the same direction she was.

But no one she recognized.

Would she see Jason in the cafeteria this morning? If so, what would she say to him?

Heck, he was the one who owed her an explanation. Maybe even an apology for playing games with her that way.

Unless it was real....

No, she wouldn't go there.

She was soon immersed in the crowd entering the cafeteria, then stood in line. Though not especially hungry, she decided that comfort food wouldn't be a bad idea. Never mind that she usually scorned pampering herself in any manner.

She paid for her pancakes, bacon and coffee then scanned the compact eating area.

And saw no one she recognized.

She shoved away the pang of regret that Jason wasn't there. She wasn't looking forward to their inevitable confrontation—was she?

Well, maybe a little.

Maybe he would be kind enough to provide an explanation, one she could buy—and one that wouldn't make her feel like an utter fool.

No Alpha Force members were eating here at the moment, at least none she'd met. Did that have some significance?

She would find out. She'd learn all she needed to restore her sense of sanity and well-being.

For now she headed, tray in hand, toward a small table where the folks eating there all wore lieutenants' insignias. Were any of them members of the Ultra Special Forces Team, or could they be Alpha Force people she hadn't yet run into?

"May I join you?" she asked, stopping at an unoccupied chair.

"Sure," said a female lieutenant whose name tag read Swainey. She held out her hand as Sara sat down. "Vera Swainey." She looked at Sara expectantly.

"I'm Sara McLinder," she said.

The others at the table introduced themselves, too—three men and another woman.

"Are you all stationed here?" Sara asked.

"That's right," said Lieutenant Manning Breman. "You?"

"I just got here yesterday. I'm aide to General Greg Yarrow, who'll be stationed here on temporary duty for a few months."

The friendly atmosphere at the table suddenly seemed to freeze into icicles of stares.

"You're with Alpha Force?" Manning asked, his tone stiff.

"That's right." It wasn't exactly true, but she hated the antagonism that seemed to waft around her. Maybe they'd explain if she pressed. "Tell me what's going on here. I get the impression that your unit and Alpha Force aren't exactly buddies."

"You could say that." Vera's voice was also chill. "We were recently assigned here and assumed that— Oh, wait. I see the person we were saving that spot for. Cal, come over here." She sounded relieved as Cal Brown, the lieutenant whom Sara had met on her floor in their BOQ yesterday, approached with a tray of food.

There were plenty of empty chairs at nearby tables that Cal could pull up to their table. But all eyes of those seated there remained on Sara, as if demonstrating that she had outstayed her welcome.

"Here," she said to Cal as she stood abruptly, picking up her tray. "Have fun with this group. I certainly didn't."

She strode away, chose a small table near the door and sat down by herself.

She glanced at her watch. It was seven o'clock. She would phone General Yarrow soon. Warn him about the extent of the friction between the two primary units stationed here at Ft. Lukman.

Find out when he was planning on arriving that day.

She wouldn't, of course, mention what she had seen, or thought she had, earlier that morning.

But when he arrived, she would talk to him as soon as possible. Maybe even show pictures.

He could tell her more about Alpha Force. He had, after all, warned her to expect a different atmosphere and different kind of unit. Had even hinted at what she'd seen.

He knew what Alpha Force was about. She had just preferred not to imagine that what he hinted at could be real.

Now she knew better—and she hoped he would explain it to her.

Jason sat back on the uncomfortable folding chair, surrounded by colleagues, both shifters and not. He looked around the small basement office in the main Alpha Force building at the far end of Ft. Lukman.

This was where they always met on the morning after a full moon. Other meetings were also held here for Alpha Force members in the secured laboratory area.

On the first floor, dogs were housed—those used as the cover, when necessary, for wolf shifters. Jason had a dog assigned to him: Shadow. He also enjoyed helping to train them in his spare time, although not today.

All the dogs had remained in their nice, well-maintained kennels last night—unlike the shapeshifters of Alpha Force.

"We need your report first this time, Jonas." Major Drew Connell, Jason's oh-so-perfect cousin, stood at the front of the room. He looked worried.

He'd really worry if Jason told him what he'd done that morning. Therefore, Jason wouldn't mention it.

"Everything started out fine," Jonas Truro responded as he stood up from his seat in the first row of four. He glanced around the group of shifters and aides who were present. "All our wolf shifters chose not to take the version of the elixir that would keep them in human form. Instead, everyone drank the kind that helped with human cognition while shifted but didn't stop them from changing. Our cougar shifter Colleen did the same." He nodded toward the woman who sat in the same row as Jason, a few people over.

The elixir was good stuff. Both formulas were. Jason gave the unit, and especially Drew, a lot of credit for that.

Now premixed bottles of both kinds were stored in a special refrigerated room nearby, even as Drew continued to upgrade the formulas for each.

Jason listened with interest as Jonas described everyone's change in the clearing in the woods that had been previously selected, then how he stayed with the wolf pack as they roved areas also designated in advance. With the Ultra Special Forces Team there for the last month, it had become impossible to have the run of the entire base while in shifted form when the moon wasn't full. At least last night, with the moon full, the USFT personnel had been told to stay in their quarters...without being told why.

Jason had no doubt that some, if not all, of that unit already suspected the true nature of Alpha Force. They probably scorned it—or feared it. But the official position for both units, at least for now, was to stay separate in all training exercises and otherwise. No joint exercises yet, although that was intended for the future. When? Peons like him weren't kept informed about such important matters.

"There was one incident," Jonas said. "Minor, but everyone should be aware of it. Lieutenant McLinder was wandering around outside around midnight and saw the pack. I shooed her back inside, but maybe someone should talk to her about maintaining silence about what she saw."

And about what she saw around five in the morning? Yeah, she definitely should stay silent about that, Jason thought. And probably would, even without being cautioned. He strongly suspected she wasn't about to announce to the world, *her* world, what she had observed. Even though he'd seen her taking pictures.

She might talk to him about it, though.

If so, he was ready. Very ready.

"Our next exercise will probably be later this week," Drew was saying. "We'll decide who'll shift and who won't. That will also dictate which of our aides and cover dogs—and cat—are needed."

He talked a while longer. Jason had started to tune his cousin out when a knock sounded on the office door.

It startled Jason, and probably everyone else in the room. They exchanged glances.

Before Drew could look outside to see who it was, the door opened.

Lieutenant Sara McLinder walked in.

Though she wasn't extremely tall, her straight stance and the glare in her blue-green eyes had her dominating the room in that instant.

She was definitely a good-looking woman. Or maybe his opinion was colored by what he knew she'd seen…and, perhaps, enjoyed.

"Sorry," she said. "I'm obviously interrupting something. But you all should know that General Yarrow will arrive here at Ft. Lukman around ten o'clock this morning."

Sara wasn't sorry at all about interrupting this meeting, whatever it was about. It clearly involved Alpha Force, since she recognized most of the people who sat staring at her.

Including Sergeant Jason Connell. He was as great-looking as she recalled, of course—even with his clothes on. Seeing him in person again only stressed that she couldn't have imagined what she'd observed…

could she? Under his camos, his shoulders were broad. His face was incredibly handsome, and the small streaks of silver in his dark hair only added to the appeal of the package.

She met his amused golden eyes only briefly, then turned back to the major.

The family relationship was apparent between the two men. Major Connell also had gold eyes and flecks of silver running through his dark hair. He was nice-looking, too. Maybe a little older than Jason. But not nearly as handsome.

More quietly than her earlier pronouncement, she said to him, "Major Connell, you know I'm here representing General Yarrow. He even gave me his card keys to get into this building and the lab area on his behalf. If this is an Alpha Force meeting, I should have been invited."

"I know your assignment, Lieutenant. You'll be invited to all meetings necessary to what the general, and you, are here to accomplish. This was a recap of some prior exercises and I didn't think it appropriate for you to waste your time."

"I'll let the general decide what's appropriate for me." She kept her expression neutral, though her words weren't.

"I understand." The major turned back to the group. "I think we're through here," he said. "Everyone is dismissed."

Especially me, Sara thought. But she didn't complain. Not yet. Nor did she ask any questions.

She had contacted the general, though, and she was

really glad that he would arrive in only a couple of hours.

She would be there waiting for him.

For now, she scanned the group until her eyes lit again on Jason Connell, who was approaching the major.

Did Major Connell know what Sara had seen last night? Had Jason told him what he had done?

Surely the major knew who, or what, his own cousin was…assuming Sara hadn't imagined it all.

Should she simply ask the major? Maybe, but she wanted to talk to General Yarrow first.

And preferably to Jason even before that, to gauge his position about the incident.

Not now, though. He was engaged in a conversation with the major. Time for Sara to leave, along with the rest of the group.

Outside the door she feigned answering her cell phone but hung up as Jason came through.

"I'd like to talk with you, Sergeant," she said, inserting her most formal military quality to her voice.

"I'll bet you would, Lieutenant." There was humor in his tone and a suggestive smile on his face. "Would you like to go someplace where we could…talk alone?"

She felt her face flush. "No, thank you. But I would like for you to give me an official tour of this facility."

"I can only do that on the major's orders, Lieutenant." This time, he sounded serious.

Which suggested further to Sara that she was being kept outside the Alpha Force loop for now. She was a superior officer, yet he was refusing to obey her while giving a good excuse. That would surely change when the general got here and ordered everyone to cooperate with her as well as him.

"Then come with me, please. There's something I'd like to show you." Not really, but she decided to lead him back to the area where he had shown *her*...a lot.

"Yes, ma'am." His tone again suggested he was thinking about exactly what she was.

He didn't comment as they walked up the stairs to the main floor of the building. There, she stopped in the kennel area to look at the dogs she had been told were there.

They were all of moderate size, and most resembled the animals she had seen last night: wolves.

"I like dogs," she said casually. "Do you, Sergeant?"

"Yes, ma'am," he responded, smiling. "Especially those guys. My favorite is Shadow."

He reached inside the chain-link fencing of a nearby kennel and stroked the head of the closest dog inside, whom he introduced as Shadow. Sara couldn't help thinking that this dog in particular bore a strong resemblance to Jason in wolf form. Could he somehow have pulled a prank on her after all? But how?

"Any kinds of dogs you like better than others?" Jason asked.

He probably wanted her to say something like the kind she'd seen last night—and especially that morning. But that wasn't something she intended to admit.

"Small ones," she said. "These guys are cute, but they look difficult to walk and control. I like dogs that I can train and manage." Oh, Lord. She knew she was stepping into a nasty mess that had nothing to do with dog excrement. He could read a lot into her words if he chose. Maybe that was a good thing, if he really was what she suspected. But there was no way she would ever admit to him that what she had seen had touched her libido, gotten her most intimate parts simmering.

"Sounds like a very interesting way to treat your… dogs," he said. "I'd be glad to teach you how to work with these guys—or any others."

She'd had enough. They were outside the building on a walkway that led toward the woods in one direction, or toward the BOQ in the other. "I've got someplace I need to go now," she said. "See you later, Sergeant." She stood straight, looking at him, until he saluted her. She saluted back.

"Yes, ma'am," he said so officially that it sounded facetious, then he whirled on his heels and strutted off.

Sara headed back toward her quarters. She would find something productive to do until it was time to go meet the general.

At around nine-thirty, Sara realized she had actually gotten something accomplished in a short time, although not what she had intended.

For one thing, she had thoroughly searched Google on her laptop to see if she could find any information to suggest that shapeshifters could be real.

Of course there was. The authors could all have been credulous fools who wanted to believe, so they did. Nothing stood out to her as proof.

There were also a lot of websites ridiculing the whole idea.

She logged off the computer and left it on the small table in the kitchenette in her quarters. Then she checked herself in the mirror. Almost time to go wait for the general.

She'd decided to meet him right away, before he had time to talk with anyone else.

Soon she headed down the stairs in the BOQ and out the door. She walked toward the front gate.

And got waylaid by Jason. What was he doing out here?

He soon told her. "Hello, Lieutenant. I'm the general's unofficial greeter from Alpha Force. Is that why you're out here? I'm supposed to call Drew—er, Major Connell—and let him know when the general arrives."

"Won't the security guys notify the major?" Sara asked.

"Probably. But those were my orders."

"Okay. We'll both wait for him, then." She didn't want to wait with Jason. He would be a big distraction. He would keep her from asking the general questions right away, too. But she nevertheless walked with Jason toward the base's front gate.

She saw a few other soldiers walking around and some cars cruising the nearby roads. But she was extremely aware of Jason's tall, masculine presence beside her.

Especially when he said in a voice tinged with suggestiveness, "How are you enjoying Ft. Lukman so far, Lieutenant?"

"It's fine, Sergeant. I intend to get a lot accomplished here. Learn a lot, too."

"About Alpha Force?"

"That's right," she said. "I have some ideas already about how it can be improved, and I intend to let the general know."

She sensed Jason's hesitation beside her, but she wiped the grin off her face before she turned to him. His expression now was grim, not suggestive of anything but worry.

Good.

She looked again toward the guard gate, just in time to see the general's old, classic Jeep stopping. His ID was apparently approved right away, since the large gate opened inward and the general drove through.

Continuing to drive slowly, he approached the area where Sara and Jason stood.

And then Sara spotted smoke pouring out of the car's back end.

Chapter 4

What the hell? Jason didn't need Sara's frantic shouts of fear, magnified by his canine senses, to spur him to dash to the burning vehicle that suddenly veered off to the side.

He assessed the situation as he ran toward the front of the car. He kept all assumptions and fears, all emotions, in check. Now was only a time for action.

He had worked on the general's Jeep a couple of times when the old man had come to Ft. Lukman for meetings since Jason's recent enlistment. It was an early 1990s model Jeep, not quite old enough to be a classic, but still an admirable aging vehicle.

The gasoline tank was in the back—near where the smoke was pouring from, but down low, beneath the axle. That model's gas tank was built well, to prevent catching fire from sparks off the road or otherwise. Everything should be fine.

Except that the tires were flammable. So were the seats, the carpeting, the safety belts…

And right now, there was plenty of smoke. What remained of the canvas cover could confine a lot of it inside, enhancing the danger of smoke inhalation by the general.

Plus, depending on the location and intensity of the fire…well, despite the built-in precautions, there were no guarantees that the gas tank wouldn't explode.

Jason aimed for the driver's door, shoving his hands in his pockets as he ran to check for anything useful. Despite his dedication to working on cars, he didn't coincidentally happen to carry tools that people were supposed to keep in their glove compartments to shatter windows in emergencies. All he had were keys. A pocket knife. His cell phone.

Nothing likely to be helpful.

Was the general still conscious? The haphazard way the car now progressed suggested otherwise. Yet if he was, maybe Jason could get him to turn off the engine and take the thing out of gear. Push the button to unlock the driver's door.

For now, he would assume the commanding officer remained alive. He had no evidence he wasn't… at least not yet.

The stench of burning rubber and more grew even ranker as he arrived at the vehicle, but Jason ignored it. He also ignored the shouts of other people. All behind him? He saw no one closer to the car than he was.

Unsure what was searing hot and what wasn't, he yanked off his camo shirt and wrapped it around his right hand.

He reached the door and looked in. Smoke. Lots of it. But in the middle of it all, Jason could see that the general appeared conscious—barely. His eyes were open. His hands? Moving, but not in the right direction to get him out of there.

Jason first tried to yank the door open, to no avail. He pounded on the window to get the general's attention. "It's locked!" he shouted as Yarrow's head jerked toward him. Had he heard? Was he aware enough to understand?

Yarrow, one hand at his mouth as he coughed, turned toward the door. In a moment, Jason heard a click that probably wouldn't be audible to someone with normal human hearing, but with his acute senses it sounded nice and loud. He again tried the door.

This time it opened.

He coughed, too, as smoke smothered his face and his ability to breathe. But it didn't completely mask visibility.

"Let me help," said a familiar female voice from behind him. Sara McLinder. The lieutenant had kept up with him.

"Stay back," he said as he leaned inside.

But she apparently wasn't used to obeying orders from lower-ranking soldiers. As Jason leaned in and grasped the now-limp body of the general, he was suddenly glad that was so.

He needed to get the CO out of there fast. In moments, as he thrust his hands under the general's arm-pits and heaved him out, he found Sara, despite also coughing, grabbing the legs and swinging Yarrow even farther from the frying car.

Others who'd caught up with them, Lieutenants Seth Ambers and Grace Andreas-Parran, also helped to form a stretcher of human—well, somewhat human—arms.

Grace was a doctor as well as a shifting member of Alpha Force. It was still too soon to have her check the general's condition, though. Awkwardly but quickly, Jason helped the group maneuver the general's barely conscious body far from the car and within a parking area near the base's entry kiosk.

The harsh smell of the fire suddenly multiplied, and so did the background odor of oil as the flames apparently reached the engine. How secure was the gas tank now?

Jason swiftly noticed that he wasn't the only Alpha Force member helping here whose eyes had widened as their noses lifted.

And then, *kaboom!* As loudly and completely as any explosion in an action movie, the general's car detonated.

"Sir? Are you okay? Greg?" Sara wasn't certain where the tarp had come from on which they gently laid the general down on the hard parking lot surface. Maybe from one of the vehicles parked nearby. It didn't matter.

What did matter was how her boss, commanding

officer to many of those present at Ft. Lukman, was doing.

Was he still alive?

He hadn't responded to her queries, which she knew sounded pitifully plaintive. Maybe he couldn't hear her. She wasn't right beside him now. Not the way things had worked out as the group of them had laid him down gently.

She therefore maneuvered around on the periphery of the tarp to be nearer to his head, not exactly elbowing others out of her way but coming close to it.

She prayed she didn't imagine it, but the general's chest seemed to be moving slowly, indicating he was breathing.

"General Yarrow? Sir?" she said, louder this time and definitely closer to his ears, not caring that her voice broke as she addressed him.

He was her mentor. Her friend.

And he might be dying.

Sure, she was a soldier. She had joined the military prepared to go into combat. To lose comrades in arms, if necessary.

But not here, on U.S. soil.

And not this very kind, very wonderful man.

She moved even closer, only to find her way blocked by Jason. "You probably haven't met Lieutenant Grace Andreas-Parran yet," he said to Sara, gesturing to the woman in camo uniform, like all of them, who knelt at the general's other side. "She's a medical doctor as well as a member of Alpha Force."

"Oh." Sara knew what Jason wasn't saying. She

needed to back off. Let the doctor do what she could for the general.

Grace was slim and attractive, with blond hair so pale that it almost looked silver.

More important, her luminous brown eyes were narrowed as she concentrated on scanning the general's body. From what Sara could see, his camo uniform was intact. Unsinged. Maybe he hadn't been burned.

That didn't mean he would survive. Smoke inhalation could kill people. And so far Sara didn't know if he'd suffered any other kinds of injuries.

"Was he hurt?" she asked Grace. "I mean, besides being in a burning vehicle."

"Not sure yet." The doctor's long fingers moved rapidly along General Yarrow's prone body, clearly checking for injuries along with her concentrated gaze. "You're his aide, aren't you?"

"That's right," Sara said.

"Are you aware of any medical conditions he may have—heart related or otherwise? It'll help diagnose and treat him if we have all his information."

"I don't know of any. He's not exactly forthcoming with that kind of stuff, but I've made him occasional appointments for checkups at Bethesda Medical Center. I can call there."

"Just get me the contact information. With privacy issues, they're more likely to let me know matters like that."

Which peeved Sara. She was almost like family to the general. But Grace was right. She was the doctor.

She was the one they'd talk to about anything needed to save Greg Yarrow.

Sara was aware of Jason's presence right behind her. He must have heard the conversation. He rested his hand firmly on her shoulder. To warn her to back off? But the contact seemed more comforting than cautionary.

Under other circumstances, Sara wouldn't allow him to touch her at all. She was his superior officer. They were on duty.

But at the moment his touch somehow helped her to survive this horrendous situation.

She heard a lot of voices near them, too, and looked around to see other soldiers she had already met here. Some, like Seth Ambers, Colleen Hodell, Rainey Jessop and Jock Larabey, were members of Alpha Force. Others, including Lieutenants Cal Brown, Manning Breman and Samantha Everly, were members of the Ultra Special Forces Team.

All circled the general's vulnerable body, staying respectfully back.

"Hey. What the hell happened?" That was Major Drew Connell, who maneuvered his way through the crowd.

"He's a doctor, too," said Jason into Sara's ear. "A damned good one."

She already knew that Drew, CO of the unit, was also a physician. "Great." She turned to look toward Jason. His expression was bland, but his gaze, as he looked at her, seemed surprisingly sympathetic and she felt tears rush to her eyes. "Two Alpha Force doctors right here?" she continued, needing to say something else to demonstrate that she wasn't some emotional wimp. "The general's in good hands." Sara prayed that was so.

A siren sounded in the distance. "Good," stated Drew Connell. "I called 911 immediately."

"I did, too," Grace said. "The general needs to be checked out by EMTs with appropriate equipment, then transported immediately to the nearest emergency facility. That's at the Memorial Hospital in Easton, isn't it?"

"That's right," said Drew.

"What…" The word was soft but interjected into the conversation from below them.

The general!

It was all Sara could do not to push her way through all people, doctors or not, to get closer, to hear what Greg had to say.

Only…was it good for him to expend energy trying to talk?

The wail of the siren grew closer. It would be even more difficult to hear him, anyway.

But his eyes opened. They looked around, cloudy and dazed—not at all the usual strong expression conveyed by the powerful and confident CO.

"What happened?" he said. His voice was loud enough now to be heard. He began moving, as if wanting to sit up.

"We're not certain yet, sir." Drew held him gently on the ground. "Please stay still for now till we can check you better for injuries. Your car caught fire and we're going to get you to the nearest hospital for an examination as soon as possible."

Which was a good thing. Sara had learned, from the general's initial description of Ft. Lukman, that it held an infirmary with high-tech equipment. But that couldn't compare with a genuine medical facility staffed by specialists and nurses. Greg Yarrow was entitled to the best care possible.

"Fire?" The general's look somehow hardened, despite the overall laxness and pain in his features. "Hell." That apparently cost him a lot of effort, since he grew silent again.

The siren was extremely loud now. Sara saw the ambulance screech up to the entry kiosk that, only a few minutes earlier, had admitted the general's now-destroyed car.

The EMTs were allowed in immediately. They quickly gave the general an initial exam, and then loaded him into their vehicle. Lieutenant Grace Andreas-Parran and her husband, Lieutenant Simon Parran, who had just joined the group around the accident site, got into the ambulance with him. Jason also let Sara know who the newly arrived man was—and that he was a doctor, too.

"There are a lot of medical doctors in this unit," Sara said. Did that have something to do with their apparently woo-woo nature, or did their backgrounds somehow help to mask what Alpha Force was really about?

"Yeah, there are," Jason responded. "In case you're wondering, those two are especially appropriate to go with the general. They recently returned here after dealing with an ordeal of their own." Sara had heard about that from the general. "They'll take good care of him."

Major Drew Connell stood beside Sara and Jason, along with some Alpha Force members Sara recognized and other people she didn't. As the ambulance pulled out of the gate, Drew turned toward them.

"So, cuz," he said to Jason, then gestured toward the smoldering hulk of the destroyed car. An emergency truck with a Ft. Lukman sign on the side had pulled up and was spraying the wreck with chemicals, presumably to put out the fire. "I doubt there'll be much left to examine, but when those guys are done I want you to take a lot of pictures. We'll need to secure the wreck where it is temporarily, but I want you to move it ASAP into a secure part of the main parking structure and cordon it off so no one can reach it till I get a good forensics team here to check it out. I need to know exactly what happened. Vehicles like that don't just catch fire for no reason. You okay with that?"

"Is that an order, Major?"

"It sure is, Sergeant."

Jason offered up a halfhearted salute along with his grim smile that looked right at home on his sharp-featured, too-handsome face. "You've got it, cuz. Er, sir."

Sara didn't smile, even though she recognized the lightness in the exchange between the two cousins as most likely their way of dealing with this terrible event.

At least the general had survived. But now, as Drew had suggested, they had to figure out what had happened.

She wasn't certain how, but she intended to help.

She would do all that she could to bring to justice anyone involved with endangering her CO.

One of the first things Jason had done after enlisting in the military, and showing up at Ft. Lukman for a very specialized form of basic training, was to check out the closest auto-repair and maintenance facilities.

Jason understood from even before he enlisted that his primary official assignment would be to take care of Ft. Lukman's vehicles, which was what he knew best…besides shapeshifting. Oh, and stealing cars— but that would remain in his past. Like it or not, he'd started over here, as a member of Alpha Force.

The base didn't have much in the way of auto-repair equipment for him to use, though. He'd bought some of the basics. But he had also needed to figure out where he could rent what he'd need only occasionally.

As a result, he had an immediate answer when Drew asked, "Any idea how you're going to move that thing?"

They both watched the base security guys who'd finished spraying the damaged vehicle with foam to end its smoldering.

"Sure do," Jason said. "There's a well-equipped service station in Mary Glen that has a car-carrier tow truck to haul in wrecks or whatever. I'll see if I can rent it. If not, I'll get the owner to bring it here and move the carcass for us."

"Sounds good. Meantime, I'll keep an eye on that hulk to make sure no one plays with it. We don't want any further destruction of evidence of what caused the fire, especially if it was somehow deliberately set."

Jason turned to walk through the substantial group of onlookers still hanging out despite dissipation of the excitement. Sara McLinder remained among them. In fact, the lieutenant hadn't moved, and he couldn't read the expression on her beautiful but clearly sad face as she continued to stare in the direction where the general's ambulance had departed. But it held more than sorrow. Anger? Determination?

Hell, he wanted to find out what she was thinking. He approached her and asked impulsively, "Hey, Lieutenant, you haven't been here long enough to visit our nearest town, Mary Glen, have you?"

She turned toward him and blinked her amazing blue-green eyes as if she'd just been brought back to awareness from some kind of dream. "No," she said slowly, as if wondering why he asked, "I haven't."

"Okay, then, come with me while I pick up a truck to move that thing. We won't stay long, but at least you'll get a sense of the place." He paused then drew nearer and said in a confidential tone too soft for nearby members of the Ultra Special Forces Team to hear. "Oh, and by the way, some of the townsfolk even believe in shapeshifters. I'll tell you all about them on the way."

Sara was fascinated.

First of all, she liked that, riding beside Jason in his souped-up, old, red Mustang, she could pay much more attention to the road leading away from Ft. Lukman. It was surrounded by gorgeous, thick woodlands composed of trees including mature oaks as well as evergreens.

The road was basically two-lane—barely. They made a sharp left turn at the edge of the base, and Jason swerved to avoid some stones on the pavement.

Sara was definitely an urbanite, but she still found the area charming and attractive. Definitely worth visiting.

But not under these circumstances.

"How far is Mary Glen from here?" she asked Jason.

"Not far in mileage." He glanced toward her from the driver's seat for only an instant before redirecting his eyes back to the risky road. "Light years away in attitude."

"I suppose you're going to explain," she said.

"I suppose I am." He grinned. And then he began telling her an utterly wild tale about Mary Glen and some murders that had been committed there over several years. "I don't have firsthand knowledge of this," Jason said, "But my cuz Drew told me about it. It's how he met his wife, Melanie, in fact. Now they even have a kid—little Emily."

"Really?" Sara said. "Now I'm getting interested."

"Okay, I'll tell you about it. First of all, he said a lot of townsfolk bought into the legend of shapeshifters living in the area. I don't go to town a lot, but I gather some of its citizens still believe the story. If nothing else, they liked the legend because it brought tourists—and, in fact, it's one reason Ft. Lukman was established so near Mary Glen, as only loonies like them would buy into the rumor that anyone had seen shifters in the area. Other people here, though, hated both the idea and shapeshifters."

He explained how the parents of Lieutenant Patrick Worley, one of the members of Alpha Force, had been killed by silver bullets, about a year apart, theoretically because they were werewolves.

"And in fact, Dr. Worley, senior, was a shifter. After he died, Patrick sold his dad's veterinary practice to Dr. Melanie Harding—Melanie Harding-Connell now, my cousin-in-law. Drew's wife."

It seemed that a cult of shapeshifting groupies used to hang out in Mary Glen hoping to see, and perhaps dispose of, some shapeshifters by shooting them with silver bullets. Maybe some still did.

"That's an absolute myth, though," Jason added. "Shapeshifters can be killed just like regular people, by any normal kind of ammunition."

Sara just rolled her eyes but didn't comment.

In any event, back then someone had shot Drew's cover dog, Grunge, who was found injured by Melanie, and, excellent vet that she was, she had saved the dog's life—while endangering her own as an apparent shapeshifter lover. She'd proven to the town that Grunge was not Drew in shifted form. Drew, of course, never admitted to shapeshifting—especially not to that wacko group of people.

Eventually, after more killings, the perpetrator was finally caught. Things around Mary Glen—and around Ft. Lukman—had settled down to a relatively peaceful existence.

Until now.

"Do you suppose anyone from town could have sabotaged the general's car?" Sara asked.

"Possibly, but that all happened a while ago. I'd bet instead that it was a member of our new best friends, the USFT."

"But why?" said Sara.

"When we figure that out," Jason replied, "we'll probably know who it was, too."

Their discussion was enough of a diversion for Sara that the drive to the main street of Mary Glen, Maryland, went quickly.

So shapeshifting was real. Jason certainly sounded convincing.

He had looked even more convincing....

The car-carrier truck was definitely available for rent. At the right price. At the right *high* price.

But hell, Jason thought. Uncle Sam would be footing the bill, not him.

And the vehicle, with its black, shining cab in front and car-size, ramplike bed in back—along with a hookup to pull a car onto it—was exactly what he needed.

Sara didn't seem impressed, but he figured she wasn't a vehicle aficionado, at least not the way he was. He haggled for a few minutes with the owner of the service station that owned the truck, though, so she'd figure he was a good military guy who wanted to save his employer, and his country, some money.

After more discussion, he locked his beloved Mustang in a relatively secure-looking garage area.

He then returned to the truck, opened the passenger door and took Sara's hand, helping her climb inside.

He liked touching her warm hand, feeling her firm grip.

Wondering what it might feel like elsewhere on his body…

Hell, what was he thinking? Why had he even taken this woman along with him? It wasn't in his nature to feel sorry for someone who was apparently suffering in sympathy for a downed friend—in this case, a superior officer.

But he had enjoyed her company. Too much.

"This thing rides amazingly well," Sara said as they headed back toward Ft. Lukman. Then she paused. "But I really like your Mustang."

Okay. If he hadn't already been attracted to her, Jason knew he would be now.

But, he told himself, just because she was beautiful and sexy and fun to tease—and talk to—and he'd inhaled her light and appealing citrus scent on their entire ride to town, and even though she liked his car, that didn't mean he could let himself get involved with her.

She was an officer—a non-Alpha Force one at that. She seemed completely by the book. Ready to obey all orders of her commanding officer, the injured general.

Horrified that she'd seen Jason shapeshift and now trying to ignore it.

And he was just a military peon.

One who happened to be a shapeshifter, and proud of it.

* * *

Their ride back from Mary Glen wasn't as enjoyable to Sara as going the other direction.

Surprisingly, she had been enthralled by Jason's glib tale about the quaint small town and its foibles. Not that she'd liked hearing about murders and strange shapeshifter groupies, but the way Jason had described the amazingly squirrely people had captured her interest.

But on the way back, it seemed as though he'd exhausted his interest in the town—and her.

Even so, their being cooped up in the small cab of that truck hadn't seemed uncomfortable.

Sara hadn't let it.

Her verbal encouragement hadn't spurred Jason to tell more stories about Mary Glen, or even himself. Maybe he didn't want to talk to her about his shapeshifting. Maybe then he would have had to explain what Alpha Force was really about.

And Sara would have enjoyed hearing it. Been relieved, in fact, to learn the secrets.

She had other questions about him, too. Why had he joined the military at all? He didn't seem enthralled by it. Was it simply to join this team of military shapeshifters?

But he was a noncommissioned officer, and many other members of Alpha Force whom she'd met so far were lieutenants and above. Why was he different?

She didn't ask. Not now. And when Jason stayed quiet, Sara had started talking about herself—and how she had become General Yarrow's aide. She'd first gotten her undergraduate degree in political science at

Kent State University, where she'd also joined ROTC. She'd always wanted to give back to her country, plus she loved the order of the military. She'd planned early on to make it her career.

She didn't mention, though, that Alan, her college boyfriend, had thought her nuts and kept trying to get her to do things outside the box. All he did was make her feel uncomfortable.

One night she'd joined Alan at a party and found him drinking, indulging in "recreational" drugs—and making out with another woman. That ended their relationship. And Sara hadn't been seriously interested in another man since then.

Which was a good thing, especially now. She would never get involved with someone like Jason. She was superior in rank to him. She had the honor of being an aide to a general, and Jason fixed cars.

And, worst of all, he was an amazingly genuine shapeshifter.

His sexy, amusing demeanor didn't make up for any of that.

"I'd really like to know more about Alpha Force," she finally finished. "And what makes it tick. General Yarrow is really proud to be the unit's commanding officer and always hinted broadly at its…unusual characteristics. One thing I do like is the camaraderie among its members." Although she knew she'd have to remind herself more than once that it was okay to call other members here by their first names instead of their ranks, as she did sometimes in private with her mentor, Greg Yarrow. She'd slipped, though, out of fear for him earlier today, but she wouldn't do it again.

Alpha Force was military, but its members clearly were less formal than any other unit she had associated with.

Jason shot a quick glance at her then—just as he flipped on the truck's turn signal.

They were back at Ft. Lukman, and he was about to enter the part of the road nearest the entry—just beyond where they'd first seen General Yarrow's car on fire.

Jason slowed down again, as if seeking clues. Or avoiding those stones on the road. Or both.

Sara couldn't help it. She looked around, too. The area was surrounded by trees similar to those they'd passed all along the drive. Could someone have shot something from the cover of the forest that set the Jeep's canvas on fire?

But wouldn't the guard in the kiosk have seen it?

Maybe it had been completely accidental. Maybe the people studying what was left of the vehicle would find an indication of what the general had been storing in the back that caught fire. Or maybe he was a closet smoker—though she'd been around him a lot over the past months and had seen, and smelled, no indication of that. And surely the vehicle would have been designed, for safety, for its canvas cover to withstand being hit by a lit butt, just in case.

Still, it seemed awfully coincidental for it to start burning in earnest, however it caught fire, just when the general entered Ft. Lukman.

Jason stopped at the kiosk. As he showed credentials to the guard who greeted them, Sara jumped as she heard a rapping on the passenger window beside her. She looked over.

It was Major Connell. She immediately pressed the button to roll the window down.

"Good," said the major. "You're back."

Sara felt herself quiver in anticipation. Had something else bad happened? Before asking, she looked around.

The hulk of General Yarrow's car was still there in the spot ahead of them. A couple of soldiers stood by it, rifles at their shoulders, obviously guarding the vehicle's corpse.

With the truck she rode in, there was a means of moving it to an out-of-the-way spot for further study before official disposal.

For now, though, Jason would have to steer around it.

But not immediately.

Sara stared back out the window toward Drew. "Is the general—" she began.

"He's doing okay. He wants to see you and me at the hospital ASAP."

"Fine." But Sara darted a glance toward Jason. "Only—"

"I'll get some of the guys to help me move the damaged car onto the ramp back there," he said, casually gesturing toward the back of the truck. He didn't seem at all perturbed that she'd be deserting him this quickly.

Which shot a bolt of unanticipated sorrow through Sara.

She hadn't planned on being with Jason for this amount of time.

She certainly hadn't planned on enjoying it.

But this just might be the only opportunity she would ever have to spend time with this appealing, sexy—and unattainable—man.

Ever.

And now it was over.

Chapter 5

General Yarrow's hospital room didn't impress Sara as looking any more exciting than any other hospital room she'd ever visited, except for its privacy. It was compact, with a single bed—which the general occupied—and two windows along one wall where the blinds had been opened, spilling light inside. The illumination struck the small chest of drawers where patients or their families could stow belongings. A TV hung overhead on the far wall. There were chairs—four of them, occupied now, including the one where Sara sat nearest to the general's right hand.

Appropriate, she realized.

It was all she could do to prevent herself from taking that hand in hers. To reassure him that everything would be okay.

Ridiculous. He was the one used to dictating the status of how whatever was happening each day played out. Plus, he was still her commanding officer. He would be shocked if she treated him like her friend or relative, no matter how fondly she thought of him.

Major Drew Connell and Sara had arrived only a couple of minutes ago. They'd entered the room and sat down in the seats as the general directed. The other two were occupied by Lieutenant Simon Parran and his wife, Lieutenant Grace Andreas-Parran, who'd obviously done a good job of accompanying the general here and ensuring that he was seen quickly in the emergency room.

Fortunately, his injuries were not life threatening. Grace had met them at the door and briefly informed them that General Yarrow had suffered a substantial amount of smoke inhalation. He'd been coughing and complained of a headache and shortness of breath. He was currently being treated with oxygen that he inhaled via tubes placed in his nose. Otherwise, he was fine.

He looked ashen, though, as his head rested on a pillow at the top of the raised back of the bed. His paleness was emphasized by the unmitigated blackness of his full head of hair—now more askew than Sara had ever seen it before.

But his light brown eyes were flashing, as always—ensuring that anyone on whom he directed his gaze knew exactly who was in charge.

"So where is the shell of my car now?" he demanded of Major Connell. The general, in his blue-plaid hospital gown, was the only one not dressed in camo attire.

Sara wasn't used to seeing him in anything but his casual uniform, jeans and T-shirt during off hours, or, occasionally, something more formal.

"By now it should be secured in an area within the base's main parking garage, sir," Drew said, leaning toward him. "Lieutenant McLinder went with Sergeant Connell to rent a special flatbed vehicle to move it, and they arrived back at the base just in time for the lieutenant to accompany me here."

The general nodded his approval toward Sara. The gingerness of the movement might not have been obvious to the others in this room who didn't work with him daily, but Sara could tell that he was in real discomfort—and trying to hide it. They all were doctors but she knew the general better than any of them.

She was his primary aide and hoped she would continue in that position for a long time to come.

But maybe not where he had intended, most recently, to station himself—Ft. Lukman.

An image of Sergeant Jason Connell flashed through Sara's mind, and she willed it away. If they didn't return to the base housing Alpha Force, then she would never see the gorgeous, devil-may-care noncom again. In either of his forms.

Either of his forms? Heck, the fire in the general's car had taken precedence in her mind over all else—even pondering how strange, and outrageous, the reality of shapeshifting was.

Not seeing Jason again would definitely be for the best.

"What's the next step, then?" the general asked.

"I presume you're having the remains examined by someone who'll be able to tell me what happened to the damned thing."

"I will, sir," Drew said. "I'm just having a little difficulty deciding on the right kind of forensics team for this. I of course don't want to use a civilian team, and because of the…well, delicate nature of the units stationed at Ft. Lukman and their relationship, I want to be sure I get the right kind of expertise in place, with complete discretion. And honesty."

"In other words," Simon said drily from his seat on the opposite side of the general's bed, "you want to bring in someone who won't either be ready to reveal any unusual things he may see—like shapeshifting— or afraid to point fingers at our new best friends, the Ultra Special Forces Team."

Simon was a tall man, whose straight, dark eyebrows matched his wavy, thick hair. Sara had noticed how often he shot glances toward his wife. She knew they were newlyweds, and had also heard, as a result of the general's grumblings, some of the awful details of their kidnapping while on their honeymoon.

Fortunately, other members of Alpha Force, primarily Simon's brother, Lieutenant Quinn Parran, and Grace's aide, Sergeant Kristine Norwood, had helped to bring them home—although their involvement hadn't been strictly in accordance with military protocol. That hadn't pleased the general—but Sara thought his irritation had been more for show in his position as commanding officer of Alpha Force than his real feelings.

What Simon had just said worried Sara, who liked everything military to be by the book. That included all units being…well, ordinary—even if she already knew that Alpha Force was anything but.

Plus, all military units should unquestionably keep any rivalry under control for the good of the country.

Assuming rivalry was what was going on at Ft. Lukman. If so, it was way out of hand in the event it had been the reason for General Yarrow's injury.

"You think they're responsible for this?" Sara demanded, recalling how Jason and she had already discussed that possibility. Her initial experiences with members of the USFT unit, in the cafeteria, in the BOQ and otherwise, hadn't been especially cordial. In fact, she'd sensed a lot of animosity from that team without understanding why…although maybe they simply mistrusted another military unit alleged to have woo-woo stuff affiliated with it, like shapeshifters. She could understand that. But all military troops had to act for the good of the country, not in accordance with their own suspicions or misgivings.

Surely no one within the USFT would intentionally do something to harm the commanding officer of another unit…would they?

Simon appeared ready to say something affirmative in response to Sara's question, but the general waved his hand dismissively. "Unknown, at least for now. That's why we have to be sure to handle the investigation appropriately."

"Do you have any suggestions about who should investigate your car, then, General?" asked Grace, who was seated beside her husband, opposite Sara.

Before he responded, Sara broke in. "I have an idea, sir. At least for starters. We can keep it low-key at first, but there's someone stationed at Ft. Lukman who apparently has an excellent background in working with cars. If we get him to do more than just move the vehicle—"

"You're talking about Sergeant Jason Connell, aren't you?" Simon's tone was neutral, but there was something troubling about the way he avoided looking toward Drew—cousin to the soldier under discussion.

"That's right," Sara agreed. "I understand he's an expert in fixing automobiles. As long as he doesn't do anything to obscure any evidence needed to be confirmed by a neutral third party, why not have him start the investigation? Major Connell already directed that he take a lot of confirming photographs while the car was still at the scene of the event. They can be shown to whoever conducts the official investigation later, too." She didn't call what had happened an accident. With that intense a fire, she suspected it was anything but.

"I don't mean to insult your cousin, Drew," cut in Grace, her gaze now on the major, "or offend you, but—"

"But you're going to, anyway." Drew turned to Sara. "You're probably not aware of the full situation with Jason, Sara, but—"

"But he's a car thief," broke in Simon.

"*Was* a car thief." Drew's expression darkened as he turned toward the lieutenant. "He enlisted in the military and joined Alpha Force as part of his penance for past misconduct."

"Right. It didn't hurt that joining up kept him out of prison." Simon was smiling now. "Hey, we understand. Far as we know, he's now a model soldier. A fine member of Alpha Force. We've seen him do great things with the unit's automobiles that need servicing. But—"

"I assume you're not suggesting that he could have been the one to somehow booby-trap my car, are you?" asked the general drily. "Why would he?"

"Why did anyone?" countered Simon. "Assuming it wasn't just spontaneous combustion."

Sara tuned out of the discussion for a moment, digesting what she had just learned. Sergeant Jason Connell wasn't merely a car lover and outstanding mechanic. He had apparently been arrested, and maybe convicted, of being a car thief. He must have agreed to join Alpha Force and throw himself under the scrutiny of his well-regarded cousin Major Drew Connell, a commissioned officer and a medical doctor to boot, to keep himself out of prison.

And this was the guy Sara had found so sexually exciting?

Hell, even if he was sexually exciting, everything she learned about him made him even more of a wrong choice for involvement.

Even so… "General, sir, I didn't know all that about Sergeant Connell. But he is a member of Alpha Force, and you're its commanding officer. He has a good reputation for working with cars, and he obviously isn't going to steal what remains of your Jeep. Sir—" Sara turned to Drew "—as I said, you've already ordered that photos be taken. You've also said that the remains should be kept in a protected area. You can additionally order that some of the other soldiers on base, maybe more security team members who aren't part of Alpha Force or USFT, assist Sergeant Connell, and be there the whole time he's conducting his investigation. Although—" She looked back at the general. "If he was involved, and there was anything he could steal off the damaged car and hide, he'll have done that already."

"True," said General Yarrow. "And I wouldn't have approved acceptance of the sergeant into Alpha Force if I'd thought he was still any kind of risk. Although having someone watching to confirm he doesn't do anything wrong with my former vehicle now is a good idea. In fact—"

Uh-oh. Sara didn't like the general's smile. She had seen it before when he was about to give an order that he knew the recipient would hate.

He was looking at her.

"Lieutenant McLinder, I hereby order you to work with Sergeant Connell to find out what the hell happened to my car—and to make sure he does a good job of checking it out."

Her shock must have shown on her face, since, for the first time that she'd seen after the explosion, General Yarrow actually laughed. So did the other three Alpha Force members in the room.

Then the general grew serious. "One thing, though. I'm pretty sure you already know it, that you've seen some things you didn't expect despite my warning before you preceded me to Ft. Lukman."

"Are you about to tell me that Sergeant Connell is a shapeshifter, sir?" Sara tried to put levity and nonchalance into her voice, but knew she failed miserably. She looked, one by one, at the three Alpha Force members now in her presence, all medical doctors and commissioned officers. "I don't know if everyone in Alpha Force is a shapeshifter," she said, "but I now believe that some of you are. And that includes Jason Connell. So if you—"

General Yarrow raised his hand in a sudden gesture that she recognized was intended to command. She immediately shut up.

Which was a good thing, since a voice sounded from behind her. "General Yarrow. Greg. We just heard and had to come here to make sure you were all right."

Sara turned. In the doorway were a couple of the USFT members she had seen in the cafeteria. They were preceded by a short, stocky man also in camos, his insignias indicating that he was a general. He'd been the one to speak.

"I'm fine, Hugo. Everyone—" General Yarrow's gaze took in the Alpha Force group around him as he gestured toward the newcomers "—this is General Hugo Myars, commanding officer of the Ultra Special Forces Team. I'm sure you've met some of his team members." He nodded toward the not especially friendly officers Sara had previously spoken with.

Myars maneuvered his way around the representatives of Alpha Force, while his backup remained near the door, their caps respectfully doffed and in their hands. "I know our people aren't merging as well as we'd initially hoped, so the exercises we planned are on hold, and now this. But I'm here to let you know, Greg, that the USFT and all its team members wish you a speedy recovery, and we're ready to work with Alpha Force as soon as we can start conducting joint training sessions."

Nice gesture, Sara thought.

Unless, of course, this was just General Myars's way to try to disguise the fact that he, or some of his subordinates, were the ones who'd set fire to General Yarrow's car.

But if so, why?

And did this unanticipated get-well visit make what Jason would find in the Jeep's remains even more critical…because it would point right to these apparently kindhearted fellow soldiers?

Jason couldn't help it.

At the moment, he stood alone on the hard concrete of Ft. Lukman's main parking garage, arms crossed, enjoying the rare and temporary solitude. Thinking.

He was in the military now. That usually meant having too many people around.

Although there were some people—one in particular at the moment—who he admitted to himself weren't so difficult to be near. But not just now.

He loved cars. They had a purpose, were understandable and followed logical rules.

They were indifferent to the fact that he was a

shapeshifter, didn't care that he had made some mistakes when he was younger—well, except that he'd occasionally taken some cars away from their real, and possibly abusive or ignorant, owners.

He particularly loved those cars that could be considered classics.

That didn't necessarily include General Yarrow's aging Jeep, but Jason had seen, when he had serviced it before, how the general had babied it. Kept it in excellent condition.

Let experts—like Jason—work on it.

Now, though, it was gone—a pile of mostly metal debris. Smelly, fire-scarred, isolated wreckage that Jason was currently examining, all by himself.

He had done as ordered and found a rare location within the main garage that contained only a few spaces, an area on the third floor where only the top brass were authorized to park. A secure enough area that, by closing a garage door and erecting a barrier comprised of excess metal and wood from recent construction on the base, he'd been able to jerry-rig a portion into a pretty secure area after hauling the wreckage there in the truck he'd rented.

He'd been there for a while now, initially just staring at what was left of the deceased Jeep.

As he'd been told, he had found some security guys who were not members of either Alpha Force or that damned Ultra Special Forces Team, and given them orders to show up in about an hour to guard the general's former car.

That was one good thing about being a sergeant.

Even though he was a noncommissioned officer, there were some folks who were of inferior ranks, and he could give them orders.

On the other hand, there were plenty of people of higher rank than him.

Like that gorgeous, sexy lieutenant. He hadn't wanted to think about her now, but she had insinuated herself into his mind, anyway.

And that stirred some of his most sensitive body parts. Bad time to allow her into his thoughts.

No, right now he ached to dig into the mess and figure out exactly what had happened. And not just because the senior commanding officer of his very special military unit had been in the vehicle when it caught fire.

No, it was even more because he gave a damn.

But Drew wanted a completely unbiased review, by non-Alpha Force investigators, of what was left, in case it contained evidence that pointed to someone's having caused the damage.

Someone like one of the members of that other major unit at Ft. Lukman, whose members had decided to look down their snooty human noses at their rival team here that they didn't understand at all, except to believe it inferior.

Little did they know.

But would they have tried to kill the superior officer of that unit? If so, why? And how had they set that fire?

Jason had changed into a well-worn T-shirt and jeans so he wouldn't appear to be doing anything official. Plus, he didn't want to mess up his uniform.

As he'd intended all along, he now approached the charred mass from the rear.

That was where the smoke had first appeared, or at least that was what it had looked like while watching the general drive through the gate.

He studied it first, then drew closer, knowing he'd better not touch it or move anything around. He wasn't an expert in finding evidence, and he might ruin any that happened to be there.

But he knew cars, damn it. And he particularly wanted—

"Hello, Sergeant Connell."

He forced himself not to jump out of his skin—his human skin—despite being startled by the familiar, strong female voice from behind him.

Instead, he pivoted to see Sara McLinder walk through the only door to this area that he had left accessible.

"Lieutenant." He nodded in acknowledgment but didn't want her here. Did he? The sight of her slim body, sexy even in her unisex camo uniform, made him want to approach her and do a lot more than salute.

He stayed where he was.

Especially because he anticipated that she was there to give him orders—like, get away from the damn wreck. Go somewhere else. Obey what she said, just because she could tell him what to do.

"Sergeant—Jason," she said. "Do you have a camera with you?"

He nodded. "I took a lot of photos before having

this thing moved here, like my cuz said." He'd have done it, anyway.

He'd wanted the reminder of how this poor vehicle had ended up immediately after its destruction.

"Good. Let's take some more right here before we start."

"Start what?" He didn't even attempt to hide the suspicion from his tone.

But that only brought a smile to her lovely, smooth features. A smile that emphasized the natural pink-ness of her lips that wasn't enhanced by any lipstick.

Lord, how he'd love to taste them…right now.

"Drew knows a lot better than I do about your skill in working with cars, but I've been impressed with what I've seen and heard. You should pretty much only look, and touch only what you have to—and take a lot more photos so that, when any experts are brought in, they won't say that any evidence has become so tainted that they can't draw any logical conclusions. But even unbiased investigators might miss something a car expert wouldn't. So I've gotten your cousin's approval to ask you to conduct an initial investigation."

"You did that for me?" Jason's look was smug and sexy as he aimed a smile at her. "I didn't know you cared."

Sara shouldn't have told him she'd been the one to convince Drew. The guy obviously assumed that she'd done it because she was attracted to him.

Not that she'd admit it to him…but she was.

She raised her chin as she shook her head in a slowly

skeptical denial, staring him straight in those gorgeous golden eyes. "I don't—not about you. But I do care about General Yarrow, and I want to make sure we get all the answers in case this wasn't simply a terrible accident."

"So you think his car was sabotaged." Jason's words sounded more like a statement than a question, even as his expression grew serious.

"I believe it's a real possibility, so I want to know the truth." She pulled her own camera and some rubber gloves from the tote bag she had carried, then set the bag on the concrete beside her. "Besides, I'm here to observe...and help."

His turn to look skeptical. She didn't like that at all. "Just how do you plan to help?"

She wasn't about to tell him she was under orders to supervise him—not unless that became necessary because he looked about to screw things up. With his apparent ego, it would be better to let him think he was in control. *Think* being the operative word.

"Observation is the main thing. And taking pictures, too. In fact, since you've already taken some, I can be in charge of the rest, at least for now. Plus—well, if you need assistance I'll see what I can do. I can at least hold things out of the way, act as a second pair of eyes, whatever."

He nodded. "That sounds doable."

"Fine. Let's get started. Put these on first." She handed him one pair of the rubber gloves, keeping a second for herself. Then, drawing her gaze abruptly away from Jason, she strode toward the pile of metal remains, aiming her camera and snapping initial pictures.

This was the same camera she'd used to take pictures of his shift. She had already downloaded them onto her laptop computer and made a backup copy, password protected both files, then erased them from the camera.

Alpha Force's cover would not be blown by her.

Taking closer pictures of the Jeep now would be better, though. "Why don't you do this in a narrative?" she suggested. "I have a lot of memory left on the card in this camera and can take videos."

"Good idea."

Great. They seemed to be in agreement. For the moment, at least. And the division of labor seemed reasonable.

Sara considered herself fairly competent with a camera, but less so with a car.

Even so, she wanted to do a damned good job of supervising Jason as he conducted his preliminary analysis of what had happened to the Jeep to cause it to catch on fire.

Maybe even help with it herself.

Assuming, of course, that the fire hadn't destroyed all indications of its initial cause.

Jason began at the rear of the hulk. There was nothing left of the canvas that had once been the removable exterior covering, but the metal framework, blackened and curled in places from the heat, remained mostly intact.

"Is it cool enough for you to touch anything?" she asked.

"Yeah, it's fine now." He was already bending over the back of the thing, mostly looking. But then he probed a few places with his fingers.

For the next few minutes, Sara mostly recorded and listened as Jason used his knowledge of cars to study every centimeter of what he was able to see and described what he was doing.

At first, he apparently saw nothing that he seemed to think was out of place in the remains of a burned-out Jeep.

At one point he asked, "Do you happen to know if General Yarrow was carrying anything in the bed here?"

"He didn't mention anything."

"Well, we'll need to check with him. I see a few things that are definitely not part of the car, but they don't look especially dangerous, either."

Without moving them, he pointed them out to her. One was the burned carcass of what appeared to be a battery, and the other was a small piece of metal that could have been from a child's toy, maybe even a model of the Jeep, judging by its angles.

Then there was what was probably the remains of a steel fishing rod and a lure box containing what once had probably been hooks but were now just melted puddles of metal. Some additional small, melted clumps of metal. Nothing useful or conclusive. In the passenger seat were the remains of what must have been the general's overnight bag, still partially intact.

Sara dutifully continued to shoot the video, recording Jason's mention of each item and exactly where it lay in the midst of ashes and other debris.

She was impressed with Jason's meticulousness and attention to detail in the ruined Jeep. He pointed out the parts he recognized, those that were no longer recognizable but had qualities that allowed him to make assumptions, and more.

He occasionally asked for her to gently touch something, holding it out of the way so he could pry even farther into some inside area. She shot more pictures of each of those areas when her assignment was complete.

Eventually, after more than an hour, Jason was through.

"I know it'll all be speculation," Sara said, holding the camera on Jason, "but do you have any initial opinion about the origin of the fire?"

His handsome features grew even sharper as his expression hardened. "Nothing conclusive, nothing I can point to that proves it was anything but some odd mechanical failure or spontaneous combustion or unavoidable accident," he said, "but despite finding nothing obvious during this first examination, I knew this Jeep well after servicing it for General Yarrow. I believe this was somehow deliberately sabotaged, set on fire. And I'll do anything I can to find proof."

Sara turned off the camera and looked at him, seeing the frustration and sorrow on his face. She wanted to do something to comfort him, but all she could do was to acknowledge her agreement. "That's my belief, too," she said quietly. "But since you didn't see anything to hang that opinion on—"

"I will," he said grimly. "Count on it."

Chapter 6

Jason used his cell phone to call the head of the small base security team. Time for them to guard the car's remains. It was getting late on this very busy day.

Sara waited with him, concern furrowing her brow beneath her short cap of blond hair. He'd never thought frowning sexy before. But, as unfortunate as it was, everything about Lieutenant Sara McLinder made him ache to touch her.

Everything including her light citrus scent.

And the way she'd jumped in to help him study the Jeep. Concentrated on taking videos. Essentially interviewed him to preserve his thoughts and actions in case they helped lead to what the hell had caused the vehicle to catch fire.

Everything including the way she now pulled her phone from her pocket often to check the time.

Yes, even that was sexy and taunted him to get up close and personal with her, encourage her to relax… and more.

Not that he'd ever give in to those urges. She wasn't exactly the kind to appreciate them.

Soon, three men on security detail—all privates, none a member of either of the primary units at Ft. Lukman, and all vetted to be trustworthy—arrived.

No chances were to be taken with the Jeep's carcass, even though Jason felt certain he'd done a pretty good job checking it over. There just wasn't anything useful to be found.

But the general would want to see it once he was feeling well enough to return here. Maybe he'd examine the remains himself. And, most likely, he would call in his own most trusted military forensics experts to confirm Jason's conclusions—or at least he'd have to consent to whoever was given the assignment.

"Let's go report to my cuz," he finally said to Sara as they left the garage. "We can show him the photos, see what he wants us to do with them." He kept his tone casual, sergeant to lieutenant.

"Fine," she responded in her characteristic clipped tone. Why did he find that sexy, too?

Sara kept pace with his long strides across sidewalks toward the building near the entry gate that housed the offices of the base's commanding officers.

That included General Yarrow's. Jason had seen

his specially furnished office here on the senior CO's earlier visits.

Drew had an office there, too. It was down the hall of the building's second floor. That's where Jason headed now, along with Sara.

But he hated having nothing conclusive to report. Especially since Drew had initially put him in charge of moving the damaged vehicle, but also agreed that he should start the investigation into the fire's cause. Thanks to Sara.

Of course Jason wasn't sure why she'd promoted the idea of having him check out the Jeep first. She clearly was uncomfortable with who, and what, he was.

They passed other soldiers on Ft. Lukman's sidewalks, some from Alpha Force, some from the Ultra Special Forces Team and others among the few miscellaneous soldiers with high security clearances who also happened to be stationed there. Jason saluted appropriately. So did Sara.

Jason recalled his first days after enlisting, getting used to such stringent protocol. He'd wanted to rebel, but knew that being there, following the rules, would be all that could keep him out of prison. He'd kept telling himself it would eventually be second nature to him.

Even now, it wasn't entirely, but he'd gotten used to it. He'd even gotten used to his own ambivalence about being in the military. Sort of.

Sara said nothing, not at first. But as they reached the building, she stopped and turned toward him. Her expression appeared troubled. He wondered again why such an unsexy look on her face made his downstairs body parts want to stand up and salute.

She shook her head then and tossed him a smile that seemed anything but happy. "You know, as we walked here, I kept looking at everyone I didn't yet know, wondering if he or she was part of Alpha Force, and, if so, whether they were shifters. And you know I'd been fighting any belief in people…like you. Even though, having seen you, I now know the truth."

He realized how much that stuff that she considered woo-woo, yet real, must really bother the by-the-book officer. Growing up the way he did, knowing that his kind needed to hide from most of the world to stay alive, he should have despised her.

He didn't. Instead, he kind of understood. And wanted to help.

"A lot of Alpha Force members are away right now, either on missions or vacation, so you've probably met everyone in our unit who's here at the moment. Tell you what, one of these days maybe we'll have a little talk not only about Alpha Force but shapeshifting in general. It's always been fascinating to me, even though I'm part of it. Maybe learning more will make it easier for you to deal with, too."

She sucked in her full lips pensively. He wished for a moment that he could do the same…in a nice, hot, endless kiss. But he just waited for her response.

"I'd like that," she said, then pivoted and headed toward the building's front entrance.

They walked up the stairway to the second floor. General Yarrow's office was right there, and Jason noticed Sara's glance toward its closed door, with the CO's name on it, before she accompanied him down the hall to Drew's office. His cuz, too, had his name on the outside door. Jason knew that this office, a new one for Drew, was mostly for show and convenience.

Drew spent most of his time when present at Ft. Lukman in the downstairs lab area of the building near the outer edge of the base. His primary office was a small one there, too—the one where the recent Alpha Force meeting had been held.

Sara, who had slightly preceded Jason, knocked on the door, but he didn't wait for a response. He opened it and walked inside, holding the door open for the lovely lieutenant.

She blinked at him in irritation but he turned immediately toward the standard-issue desk at the far side of the room. Drew sat behind it, also glaring at him.

"Come in," Drew said through clenched teeth.

Jason just smiled. "Don't mind if I do." Again without waiting, he approached Drew's desk and pulled out one of the two chairs facing it, both with gray tweed upholstery attached to a light wood frame, and motioned for Sara to sit.

She hesitated, as if not comfortable with the gesture, but then complied without comment.

"Okay, you two," Drew said, and Jason was glad to see that Sara didn't cringe at being grouped with him in Drew's upcoming inquiry. "I gather you didn't find anything particularly helpful, but give me a rundown."

Jason did, starting with the photos he'd shot before

relocating the charred remains, then annotating the narration they presented when Sara ran her videos.

Drew was silent for a moment when they finished. "Maybe I am trying to make a bigger deal of this than it warrants. General Yarrow was injured, but he's okay. In fact, I understand he'll be well enough to return here as early as tomorrow. If there's no evidence that the fire was deliberately set—"

"Then someone was damned good at setting it," Jason interrupted. From the corner of his eye he saw Sara glance toward him. He caught her gaze, and they both gave slight nods.

"Then that's what you think, too, Sara?" Drew asked.

"Until someone proves that it was just some stupid little thing like the sun shining on a piece of glass inside and heating a spot on the canvas cover till it ignited, or the general just unfortunately passed a smoker who happened to flick a butt at just the wrong angle— and, yes, I can see from your expression that you're as dubious as I am about those—then I'm going to assume the worst. We're not experts, but I'm sure you and the general can find some guys who do this all the time. I'd just request that you keep me informed about anything they find."

"Me, too," Jason said, wanting not only to support Sara but to hug her, as well.

She had expressed everything he'd wanted to, and then some.

If she let herself, Sara knew she would feel depressed as she left the major's office with Jason.

They headed back toward the stairway that had taken them to this floor, then down the steps. Jason's footfalls were light, sounded carefree as he took those steps a couple at a time.

Their discussion with Drew must have pleased him more than it did Sara.

The good news was that General Yarrow was improving, might even be there, at Ft. Lukman, tomorrow.

The bad? Well, nothing that she didn't already know. No news wasn't necessarily good news.

And now it was very late in the afternoon. Sara hadn't yet formed any friendships with other officers at the base. She wanted to, at least with members of Alpha Force, and might be able to call on one or two and invite them for coffee or whatever to get to know them better.

She didn't even want to try with any members of the Ultra Special Forces Team. She might have a lot more in common with them than with Alpha Force members, but the animosity between the two units remained almost palpable—and she had come here to help the general work with the unit reporting to him.

"Hey, Lieutenant," Jason said as he held the building's door open for her to exit. "What're you up to now?"

Had he read her mind? Or was her dejection obvious?

She pasted a smile on her face as she looked at him. Then it turned more genuine. It was hard to stay depressed in the presence of a guy so great-looking, so cock-sure of himself, who teased sexily with every gaze of his golden eyes.

"Just thought I'd head back to the BOQ and do some reading. I'm tired of excitement for now."

"Well, if you'd like just a little more excitement first—fun stuff, nothing heavy—you could join me. I'm heading over to the kennel to pick up my best friend."

She tilted her head at him, slightly puzzled. "I assume, if you're going to the kennel, that it's—"

"Yep, my cover dog, Shadow. I've been letting him hang out with his buddies much too long lately. It's time he spent some quality time with me. And with you, too, if you're interested."

"Cover dog?" She had thought Shadow resembled Jason in wolf form but still… What did that mean?

"You've been at the kennel, seen some of the dogs," Jason said. "They're mostly trained for K-9 uses, security and bomb sniffing and all that. But in addition—well, all of us shifters have a pet who looks like us in our animal forms. That helps confuse people who don't really know, or understand, what Alpha Force is about. If they happen to see a wolflike dog, they're much more likely to assume it's a wolflike dog than a shapeshifter. Same goes for Colleen Hodell's cougar-resembling cat. Smaller, of course. She keeps Puka in her BOQ unit."

Fascinating, Sara thought.

"With all that was going on," Jason continued, "I figured Shadow would be better off there, with company, than hanging out with me, but I miss the guy, want to spend some time with him."

"Sure," Sara said. "I'd love to play with Shadow."

And you, too, she thought, but didn't say it. Yet suddenly she felt much more lighthearted because she wouldn't be alone, at least not for now.

Knowing she'd be in Jason's company a little longer had nothing to do with it.

She loved it!

While Sara was growing up in Cleveland, Ohio, she'd had a dog—a small one, a Shih Tzu mix named Sissy, who had loved to play fetch with nylon bones. She'd been a sweetheart. Sara had missed her as much as she'd missed the rest of the family when she'd left home to attend Kent State to study political science— and to join ROTC, since she'd known she wanted a career in the military.

Sissy was gone now, and Sara hadn't gotten to know the dog her parents had subsequently gotten from a rescue organization very well, mostly because she visited so infrequently.

She'd forgotten how much she enjoyed dogs—until that afternoon.

Jason and she each had a dog leashed beside them as they left the building housing the kennel on its main floor. Jason's was, of course, Shadow.

He had also gotten her a dog for companionship that afternoon. "This is Duke," he'd told her as he handed her the leash of a large shepherd-wolfhound mix. "He's the cover dog for the second in command stationed here at Alpha Force, Lieutenant Patrick Worley. Patrick's been on vacation with his wife, Mariah. She's a nature writer and they went back to Alaska, where they met, for a couple of weeks. They're due back tomorrow, but we've all been exercising Duke in the meantime."

And now, Sara was running with dogs and Jason on the neatly trimmed lawn beneath canopies of trees, and between some of the cookie-cutter low buildings that filled Ft. Lukman, including the one that housed the general's, and Drew's, offices. The one holding the kennel—and the lab areas below—was on the periphery of the rest.

Sara knew she was a bit out of shape despite all the calisthenics she performed as a matter of course nearly every morning at home, as part of her military regimen. But she hadn't run like this for—well, forever.

"Please, wait!" she finally cried to Jason, who was ahead of her with Shadow. Duke tugged on his leash to catch up. "I need to rest."

"Is that an order, Lieutenant?" Jason called. He'd turned and was running backward. At least his pace was slower now.

"That's an order," Sara gasped, stopping altogether. "Duke, come here."

"Here, let me give you a lesson in training these guys." Jason was suddenly right beside her, and the dogs, too, had stopped. Both large canines were panting heavily. So was Sara. Jason barely seemed out of breath, although Sara did see patches of perspiration near his armpits, and his forehead, too, was damp.

She must look awful, she thought—definitely sweaty and breathless and generally a mess.

So why, when Jason looked at her, did he smile so sexily?

Hell, she knew why. That was his usual look. But if he was totally turned off by her, he was kind enough not to show it.

Which in a way was too bad. Maybe it would make her stop lusting for this highly inappropriate soldier.

"Okay, Shadow." Jason stood straight as he looked down at his dog. He raised one hand and pointed to Shadow's rear. "Sit." The canine obeyed immediately. "Now you try it with Duke. That's elementary, and they've all been taught the same commands."

Sara did so and found herself surprisingly pleased when Duke sat, stood and gave her his paw, all on command. "Is he trained for any of the K-9 things you mentioned, like sniffing out drugs or whatever?"

"Sure. They've all been taught some of that, too. A few are real experts, and they're used when that kind of help is needed. But most of these guys are just excellent camouflage pets." He paused. "Are you ready to take Duke back to his quarters? I'm keeping Shadow with me tonight."

So he would have company, even though it was just a dog.

Sara would be on her own—which never used to bother her. She'd find male companionship now and then when she wanted some, but not here, of course.

"Tell you what," she said. "I saw an outdoor eating area at the base cafeteria. Why don't we grab dinner together with both dogs—part of their training, of course." And definitely not fraternizing. Or at least arguably not, if anyone called her on it.

"Fine with me." Jason gave her one of those hot grins again, as if he knew exactly what she was thinking. "You hungry now?"

"Hungry enough." Under other circumstances, she'd go shower and change clothes before having dinner with a great-looking guy.

But now, it was better if she stayed grungy and unalluring. Much better.

Because even if she hadn't yet been able to get her attraction to Jason completely under control, at least he couldn't possibly find her appealing.

Jason kept the dogs company while Sara went inside to grab her dinner.

He'd have liked to have accompanied her, even paid for her meal, but it was better this way.

No way could it look like a date.

Especially since the cafeteria was filled with both Alpha Force members and those from that damned Ultra Special Forces Team.

Jason sat at a table for two, bending over and petting the dogs. Talking to them.

It kept him from having to speak with anyone nearby—who mostly seemed to be USFT guys. Too bad he didn't know what their special skills really were. What the hell made them more ultra than regular Special Forces?

He wasn't about to ask. Probably no Alpha Force

member would. Better that both units keep pretty much to themselves for now, till given orders otherwise to start whatever joint training was planned for them—although he had no doubt that these guys had at least some idea what made Alpha Force so special.

"They've got Salisbury steak as their special tonight." Sara had returned, carrying a tray, and Jason inhaled the aroma of the dish she had mentioned. Smelled good. He figured he'd get some, too, instead of his usual T-bone here.

This cafeteria was used to serving Alpha Force members red-meat entrées.

"Did you get enough to treat these fellows?" Jason gestured toward the dogs, whom he'd given commands to lie down and stay. Their noses were in the air, though—both of them.

"I didn't think people food was good for them."

"Not as a general diet, but treats don't hurt. I'll get a little extra."

He went inside. When he came out again with his tray a few minutes later, the dogs hadn't moved.

A couple of those damned USFT guys had, though. They were close to Sara, apparently hitting on her. Both were in camo uniforms, and they also wore the insignias of a lieutenant and a captain.

Her rank and above.

She seemed friendly enough to them, too, chatting. He focused his excellent hearing on the conversation before joining them.

Sounded innocent enough—maybe. They were asking about her work for General Yarrow, what had happened to his Jeep, how he was doing.

Did these guys already know? Were they trying to learn how much Sara knew?

Oh, but she was cagy in the responses Jason heard, though. All she said was that so far she'd heard of no indication that the fire in the vehicle had been anything but some kind of weird accident. And since the general was okay, that was all she needed to know.

Jason took that opportunity to sit back down across from her.

Shadow and Duke stirred. He looked at them both and said, "Stay," and they did.

"So how's the Salisbury?" he asked Sara, ignoring the others.

"Pretty good." She hesitated only a moment before saying to Jason, obviously for the benefit of the other officers, "So after dinner you'll teach me the commands you use for getting these guys to fetch?"

"Sure will," he said, and smiled at her.

And loved the way she smiled back.

Sara hadn't imagined that having dinner with Jason would turn into a land mine of possible dangers, but it had, at least in a way.

She didn't, couldn't, trust those USFT guys until what had happened to the general's car was explained, but she'd been trying to both answer their questions and interject some of her own to find out if they were just stringing her along while knowing the answers themselves.

But there'd been no indication of that.

And she had of course wanted to make it clear that she wasn't simply fraternizing with Jason.

So why did the idea feel so good?

The USFT group returned to their prior table. Jason and she took their time finishing their meal. Jason even gave her some of the meat he'd saved to give to Duke, while he did the same with Shadow.

And then they left.

Sara would have loved to take Duke back to the BOQ as her companion that night, but Jason had already said that his master, Patrick Worley, would probably be back soon. No sense for her to get any more involved with the dog—either for her own sake or for his.

She enjoyed the way they sauntered, though—Jason and her and both dogs—back to the edge of the base and the kennel.

She felt almost mournful putting Duke back in his enclosure, even though he went leaping inside to be greeted by other base canines.

Then she walked back out again with Jason and Shadow.

It was starting to get dark. "We'll accompany you to the BOQ," Jason told her. "Not that I anticipate anything bad happening on the base, but in case you need backup we'll be there."

She didn't need backup. But she appreciated their company—for more reasons than gentlemanliness on the part of Jason, which she figured wasn't his normal demeanor.

Was he, after all, as attracted to her as she was to him?

On one level, she hoped not. It would only make it harder for them to stay apart, as they had to do.

On another level...well, why shouldn't it be as difficult for him as it was for her?

"Lovely night tonight," she said to make conversation as they strolled toward her quarters.

"Yeah." By the location of his voice, she could tell he was looking at her, and she felt herself begin to blush.

"Glad the general might be here tomorrow." She hoped that her change of subject would be a turnoff to him. It was to her.

Kind of.

She knew what would be a real turnoff to her. "So when will you be shapeshifting again? I've heard that you Alpha Forcers don't always have to wait until a full moon."

"That's true. And I don't know."

When they reached the front door of the BOQ she looked around, hoping someone else would be there so the parting would be brief and simple.

They were alone.

She bent and patted Shadow. "Good night, guy." She stood again. "And good night, Jason."

She didn't expect it...did she? But he leaned down toward her and planted just the hint of a kiss on her mouth—leaving her wanting more. Much more.

"Good night, Lieutenant." He backed off, grinned and sauntered away, whistling an unidentifiable tune.

Chapter 7

Turning away from the BOQ, Jason yawned. He didn't bother covering his mouth. No one was around except Shadow, and the dog wouldn't be offended.

And besides, yawning in the face of an officer might only make him feel better.

Not if it was Sara McLinder, though. He'd much rather leave a favorable impression with her. Like that kiss.

Too bad he hadn't dared more with her...yet. But his body was still reacting to that little peck.

It had been a long day. A lot had happened—starting from when the general's car had caught fire.

Jason knew he was dog-tired. Loved that expression. It certainly fit.

But feeling that way wouldn't stop him from what he still had to do.

He stepped up the pace as he and Shadow headed back toward the building housing the kennels…and the labs. While hurrying, he called Noel Chuma.

"Is Simon Parran doing anything tonight?" he immediately asked when the guy, not a shifter but one really good aide to some of those who were, answered the phone. At the moment, Noel was assigned both to Lieutenant Simon Parran and to Sergeant Jason Connell.

Jason never had to guess who had priority in the case of a conflict.

"Nope," was Noel's response. "Are you?"

"Yeah. You near the lab?"

"I can be there in five minutes."

"Me, too. See ya there." Jason ended the connection.

He had lied to Sara. She'd asked if he planned to shapeshift anytime soon. He'd claimed he hadn't decided on a time.

But he had already intended to shift tonight. He still needed answers about the damage to General Yarrow's Jeep. They all needed answers. And his plain, ordinary human senses weren't nearly as much help as his enhanced wolfen senses might be.

"Hey, boy," he said to Shadow as they finally reached the door to the building they'd been heading toward. The dog's tail wagged. "I'll leave you with your buddies again. If all goes well, I'll be back for you in a little while and you'll go home with me."

Not that his quarters, in the building housing the base's NCOs, were especially lush. But he liked having Shadow around for company and believed that his dog, too, preferred being out and about, at least some of the time, rather than hanging out with his canine pack.

Jason swiped his key card and they entered the building on the main floor where the kennels were located. By the time he had let Shadow into the large enclosure with his closest canine friends—including Duke, who greeted him nose to nose once more—Noel Chuma had caught up with him.

Noel had dark-toned skin. Though he was on the short side, he had the build of a guy who worked out a lot. Maybe that was how he made up for not having all the abilities of the Alpha Forcers he helped. He hadn't bothered putting on his uniform that night, but instead wore a black T-shirt over equally dark jeans. The better not to be seen when Jason left him in the woods later.

He'd also thrown a backpack over his shoulders. "Hi, bro," he said. "Let's go downstairs. I need both a light and some elixir."

"Sounds good."

At the door to the stairway, as Jason prepared to swipe his other key card, he noticed some scratches in the paint. "You seen this?" he asked Noel.

"No." The other man bent down to scrutinize the area. "You think someone tried to break in? One of those USFT guys?"

Alpha Force had beefed up security in this building when they'd anticipated the arrival of another unit to be stationed at Ft. Lukman. There were two types of key cards—one to enter the kennel area upstairs, which were given out to nearly anyone who might need to help out with the dogs, and a second kind to get down to the highly classified lab area. Not many of those were available.

And it now appeared that someone who didn't have the second kind of key card had gotten frustrated about that.

Too bad they'd decided against using security cameras—but there was too much of a chance that pictures taken of shapeshifters could get into the wrong hands. Or even on the internet.

"Could be one of them—although as far as I know they're not aware of the importance of the lab facilities down there. Tell you what. You tell my cuz about this while I'm shifted, okay?"

"Yeah."

They headed downstairs and emerged about five minutes later with all Noel needed in his backpack, closing and locking the door carefully behind them. Without discussing it, they both walked straight into the depths of the woods nearest the building, which was in a remote site on the base.

There, Jason drank the elixir and stripped while Noel aimed the light at him. Immediately, Jason felt the initial throes of his shift.

"Have fun," Noel called. "And be careful. I'll call Major Connell and hang mostly near here, but I'll be around if you need me."

Jason answered with an acknowledging growl.

Jason bounded even farther into the cover of the thick trees then followed the inside of the base's fence around its perimeter. He didn't have time to revel in his wolfen state. Not at this moment. But he loved the feeling. Always.

Right now, he needed to get to the area around the main entrance where the fire in the general's car had first been noticed.

It was dark, late enough that not many people were out walking the grounds either on official security patrols or otherwise. Good. He barely had to hide. And some of those he saw were part of Alpha Force so there would be no repercussions, even if they noticed him.

He reached the area closest to the BOQ, though there was another building paralleling it that was nearer to him. He spared a quick glance and sniff in that direction.

Too far and too late to smell the appealing scent of Sara McLinder. She had to be inside, in bed.

Alone? Probably. Even so, he uttered a low growl at the thought she might not be, then made himself hurry forward. He had much to accomplish.

There were more bushes for camouflage near the entry drive and its security kiosk. He waited for a minute, his long, smooth muzzle in the air, inhaling the smells. He doubted that any useful scent would remain, though it had appeared that the general's car had first started to burn in this area, or just beyond.

Vehicle odors here. Some human scents. The nearest trees and other vegetation. The merest hint of the residue of the smell of fire.

Nothing helpful.

As always, 24/7, there was a guard inside the kiosk.

Of course the guards had high security clearances. Although none were Alpha Force members, they knew that some delicate and highly covert training exercises were held inside this fence. They also knew to ignore anything...unusual. And absolutely to keep it to themselves.

Even so, Jason was cautious as he slunk under the fence and outside the base. He knew the most likely way the general would have approached the entrance. He stayed hidden in the surrounding trees as he trotted along that route, once more using all his special senses to identify anything unusual.

Unlikely, of course. He'd found nothing in the car that explained what had happened. It was improbable that someone had hidden an incendiary device inside the Jeep before the general left D.C. The idea that a person just outside here could have somehow done something to set the fire...

He had driven past this area before, seen and sensed nothing unusual, but he'd been in other vehicles and not particularly close.

Now though—

Wait! Jason found himself coughing, his head nearly touching the ground as he inhaled...what?

He had just reached the corner almost a half mile from the base's entrance where the general would have turned off another road. There was a stop sign. Stones on the street and at the roadside that Sara and he had noticed before.

Had they been thrown onto the road to slow the general's car?

There were lots of trees around. Places where some-one could have hidden, then somehow lobbed some-thing into the back of the slowed vehicle?

Jason couldn't focus on his speculation, since he had not stopped gagging. Fortunately, whatever it was did not negate the effects of the Alpha Force elixir that allowed him human consciousness, but there was something on and in the ground that reeked. Made him feel ill.

Was the area rigged for this purpose: to prevent an Alpha Force shifter from scenting someone, some-thing, that would give a clue to what had happened to the Jeep?

Jason was sure of it—as sure as he could be about anything while feeling so miserable. Too bad he couldn't hold his breath. Would that help?

It was dark here, no streetlights, so he couldn't even attempt to use his most vital human sense and look around for anything causing the problem.

He would come back, in daylight, in human form.

Then maybe he would find answers.

For now, he coughed some more, and headed slowly back toward the base's entrance.

Sara felt exhausted after such a stressful day—a day that had ended with that kiss, admittedly fairly tame, by Jason Connell.

She'd tried lying down on her sofa in the BOQ, reading to put herself to sleep by the light of a table lamp. She had even chosen another complicated book on military strategy.

It didn't help—not any more than her attempts to sleep on the night of the full moon after seeing the pack of wolves she now knew to be Alpha Force shifters.

Was that why she couldn't sleep now? Was she thinking too much about Alpha Force? Shapeshifting?

Jason?

Of course not. She was worried about General Yarrow and what had happened to him earlier that day.

Not that she could do anything about that now... could she?

Hell. She wasn't sleeping, anyway. She hadn't even changed out of her camos.

Why not just go outside and take a short walk to exercise and wear herself out?

She slammed the book down on the low coffee table, stood and headed for the door.

She didn't want interaction with other people, so she took the same set of stairs she'd used before to avoid the main doors.

There was a light outside the door where she exited. Off to her right was the building's primary entry, so she decided to go left.

Especially since a couple of officers she recognized stood just outside the main door, talking. One was Lieutenant Manning Breman and the other was Captain Samantha Everly, both members of the Ultra Special Forces Team.

But before Sara started off, she heard something in the distance. Someone coughing? It sounded more like a sick animal.

Not only that, but she saw a movement in the gap

between the two low buildings between the BOQ and the trees that lined the base's outer boundaries. Something low.

The size, perhaps, of a wolf. A wolf that resembled Shadow, Jason's cover dog.

Which meant it resembled Jason, too, at times. Not that her brief glance could tell her that for certain....

Making an immediate decision, Sara changed her mind and approached the two from USFT. No sense taking chances about their noticing the creature sneaking around in the not-too-far distance.

Just in case.

"Hi," she called, loudly enough for the wolf—or whatever—to hear. "I couldn't sleep. You, too?"

In the artificial light, Manning Breman looked moderate in height and chubby-cheeked, and he immediately smiled when she approached. "Yeah, I just came out here to—"

"To meet with me," Samantha broke in. She, on the other hand, wasn't smiling. She was about Sara's height but a lot curvier in her uniform, and her light brown hair was gathered with a clip on the top of her head. "We had some planning to do for our next USFT exercises." She looked tellingly at Sara, as if ordering her to leave. She was a captain, so she could actually give that order if she chose to.

For the moment, though, she didn't—and Sara wanted to waste more time. "Really? What kind of exercises do you do? I know you're special forces, but I have to admit my ignorance. I don't really know anything about your unit, and—"

"Well, it's nothing like your damned Alpha Force," Samantha said. "No claims, or actuality, of any woo-woo stuff. We're just damned good soldiers with strategic and fighting skills that are highly classified. All I'll say is that we're the best, in fact, chosen from other special-ops teams. But we're not about to tell you anything else, Lieutenant."

Sara felt affronted. On the other hand, it was in the best interests of General Yarrow, Alpha Force and even herself not to antagonize any members of this unit—for now.

"I understand," Sara said. "Sorry. I'll leave you alone now." She noticed Manning's frown at his superior officer until Samantha looked his way. He gave a brief shrug of his narrow shoulders in Sara's direction then aimed a concerned expression toward the woman beside him.

Apparently, the guy didn't necessarily agree with his boss, but he obeyed military protocol and didn't voice an opinion.

Sara turned and strode off. Instead of the walk she had planned around the building, though, she decided to head in a different direction.

Down the center road of the base.

The one that would take her to its farthest building, the main quarters of the cover dogs, and hidden laboratories, of Alpha Force.

In case she was right about the nature of the animal she had glimpsed and heard, she believed it—he?—would be heading there.

* * *

Jason was in a downstairs lab. He had just changed back to human form and lay on the cold, hard floor. He hadn't even wanted to go into the small office to sit on a more comfortable chair.

Noel had ushered him down there after seeing the wolf's condition, helped him into his clothes, made a call or two.

"So," Noel said. "You okay? That looked like a pretty rough shift, and you weren't looking so great before, either."

"Something was definitely wrong," Jason said then coughed again. "Suspicious," he managed to hack out.

"What was it?" He looked up at the sound of the female voice to see that Sara had joined them.

Sara. She must still have the general's key card to get down here. What had she been doing outside her quarters?

Talking to those USFT people? Was she conniving in some manner with them?

Even if she was, she had managed to help him that night.

And she surely was much too smart to collude with them in public.

"Don't know." He coughed again.

"Don't try to talk," Sara said. She looked toward Noel as if to get his concurrence.

"That's right. Tell us later what happened. Right now, just relax."

He continued just to lie there and listened as Sara,

bless her, explained to Noel what had occurred from her perspective.

"I didn't know for sure it was Jason, or even a shifted Alpha Force member," she said, "but I heard a strange noise like coughing then saw the form of a canine in the distance. I'd noticed a couple of the USFT people standing outside the BOQ and figured I'd better distract them, just in case."

Jason couldn't stay quiet at that. "I saw you. Wondered. Thanks."

At her bright, pleased smile, he wanted to kiss her again. Only better.

Instead, he just coughed.

"Are you going to be okay?" She sounded worried.

He nodded. "Just wish I knew what it was." Each word came out softly and slowly as he kept trying not to cough.

"We'll figure it out." This time, the speaker was Major Drew Connell, who'd just arrived. "Let me examine you, maybe run some tests." His cuz was obviously wearing his medical hat at the moment, which pleased Jason.

"Fine," he said. "Noel, would you walk Sara back to her quarters?"

"Sure," his aide said, though he sounded worried. "Unless you think I can help here, sir." He was obviously talking to Drew.

"I think you can help best by doing as Jason suggested. Then return here and we'll talk about what we find."

"And you'll let me know, too?" Sara asked.

"Absolutely."

Chapter 8

The walk back to her quarters with Staff Sergeant Noel Chuma felt tense to Sara—and not because of her companion. Noel seemed like a nice enough guy who stayed friendly while constantly surveying their surroundings, doing his job of protecting her.

Maybe his efficiency was part of what disturbed her. It was as if he assumed there were people—or whatever—watching them, ready to attack.

She wished she could refute that possibility.

Instead, she decided to talk to him, without, hopefully, distracting him too much.

"How did you get recruited into Alpha Force?" she asked.

"I like challenges." He glanced down at her beneath the dim light with a huge grin. "And what could be more challenging than helping out a whole group of shapeshifters?"

That gave Sara pause. "Then you knew about them before you joined?"

"I was already in the military, spent a year deployed to Afghanistan, and figured I'd had enough combat experience to ramp my military career up a notch. I started asking around, learned that there was this highly covert unit that needed some extra guys, so I threw my name onto their list of possibles. I heard from Major Connell a couple of days later. He came to see me at my base in Texas, which seemed unusual. I assumed I'd be the one who'd have to travel. I guess I answered his questions okay since he put me at the top of his list. That was when he started asking really weird questions about what I believed about people and the universe and things, or creatures, that were unusual. Guess I did okay there, too, since he offered me the position—after swearing me to absolute secrecy. Now, here I am!"

And so was she, Sara thought. She had also been vetted—by General Yarrow before he took her on as an aide. But he hadn't been as upfront as Noel described about the units that were under his particular aegis.

She might never have known about Alpha Force and what it really was if he hadn't come to trust her implicitly.

Was she happy now? Well, she liked that he did trust her. She liked working with the general.

But did she like being here, in this situation, being

surrounded by people whose characteristics still seemed unreal, no matter what she'd seen?

Amazingly, the answer was yes. Or it would be if they figured out what had happened to Greg Yarrow and his vehicle, and resolved that satisfactorily.

Including finding out what had sickened Jason, in wolf form, that evening.

They reached the BOQ, and Noel offered to accompany her to her unit to make sure everything was okay. Sara still felt somewhat spooked, so she agreed.

All seemed fine. It was empty. At this late hour, they didn't even see any other building occupants up and about.

Noel left after a pleasant goodbye, leaving Sara wishing things had turned out way differently that day, on many fronts. But at least the general would be okay. And it was still much better that Jason hadn't been the one to walk her home.

Jason. How was he doing? Well, she could always call, as an interested superior officer, to find out.

As she pulled her cell phone from her pocket, it rang.

It didn't show a name—but the number had a local area code.

"Hello?" she said.

"Sara? It's Jason." There was still a raspiness to his voice, although it could just have been the connection. "You back at your place?"

"Yes. Our walk here was uneventful, and Noel just left." She paused for only a second. "How are you feeling?"

"Mad."

"I mean—"

"I know what you mean. Nice of you to ask. I'm fine. And I also want to find out what caused that re- action. Fast."

"Then you'll be—"

"Checking it out tomorrow, after a good night's sleep."

"I'll help," Sara said, not sure what she could do that would be useful. But whatever it was that had af- fected Jason so badly had to be related in some way to the cause of the burning of General Yarrow's car.

She wanted answers—and, she realized, not only because the general had been harmed. She sought ret- ribution for Jason's sake now, too.

Just because he was a member of Alpha Force, on the general's team, she told herself—recognizing it was at least a partial lie. She cared about what happened to Jason—more than she should, and for reasons she didn't want to think about.

But she did think about them when Jason prepared to hang up. "By the way," he said, his tone soft and somehow amazingly sexy over the phone. "I called to make sure you got there okay, but I also wanted to thank you."

"For what?"

"For having my back. If you hadn't distracted those USFT guys, they might have noticed a coughing wolf sneaking around the base. Not good."

She considered sloughing off what he said, but re- alized he not only was right, but that she appreciated his acknowledgment, too. "You're welcome," she said, equally softly. "I know you'd do the same if the situation warranted it."

"Count on it," he said with no hesitation. Then he paused. "So…see you tomorrow."

"Absolutely," she said. "We'll try to figure out what you breathed in while you were shifted."

"*I'll* try to find out," he contradicted sharply. "There's no need for you—"

"I'll be helping out, Sergeant." She used a no-nonsense military tone.

Another pause. Then, "Thanks, Lieutenant." And he hung up.

Leaving Sara wondering if she had made a mistake.

She wondered that far into the night.

Jason slept on and off that night in his small, private quarters. He told himself that his intermittent coughing, which hadn't completely gone away, was what kept waking him.

Or maybe it was Shadow's restlessness. He had brought his cover dog back when he'd left the building housing the lab and kennels. He was glad for the company. Shadow was his real bud. Gave him affection without asking anything from him but pats on the head and treats.

But Jason knew that it was partly irritation that kept him from sleeping soundly.

He recognized that he had to talk to Drew about the strange scratches on the door to the lab.

But even more, there was the stark reminder that

Sara McLinder wasn't just a woman who happened to be hot and attractive to him.

No, she was definitely hands-off. A superior officer. The kind of woman who thrived on giving orders.

Well, he may have had to buckle under and join the military to redeem himself. Stuck himself into a position where he had to take orders, since that was preferable to prison. Maybe even stay for the rest of his life, since he wanted continued access to the Alpha Force elixir.

But that didn't mean he had to like all aspects of it. Or to feel attraction to a woman who could force his submission by just tossing words at him.

No matter how much she turned him on.

He eventually gave up and got out of bed around six-thirty. He showered, put on his uniform and took Shadow for a walk.

Lots of people were up and about already at Ft. Lukman. Some were Alpha Force members, wolf shifters who were also walking their cover dogs, including Seth Ambers and his dog Spike, Marshall Vincenzo and his dog Zarlon, and Jock Larabey with his dog Click.

"Morning," Jason said as Shadow and he caught up with them just outside the base's primary office building. The dogs all traded greetings by sniffs.

"Heard about what happened last night," Marshall said in a low voice. He was a generally quiet guy, about Jason's height and built even more muscularly—had spent his childhood, while not shifted, doing martial arts, Jason had heard. Zarlon looked more like a German shepherd than most of the cover dogs, and Jason had seen that Marshall, too, resembled a shepherd when shifted.

"Yeah," Seth said. "You okay?" He, on the other hand, looked more like a football player while in human form. Spike resembled a wolf and had a hint of wildness about him, but he obeyed Seth just fine.

Jock gave a nod toward Jason, lifting his massive shoulders as if he was ready to hear the worst. His dog Click had a touch of German shepherd in his wolf appearance—but that was okay, since so did Jock while shifted. "What we heard sounded bad, but you look all right. Are you?"

Jason figured he might be asked how he felt a lot today. "I'm fine. I just want to figure out what happened."

"We all do," Seth said. He might even more than other Alpha Force members. From what Jason had heard, Seth had been injured months ago during a training exercise with another military unit—while in wolf form, too. "In fact, there's already a contingent of people who met at the labs early this morning for orders and information. They're already preparing to collect samples of dirt and vegetation in the area where you were walking. They're also looking into whether someone tried to break into the lab and said you reported scratches on the stairway door. Didn't they contact you?"

"No. Where are they now?"

"Still at the lab," Jock answered. "Drew was there— said you'd described where you'd been checking things out while shifted last night, so I guess that was why no one got in touch with you. They probably figured you ought to rest."

"Like I said, I'm fine," Jason responded, holding back his irritation. He didn't like people making assumptions about him any more than he enjoyed taking orders—but the latter was a necessary evil as long as he stayed in the military. The former? Total garbage. "Think I'll go see if I can give them any more info before they go off on some wild-goose chase."

He gave his usual halfhearted salute to the three lieutenants, aiming it even more toward their dogs, who probably deserved it more than the humans. Then Shadow and he stepped into high gear to hurry to the lab building.

When they got downstairs to the small office near the spacious lab facilities, Sara was there with Drew, Jonas Truro and Colleen Hodell.

"Good morning, cuz." Drew appeared surprised to see him. The others, too, sounded as if they hadn't expected him.

"What're you up to?" Jason asked.

"We were just going to try to retrace your steps yesterday," Sara said. "While you were shifted. When you inhaled—whatever. That's what we intend to find out. Just in case—well, we've been speculating that it was intentional. That someone who knew about Alpha Force's nature, and its wolf shifters, planted something to hide evidence of what they did to set the general's car on fire. We decided to collect a lot of samples this morning from the route you took." How could she look so calm and concerned in the face of the perfidious act she was engaged in? That they all were doing—solving his issue without even asking his advice.

But Sara's involvement was the most biting of all. Which didn't make sense. Jason should have been more upset about Drew's cutting him out.

"And how, exactly," he said, "do you intend to retrace the steps of someone without asking that someone exactly where he walked?"

"You told me most of it last night," Drew said. "I did look at those scratches on the door, too, by the way. We'll be doing more investigation of that, too."

"And I saw you on at least part of your walk while ill," Sara reminded him. "Plus, we spoke with the general to confirm the last part of his route before he turned into Ft. Lukman."

"I've just been handing out some sanitary and sealable containers from the lab for collecting samples," Drew said. "I figured this was a good group of people to conduct the examination. Jonas has a medical background, Colleen—as a shifting feline—won't necessarily react the same way to a contaminant as a werewolf, and Sara—" He seemed to hesitate.

"I just insisted on being included," she said, "as a key representative of General Yarrow." She stared with her flashing blue-green eyes, as if challenging him to tell her to bug off.

Which he wouldn't. In fact, he found her dedication admirable, although he'd never admit that to her.

"Fine," he said. "I insist on being included, too, as a party with a whole lot of interest in what happened. Besides, it won't hurt to have a shifter in human form along to check out the odors without having the even more acute senses of a wolf."

The entire group soon walked up the stairway from the underground lab, all of them carrying paraphernalia for collecting dirt samples.

As they started along the walkway toward the base's entrance, Jason found himself beside Sara.

Not that he'd planned it that way…or had he?

"Guess you got your way," he said to start a conversation—or argument, whichever worked out.

"What do you mean?" Her tone sounded innocuous, as if she didn't recall pulling rank on him over the phone last night.

"I mean, here you are, helping out."

She glanced at him with her sparkling eyes, which again contained a challenge. "Yes, I am. Any problem with that?"

"No, ma'am." He gave her a salute that arguably looked real, then glanced around. The others were ahead. It might look as if he gave a damn if he stepped up his pace to catch up.

Sara stopped altogether, reaching to grasp his arm. "Look, Jason, I didn't intend to start a war between us, but my assignment as an aide makes me want to know everything, solve all problems and…" She looked away. "I was worried about you yesterday." She glanced back, raising her chin almost belligerently. "If I'm going to be hooked up with Alpha Force for a day, or a week or month or longer, I intend to do all I can to help it and all its members. That includes helping to discover sources of anything that can harm any of you, to the extent I can. So if you don't like that, tough."

To his chagrin, he did like it. He liked her.

In fact, at this moment, he had a much-too-strong urge to kiss those defiantly pursed lips once again.

Instead, he just grinned. "Oh, I do like it, Lieutenant, ma'am. If anyone can solve this mystery, I'll put my money on you."

But it didn't appear that this mystery would be solved any more quickly than determining who might have tried to get into the lab area, Sara thought a while later as she stood with Jason, Jonas and Colleen near the stop sign about half a mile from the entrance to Ft. Lukman. She had hooked the straps of her backpack over her arm so she could access its contents and stick whatever she collected into it most easily.

The general would have made a right turn here onto the final road to his destination. Since he'd have stopped, this was a logical place for someone to do... well, whatever was done.

Especially since Jason had noted that this was the vicinity where he had first inhaled whatever had made him ill last night.

Jonas Truro, despite being trained as a medical doctor, dug in like a regular enlisted guy to pick up some of the stones they'd noticed before and examine them minutely, hanging on to only one or two that he said were just samples. He threw the rest back along the roadside with a shake of his head and a shrug. "They seem like regular stones to me."

And Jason, even with his enhanced senses while in human form said he didn't perceive anything about the rocks other than usual natural odors.

Sara had been watching Jason carefully, trying to guess, from his expression and demeanor, not only if he sensed anything off, but also if he was feeling okay.

He glanced back often, sending her looks that seemed both exasperated and challenging, as if still not thrilled that she had insisted on coming along. She kept her expression neutral, but she would have loved to challenge him right back.

Trees grew close to the roadside, with decaying vegetation between the trunks. Jason again gagged despite his senses being so much less acute than when he was in wolf form, so it was up to nonshifters Sara and Jonas, and cougar shifter Colleen, to collect samples of stones and dirt and plants—mostly dead leaves and grass—and even a few pebbles.

If there were traces of something placed there to veil evidence of who had been there and what they had done, something shifted werewolves might otherwise have noticed and possibly even figured out, it would need to be ID'd in tests that would analyze those samples. And that could take time.

In the meantime, whoever was guilty of placing it there, and doing whatever was done to the general's car, would be free. Maybe escaping, or maybe hiding in plain sight at Ft. Lukman. A member of the Ultra Special Forces Team? If so, why?

Or perhaps there was another culprit or motive that Sara hadn't yet considered. The guilty person could even be an Alpha Force member, but what motive could they possibly have?

"I think we're through here," Jason finally said, but Sara was glad when he added, "Agreed?" at her sideways glance. Maybe he needed reminding, but at least he had acknowledged, in some manner, that he was in the presence of superior officers.

And then he coughed again.

He may have tried to hold her back, but the reality was that she should have pulled rank and not let him come along. He had no business being here, where he'd come across something harmful yesterday.

On the other hand, his presence was helpful, since he'd been able to point out precisely where he had prowled in wolf form, and where he had first sensed whatever he had inhaled.

"Yes," she said, "but let's walk exactly the path you took to get back on the base, from here till we get to where I first spotted you opposite the BOQ."

"I'm fine with getting away from here, too," said Colleen Hodell. She was a friendly, pretty woman with pale feline eyes that seemed almost translucent. Her tawny hair, though layered, was longer than Sara's and had become mussed in the slight breeze wafting around them. She had stayed with the group yet wandered toward the fringes of the areas they explored as if believing the answers were even less obvious than the others might have considered. "My other senses are different from those guys', but I feel a bit like gagging, too. Damn, it's frustrating to be here and know this is a vital location for what happened to General

Yarrow and only be able to pick up dirt, not find anything helpful."

"I'll second that." Jonas Truro had started out wearing a camo cap over his dark hair but he'd taken it off and shoved it into a back pocket. His frown appeared as exasperated as Sara felt. They were supposed to find something here. And maybe he, as a doctor, figured he'd have better insight into the chemical reaction Jason had suffered.

But apparently he didn't—although he had collected the bulk of the samples they were returning with. Like Sara and Colleen, he was carrying the pack that contained all he had gathered.

They all walked back together to the base's gate where they checked in with the sentry guarding the entrance.

"I want to get all the samples right to the lab for handling," Jonas said.

"Good idea," said Colleen.

"I'd still like to retrace my steps of last night," said Jason, "in case something useful comes to mind."

She knew better, but Sara had seen Jason's difficult trek through the base yesterday. What if he suffered a relapse, despite being in human form?

Or was she just looking for an excuse to stay with him?

Either way, she said, "I'd like to continue this recon as we discussed before and follow everything Jason did last evening to look for additional evidence. Can you take my samples with you?" At Colleen's nod, she handed the other woman the backpack containing the sealed packages and tubes filled with all she had collected.

The other two hurried along the road toward the far side of the base—and the building containing the underground lab. Did they have enough technical personnel and expertise to conduct all the analyses here? Maybe, Sara thought, since apparently they did all their own blending of shapeshifting formula there. But analysis and creation could be quite different.

Well, that definitely wasn't her expertise.

Organizing was. So was following through.

"Okay, let's trace your exact footsteps from last night," she told Jason.

He grinned down at her, but his expression appeared wan. "My pawprints, you mean?"

"Yeah," she said, finding herself smiling at the reminder rather than recoiling at it. Interesting.

Instead of strolling down the road, they went behind the low buildings on the base's far side. Part of the area was paved, but a lot of it abutted the narrow groves of trees that formed the perimeter of Ft. Lukman inside its fence.

Jason's gait was slower than Sara had seen it before in human form, and she kept her pace equal to his.

They had almost reached the area between buildings where Sara had spotted Jason last night when he said, "You know, I thought I smelled something else when I got here, but I was feeling too awful to check it out."

"Let's look now," she said.

Together they entered the forested area. Although it was daylight, once they walked into this place of heavy growth they were surrounded by shadows. Sara heard the singing of several species of birds, overlying other soft sounds like small animals scurrying around dead leaves at the base of the trees. No one could say this place was anything but fully alive.

"Do you smell anything unusual now?" she asked. All she sensed was the green, healthy scent of growing trees, interspersed with some heavier, darker odors of decaying undergrowth. But she realized that her sense of smell was nowhere near as acute as his.

"Nothing unusual," he said. Even so, he walked farther into the forest and Sara followed. "I just wish… well, whatever happened must have been centered on the road outside, like we thought. I'm just mad at myself now for not having protected myself from whatever was left there. I already suspected some kind of terrorist act or sabotage or—"

"It's not your fault," she interrupted sharply, then paused at the way his golden eyes widened. They'd both stopped beneath some fairly low branches, in shadows.

He might have been surprised at her outburst, but she, too, had been surprised that this jaunty, devil-may-care guy actually did care. Blamed himself for the harm that someone else had caused him. At least he wasn't blaming himself for what had happened to General Yarrow…was he?

"I know it's not my fault," he said softly, his gaze grabbing hers and latching on with a hot intensity that seemed to come out of nowhere. Or had she anticipated—hoped for—it all along? "But thanks for the vote of confidence."

She opened her mouth to say something casual, but nothing came out. Not while she continued to look into his eyes, see the heat blazing between them, feel a sensuality rising within her from far below that didn't belong in this cool, neutral surrounding. That didn't belong inside her at all.

Sara wasn't sure who moved first, but she was suddenly engulfed in Jason's strong embrace. His mouth came down on hers, softly at first, then picking up heat and fierceness and intensity that she felt helpless to do anything about but respond in kind.

No. She never felt helpless. This was exactly what she wanted, precisely where she wanted to be: in Jason's strong, sexy embrace. Kissing him as if there were nothing, no one, in the world but them. As if their attraction was fiery and wonderful and inevitable. And not forbidden by who, and what, they were.

Their lips parted, their tongues met and teased and tested one another as if in anticipation of a mind-blowing sexual encounter.

Sara felt the hardness of Jason's erection press against her and pushed harder toward him. If only...

But as her hands raced under his clothes and up his back to clutch his heated flesh, she heard, in the distance, the sound of conversation. Someone must be on the sidewalk on the other side of the nearby building.

Or so she hoped. Surely they weren't any closer.

But the sound brought her back to reality. Instead of pulling him closer, she pushed him away.

"I—I'm sorry," she gasped. "This wasn't right."

"Oh, I'd say it was very right," Jason muttered.

"I mean—"

"I know exactly what you mean." He looked down with both heat and sorrow in his gaze. "Nowhere to go from here but back to the lab, right, Lieutenant?"

Sara closed her eyes at the jab, the reminder that she didn't really need—that even ignoring that the hot, enticing, utterly sexy man who'd kissed her was also a shapeshifter, their lives, their careers, their military ranks made it impossible for them to do even what they had done, let alone follow through and engage in the hot sex suggested by their heated embrace.

"Right, Sergeant," she finally said, putting as much strength and distance as she could into her voice despite her continued breathlessness.

Without looking at him again, she hurried from beneath the trees and onto the path behind the nearest building.

She thought she heard Jason following but didn't turn to confirm it. She walked between two buildings, ironically in about the same location as she had spotted Jason yesterday. She reached the sidewalk nearest the road through the base where a few other people strolled on the sidewalk ahead of her.

And as she looked toward that road, she saw a car carrying General Yarrow drive by.

Chapter 9

Sara had peeked into General Yarrow's Ft. Lukman office before but hadn't gone inside.

Not without the general there.

But now he had arrived. Safely, this time. He still looked pale in his camo uniform as he sat behind his attractive antique mahogany desk. Maybe even frail, although she would never dare to tell him that.

At the moment he was chatting with Major Drew Connell, who sat on one of the couple of chairs facing the desk.

A short while ago, as Sara had neared the base's main office building, she had seen the general being helped from the car being driven by an enlisted man—who'd presumably picked him up and brought him here from the hospital. Drew had obviously been expecting him and accompanied the general into the building.

From what Sara had seen, still at a distance, the general had refused further assistance, even an arm to hang on to.

Sara hadn't asked for an invitation. She was still the general's aide. She had turned quickly to see that Jason had followed her here. She gave him a quick nod that she hoped appeared dismissive, even though her glance settled, for just an instant, on those lips that had created so much emotion—and desire—within her.

Wrong. How wrong that had been. And the general's presence only reinforced how foolish she was.

Despite how good that kiss had felt…

She had quickly reached the building, then hurried up the stairway to the general's second-floor office.

She'd wanted to interrupt his conversation with Drew. Maybe even to hug him in relief that he was okay.

But that was almost as inappropriate as her sharing a kiss with an enlisted man.

Instead of doing anything else, she had simply come in and saluted General Yarrow. He had saluted back as if all was in order and nothing bad had happened.

"Have a seat, Lieutenant," he had told her.

"Yes, sir." She had quickly obeyed.

Now she remained there quietly as he continued to talk with Drew.

She liked the general's office. It suited him, with its decor that spoke of his love of both the United States and history. The U.S. flag that hung on the brass pole behind his desk was similar to the one he had in his much more formal office at the Pentagon. Nothing else resembled his usual digs. Oh, sure, she recognized a lot of old books on the sumptuous wooden shelves behind him—the ones with military history and regulations.

But then there were the antique-looking volumes of old classics, from Bram Stoker's *Dracula* to Jules Verne's *20,000 Leagues Under the Sea.*

And was that what she thought it was? Before coming here, she would only have laughed had she heard he had an original script from the classic movie *The Wolf Man.* Now she recognized how fitting that was.

"Our investigation is still inconclusive, Greg." Drew brought Sara's attention back when he looked at her for confirmation. His golden eyes, so like his cousin's, flashed as if he was furious that such an event could have occurred under his watch.

"That's right, General," Sara said. "But we're still working on it." She related how Sergeant Jason Connell and she had brought a vehicle back to the base to move the remains of the car, and how automobile expert Jason and others had studied those remains. She caught Drew's expression as she described all his cousin had done so far.

Then she looked at the general. Her CO looked older now than his actual age: sixty-four. He took good care of himself, and most of the time he appeared younger, possibly because his hair was really black—and from what she gathered, he didn't do anything to keep it that way. It had receded quite a bit, though, around his temples.

He frowned a lot even before—although right now the expression seemed etched into his long, lined face.

But he needed to know everything, at least all that was related to what had happened to him. As far as Sara knew, Drew hadn't mentioned to the general the scratches on the door to the lab. Maybe he'd already had someone examine it and determined it was nothing.

Taking a deep breath, Sara told the general about seeing Jason in shifted form last night after he'd gone to the area near the base where the car might have been ambushed.

"That's why we think this was an intentional act of sabotage," Drew said.

"Especially since Sergeant Connell was taken ill after visiting that site," Sara added, then described Jason's coughing and how she had accompanied him, and other Alpha Force members, to that area to collect samples that were being analyzed.

"I see," the general said slowly when she was done. He leaned forward, folding his arms on the top of his desk as he looked at Sara. She expected more questions about the investigation.

Instead, his expression lightened. He even smiled. "So Sara, what's your opinion of shapeshifters now?"

She stared at him. What did he expect her to say?

When she remained silent, he continued, "Just wondering. Every time I hinted at the real nature of Alpha Force after you started reporting to me, you laughed it off."

"I'm not laughing now," she said, keeping her tone bright. "It's really amazing."

She wasn't about to give an opinion of shapeshifting, let alone the existence of a military unit like Alpha Force. In fact, at this moment she wasn't really sure what her opinion was.

Except that, as she considered it, the face of Jason Connell—and the feel and taste of his lips on hers—insinuated itself into her mind.

She felt herself start to flush and looked down at her hands, hoping that neither of the others in the room noticed.

"Amazing, huh?" The general sounded amused. But then his tone hardened enough to make her look up. "I'd just like to know whether the *amazing* nature of Alpha Force is what caused someone to mess with my Jeep. I loved that old thing."

"They messed with you, too, General." Sara knew her anger and indignation were clear from her tone. "I'm sorry about your car, but…well, you could have been killed."

"And whoever it was apparently went to some lengths to conceal his identity and method—especially from anyone, human or otherwise, with keen senses," Drew said.

"Yeah, looks that way," agreed General Yarrow. "In fact, I'd like you to contact your cousin and tell him to come here now, Drew. I want to talk to him more about what he sensed when he went in shifted form to check it out."

Meaning that Major Connell would be bringing Sergeant Connell to this office. While Sara was here.

Only a short while after they had embraced in the woods. And kissed.

Lord, how they had kissed....

"Well, it sounds as if you have a lot to discuss," Sara said. "You won't need me—"

"Yes, we do, Lieutenant," the general replied sharply. But the expression he leveled on her looked curious. And shrewd. "You were helping in the investigation. I want you to join in our discussion. Unless you have something better to do?"

"I'll do whatever you'd like, sir," Sara said. Within reason, of course, although she wasn't about to tell him that.

But she did have something better to do. Almost anything would be better than being in Jason's presence at this moment.

The general's gaze had not moved from her face as he said, "Then stay here, Sara. It'll be good for all of us to get both your take on things and Sergeant Connell's." His smile broadened, then faded.

She now believed in shapeshifters. What about mind readers?

Or was she just being much too obvious in her demeanor and desire to get away before Jason arrived?

"Drew, give Jason a call. Sara, you hang out here for a short while, at least, and see if you can contribute to what the sergeant says. Then you can leave, if you'd like."

"Yes, sir," she said formally.

And then she sat and waited as Drew called his cousin.

* * *

When Jason's cell phone rang, he wasn't surprised to see that the caller ID said it was his cuz.

He had seen General Yarrow being chauffeured onto the base in a black military-looking car that looked nothing at all like his Jeep.

He wondered whether the general would do something about the loss of the car he'd seemed to care about so much. Get another Jeep?

Jason would be happy to discuss possibilities with him.

But following the general when he'd spotted him hadn't been an option—first because he was a general and probably had little interest in talking to a lowly sergeant who fixed cars.

Second because Sara had seen him, too, and clearly was following the general to wherever he ended up on the base.

At the moment Jason was in the underground lab where Colleen Hodell and Jonas Truro had taken the samples of dirt and leaves and all they'd collected from near the road to analyze what had made him cough and feel sick.

But he'd half expected the call from Drew.

He said hi, listened, then said, "Be there in a little while." Then he turned to Jonas.

They were in one of the large, sterile labs. Jonas, who worked on the shifting elixir, had started an initial analysis of what they'd found.

"Anything helpful?" Jason asked. He'd let both of

them down here using his own key. Neither had mentioned the scratches on the door.

"Not yet. And our facilities are more for trying new formulas out, not figuring out what other stuff contains." He was dressed all in white in a clean-room kind of outfit that contrasted with his moderately dark-toned skin, including a hat holding back his wavy, black hair.

Jason wore something similar, as did Colleen. Wearing all that white clothing made the feline in human form seem almost ethereal. Interesting, Jason thought. With her pale skin showing but not her tawny hair, she looked more like what she was than she normally did: a shifting cougar.

She'd been in the lab before. All Alpha Force members spent a lot of time here. She'd seemed fascinated by the experiments that Jonas had launched into right away. Jonas had been part of Alpha Force for a while and knew his way around this facility. Though he wasn't a shifter, he sometimes acted as a shifter's aide—and also helped Drew modify and even test his newest formulations of the elixir.

"I've got to go now, at least for a little while," Jason told Jonas. "The general's back and Drew wants me to join them to talk about what's been going on."

He didn't mention that Sara was there. If he did, he'd undoubtedly think about the kiss they'd shared.

That kiss he should have restrained himself from.

Too many complications now—including the fact that, given the opportunity, he'd do it again.

"Good." Jonas shook his head. "So far I'm not finding anything helpful, but even with my medical background I don't really feel competent to figure out how whatever may be contained in these samples led to your reaction. We'll need to send everything to another lab."

"What kind of lab?" Colleen asked.

"I don't know yet, but someplace with professionals who are a lot more sophisticated in analysis of possible toxins than anyone here is."

That was definitely out of Jason's realm of knowledge, too. He could analyze pretty much anything having to do with cars and most other vehicles. But though he didn't know what had caused his problem, he damn well wanted to find out.

In fact, he had already scheduled an examination with both Drew and his wife, Melanie, a veterinarian. He would have both the human physician and the animal doctor do what they needed to ensure there wasn't anything nasty lurking inside him.

But that was later tonight, when he could shift in their presence.

Right now, he had a meeting to attend—one that might be a hell of a lot more difficult.

Sara would be there.

Oh, yeah. She was there.

Was she ever.

When Jason arrived, saluted the general then asked after his health, Sara remained seated. As always, she looked beautiful.

But remote. She barely glanced at him despite that damned kiss he'd stolen from her.

Well, hell, she'd participated, too. And now she

acted like she'd never even seen this lowly sergeant before.

He'd do something about that…sometime. When he could. But not now, with his cousin Drew greeting him effusively and dragging a chair for him from a neighboring office.

Which his cuz ironically placed between his seat and the one still occupied by Sara.

What else could Jason do but sit down there? Toss her a half smile. Then turn all his attention back to the general.

"Thanks for asking about how I'm doing," General Yarrow said from behind his awfully nice-looking, old desk. In fact, Jason considered him an awfully nice-looking, aging military geezer. Even though, at the moment, he looked nearly as pale as the white stripes in the flag hanging behind him. "Now I want to hear how you're doing. I heard you may have inhaled something harmful while trying to figure out what happened to my poor Jeep."

"Yeah, maybe." Jason gave a brief description of his shift last night to check things out, his finding nothing useful but smelling something intense and awful while in wolf form that led to his coughing spree.

"Several of us accompanied Sergeant Connell back to the area where he first smelled whatever affected him," Sara added before Jason got into that part.

"Nothing conclusive there, either, General," Jason said. "I figure, though, that the fire was somehow set by whoever disguised his scent that way. That only makes me even more determined to figure out what was done to your Jeep. I liked the damn thing—and I'm sure that's nothing compared with your feelings for it."

"Thank you, Jason," the general said. "I think we're all as determined as you to figure out what was done to cover up how my car was sabotaged. You could have been harmed, too." He looked at Drew. "I assume your cousin's health has been checked to make sure no on-going problem was triggered."

"I'm feeling fine," Jason broke in, then sagged a little. "But I'm letting them do a complete analysis of everything inside me tonight—in both forms." Not that he looked forward to it. But it was necessary, though the coughing had stopped and he felt no further effects.

As a car expert, he knew that people who had car problems were better off having the vehicle checked out for residual issues. Same went for living beings—especially shifters. It wasn't like he could just drop into any medical clinic anywhere if he started to show symptoms again later.

Besides, he might as well take advantage of his cousin's being a doctor.

Sara had turned to stare at him. Her amazing blue-green eyes looked as if they might be trying to disassemble his brain to learn what was inside.

"But it's just a precaution, right, Ja—er, Sergeant?" she asked. "You said you're feeling okay." As if she realized that she sounded as if she might actually give a damn about how he was feeling, she added, "I'd really hoped to find out what gave you that coughing problem. I felt…involved with it, you see, sir." She related how she had noticed the slinking wolf in the distance when she was outside the night before.

Before she added in how she had assisted him at the time, Jason inserted, "Lieutenant McLinder helped me a lot then. She distracted a couple of members of that Ultra Special Forces Team who happened to be outside at the same time."

"Oh, yes. That's one of the reasons I'm here," General Yarrow said. "Why I headed to Ft. Lukman in the first place. I've set up a meeting with the commander of the USFT at this facility—General Myars. I know that relations between the two units are rather strained and I want to see what we can do about it so we can start our planned exercises."

"I respectfully suggest that the solution is to have those…er, difficult troops deployed elsewhere, Greg, and plans dropped for our working together." Drew leaned forward in his chair. Jason knew that look on his cousin's face. It meant sincerity, determination— and definitely intention to be heard. "I know they've all been vetted, so their suspecting that the other unit they're interacting with here has shapeshifters should be fine, since they supposedly understand how covert things are, but, well, someone may have attempted to break into the lab." He described the scratches on the door. "Maybe they know more than we think—or are taking steps to find out."

"I gather they're also doing things that must be kept completely under wraps." General Yarrow shot a glance toward Drew. "Scratches, huh? But no indication they got inside?" When Drew shook his head, the general continued, "Well, it's mutually beneficial, not to mention useful to the U.S. military, to have them stationed here right now. We'll just need to direct our security forces to be more on alert."

"I understand, sir," Drew said. "But to have two units functioning so closely together with apparent animosity from one toward the other—"

"And from that other right back at 'em," the general said. "Look, that's one reason I'll be meeting with General Myars. I want to find out if we can find common ground between Alpha Force and the USFT. Encourage military camaraderie and get all of you to work together—the usual."

"But what if USFT members were involved in sabotaging your car, sir?" Sara's voice was quiet, but it lacerated the peacefulness of the conversation.

Jason admired her for bringing up the obvious, especially when it clearly wasn't what the general wanted to hear.

"It's possible," he admitted.

"Even probable, Greg," Drew said. "Who else around here would have wanted to harm you?"

"You, of all people, can figure that out, Drew," the general shot back. "It's been a while, but you were right there in the middle of the animosity between the visitors and residents of Mary Glen due to their legends about shapeshifters."

"You're right, of course—at least back then," Drew agreed. "There were both werewolf fans and haters around at the time who thought shifters could be real and hanging out around town. But we resolved that.

Some were killed—and we caught who was committing the murders for motives of their own."

"But some remaining townsfolk may not yet be appeased," Greg said, "and even then there was some speculation in Mary Glen about whether there were shifters at Ft. Lukman."

"Could be," responded Drew. "We won't eliminate any possibilities for now."

"Good," said the general. "Right now, I want you to walk me through everything that happened and what you've learned about it. Let's start with a visit to my poor car. Then we'll walk the path. Agreed?" He looked at Drew.

"Fine, General. I'll come along. But Sara and Jason know a whole lot more about it than I do, so we'll follow them."

Sara felt even more uncomfortable now. She was essentially under orders to be in Jason's presence, so that helped. No one would officially question their being near one another.

But she definitely questioned the wisdom of that.

She hung back, following General Yarrow and Jason, who took the lead as they walked from the office building toward the garage where the Jeep's hulk was stored.

"Everything okay, Sara?" Drew's voice from beside her startled her, even though she was aware of his presence.

"Yes…more or less," she said, wishing she could be candid with Drew. Ask a few questions.

His wife, also a nonshifter from what Sara had heard, had been in a similar position to her. Well, not exactly. She had apparently fallen in love with a werewolf, then married him and they had a child, a little girl.

Sara was merely attracted to Jason. But Melanie Connell hadn't been in the military so there'd been no policy against fraternizing to keep them apart.

And…well, hell. Drew was a good guy. A doctor who had the best interests of the troops below him as well as all shifters at heart. He was even the person who'd mostly developed the elixir all the shifters in Alpha Force now relied on to help them control what they did and their consciousness while shifted. He was nice. Intelligent. By the book.

And then there was his cousin Jason, who had joined the military under duress—to keep from going to prison for car theft, of all things.

Sara should focus on that, and not all the man's intelligent analyses of what had happened to the general and his car.

Nor how hot Jason was.

She'd heard of another couple, Lieutenant Quinn Parran and Staff Sergeant Kristine Norwood, whose fraternizing was simply being ignored here at Ft. Lukman, thanks to the unofficial camaraderie of Alpha Force. But Sara wasn't really an Alpha Force member. She wasn't actually stationed here, and her presence was temporary.

No, fraternizing wasn't her destiny.

They'd reached the parking-lot building. Jason had

directed them all to the entrance nearest where the car's remains now lay and used a key to open it.

He held the door open for the general then for Drew…and Sara. She met his glance—and was dismayed to see how icily he looked at her.

Obviously he, too, had decided to back off.

Which made it a little easier for her to talk to him… through the unwanted sorrow she felt at his attitude.

"Thank you, Sergeant," she said softly as she walked by him.

And felt a tiny stab of pain in her butt, as if he had pinched her.

She gasped and turned back to face him, but he had already let the door shut and was passing by her to catch up with the general.

He led them all into the secluded area where the Jeep's hulk still rested. A uniformed guard still stood there, a private whom Sara had seen and talked to before named Kerry Browning. He had been the sentry at the gate when General Yarrow's car was set on fire. He saluted them, and Jason told him it was okay to take a break while he showed the general what was left of the car.

Without looking at either Drew or her, Jason started walking around the remains with the general, pointing out the charred elements of the front first, the wheels with burned tires, the engine compartment then the driver's seat where the general had been sitting when the Jeep caught fire.

After that, they walked to the back of the chassis and Jason showed the metal framework that had supported the canvas cover, which no longer existed. He went to a storage trunk with a lock on it where all the ashes, and the residue of the items found in them like the general's fishing pole, overnight bag and other stuff, had been stored.

Then Jason went through the scenario as he said he believed it had happened, where the canvas had caught fire first then the flames had moved through the vehicle, causing the general's smoke inhalation and more.

"Very interesting," Greg said as Jason finished up. "And thorough. But we still need answers."

"We're still working on that, Greg," Drew said. He explained the investigators who were due to arrive the next day from D.C.

While they talked, Sara found herself beside Jason. She shot him a look that she hoped appeared withering, as if she were responding only now to what she thought she had felt.

A pinch on the butt?

She must have imagined it. Jason appeared so interested in the others' conversation. So serious. And innocent.

She took a step toward Greg and Drew so she could hear them better, only to have Jason take the same step beside her.

She turned to look quizzically at him.

That was when he gave her a wink.

Chapter 10

General Yarrow seemed tired after their visit to what was left of his car. Maybe his fatigue was partly depression, but Sara knew better than to ask something like that. Instead, she did what any good aide would do: she told him to go rest while she set up the meeting that was the reason he had originally come to Ft. Lukman.

Walking with the general to discuss plans also gave her a good excuse to avoid Jason, who remained, for now, with what was left of the vehicle. He couldn't get away with that pinch, but she hadn't yet figured out how to deal with it.

"How would 0900 tomorrow morning be, sir?" she asked as she accompanied the general to the BOQ. His quarters were in the same building as hers, but it held a wing for VIPs. "Or is that too early?"

He'd already said that General Myars was planning to arrive at Ft. Lukman this evening. She wanted to arrange things for the convenience of her CO.

"That should be fine—on the late side for Hugo, if anything. Liking to start working early in the day is about the only thing we see eye to eye about." The general's smile appeared wry, and Sara wondered how the conclave between the two senior officers would work out.

"And let me confirm this," she continued. "You want it to be a one-on-one session between General Myars and you."

"At first, yes," the general said. "I want a brief meeting with Hugo and then get everyone in both units together to talk, clear the air and exchange information."

"If all goes well," Sara couldn't help saying.

"It will go well," the general responded grimly.

They continued to discuss plans for the meetings as they approached then entered the building and climbed the stairs to the second floor. They stopped outside the general's apartment. Even the hallway in this wing appeared more sumptuous than the one outside Sara's regular officers' digs on the same floor at the far side of the building. It might as well have been a world away.

He didn't invite Sara inside, which was fine with her. He unlocked the door then said, "First get the place confirmed with Drew. We'll meet in my office for the initial meeting then go to the large assembly room when we get everyone together."

"Yes, sir," Sara said, making a mental note.

"Then call Hugo. Make sure you make it clear you're

contacting him on my orders. Otherwise, he probably won't even talk to you. Feel free, by the way, to
tell him to call me to confirm that. Either way, give
me a call after you've spoken with Hugo and let me
know if we're on. Once we're square with a time, contact Drew and have him get our Alpha Force members
there, too. Oh, and here. These are for you." He handed
her a set of card keys that he said were duplicates of
his that would let her into the kennel building and the
labs below, which she had already returned to him. "I
know I don't have to remind you to keep these to yourself, but you may need to set something up in the lab
areas sometime."

Sara was glad but a little surprised. Only the general, and those members of Alpha Force with a need
to work in the labs, had key cards to get there. All,
though, had access to the kennel floor above.

That was that. Sara had already programmed Major
Drew Connell's number into her smartphone, so as
she headed down the hall to her own quarters she
called him. No problem there, setting up the time and
place. She was also able to get the number for General Myars's aide, Captain Rynton Tierney. She needed
to use appropriate protocol to get through to General
Myars despite being under orders to speak to him.

She entered her apartment and sat on the well-worn
couch in her main room before calling Captain Tierney. She wished she'd brought a cup of coffee from the
cafeteria. She didn't have any to brew in her kitchenette, which was fine since it wasn't equipped with a
coffeemaker, anyway.

She heard background noise in Tierney's phone. "We're on our way to Ft. Lukman now," he said. "In the car. I'll hand the phone to General Myars."

Just like that, Sara was able to schedule the meetings the next day that General Yarrow had requested. "We'll be at Ft. Lukman within the hour," General Myars said. "We've already arranged for quarters while we're there." His tone suggested he wasn't pleased about it. "It's not the night of a full moon, but I understand that isn't necessarily a prerequisite. You can tell General Yarrow that I do not wish myself, or anyone in the Ultra Special Forces Team, to be subject tonight to little green men—oh, I mean attacking werewolves or whatever."

And then he was no longer on the line. Probably a good thing, Sara thought. The animosity had been almost palpable.

She called Drew back to confirm everything so he could get the Alpha Force members primed to attend the all-hands meeting the next day.

"Something wrong?" Drew asked.

"Just…well, I'm not holding out a lot of hope for the meetings to go well." She related her conversation with General Myars to him.

"Sounds like, even though he was polite enough to visit General Yarrow in the hospital, Myars isn't overly fond of werewolves." Drew sounded half-amused—and half-angry, if Sara was any judge of it over the phone.

"My take on it, too," she agreed. Apparently, even if not all USFT members knew about the Alpha Force shifters, their CO was aware of the nature of the unit.

"Is General Yarrow available to meet me again tonight?"

Sara told Drew that she had accompanied him to his quarters.

"I'll give him a call. I'd like to strategize with him. You, too. But you'll need to come to our labs. My wife, Melanie, and I will be conducting some tests on Jason—we want to make sure that whatever my cousin inhaled is out of his system with no lasting effects, in either of his forms. It's not something we want to delay anymore, so we've got him joining us tonight."

Sara paused. Did she want to see Jason at all? Even if she did—well, he would be transforming into his wolfen form then back, if she understood what Drew had said.

In a way, that might be perfect. She felt much too attracted to him as a human, and watching him shift once more might be enough to permanently end that attraction.

And that was exactly what she needed.

"I need to call General Yarrow to confirm that we have things set up," she told Drew. "I'll ask him to join us tonight at the lab. What time?"

"Nineteen hundred hours."

Which was only a couple of hours away.

"Fine," Sara said. But she would not look forward to it.

Jason didn't really want to do this. "I'm fine now," he told Drew, who'd made him take a seat in a downstairs laboratory on one of the most uncomfortable chairs he'd ever sat in. It was plastic and canvas, faced a small desk in the large lab with its complicated layout and it sucked.

Or maybe it was the anticipation of what was to come that made Jason feel so uncomfortable.

It was early evening. Jason knew he had to take some of the elixir in a short while so he would shift here. That was the only way that his cuz and cuz's wife could do a thorough inspection of him to make sure that whatever he'd breathed in last night was all the way out of his system.

"We'll make sure of it." Drew looked like the damned soldier he was, in his camo uniform—and yet, he had put all the garb over it to prove he was a doctor, a white lab suit.

His wife, Melanie, was a pretty lady, with bright blue eyes and long brown hair she had fastened back behind her neck. Nice, too—full of sympathetic smiles. She'd left their daughter, Emily, at home with a trusted neighbor who babysat so she could come here and help out.

No camo uniform on her, but she wore a similar lab outfit—because she was a veterinarian.

"Okay," Jason said resignedly. "Get it done."

Drew's turn first. Using standard medical stuff Jason had seen before, he checked Jason's heart rate and blood pressure. "All seems fine there." He sent him to the adjoining bathroom with a small container so he could provide a urine sample. But then Drew took out what Jason hated: needles. He looked away when Drew pulled his arm straight, used some kind of cleaning stuff in the crook of his arm and drew blood. "I'll analyze this tonight," he said.

Which Drew could do on his own. Jason's cuz was more than a medical doctor for humans. He was the one who'd taken the old, standard family elixir that helped a bit while they were shapeshifted to allow shifting outside the full moon—when it was effective—and turned it into something that not only worked all the time but did a damned good job, plus it let every shifter who used it keep their human awareness while in their alternate form.

In addition, thanks to sometimes incorporating another formula developed by a different Alpha Force member, Dr. Simon Parran, they were working on being able to avoid shifting during full moons, as well as other improvements.

Jason wasn't the only one who was happy about that.

When Drew was finished drawing blood, he patted Jason's back. "You can breathe again, cuz. For now. But we'll want you to shift in five minutes so we can check you that way, too."

"Fine." Jason continued to sit for a short while longer, staring out over the lab. It was full of shiny metal cabinets with glass doors that Drew said were always kept locked, even though the bulk of the already prepared elixir was now kept in a secured refrigeration unit down the hall. Some cabinets had equipment on top—really sophisticated-looking microscopes and stuff Jason couldn't identify but figured it was state-of-the-art. Computers, too, on shelves here and there. The place was inevitably kept clean and sterile, the better for ensuring that the amazing elixir could be brewed without any contamination.

As Jason sat there, he thought he really was still unwell. He was hallucinating—wasn't he?

For two people had just entered through the lab door. General Greg Yarrow…and Lieutenant Sara McLinder.

What were they doing here, especially now?

This was his time here to ensure he was okay.

And he was just about to shift into wolfen form. Surely no one thought he'd do that in front of these nonshifters—even though he'd already shifted before in Sara's presence. But it had been his choice then. He'd wanted to have some fun with her.

It wouldn't be fun to tease her here, in the presence of all these other people, particularly when his shift would be for medical purposes.

Some other time, though…well, sure, it would be enjoyable to do that again.

Especially after that kiss.

"Hi, General, Lieutenant," he began, drawing himself to a stand.

But before he could get closer, Drew and Melanie had positioned themselves between him and the newcomers. "Welcome," Drew said. He turned briefly, glanced at Jason, then back toward the others. "You know, General, this is not the most auspicious time for you to observe another shift here."

Which implied the general had seen shifting here at Ft. Lukman before. But it hadn't been Jason who had changed then.

"No," the general said, "but with our meeting coming up tomorrow, I want to observe a shift generated by the most current version of the Alpha Force elixir in case I have to describe anything about it."

"Or defend it." Drew didn't sound happy about that.

"That's right."

Melanie got closer to her husband and put her arm around his waist. "If those special forces guys don't like the idea of shifters, they don't belong here," she said to the general.

Jason could see Sara at General Yarrow's side. Her eyes widened as if she couldn't believe that someone would confront her commanding officer that way.

But of course Melanie wasn't a member of the military despite her close affiliation.

"Maybe not," the general said with a shrug. "But they are here, and we need to do the training for the planned joint mission as soon as possible."

"Even if they're willing to harm you and Alpha Force members to make some kind of point—one we don't even get?"

That surprised Jason. It was Sara this time who confronted her commanding officer. Not only that, her gaze had slipped from the general to Jason, as if she might actually give a damn that he'd possibly been harmed.

An unwelcome yet enjoyable warm and fuzzy feeling swept through Jason. He shot her a quick smile. For an instant, she returned it then seemed to catch herself and resumed the grim, remote expression she'd had before.

"Hey," Jason said. "Bring on that super elixir, cuz.

I'm ready to give the general and lieutenant a demo of exactly how wonderful the stuff is right now. And I can't wait till Melanie gets the chance to give me her best veterinary checkup and extract some of my most vital bodily fluids." He winked at Sara, who stared at him in apparent shock.

Then he strutted across the lab to the refrigeration unit where small amounts of elixir were stored.

He was in wolfen form.

Unlike how he usually behaved during a shift, when he almost always was outdoors and able to prowl, he was confined in a room with others.

Mostly nonshifter humans.

No specially designated aide had assisted him. Drew had handed him the elixir. He had drunk it, then walked beyond the rows of sterile cabinets to take off his clothes.

Drew had also followed with the light needed to effect the shift and aimed it at him. General Yarrow had been with him, watching the whole thing.

The shift had commenced nearly at once. That was when both Melanie and Sara had joined the general and Drew.

Jason's shift had occurred in front of all of them.

He had tried to observe Sara's reaction—especially at first, when his still human organs would be visible to her—but his discomfort shifting, and the presence of other people, distracted him.

When it was finished, she hadn't run screaming out of the room. Neither did she regard him with contempt.

But she did regard him with... He wasn't certain what she was thinking.

Immediately, Melanie Connell had started her poking and prodding of his wolfen body. Even drew blood and saliva and urine, although peeing into a cup while shifted was far different from doing it in human form.

And then she was finished.

He sat on the cold floor of the lab, relatively motionless despite wanting to run.

But his dosage of elixir had been small, so he knew he could change back fairly quickly.

That was when he would learn what Sara McLinder was thinking.

It was all a scientific experiment. Neutral observation of an interesting phenomenon. Yet another act in her capacity as General Greg Yarrow's most trusted aide.

Sara had nearly been able to convince herself of that when they had all watched most of Jason's initial shifting into wolf form. That was something the general had really wanted to do, so what could she do but stay by his side?

And then, after all the veterinary tests Melanie conducted on Jason, it had been time for him to change back.

Right there, in the lab, since General Yarrow had also wanted to see that.

As a result, Sara had gotten to see a lot. More than she wanted? Well…yes and no.

Close up this way, it was fascinating.

In this very controlled, very human, very clean environment on a pristine white floor: a body changing, from a man, standing then crouching while arms and hands changed to legs and paws in a more compact form. A muzzle, hair erupting everywhere. Low moans and growls of discomfort and pain.

And then a wolf.

Afterward, back again. Similar, in the opposite direction. That was where Sara could have lost control if she hadn't considered in advance how to handle this.

For when it was over, there was Jason in all his naked glory. Again.

Only for a moment, of course. Well, several moments in which Sara pretended to look elsewhere while Drew brought a blanket over to cover strategic areas as he handed Jason his clothes once more.

Jason seemed a little out of breath even after he'd donned his clothes. As if they'd planned it in advance, they all headed for the small lab office area and took seats around the desk. Four of them were clad similarly in their camo uniforms, but Melanie, who, like Drew, had removed her lab jacket, wore a button-down shirt over navy slacks.

"Good," General Yarrow said at once. "Not that I'm any kind of expert, but the shift looked quicker, more controlled, than I've seen it before." He looked toward Jason. "How are you feeling? I take it that nothing you inhaled before inhibited the process, but are you inclined to cough any more than usual, or is there any other difference that you sense?"

"No, sir," Jason said. "I'm really feeling pretty well

now—subject, of course, to how Drew and Melanie tell me I should be reacting."

They all laughed. Even Sara, who had once again wound up sitting beside Jason. She hadn't planned it. Had he? Drew was the one behind the desk, since the lab was his venue.

She tossed a glance at Jason to find that he was leveling a look at her, too. Was he challenging her to say something?

It wasn't as if she hadn't seen him shift before.

General Yarrow was the one, though, who got her to talk. "So, Sara," he said, "I've no doubt that you believe in shapeshifting now." His tone was teasing and ironic, like a father who'd told his skeptical kids there was a Santa Claus and had introduced them to a store version at Christmas.

Bad analogy, Sara thought. First of all, most kids continued to believe in Santa for a while, even after they're told Jolly Old Saint Nick is just a myth.

Shapeshifting was definitely real, even though she hadn't believed in it at all when her paternalistic commanding officer had hinted about it before.

She'd now seen it herself. Several times.

"Yes, sir. In fact, as I'm sure you know, I've believed in it for a couple of days. But you have to admit that, in the regular world before I met Alpha Force, it wasn't odd of me to have my doubts."

"Not odd at all," Jason said. "But isn't it more fun to believe?" His lowered brows and grin made it clear he was teasing. Maybe even trying to remind her of his hotness during the process when he was unclothed and his masculine organ was so erect—and so obvious.

"Definitely. You know, I really like dogs. Haven't been able to own one since joining the military, but it's fun to be around them here—or at least canines of varying types." The look she tossed back at him was all innocence, as if she hadn't gotten what he'd been trying to do.

He laughed. "Any time you want to work with Shadow and me, or any of the other dogs, you're welcome. And you know we shifters are generally assigned assistants who help by bringing our elixir doses and lights along to wherever we need them. Why don't you give that a try one of these days, too?"

"I just might do that," Sara shot back, then hoped her small flinch wasn't too obvious. She was acting as if the two of them were alone, not in the company of others, including her commanding officer.

"Really? Interesting thought." General Yarrow's lined face grew pensive. "I could possibly assign you to stay here on a longer-term, temporary-duty status once we reach whatever agreement we work out with the USFT, to make sure it is honored. You'd have a dual function of working directly and deeply with Alpha Force to be able to assist even better with my reports— as shaded as they are—to the highest-ranking officials who supervise these special units."

Uh-oh. That wasn't what Sara had intended. Staying here? Being assigned to work closely with Alpha Force, with Jason on indefinite TDY? Bad idea.

And yet she found the idea intriguing.

"Well, everyone, I need to go take Jason's samples to my clinic for analysis first thing tomorrow, and then I have to go home and get Emily," Melanie said. "Would any of you like to join us for dinner?"

She had stood and was regarding all of them, Jason included. But Drew nixed that invitation—as well as the implied one to Sara. "Sorry, but I'd really like the general to come to our place so we can talk. Maybe we can invite all of you some other time."

"That's fine," Sara said, not wanting Melanie to feel uncomfortable. Although, as the wife of a military officer, she probably felt outranked now and then, anyway. And since that officer was not only a member of Alpha Force but also a shifter himself—well, Sara felt sure that Melanie knew how to cope with situations that Sara couldn't even imagine. "I was planning on just grabbing something light at the cafeteria and taking it back to my quarters. I want to go to bed early so I'll be rested to assist with anything I'm needed for tomorrow."

"You can go ahead, Mel," Drew said. "I'll also do my analysis first thing tomorrow, since Jason seems to be okay. The general and I will join you at home soon—right, sir?"

That was fine with General Yarrow. Sara decided to take the opportunity to leave then.

So did Jason. She felt a little uncomfortable as they walked out together.

"Want to grab dinner in the cafeteria?" Jason asked, staying much too close beside her as they walked up the stairs to the main floor.

No, is what she thought. *Bad idea.* But what she said was, "Sure." And in fact, it wasn't really a bad idea, if she might be staying at Ft. Lukman for a while. Getting to know some of the other Alpha Force members better in a group setting couldn't hurt. And in preparation for the meetings tomorrow, it also wouldn't hurt for her to watch the reactions tonight from any USFT people who were there and potentially further brainwashed by their general.

Surely Hugo Myars wouldn't be at dinner there—would he?

He wasn't. In fact, not many members of the other primary unit at Ft. Lukman were in the small facility that night. Probably a good thing.

But Staff Sergeants Noel Chuma and Rainey Jessop were there, as were shifter members of Alpha Force Lieutenants Seth Ambers, Colleen Hodell, Jock Larabey and Marshall Vincenzo. They'd taken a table in a corner, and Jason pulled a couple of additional chairs up to it before Sara and he got their dinners from the cafeteria line.

Sara chose a large chopped salad with steak chunks in it. The steak theme remained major here—undoubtedly because of at least some of the troops stationed on this base. In fact, almost all of the others had brought beef dishes of one kind or another to the table.

She mostly listened to the dinner conversation—which primarily centered on grumbling about Alpha Force's relationship with USFT and how no one was looking forward to tomorrow's meeting. They also talked a bit about their respective backgrounds, what the shifters' lives had been like before joining Alpha Force. They'd all had practice being secretive, but some had had easier existences than others.

Sara couldn't help looking at the shifter members with a different focus now. Not only had she seen Jason shift up close and personal today, but she might also be taking on, at least now and then, the function that Noel Chuma and Rainey Jessop had in assisting shifters.

She still wasn't sure how she felt about that.

But everyone treated her as a comrade, not with the remoteness she had concerns about since she unabashedly represented their commanding officer, General Yarrow.

She liked these people.

She wondered how their unit was trained to assist the rest of the U.S. military, but the general had indicated, before she believed in shifters, that the group was working undercover in some very interesting situations—and had already helped to thwart biological warfare and other major threats.

And now she could be, indirectly, part of that very useful function.

Eventually, they all finished. Time to leave.

With Jason? Yes, it seemed that he intended to walk her back to the BOQ, notwithstanding the fact that she had other officers here who could keep her company.

Although…as they started to walk past the enclosed parking structure that housed the remains of the general's car, Jason looked at her. "There are a couple of things I thought of that I'd like to check out on the car," he said. "Care to join me?"

There was something in his look that she couldn't quite read. A challenge?

Well, if she was going to remain part of Alpha Force, even for a short while, she had to stand up to Jason's challenges and then some.

Even more, she had to master the deep sexual attraction that stirred her insides with just the slightest heat of his gaze.

"Sure," she said. "Let's go."

Chapter 11

"Here we are." Jason turned to Sara as they reached the main entrance to the post's parking garage. "I'll call ahead and warn the guard that we're coming."

She looked at him quizzically. "Okay, but I'm still not sure what we're looking for tonight."

"I have a couple of ideas I want to test." Jason pulled his phone out of his pocket before she could ask anything else.

Only one guard was stationed outside the room where what was left of the general's car was stored, since that room was secluded and locked. Jason had access with a key, but the couple of times he'd visited here, he'd called the guard first on his cell phone, warning that he was about to get company.

Jason had made sure he was on a first-name basis

with each of the guards he'd met who were charged now with the duty of ensuring that no one disturbed what little evidence there was on what had been done to General Yarrow's prized Jeep.

It was only a little more than a day since the incident, and the military crime-scene team Drew had finally zeroed in on wouldn't be there until tomorrow, or maybe even the next day.

Jason doubted they'd find anything he hadn't already seen, but hey, that was their expertise. Maybe, if they got their butts in gear and arrived, they'd actually figure out what had happened.

And who'd done it.

Meanwhile, his mind had been working double-time on things he may have missed when he'd looked before. Though he couldn't come up with anything he should have done differently. Maybe he needed to look again at the small stuff, in case he'd missed something while preoccupied with his coughing spree. Surely there'd been something important he hadn't focused on.

Sara and he hurried up the stairs to the third floor, then exited the stairwell. The room was at the far side of the garage, not far from the ramp they'd taken when they used the rented truck to bring the remains inside. Jason didn't wait for Sara to keep up. He just hurried toward his destination.

As anticipated, a sentry stood there with arms crossed, a weapon on his hip. When he spotted the two people approach, he snapped to attention, his hand over his gun. Then he relaxed and saluted. "Sergeant Connell," he said then looked toward Sara.

"This is Lieutenant McLinder, Kerry. Like I told you on the phone, we need to go see the general's car again."

"Yes, sir. Hi, Lieutenant McLinder." Sounded to Jason as if they'd already met. For now, the private stood out of the way, allowing Jason to hold the door open for Sara.

Inside he flicked on the lights. In the center of the room, where they'd left it, was the mess of charred metal and more.

"What are we looking for this time?" Sara had moved around him to approach the hulk.

"Wish I knew," Jason said. "But I've got to have missed something before. And it sure would be handy to have whatever that is with us at the meeting tomorrow. Whoever did this has to be a USFT member, and I'd love to wave evidence in their faces to see whose reaction gives them away."

Sara turned toward him again. She was smiling, the expression lighting up every inch of her gorgeous face beneath that sexy cap of blond hair. "Love the idea, but I don't think it'll happen. Even if we find something, whoever did it has to be craftier than that. He—or she—will look at that piece of evidence with an expression as bewildered and innocent as everyone else's."

"Ah, Lieutenant, you forget. A quarter or more of the people in that room'll be shifters. We don't rely on looking at someone's face or even body language to tell us what they're thinking or feeling."

"You mean that—"

"Fear has a scent, and we're all familiar with it." He grinned.

Dumb, but he felt a swirl of pride inside as she flashed him an even broader smile that he read as admiring. "Know what?" she said. "We're going to find something here today that you can wave tomorrow to see the reaction—even if we actually come up with diddly squat."

His turn to look at her with admiration. They were definitely on the same wavelength.

He found that idea to be hot. In fact, he found everything about Sara to be hot.

They spent about half an hour going over the car again. Once more, they wore latex gloves and held flashlights. Lots of seared and melted metal, ashes, pieces and puddles and ruined rubber and the kinds of things Jason expected and had noticed before. He didn't see any more paraphernalia that the general might have been transporting in the back of the car.

Jason had already interfaced with the soldiers charged with initial checking out and photographing the scene before the car was moved, who'd looked into the general's overnight bag that had been in the front seat with him. They'd found nothing with the remains of the general's clothing and personal items beyond what Jason had already noted there—and none of it had provided any clue as to what had gone wrong in the Jeep.

No indication that anyone had set the general's miscellaneous stuff to smoldering before he'd gotten on his way here.

Then Sara and he got into the box at the side of the room where ashes and debris were stored, stuff like the remains of the general's fishing pole and hooks and other unidentified metal items.

Sara knelt on the hard floor beside him, also scanning the detritus with her lovely blue-green eyes as if this additional viewing would somehow yield results.

Her sigh told him that she felt as ineffectual as he did. Why did that feel so appealing? He wished he could reassure her that she was a big help here—but knew that wouldn't go over well. Not when they weren't finding answers.

Jason wished, for a moment, that he was in wolfen form. Might he smell something that would be helpful?

Just in case, he closed his eyes and let the smells filter into his nose as he inhaled, carefully and slowly. There was no indication that whatever had triggered his bad reaction was present, but he didn't want to take any chances.

Scents were merged here, but he could tell the difference between the ashes of the canvas and the odors of charred metal, burned rubber and the rest.

And yes, there was more. The fishing line? Maybe. There were several smells he believed to be melted plastic.

But that proved nothing.

"Anything interesting?" Sara said from beside him. When he opened his eyes, she was watching him intently, as if trying to vicariously participate in what he was doing.

He enjoyed that look, her seriousness. The way the

intensity of her expression made him feel as if she were studying him, getting inside him, wanting more of him.

That was only wishful thinking...wasn't it?

"Maybe," he said. "But nothing I can really follow up on, at least not yet."

"So we'll just wing it tomorrow," she said decisively.

He liked the way she said *we*. And the way she tilted her head, as if soliciting his agreement.

"But I can't help agreeing that we're missing something," she added. She turned back toward the box of debris. "Maybe the experts will figure it out when they sift through these things, but I wonder if there's something in here that the general couldn't possibly have had in the back with his stuff."

"Let's make a list of what we find. Take a few more pictures. We'll run the details by the general tomorrow. All he saw, when he was here checking over what was left, was the big picture. Maybe seeing and hearing about the small stuff will trigger him to suggest more clues."

"Good idea."

They spent another fifteen minutes there. Sara moved from angle to angle and shot photos, and Jason made the list of items they surveyed. That seemed backward to him. He was the kind of person who took action, not the kind who kept track of things. But Sara seemed happy this way, so he didn't object.

Task completed, she stuffed her camera back into her pocket. She looked so woeful that he wanted to kiss her, to distract her from all that was bothering her.

Hell, why give himself an excuse? He just wanted to kiss her.

"Guess we're done here," he said unnecessarily.

"Guess so," she agreed.

As they both headed toward the door, Jason said, "Sounds like I still won't have an opportunity to return the truck to that service station tomorrow and retrieve my own car. I've been in touch with them but I'll have to make sure it's still okay with them. Uncle Sam's paying for the rental, but I can't help worrying about my Mustang."

Her smile was broad and amused. "I'd worry about it, too, if I had a great car like that."

"You really like it?" He felt himself lighten inside. Well, anyone with a brain and a heart would like that red, classic delight of his.

"Of course," she said. "I told you so before." As their eyes met, he felt some really top-grade tingling way down in his body. Tingling that told him her attitude—everything about her—was making him hot.

"I still need to go get it," he said. "Right now, though, I'll check on the truck. I've got it parked on another floor."

They left the room, locking it behind them and making sure that the sentry was back on guard. Then Jason led Sara down the stairs to the second floor.

The garage contained a lot of cars parked in parallel rows but was devoid of other people at this late hour. The truck was right where Jason had parked it, at the end of a row near a concrete wall where it wouldn't get in anyone's way. All looked fine with it.

Jason glanced around. "Is your car here?"

"No. I've left it in one of the outdoor lots near the BOQ."

"Well, we can still check on one of my other cars."

She blinked at him. "How many do you have?"

"Two here. A few more with family back home in Wisconsin, where I grew up."

"Legitimately acquired?"

He stared, offended, till he saw the twinkle in her eyes. "Some are. Some I stole."

"Really?"

"No," he said, grinning. "Like I told you before, the ones I stole have been returned to their rightful owners, damn it."

Her look suggested that she was trying to feel shocked but not succeeding. He liked that teasing look. In fact, there wasn't much about her that he didn't like.

"Let me introduce you to the other vehicle I brought here," he said. "I even bought it in Maryland a short while after I arrived."

He motioned for her to follow. He led her to a silver Toyota hybrid SUV that he'd bought used but in pristine condition. It was useful—and it was a gorgeous hunk of car.

"Nice," she said, and her sincere and impressed tone got to him.

"Yeah, nice," he said and took a step toward her.

What was it about this guy that turned Sara into a totally different person every time they were together?

She wasn't a car groupie. She just considered them

handy transportation. But she knew that Jason had gasoline in his veins, a love for cars that at one time, at least, had gone way beyond sensibility.

And now…now he was up close and personal with her. Right beside this nice, utilitarian but attractive vehicle that he apparently owned.

Not only that, but he was *really* up close and personal with her. If he took just one more step—

He did take it. And suddenly, she was in his arms.

His kiss was astoundingly hot and sexy as he thrust his tongue into her mouth. She felt like melting and exploding, all at the same time. She responded with gusto, expecting—wanting—more. Lots more.

But just as suddenly, he stepped back.

"Don't see anyone around, but you never know," he said huskily. "Care to see my accessories?" He winked one of those golden eyes of his and she was lost.

Her own return laugh was soft and full of…what? Challenge? Sex?

Hell if she knew. But in only moments she found herself entering the back of his car. The seats were already down, forming an upholstered bed that looked much too enticing.

Especially with Jason's hands guiding her inside.

She didn't resist. Didn't want to resist—although she did take one furtive look around to ensure that they were still alone.

And then there they were, with the door closed behind them, both kneeling on the SUV's bed. Jason wasted no time in taking Sara into his arms. Kissing her again—so hard and so sexily that she nearly toppled over.

Which wasn't a bad idea. The surface was softened by the light upholstery, but it wasn't particularly comfortable for kneeling, even in her camo uniform's slacks.

But instead of lying down, Sara just snugged herself closer to Jason's muscular body. Awkward? Yes. But even so, against him this way, she could feel how hard he was below. Without thinking, she urged her own body even closer and heard him moan softly.

That did it. She wanted him. Wise or not. Forbidden or not. Or maybe that was a factor in wanting him. Rebelling against who and what she was? She'd never done that before, but maybe, just maybe, she was starting now.

She pulled back enough to start unbuttoning the top of his uniform without breaking their kiss. Turned out he had the same idea, for suddenly her shirt was open and pulled back, baring her to him.

Only, when she got through unbuttoning him, she was enthralled by the sight of his hard, wonderfully toned chest. Apparently servicing cars, or being in the military, or both, sculpted this sexy man's muscles into perfection.

She, on the other hand, wasn't completely naked above—not at first. But she felt one of his hands touch her breasts, rub against them so her nipples hardened, and then her bra was off, too.

"Sara," Jason gasped, laying her down gently onto the carpetlike surface. He sucked first one breast, then the other, into his mouth as his tongue teased her nipples.

She was far from passive, even as she moaned at his utterly sensual activities, his gentle attack on her vulnerable, eager body. She reached into his pants, grasping his hard erection and pumping it gently with her hand.

He moved so quickly that she was barely aware of it, but in moments he was naked against her. She imitated his motion, and the rest of her clothing was gone, too.

And then he touched her, right there in her most sensitive area. Grasped her, rubbing gently, moving one finger, then more than one, inside her in imitation of the sex act that she suddenly craved.

Only— She couldn't, could she? Not without protection, even with a being who was entirely human, and his differences from her, although not obvious now, suddenly leaped into her mind.

She stiffened.

"Wait," he said. He let go of her, leaving her bereft despite thinking it was for the best. But as she watched, he wriggled between the two rear seats and up into the front of the vehicle. Lord, what a view. His long, sinewy, hard legs ending in a tight butt she wanted to stroke and squeeze, but she couldn't reach it. Not now.

She heard the glove compartment open, and in seconds he had retaken the position he had just left—almost. She saw him struggle to open a small package but his hands were trembling and he was taking too long.

But he was prepared, bless him.

"Let me," she said, taking the condom from him.

She got the wrappings off—and had the additional pleasure of sliding it gently, teasingly, onto him.

With a growl that was entirely human, he repositioned her onto her back and thrust inside her. He was still, as if savoring the moment, and she did the same.

And then he started pumping, gently at first and then with more and more intensity. She groaned in ecstasy, and when she finally reached the most amazingly powerful orgasm of her entire life, she had to stifle a scream.

Minutes later, or was it hours? Sara still lay on her side on the stiff, uncomfortable surface at the back of the SUV. She was breathing deeply and erratically, and the fact she was facing the similarly still—but really ripped—body of Jason's didn't help her calm her respiration.

She still felt damned attracted to him. If she weren't so exhausted, maybe she would attack him again and engage in more feral, uninhibited, mindless sex.

Only…well, she wasn't really mindless.

Even so, her gaze locked on to his for a long moment, and she knew that, if she let herself, she would be absolutely hypnotized by his smug grin.

As if the words were extracted from her by some kind of woo-woo sci-fi mind meld, she heard herself say in an irregular voice, "That was amazing."

But at the same time, reality was starting to reinsert itself into her mind.

Yes, he was one damned sexy guy. What she'd experienced was incredible.

But he was a subordinate in the military, which made what they'd done forbidden—especially for someone like her, who toed the line implicitly. Or always had before.

And in addition to that little problem, another insurmountable barrier remained between them. Jason was also a shapeshifter.

"It was," Jason responded to her comment. "But there's always room to make it even more amazing... soon." As if his body responded to what he said, Sara saw his sex organ start hardening once more.

Despite her fascination, she made herself stare at his face again. But she didn't respond to his suggestion.

Once she regained her senses, she'd never want to have sex with him again.

If she ever regained her senses....

Now though, physically sated, she relaxed against him while catching her breath, and allowed her mind to glom on to the curiosity that had invaded her from the time she'd begun to believe Jason was truly a werewolf.

"You told me before that you'd let me know what it's really like to be a shapeshifter," she murmured against his chest.

He put his arms around her and held her close. "It's incredible," he said, and she felt his breath rippling the hair on top of her head as he spoke. "The change? It's uncomfortable, and yet it feels like being reborn every time. In both directions."

"Which do you like better?" she asked. "Human or wolf form?"

"Love 'em both, for different reasons." He paused. "At the moment, human's in the lead."

She heard herself chuckle. And then she said, "Did you have a hard time while growing up? Were there regular humans around, and did you have to hide who—what—you were?" *And did that, somehow, lead to your becoming a car thief?* she wondered, but she didn't ask.

"Our family was pretty much located in remote areas of Wisconsin," he said, drawing her even closer. "And yes, there were still a lot of 'normal' people we had to keep our secret from. But we weren't too far from Madison, so we were always able to shop there for stuff our neighbors wouldn't understand, even some kinds of chemicals. Over generations, our ancestors had started fooling around with an elixir to help us decide when to change and all—similar to the one Drew has been developing for Alpha Force, but his is a whole lot better, more sophisticated now, than what he and I grew up with. And its current formulation is proprietary to Alpha Force, which is one reason I'm here and will be staying, at least for now."

"How did you all… I mean, is there a whole community of shapeshifters where you're from, or only your family?" She was finding this description fascinating, which surprised her. She always had a streak of curiosity that controlled who she was…but who knew she'd find something she'd considered pure fiction—before—so interesting?

"There are a bunch of us," he responded. "Not all

are in the same area, and not all are part of our family, but we do keep in touch."

"And what do you do there about—" A sound startled her, interrupting her question, but she stopped herself from gasping aloud. A car must be driving by. She heard the noise of tires on the concrete floor and froze.

Just moving her eyes, she glanced upward. There were no lights on in the SUV. The only illumination was dim and came from recessed lighting in the parking garage. Plus, the vehicle's windows were tinted.

And Jason and she both were lying chest-to-chest— and how sexy that felt—on the folded-down backseat, way below those windows.

They had to be invisible to anyone driving by.

Thank heavens.

She looked at Jason, though, realizing that she was trembling a little. He was grinning, apparently at her horrified reaction about potentially getting caught here. She glared, but at least he wasn't moving. Although she wouldn't put it past this man to stand up, turn on the lights and flaunt all he had.

If the driver happened to be female, she'd get one hell of a show.

But fortunately, Jason was wiser than that. He stayed as still as Sara did.

In less than a minute, the noise receded and was not followed by the sound of any other vehicle.

"I think it's time to go." Sara drew herself up slightly, still hiding herself in the corner between the farthest-back side window and the rear one, and hurriedly donned her clothes.

With what appeared to be a sorrowful shrug, Jason also knelt and began to dress.

Sara tried not to look, but she nevertheless saw enough to feel regret that such a gorgeous, hard, utterly sexy body would soon be hidden from her view.

Until the next time that Jason had suggested…?

No.

There could be no next time.

Reading Sara McLinder's face was even easier than reading a car's maintenance manual.

Jason purposely made dressing himself into a show, as he'd done with his body when he had shifted in front of Sara so many times now.

Even though she'd been curious, had asked a lot of good questions about his background and all, she regretted what they'd done.

But damn, she'd enjoyed it, too.

Even admitted that—a few minutes ago. But he bet that if he asked her now, while she finished dressing as she hid as best she could inside the back of his SUV, she'd pretend she'd never meant anything of the sort. Had maybe enjoyed slumming just this once.

But that was the one and only time.

His presumption was unexpectedly painful. It challenged him, too. They would do it again. He'd make sure of it. Or at least he'd do his damnedest to seduce her sometime in the future.

The near future.

"So what do you think of my second car?" he finally asked, keeping his tone light.

"Nice," she said, although she didn't sound serious. And then, still buttoning up her camo blouse, she stopped and stared at him. "Did you plan this? Did you bring me to the hauling truck—and then this car—because you wanted us to get in the back here and...and make love?"

He could see by her rattled expression that she sought the right euphemism, one she could live with, for the various words and descriptions out there for having sex.

"I thought about it," he admitted easily. He'd thought about having sex with Sara since he'd met her. "Our respective quarters wouldn't be exactly the easiest places to get down and dirty like this, would they?"

"No. And that's a good thing." Sadly, every bit of her gorgeous body that had turned him on so much it hurt was now covered. Oh, her bustline was obvious even beneath her shirt, but her being in uniform was definitely not the most exciting view of her he had seen.

"Okay," he said. He didn't want to get into a fight with her. Not now. But he could see by her angry expression that his agreeing with her hadn't pacified her, either.

He wanted to grab her. Shake some sense into her.

Better yet, turn her on again.

Instead, he turned away and grabbed the inside handle of the vehicle's back door. He levered it and pushed it open.

"I'll get out first," he told her, which he did. He looked around to ensure they were still alone. "It's okay now. Let's go."

Chapter 12

Sara's bed in her BOQ apartment was a hell of a lot more comfortable than the bed of that SUV she'd left only about half an hour ago, alone, stalking out of the garage ahead of Jason—even though she knew he was behind her, keeping watch.

Which made her feel protected. But she didn't need protection. She could take care of herself.

So why wasn't she sleeping…again?

Last time she'd had insomnia, it was because she'd thought she was hallucinating after seeing all those wolves.

This time…no hallucination. She had just experienced the best sex of her life. With the wrong man. Or whatever he was.

He'd described his background—some of it. And

he'd even suggested they'd partake in another heated encounter someday. Another bout of unforgettable, incredible love-making with a man—yes, he was at least partly a man—who seemed to anticipate every touch, every kiss, every thrust that would make her giddy and turn her into a heap of mindless sensation.

She didn't even want to think about it.

Which meant she thought about nothing else, except for her fascination—no, her fury with herself— far into the night.

She was relaxing, at least, when she suddenly jolted to attention in her bed with the ringing of her smartphone.

She glanced at the caller ID.

Jason.

She ignored the sudden moistening and twisting down below, where he'd made her feel so good. Why would he be calling at this hour?

Was something wrong again at Ft. Lukman? With General Yarrow? Something else?

"Hello?" Her voice was all professional. At least she hoped so.

"Hi, Sara." His deep voice made her insides react even more. He didn't sound frantic or upset. But why was he calling?

"Is anything wrong?"

"Yes," he said immediately, and her heart started thumping erratically.

"Tell me."

"I can't sleep. I'll bet you can't, either. I don't suppose you'd like to get together again so we could relax one another. I'd like at least some rest tonight. Lots going on tomorrow."

"You have a lot of nerve," she spat out. "What's going on tomorrow is just one of the many reasons we are not only staying apart tonight, but what happened…well, it was a mistake. It won't happen again. Do you understand?"

"I hear you." She heard him, too—including the laughter in his tone. "Good night, Sara."

Damn. He hung up, and she'd wanted to be the one to end the call.

She felt furious—with not only him, but herself, too.

But as she lay there, rehashing not only his phone call but their unforgettable lovemaking, she found herself smiling, too…even as she finally felt sleep coming on.

Sara hurried from her apartment first thing the next morning. With the upcoming meetings, she didn't have time to obsess about what had happened last night.

As she walked down the hall toward the stairway, a door opened. Colleen Hodell ran out, almost bumping into Sara.

"Sorry," the tawny-haired lieutenant said, her felinelike eyes wide. "I'm meeting Rainey for a quick breakfast and I'm late."

"She's your shifting aide, isn't she?" Sara felt curious about how a cougar-shifter handled her role here among all the wolves.

"That's right." Colleen seemed to hesitate then smiled. "You haven't met Puka yet, have you?"

"Puka?"

"My cover cat. I keep her in my apartment rather than having her stress out among all those dogs. Come on in. Rainey can wait a few more minutes."

"Thanks."

Colleen's apartment was as small as Sara's, with nondescript but comfortable-looking furniture and a tiny kitchenette, but she had been there long enough to add some personal touches such as photos on the wall of lots of cats.

Some were wilder kinds of felines, and Sara couldn't help wondering if they were real pumas and jaguars and tigers—or if they were shapeshifter felines, like Colleen.

"In here." Colleen gestured for Sara to join her near the kitchenette. "This is her favorite spot."

The cat that lay on a fluffy, orange pillow at the far side of the narrow tile floor was large for a kitty, maybe twenty pounds. She was as tawny as Colleen's hair, and her face looked like a miniature version of a mountain lion.

"She's lovely," Sara couldn't help exclaiming. She considered herself more of a dog person, yet this cat was not only unusual but the stare of her brown eyes appeared highly intelligent. "Where did you find her?"

"I knew when I joined Alpha Force that I'd need a cover animal." Colleen crossed the floor, reached up and opened a cupboard door. She removed a box of feline treats and fed a couple to the cat, who rubbed against her leg. "My family always kept cats around that resembled us as much as possible while shifted, so I just brought Puka with me."

"Where are you originally from?" Sara said, wondering if it was any harder to keep a shifting cougar's identity secret than it was a wolf's. She now knew a bit more about where Jason had come from. Colleen had given some of her background the other night at dinner but Sara didn't recall what she'd said except that she wasn't among those shifters who now liked to complain about their prior lives.

"Oh, the Midwest."

"Is your family—"

"Yeah, they're still there."

Colleen's abruptness suggested she didn't want to answer a bunch of questions. Maybe she truly was concerned that she was late for her breakfast with Rainey. But after her conversation with Jason, Sara was curious.

"Are they all shapeshifters?" she asked. "Are there a lot of cougar shifters? I gather there are quite a few wolves. And did you have to hide from regular humans while you were growing up?"

Colleen's sigh was deep and she didn't meet Sara's eyes. "I don't generally talk much about my background." Her voice was hoarse. "You're right—there tend to be a lot more wolf shifters than feline, and there are more of us than there are other shifters, like birds. My family is small. We all shift under a full moon so, hiding—yes, that was a lot of what we did when I was a kid. I'd wanted...well, I thought my life would change a lot when I found Alpha Force and was able to join up. And it did. But..." Her voice trailed off, and Sara didn't prompt her. Maybe that was enough. "But my family," Colleen finally went on. "They're still there. It's hard for them, and I'd love to help them. I—" She turned toward Sara. "Okay, enough of that."

"Sorry for being pushy," Sara said. "But I didn't even believe there were shapeshifters before, and now that I know there are I'm really curious."

"No problem." Colleen bent down and picked up her cat. "Anyway," she continued, "Puka is mostly an indoor cat, and you can't really train cats the way they do with the dogs, so she's my furry apartment mate."

Despite her reluctance to talk about her past, she apparently had no issues about talking about her cat. "Have you ever had to use Puka to protect you as a shifter by proving there's a genuine cat around?"

"A couple of times, but not around here."

"I figured," Sara said. "Not with Alpha Force being the primary unit stationed here."

"Yeah, but even around those USFT guys...well, I know some have figured out what Alpha Force is all about."

"And they're about to learn more," Sara agreed. "Today."

"Which means we'd both better get going." She reached down and stroked Puka. "See you later, little girl."

That cat wasn't a *little* girl, in Sara's estimation. But she did enjoy watching Puka stare with interest as her best human friend said goodbye.

* * *

Jason wasn't invited to the initial preparatory meeting that morning.

He understood why. He wasn't the general or his aide, like Sara, nor a commanding officer of Alpha Force like his cousin Drew or Lieutenant Patrick Worley.

He definitely wasn't even aligned with other NCOs from that damned Ultra Special Forces Team.

Nah, he was just a peon. A mere sergeant who shapeshifted, fixed cars…oh, and occasionally helped to save a general's life.

Or spent a really great night with that general's aide.

So he just waited in the cafeteria, along with other Alpha Force members who were also eager for their part of the meeting to start—like shifters Seth Ambers, Jock Larabey, Colleen Hodell and Marshall Vincenzo, and nonshifting aides Noel Chuma and Rainey Jessop.

But they weren't alone playing with their breakfasts and speculating about what was to come. Oh, no, some of those damned USFT guys were there, too. Jason didn't know all their names, but they sat at their tables eating, drinking juice and coffee and, undoubtedly, gossiping, since they sent a lot of glares toward the Alpha Force folks, who only glared back.

And the meetings today were supposed to somehow promote accord and working together?

Good luck.

For fun, Jason decided to stick a baiting knife into the tense atmosphere. He stood with his cup of coffee and went to the row of dispensers to top it off with some hotter brew. Instead of returning to his original seat, he sat at the USFT table and gave a smile of utter innocence. "Hey, you guys going to the all-hands meeting later?"

"Yeah," said a woman whose ID tag said she was Lieutenant Swainey. "We'll be there." She said nothing more at first, but Jason continued to stare at her smoothly attractive African-American face with his goofy yet challenging smile. "Will you?" she asked, as if she had decided to follow his unspoken instructions.

"We sure will. I'm looking forward to hearing how we're all going to work together like one big, happy family." He widened that faux smile.

"You're the guy who works on cars, aren't you?" asked Lieutenant Brown. He was a big guy who'd apparently either chosen to wear his camos tight or he'd been beefing up his body since acquiring his uniform.

Jason wouldn't want to get into a physical altercation with the muscular lieutenant. But a battle of wits? Anytime.

"That's right," he responded. "You have one that needs work?"

"No, but I heard you did a pissant job of fixing your General Yarrow's."

That brought a titter from everyone else at the damned USFT table and nearly made Jason stand up and tip it onto their fat little laps.

But some of those from his own table now stood behind him. This could get out of control really quick.

He thought then of straitlaced, by the book—almost—Sara. What would she think if he primed the atmosphere here so that nothing could be accomplished at the later meeting?

Hell, he figured the meeting would be worthless, anyway. No need for him to cause any additional ill feelings right now. So instead of accusing these guys, or someone in their unit, of sabotaging General Yarrow's car, he simply said, "Yeah. Unfortunately, it was too far gone to be saved. Fortunately, the general survived."

"Yeah, fortunately." Brown's tone made Jason want to slug him.

"I need more coffee," Jason said, standing. The Alpha Force members who'd joined him looked surprised.

Hey, he'd gotten a reputation not only for talking out of turn but acting that way, too. Sometimes. When it didn't threaten his ability to stay in Alpha Force and therefore out of prison.

But these folks didn't really know him. And if he'd surprised them this time? Well, hell. That felt good… and he knew he'd do it again.

The preliminary meeting of the topmost officers stationed at Ft. Lukman was nearing its end.

It had taken place at the front of the base's assembly room, even though they all could have fit into General Yarrow's sumptuous office.

Sara understood why that hadn't happened. Her CO hadn't wanted to make it appear to the other general, Myars, that he intended to take charge.

But it had become crystal clear nearly immediately

who had not only the power here, but the knowledge and intelligence to get these people talking—and to prepare for the larger upcoming session, too.

She couldn't help wondering where Drew's "cuz" was but forced herself to cast all thoughts of him aside.

Two of General Yarrow's subordinates who were the local officers in charge of Alpha Force were inevitably present: Drew Connell and Patrick Worley, who was back on base temporarily but due to leave again that afternoon.

General Myars had a couple of his immediate reports present, as well: Captains Samantha Everly and Rynton Tierney.

Sara recalled her brief discussion with Samantha the night that Jason had been in such bad condition while shifted. The captain seemed less animated now, although she undoubtedly tried to take her cue from her commanding officer. Today, the clip holding her light brown hair was at the nape of her neck instead of on top of her head.

Sara was more interested in watching Rynton Tierney, who held a similar position to hers with the other general. He appeared less engaged than Samantha listening to the conversation. In fact, he seemed more inclined to watch the Alpha Force members from across the narrow aisle between the seating areas. Did he know, or just suspect, that some of them were shifters?

The two generals' initial conversation was standard cordial B.S., with Hugo Myars commenting on how well Greg Yarrow looked despite his ordeal the other day.

Greg, similarly, asked Myars about his trip here and how things were going with him at the Pentagon and Ft. Lukman.

Useless stuff. At first.

Sara noticed with relief that General Yarrow looked a lot better than he had even on his arrival yesterday. Maybe it was because he was no longer pale, but his lined face was florid beneath his dark hair as he faced off with his counterpart about what they intended to do at the later meeting.

General Myars looked ten years younger than Greg, despite the fact his hair was sparser and its short style displayed strands of gray within its brown. Maybe it was because he was stockier. The flabbiness of his cheeks shoved out most wrinkles. He was taller, too, though part of that height was due to the exaggerated heels on his military boots.

But once the polite initial conversation was ended, he seemed ready to shout and storm and do anything he could to rattle General Yarrow.

Including insult his subordinates.

Both generals sat at the front of the room, beyond the tiers of chairs holding underlings like Sara. She couldn't hear all they said when they lowered their voices for more serious conversation—and wished, for once, she had a few of the enhanced senses of Alpha Force members who sat with her in the first row of seats. They must have heard it all.

With the little she did hear—and the animosity emanating from Myars—Sara had a hard time staying silent and not jumping in with her own opinions and accusations. One or more of these people may have been the ones who'd ruined Greg Yarrow's prized car—and tried to injure, possibly kill, him.

Damn them.

She wouldn't ask Drew or Patrick what they heard when the two men's voices were lowered. But if Jason had been here? Well, even though she had to stay away from him personally, the bond they'd started to forge would have allowed her to ask him.

After five minutes of the heated, low-voiced exchange, Greg stood and looked at the members of the small audience.

"Here's what we decided, ladies and gentlemen." He glanced at Myars, who stood quickly beside him. "General Myars and I will each introduce our units briefly to the entire group when everyone is here and seated."

"We'll describe again what sets our units apart from each other, and from all others in the military," Myars added.

"Then we'll describe the joint maneuvers we intend to hold here," Greg continued, "demonstrating those special skills to one another and seeing how we can work together—because we've been primed about a very special, critical mission that the government intends to send us both on. That's why USFT was sent here, to where Alpha Force is stationed, to see if we could join forces and get the kind of result our government needs."

"I'm sure we can work together, sir," Samantha Everly said immediately, undoubtedly kissing up to her CO. "USFT can do anything—even if it involves danger…and weirdness."

She pointedly shot a glance toward the other side of the aisle, where Sara sat with the Alpha Forcers. Apparently, Samantha had a pretty good idea of what special abilities the other unit had.

Sara wished she knew what skills above and beyond standard the USFT members had. If they behaved this way with shapeshifters, Sara suspected their abilities were more similar to what was considered normal, even if they were somehow enhanced.

The all-hands meeting definitely promised to be interesting.

Especially because…everyone in both units was expected to be there.

Including Jason.

And his offbeat sense of humor.

Sara had a feeling that whatever the USFT's special abilities, if Myars, Samantha or anyone else in that group decided to diss Alpha Force and its highly unique capabilities, some members of Alpha Force would reciprocate in kind.

Jason, in particular, would get a kick out of making fun of them.

That was neither professional nor military, Sara knew. But even tamping down all memories of the night they'd shared, she couldn't wait to see Jason… and hear his reactions.

Chapter 13

Jason entered the administration building near the assembly room at least fifteen minutes before the session was to begin.

He wasn't alone. The other Alpha Force members he'd been with were there, too, talking and joking in the concrete-and-tile foyer till it was time to enter the room.

Jason often hung back when forced to attend meetings. Alpha Force might be an exceptionally good job for him, but, hell, it was still the military.

Only today was different. He was interested in what this session was about.

What were the special skills of those damned USFT members that made their higher-ups consider them appropriate to train, then deploy on a major assignment, with Alpha Force?

What was the point of basing them here, at Ft. Lukman, then waiting weeks before holding this kind of assembly to inform the groups what their respective future roles would be?

How had the earlier meeting gone—with the two generals?

With Sara's presence.

While waiting, his group linked up almost as if under orders to do so, ignoring the similar gathering of their rivals. Nemeses?

Jason wasn't the only Alpha Force member who mistrusted them.

"You ready?" Colleen broke into a conversation among Noel, Jonas and Rainey, who were trading humorous suggestions on how best to act like a shapeshifter's aide. They'd kept their voices low. Even if a lot of the other Alpha Forcers here could hear them, the damn USFT guys would stay oblivious.

Jason looked around and saw that the door to the assembly room had been opened. Sara glanced out before turning and walking back in.

"Showtime," Jason acknowledged. He kept his pace slow enough not to look eager to get inside. His habits were known here, including his lack of enthusiasm for meetings. No use changing that now and triggering any speculation.

There'd be plenty of speculation about the truthfulness, and completeness, of whatever they were told in the meeting.

The USFT group had noticed the open door, too, and headed in that direction. Jason turned enough to inhale their scents—standard shower soap and deodorants and the usual, but also more, caused by emotions. Sweat from fear? Heated by anger?

What the hell did they have to be angry about?

But their filing through the door was accomplished politely as they allowed others through first.

In the crowd, it was harder to scan the place to locate Sara. Yet it was almost as if he had a direct link with her—her light citrus scent, her connection with General Yarrow. All Jason had to do was check the front of the room for the two generals, and there was Sara standing, unsurprisingly, at Yarrow's right arm.

The two COs stood by chairs facing the crowd. Each gestured toward where they wanted everyone to sit.

There were a few seats left in the first row. Jason despised being up front—but it was the only way he'd get to be near Sara. He took one of those seats and waited.

Not long after his entrance, the room was apparently filled with all who were expected. Sara returned to the door and closed it. She turned before heading back to her seat, looking into the crowd.

She met Jason's eyes. She blinked then chilled her expression.

He nodded coolly, as he would toward any acquaintance, even a superior officer. Even so, she sat down in the last remaining seat in the row, which happened to be directly at his left.

Yes! But he didn't look at her.

The meeting began. General Yarrow took a step forward, placing himself a little closer to the crowd than General Myars. Myars tried to join the other man until General Yarrow's glance made him stop.

Interesting. Jason had been curious about their dynamics. Would Myars continue to take a more minor role?

"Thanks for coming, everyone." Yarrow raised his voice so it projected over the crowd. Conversations in the ten or so sparsely occupied rows of seats all stopped. He waited a moment then continued. "I know there've been a lot of questions you've all had over the past weeks, especially since the Ultra Special Forces Team arrived at Ft. Lukman. I am fully aware, and proud, that both the members of Alpha Force and USFT have been highly vetted and know not to talk about anything they know is confidential, and that has led to some…let's just say suspicions and lack of camaraderie around here. That was part of the plan. We wanted to see the reaction."

Murmurs circulated through the audience. Jason knew the other Alpha Forcers could pick up what was being said as well as he did. In fact, they were among those commenting, or swearing, or both, about the so-called plan.

Most had found seats near the front of the crowd, which meant that the USFT folks hung out mostly farther back.

Seth Ambers, in the second row, stood and saluted. "Permission to speak, sir?" The guy who looked like a moose, or at least a football player, would have dwarfed the general if they'd been closer. But Seth, a medical doctor as well as a shifter, was completely gentle...with those to whom gentleness made sense.

"All right, Seth," Yarrow said.

"I'm sure I'm speaking for everyone here when I say that we all really hope that the purpose of this meeting is not only to formally introduce the two groups, but also to explain the plan, and why we were allowed to get together with our counterparts before but not do much more than say hi."

Myars took another step toward the seats and scowled. His mouth was open as if he intended to berate Seth for daring to even suggest that the plan was anything but perfect.

But General Yarrow turned, blocking Myars as smoothly as if it had been choreographed.

Jason grinned. He used his peripheral vision to look sideways at Sara and saw her brief smile, too—although it quickly disappeared.

But General Yarrow was a peacemaker as well as a fighter. He said to Seth, "That's exactly what this meeting is about. In fact, I request that General Myars tell us all about USFT, why it is so ultra special. I'll then explain a bit about Alpha Force, and then together we'll outline the training exercises we plan here—and the mission on which most of you will be deployed if all goes well."

Jason leaned forward in his seat. So did most of the others in Alpha Force. This was what they'd all wanted to know.

"Okay," Myars said. "The Ultra Special Forces Team—you're all exactly what that name describes.

You've proven it before. And whether or not you work directly with…Alpha Force—" his tone sneered, though his face remained visibly blank. Jason glanced at General Yarrow, whose eyes had narrowed, but he, now seated, said nothing "—you will prove it again."

Sara wanted to yell at that general for not acting wholly professional. For insulting Alpha Force with his tone and attitude.

Instead, she just clamped both hands into fists.

And glanced sideways at Jason. His hands were fisted, too.

Almost involuntarily, she looked at his face. Didn't smile, but nodded her head in acknowledgment that he, too, was riled—but also acted professionally within military protocol.

He, on the other hand, shot her a very quick grin then looked at the two generals once more.

At least General Myars finally got into what he was supposed to talk about: what USFT was all about.

"All members of the unit had to pass some very tough tests. For example, their eyesight is far better than most people's."

Sara had noticed that none wore glasses except sunglasses, but she'd just assumed some wore contact lenses. Apparently not.

"Plus, they're highly trained in all special forces skills. Most important, they are the most elite of all snipers."

Myars went on to explain the extent of their vetting, their initial training, their ongoing perfection of their skills.

In other words, they'd been selected as the best of the special forces best. Some had been Navy SEALS. Some had been Army or Marines Special Forces. Some had been Air Force Special Ops.

Now they were all members of the Ultra Special Forces Team.

When he was done, the members of that highly skilled unit stood and cheered themselves. To be polite, Sara rose and found that the Alpha Forces joined her to applaud the others.

Then it was General Yarrow's turn. "I don't think it's a huge secret here, but all of you USFT folks were also chosen because of your security clearances, and understanding of clandestine operations and how to stay quiet about them."

Sara heard quiet muttering behind him. She couldn't make out what was being said, but knew that the shapeshifters in the room would hear it.

She was glad when Jason bent toward her and whispered, "Here's what was said: 'Oh, yeah. They're going to feed us that line again. Shapeshifters. Yeah, right.'"

"You know," General Yarrow said, "I heard someone comment but my ears aren't good enough to hear what was said. Drew, did you hear it?"

Major Drew Connell was also in the front row, a few people down from Sara. He stood—and repeated what had been said, verbatim. "The shifting members of Alpha Force also have enhanced senses while in human form," he said coldly, looking at the back row where Lieutenant Cal Brown sat.

The large soldier squirmed a bit, and Sara knew he was the one who'd spoken—especially when Jason confirmed it.

"And yes, the special talents of many Alpha Force members include shapeshifting," General Yarrow continued, as if he were describing the features of an outstanding new car. "What some of you USFT personnel thought was just a ruse on the recent night of the full moon was real."

No one spoke, but Sara sensed a lot of discomfort in the room. As she turned to look, she saw a number of personnel from the other unit moving uneasily in their seats.

Greg Yarrow didn't offer details about the shifting elixir, but he said that the next few days at Ft. Lukman would be critical. Obviously, those within the two groups had not yet bonded simply because they were fellow members of the military. That had been the hope when the USFT unit was first sent here. Neither group had passed that test. They had stayed separate and even seemed somewhat antagonistic.

But that had to change. Now they needed to show they could get along under many different kinds of conditions—conditions that each group would be permitted to manufacture.

If all went well, they'd then be put through joint exercises…and only then would they be told what their real assignment would be.

"Only if you've convinced us you can work well together," General Yarrow finished. "Right, General?" He looked at Myars.

"That's right," the other man said. "Otherwise, we'll call an end to the experiment, and both units will show a failure on their records."

"Permission to speak, General Yarrow?" That was Colleen Hodell, who'd sat in the second row. She was on her feet, saluting.

"All right, Lieutenant," Yarrow said.

"I know this isn't a question that'll lead to better relations between the two units, sir," she said, "and none of us wants any failures on our records. But everyone in Alpha Force will want the answer." She pivoted, first toward the people at the front who were in her unit, and those more toward the back rows who were not. "Has anyone found an answer about what happened to your car, General Yarrow? I mean—are we sure it wasn't damaged, and your life endangered, because of the lack of…well, camaraderie here?"

Jason felt the tension in the room rise. He didn't need his enhanced senses as a shifter for that. Even so, he inhaled the heated scents of anger enough that he felt his whole body tense.

Beside him, Sara also stiffened in her seat. He glanced at her and saw that her eyes were wide and worried, her full lips pursed in concern.

She looked as if she'd have shut the Alpha Force member up if she'd been able. And she clearly wasn't going to do what they'd discussed previously: hinting that they'd found a clue on the Jeep implicating USFT.

She didn't need to. Not now. Colleen had come pretty close to doing so, and the tension in the room could be sliced with a combat knife.

He didn't turn around to look at the USFT troops, but their scents suggested anger.

Of course they were all real military sorts. Unless ordered to fight—or otherwise given official approval—they'd hold it inside. And stew. And say "yes, sir" and "no, sir" and bite their tongues.

And potentially find underhanded ways of avenging their unit's honor.

Jason expected General Yarrow to respond, possibly even to scold his own Alpha Force member, to keep the peace.

General Myars beat him to it, stomping forward at the front of the meeting room. "Is that intended to be an accusation against anyone within USFT, Lieutenant? If so, you'd better be more specific—and have proof, not just insinuations."

"Sorry if I was out of line, sir." Colleen hung her head so that her light brown hair spilled forward over her face for a moment. But then she looked around again, a smile that looked rueful momentarily lighting her felinelike features. "I just meant that I would much prefer it if we weren't so—isolated here. Wouldn't it make more sense for our two units to mingle more?"

And was the fact that they hadn't before a factor in what had happened to General Yarrow—and to him, for that matter? Jason thought that was too simplified.

But sometimes the simplest answers were the right ones.

General Yarrow stepped forward, taking his place again beside the other general. "I think Lieutenant Hodell is right in what she just said." Yarrow was much too polite to hint that she might have been right before, too. "In fact, it's also my opinion that we all need to commingle more, and that has been my opinion for a while. That's one reason I came here, to Ft. Lukman, to set things right before we attempt to meld the two forces for an exercise—and then, if all goes well, in the field. So here's my order for tonight. I want each of you to pair up into groups of two members from your own unit, then hook yourselves up with one of the pairs from the other unit. You'll eat dinner together. Then later tonight, we'll conduct a preliminary exercise here at Ft. Lukman to see how your respective strengths can complement each other." He looked at General Myars. "Are you in agreement, General?"

The flabby officer said nothing for a moment, appearing as if he were trying not to throw up.

But then he answered, "Yes, General, let's give it a try."

And it would just be a try, Jason thought. He glanced toward the woman beside him. Sara looked as skeptical as he felt.

"Then…everyone, dismissed," called General Yarrow.

Interesting, Jason thought as Yarrow immediately stomped into the crowd and confronted Lieutenant Hodell. The conversations around him were immediately too loud for him to focus in on that particular one, even with his superior hearing, but he'd have loved to catch what the general was saying to the lady shapeshifter.

Congratulating her for bringing the issue to a head—or reaming her for not staying in her place?

The conversation he did hear loudest, since the participants stood beside him, were among other officers in Alpha Force, including Sara. They stood near the front of the room, keeping their voices low.

"How should we pair up?" Sara directed the question to Drew.

His cuz's golden eyes narrowed. "I don't know whether General Yarrow intends that any of us do some shifting tonight to show these…fellow soldiers…who we really are and what we can do, but just in case I think we should have a shifter and nonshifter in each group. Not necessarily our usual group of shifters plus aides, although that would be all right, too."

In what seemed like moments, they'd chosen their groups: Drew with Jonas Truro, Simon Parran with Noel Chuma and so forth.

Was Sara intending to work with Colleen when the general was through with her?

Jason decided not to wait to find out. "Would you join up with me, ma'am?" he asked, trying to act as subservient a soldier as he could. "Unless, of course, your preference is to work with Lieutenant Hodell."

He caught the horror in her glance as she looked around and saw that most of the other Alpha Forcers had decided on their partners. "I may just sit this out, Sergeant," she said.

"Whatever you say. Only…" He let his voice trail off.

"Only what?" Her lovely brow puckered.

"Well, for one thing, if we…" He leaned closer and whispered, "If we do shift tonight, all the usual aides already have paired up for this, so I'll need some help. And even if we don't—well, I'm really interested in how this works. How we get along with members of the USFT, see them strut their stuff, try to work out the camaraderie that General Yarrow's so eager to promote."

That got Sara's attention. Her blue-green eyes glanced upward, then glommed on to his as if she had been struck by what he said.

"Wouldn't you like to be part of that, too?" he pushed. "So you can report to the general how it all seems to work out. I'll bet he'd love to have an insider like you tell him about it."

Her smile was wry as she looked up into his face and shook her head slowly, as if in amusement. "You really know how to pull my chain, don't you, Sergeant?" He didn't like that she wasn't using his name, but in this location he definitely got why.

And her chain wasn't all he'd enjoyed pulling before. Although, judging by the heat in her look, she didn't need a reminder.

"Okay," she said. "We're a team for this evening. An official Alpha Force team." She paused. "It might be good this way to have an officer in charge as well as a subordinate, to show whoever we get from the USFT how Alpha Force is an excellent, smoothly functioning military unit."

Jason read into what she said. In other words, he

was to follow her lead. Her orders. Be a good member of the damned military and follow all the rules.

Not to mention showing the other guys what a great soldier he was.

Could he do it?

Hell, yes.

Especially if it got him extra brownie points with his cousin and the commanding general…

And Lieutenant Sara McLinder.

Chapter 14

This was becoming unnerving to Sara. But she could, and would, handle it. Even though it seemed contrary to most protocol she had learned since joining the military.

The protocol she had been comfortable with.

Right now she stood on the periphery of the improved areas of Ft. Lukman, beyond the buildings and at the edge of an outdoor parking lot—near where the forest within the base's boundaries began to grow.

Not far from where she'd gone her first night—and been confronted by that apparent pack of wolves.

The early-evening air was crisp, but her discomfort wasn't the result of her camo uniform not being warm enough. No, it was more internal.

Especially because she stood beside Jason, who was

acting all soldier, all professional. Seeming even to enjoy it.

To enjoy being her partner in what was to come.

That only made her even more uneasy. And not just because being with him stoked her heated recollection of the time they had spent together. And how sexy he was. And how she lusted after him no matter how much she doused those thoughts with the iciness of reality checks.

That was much easier to ignore when she wasn't with him. But she'd been, and would continue to be, in his company a lot of the time she was here at Ft. Lukman.

She wasn't alone with him, of course. She was among all these teams of soldiers who had been ordered to work hard to get along together. Ranks didn't matter.

Their units did.

And as to members of Alpha Force, the preference was that one of the pair be a shapeshifter, and the other not.

She could have said no when Jason asked to team up with her. It was probably a bad idea.

Especially since she might have to not only watch him shift, but help him, too.

"All right, everyone." That was Major Drew Connell shouting to be heard above all conversations. From what Sara could tell, everyone was at least making an effort to achieve the camaraderie that they'd been ordered to do. "Here's what we'll do."

"My cousin likes to give orders," said Jason to the two members of the Ultra Special Forces Team who were now part of their team: Samantha Everly and Manning Breman. How odd—or contrived—was it that they'd been the ones Sara had talked to in the middle of the night to keep them from seeing Jason in wolf form?

But Sara liked that Jason was acting as he should—trying to make friends with these two.

Samantha looked offended, though, at the friendliness of a mere sergeant. She kept her chin raised, which made the brown hair clipped at the back of her neck seem to dig into her. Her arms were crossed over her full chest encased in her camo uniform, and her expression seemed…well, haughty.

To Jason's credit, he didn't appear to notice.

Manning, on the other hand, seemed all graciousness. The tall, pudgy guy laughed at what Jason said. "Isn't it a downer to have to report to your own relative?"

"Sssh." Samantha scowled at them both. "We need to hear this."

Sara said nothing. Samantha was right, but she didn't want to acknowledge that to the bitchy woman.

"First thing, we'll have our Ultra Special Forces Team members demonstrate their sniper proficiency," Drew continued. "For those of you who don't know, we have an outdoor shooting range near the fence at the back of this forest area."

Sara hadn't seen the area but figured that all shifting members of Alpha Force knew every inch of the base.

They'd have seen it while on the prowl.

"Let's head there, and we'll get a demo of the abilities of the USFT members. I've heard about them but really look forward to seeing it with my own eyes."

Drew motioned for everyone to follow. The closest to him, his own temporary team, consisted of his aide, Jonas Truro, as well as USFT members Rynton Tierney and Vera Swainey.

Sara noticed some of the other teams, too—around six in all. One consisted of Simon Parran and his aide while shifting, Noel Chuma, plus two USFT members Sara hadn't met yet. Simon's wife, Grace, wasn't included in this exercise.

Another team included Colleen Hodell and Rainey Jessop along with USFT member Cal Brown and another one Sara didn't know.

They all trudged through the woods. It was still light enough to see their way around the trees, though the area was blanketed in shadows.

The shifting Alpha Force members would have no problem. The sounds of everyone's footfalls on fallen leaves, and the twittering and shrieks of birds above, along with the smells enhanced by the sudden occupation of this area, would be child's play to their keen senses.

Sara made sure to keep up with teammate Jason. For safety's sake. Not because she was happy to be in his company.

When she tripped once over a fallen branch, she ignored her impulse to grab his hand and hold on. But he seized her arm and helped to keep her upright—before quickly letting go.

"Sorry, ma'am," he said, the perfect soldier—for the moment. "You okay?"

"Yes. Thank you." She managed a glance in the near darkness and caught his amused expression. He enjoyed the show that he and the others were putting on.

Sara couldn't make out much of the conversations of the groups heading through the forest. For a moment she wished, as she sometimes had before, that she had the senses of a shifter—utterly absurd. She hadn't even wanted to believe in them, and now that she did it wasn't logical to want to share any of their characteristics.

In a short while, they reached the far side of the forest. There, Sara saw a long fence that marked the perimeter of this part of Ft. Lukman. It wasn't standard chain link but was composed of some high, substantial-looking metal material.

Which made sense if this was a shooting range. She believed the other side of the fence was public parkland. No one would want any hiking civilians injured by unrestrained gunfire.

"Okay," Drew said loudly then turned to his new team member Rynton Tierney. "Please tell us again what your unit's special abilities are and explain what they'll demonstrate here."

Every team now stood in the clearing. Were they each getting along? Well, the members were all still alive and not shouting at each other, so Sara figured they were at least pretending to be buddies.

"This area is a good one, even at twilight," Rynton began. He explained again that most of the special nature of the USFT members involved their perfect—no, better than perfect—vision and accuracy in aiming weapons. "We've all been vetted to make sure we can do even more than an ordinary sniper—and you all know that the military's regular snipers are far from ordinary."

He went on to talk briefly about how the USFT members' accuracy in aiming and more had been recognized and lauded at the topmost echelons of the military—including its commander in chief, the president of the United States.

Then it was time for a demonstration.

The special M25 sniper rifles and ammo had already been brought to the area and secured there. Rynton opened the case that had been hidden at the edge of the woods. He also introduced a couple of privates who were members of USFT, and who had acted as sentries over the equipment.

For the next half hour, while the area grew darker as night fell, each USFT member provided a demonstration of his or her prowess, firing into wooden targets in the shape of people—and never missing the area of the heart or head, or wherever else they said they were aiming, even as each stepped back to be farther away in the blackening night. Then the targets were set to moving on their platforms. Fast. The perfection of the hits didn't waver.

It definitely was impressive.

But soon—maybe too soon—it was over.

Time for Alpha Force to conduct its own demonstration.

Sara wondered how Drew intended to carry this off. She knew he'd discussed it with General Yarrow, but she hadn't been included in the process.

She hoped that, for the sake of the modesty of Alpha Force shifters, they weren't just supposed to drop their drawers and change in plain view.

Fortunately, that wasn't the plan.

"All members of the USFT, please stay here. For security's sake—and mostly because I don't think any of you really want too much information here—we'll head into the nearest building, then return in shifted form."

"What if we want to see it all?" demanded Rynton Tierney. "That's what General Myars expects."

"The shifting process is highly classified," Drew shot back. "We saw the results of your abilities and training. That's all we'll show you of ours."

He gestured for the members of Alpha Force to follow.

Sara was glad she was among them. But was she about to see a lot more nudity than Jason's?

If so, she'd handle it as she'd handled everything else in the military.

The nearest building, a storage depot, had already been organized for the night's activities. Drew's wife, Melanie, was there, and she had taken charge of the shifting elixir. There were plenty of vials as well as boxes of the lights used to trigger the shifters' changes.

Each Alpha Force team was directed into a different storage area. In each case, the Alpha Force members consisted of a shifter and an aide.

Which meant Sara would become Jason's aide.

Drew approached her before he went off with Jonas. "Are you okay with this? You've never acted as one of our aides before."

"But she did see our pack that first night," Jason reminded him. He looked oh so smug when he glanced toward her, but was the picture of military propriety when he faced his cousin.

"Yeah, and I gather she's also seen you shifting since then."

"Yes, sir." Sara nodded, not looking toward Jason. "It's fine. I can handle it, sir."

Poor choice of words, she realized immediately, and felt herself flush. What she could and would handle right now was the light, and Jason's clothing.

But she would be seeing a lot more than that which she might desire to handle…again.

Drew didn't need to know that. Fortunately, he either didn't catch her slip or didn't interpret it as she did. "Fine. If you're all right with it, that'll help a lot, since our members have already paired up. You understand that it's fairly simple. Jason drinks the elixir and removes his clothing, you shine the light that resembles the light of a full moon on him and he changes. You take charge of his clothes and return them to him when he changes back again. Because this is a limited exercise, he won't drink a lot of elixir and will shift back in a short period of time. Okay?"

"Yes, sir," Sara said. And it *was* okay.

She would make sure of it.

And keep her damned, easily ignitable lust under control.

* * *

Jason had to hand it to Sara. She did everything just right.

Which was too bad. He saw her staring only momentarily at his private parts when he stripped after taking the elixir in the small room to which they'd been directed.

"Are you ready, Sergeant?" she demanded while he stood there in all his naked glory.

Just knowing she was there, this woman with whom he had so recently made memorable and magnificent love, made his cock stand up even larger and harder than usual.

Damn, he wished he wasn't about to shift so he could take Sara into his arms once more.

But that wasn't to be.

"I'm ready, Lieutenant." He drew out the last word as if he made fun of it. He watched as she pulled out the light and turned it on.

Before she aimed it at him, he couldn't resist. He flexed himself down below, and had the pleasure of seeing her eyes widen, her lips part, her body tense— but only for a moment....

That was when his shifting started and all things within him began to change.

Jason accompanied his pack members as they all stalked into the lobby of the storage building—all shifters within Alpha Force who were on duty on base. That included the sole feline member, Colleen, now a cougar.

The rest, including Jason, were all in wolf form. The other feline members of Alpha Force and its sole avian member were not present.

Together the pack walked, one by one, out the door, their human assistants following.

Outside, in darkness illuminated only by dim lights attached to the building, waited the members of the other unit now at the base, the ones who had perfect aim with sophisticated weaponry.

Did any wish they had their guns on them now to aim at the wild animals who faced them, waiting for their reactions?

Some came forward, including their current officer in charge since their general was observing from a distance with General Yarrow while this exercise took place.

Captain Rynton Tierney drew closest, even put his hand out to touch the canine at the lead, the most alpha wolf present, Drew Connell.

Jason tensed, ready to spring to his cousin's defense if needed.

But Tierney just shook his head as he stroked the wolf like a dog. "This is amazing." Then he looked beyond the pack and the cougar toward the human aides who had followed them out. "If it's real. I've seen the dogs here at Ft. Lukman who look a lot like these animals."

"They're cover dogs. And have you seen the cover cat? I have."

That was Sara's voice from behind him. She was

speaking up for Alpha Force, this woman who hadn't wanted to accept the reality of its existence.

Jason's human consciousness was highly enhanced by the special elixir Drew had developed. He knew what he was hearing.

And if he could have, he would have turned to thank, and congratulate, Sara McLinder. Maybe even kiss her in appreciation.

But he would have to wait for that.

For now, he waited to follow Drew's lead.

Sara wasn't surprised that Rynton Tierney didn't simply accept her answer: that these shifted Alpha Force members were exactly what they seemed and that cover dogs that resembled the wolves remained in the kennel area. Colleen's domestic cat that looked like a small cougar remained in her quarters.

As a result of his skepticism, Rynton sent a couple of USFT members to the building housing the kennels. The shifted Alpha Force members could start their planned demonstration, anyway, while that part of the cover story was confirmed.

Sara knew what else was in that building, downstairs and hidden away. The USFT troops didn't need to visit there. As a result, she requested that Noel Chuma, Simon Parran's aide today, accompany them. He'd be able to ensure they saw what they were after without heading below ground level to the highly classified and critical lab area.

With Noel gone, Sara would keep careful watch

over the shifted wolf that was Simon as well as her own current charge, Jason.

Jason. In wolf form, he was sleek and gorgeous and alert, staying by her side, at least for now. Sexy? No, not this way…but somehow the idea of his having two such different personas didn't turn her libido off, not even now.

All Alpha Force and USFT members went outside together and stood in the pale glow cast from lights at the top of the building. USFT Lieutenant Cal Brown, on the four-member joint team that included Colleen, seemed particularly interested in the sleek feline, talking a lot to the cougar as if she were human—which she was. He goaded her, urging her to find prey within the darkened woods and go in for the kill as her real feline counterparts would do in the wild.

Unsurprisingly, the cougar growled and roared. But to her credit, she didn't attack the man who taunted her.

Sara marveled at the situation. She'd have heard something from General Yarrow if there'd even been any similar kinds of exercises between Alpha Force and other military units. She had heard of only one— and although she'd not been informed of all the details, she'd gathered that the humans had interacted with canines they hadn't been informed were shapeshifters.

Previously, she hadn't believed they were, either.

Soon it was time for the demonstration that had been planned in advance by the Alpha Force members. First the nonshifters gave a couple of easy commands—things that perhaps even real wolves could be taught, but only with time and patience. The idea was to prove that these creatures understood language and could react to it appropriately—better than a true wolf would do, even after training.

"Use your left paw and scratch at the bark of the nearest oak tree," Jonas Truro instructed his charge, Drew Connell in wolf form. The rest of the shifted creatures were to sit and wait, which they did.

Of course Drew did as commanded. Sara had been told that all shifting members of Alpha Force had the consciousness of their human form while changed, thanks to the elixir that Drew had blended and continued to upgrade.

Next she told Simon Parran to find the tote bag she had brought along and take the bag of rawhide dog chews out of it. She'd left it behind a bush near the storage building, and he found it with no trouble.

She offered one to each of the wolf shifters. Most, but not all, accepted the treats. Each looked at her as if in thanks. This wasn't, of course, anthropomorphism. These animals truly were human some of the time.

But they were wild creatures in more than looks, too. After all the other, easier exercises had been performed, Rynton said, "I want to give an order, too." He didn't ask if it was okay. Instead, he approached Jason.

Which made Sara stiffen. Would he perform well? She didn't want her primary charge for this night to be the one who somehow ruined the fragile détente between the two units.

On the other hand, with his contrary, sometimes anti-military attitude and offbeat sense of humor, he might decide to act like…well, a real wolf.

"Go catch some prey. I don't care what it is. A rodent, a bird—but act like what you look like. Got it?"

Sara watched the face of the wolf that was Jason. She tried to read the expression but couldn't.

Then he raced off into the forest.

The entire crowd stood watching. At least a few of them stood. Some Alpha Force shifters sat on their haunches as they followed Jason with their eyes.

Would he come back?

Their attention was interrupted by the return of the guys who'd been sent to check on the cover animals. Noel Chuma was with them.

They approached Rynton Tierney, who stood with Vera Swainey and Manning Breman.

"Yep, there were a bunch of dogs in those kennels, Captain," said one of the USFT privates. "Want to see the pictures we took?"

He did, looking at the illuminated photos on the digital camera proffered by the soldier. He passed them around, too.

He then looked at Sara. "So those cover dogs do exist, along with the…shifters we've got here."

"You still don't believe?" she challenged him.

Maybe they'd have to allow at least this man, or perhaps General Myars, to watch a shift no matter how much violation of privacy that caused.

As long as they didn't take pictures….

That was when a wolf leaped out of the forest, into the sparse light near where they all remained, waiting.

He approached Captain Tierney. There was something in his mouth—and Sara shuddered. It looked like a rat.

She expected him to place the dead creature on the ground in front of the captain's feet.

Instead, the wolf that was Jason got up close and personal with Rynton Tierney, his filled muzzle just over the guy's shoe. He stuck his nose between Rynton's shoe and his pants leg.

And let go of the still-living rat.

It scampered up Rynton's leg inside his camo trousers. That was obvious by the bulge that moved upward.

Rynton shouted, "Get it off me! Get it off!"

As some of his underlings raced to get to him to help, Sara watched the wolf sit down. Raise his muzzle in the air. A howl that sounded full of pleasure soon filled the air. And when it stopped, Sara would have sworn that the wolf was smiling.

Chapter 15

It wasn't long after Jason's return with the rat that everyone—the humans, at least—agreed it was time for the Alpha Force shifters to change back.

"You're still not going to let us watch, even after that nasty joke?" Rynton's voice was harsh. He hadn't stopped scowling since his minions captured and dealt with the rodent he'd demanded be brought back as proof of cognition by a shifted wolf.

After all that, he still didn't believe?

"Alpha Force's position is that no one outside the unit can be permitted to watch a shift, Captain," reminded Jonas Truro.

Sara had an idea, though, that should satisfy even the most skeptical USFT member. "We each assisted our charges in separate rooms before. I don't believe they have alternate entrances or exits, so you could stand in the hallway and watch them enter in animal form and come out as humans."

"That's better than nothing," Rynton grumped.

As a result, they all trooped back into the storage building. Sara noted that the cougar that was Colleen Hodell was followed by Cal Brown, who appeared much too interested in her. Fortunately, her aide Rainey stuck with them.

In a short while, they were all in separate, closed rooms once more. The walls appeared to be thick, and were fairly soundproof.

The shifters often made noises during the process that the USFT personnel didn't need to hear.

The empty elixir vials and lights had already been gathered up by some Alpha Force nonshifters and taken back to the underground lab. The storage rooms, therefore, contained only the usual shelves and boxes, plus backpacks holding the shifters' clothing.

Sara entered the room where they'd been before with only the slightest trepidation. She steeled herself to see the shift. And Jason. Naked.

She would act totally professional.

She shut the door behind Jason the wolf. "Are you ready?"

She still wasn't exactly certain what precipitated the shift back to human form. It had to do with the amount of elixir that was drunk, but apparently, the shifter also had some choice.

Jason's response was first to look at her. Then he started turning in a circle, like a dog outside tamping down imaginary grass to prepare the perfect place for its eliminations. But in moments he stopped and lay down.

That was when the shift began. His limbs began to elongate. His fur receded into his body, which grew. His muzzle lifted into the air as he moaned softly, then started to disappear and morph into his facial features.

The rest of his body began to change, too. His external canine organs became human. Sexual organs. Sexy as Sara remembered.

She closed her eyes. He should have privacy.

And she needed to regain control over her libido.

"Sara." It had only been a minute or two that she'd looked away, with her eyes closed. The word wasn't enunciated quite right, but the voice was arguably human.

She turned and looked.

There was Jason. In all his naked glory.

She quickly moved her gaze from his genital area to his face, then hurried across the room to her backpack. Damn! She should have had his clothes ready.

Or had she subconsciously awaited this moment, prolonging her ability to look at his firm, toned—hot—nude body once more?

"I'll have your things to you in just a minute," she called.

She extracted his camo uniform and underwear, then turned toward him.

He was standing there, all human. His broad shoulders were hunched a bit and he slumped, his head forward, as he seemed to catch his breath.

But oh, what a view.

She didn't even try to stop herself from looking. At least he wasn't meeting her gaze.

But if—when—he did? They couldn't take the time to make love again. Not now. No matter how much she suddenly ached to do so.

People were outside, perhaps counting the minutes until they emerged. Other Alpha Force members might already have completed their shifts and left their rooms.

Frustration or not, she strode forward, holding out his clothes. For a moment, his golden eyes met hers. He smiled…but it disappeared into a serious, formal gaze.

Still undressed, he took his proffered clothing and stepped back. "Permission to get dressed, ma'am?" he asked, not sounding at all teasing. He even saluted.

"Of course, soldier." She saluted back. Then she added softly, "Jason, I liked the way you acted out there with Captain Tierney. And I like even better… well, the way you look now."

He merely blinked, said, "Thank you, ma'am," and turned around.

Hurt, Sara watched from behind as Jason started donning his clothes.

It was one of the hardest things Jason had ever done: turning his back on an obviously sexually aroused Sara McLinder. Pretending he didn't care. That, this time, he was the one who observed military protocol.

But he'd had to do it. No way could they satisfy their

lust right now. And yes, he felt lust just by looking into Sara's interested and provoking expression.

Just that look had caused his erection to harden even more, but he tucked it into his pants.

He wanted Sara. Again. More. Often.

But that was foolish. She had apparently accepted, at least on some level, that he was a shifter. Yet the reality was that they had no future together. Getting up close and really personal more than they already had today could only lead to further frustration, and maybe even heartache.

He needed to try to find another noncommissioned officer who might accept who and what he was. Maybe even a private. Someone who was already a shifter? Unlikely in the military unless she was already in Alpha Force, but who knew?

So far, the only women he'd had relationships with had been near home. Nonmilitary, of course. Nothing serious, just companionship and sex. None had been shifters, so some of the fun had been in keeping his true status from them.

He hadn't regretted leaving any of them behind when he'd had to join Alpha Force.

He'd finished donning his clothes. Now he turned around.

Sara must have been watching him. She suddenly swung away and seemed to examine some of the shelves along the wall of this storeroom.

"Thanks, Sara," he said softly. His body moving almost involuntarily, he approached her. Touched her arm.

She pivoted, and suddenly she was in his embrace. He moved so his mouth was hard upon hers. Her arms went around his neck, pulling him down, closer, as her lips opened for him, her tongue speared out to play with his, and her soft, supple, altogether sexy body pressed close against him. Really close...down below.

He groaned, rubbing harder against her. Aching to remove those clothes again.

He was suddenly startled by a knocking on the door. "Hey, cuz, you shifted back yet?" yelled Drew.

Sara pulled away, her expression horrified. "We have to get out of here," she said. "I didn't... I mean, we shouldn't..."

"You're absolutely right, Lieutenant," Jason made himself say as coolly as possible. "Time to put all of this behind us."

They all were to return to the assembly room after the exercise was complete.

Sara stopped in General Yarrow's office on the way to report how things had gone from her perspective before walking to the meeting with him.

She planned to tell him all he needed to know including, with regard to Jason, only that he had successfully shifted in a timely way, had shown himself in wolf form to the USFT members and had then shifted back again. Oh, and yes, the general was sure to hear about that little prank Jason had pulled with the rat on Rynton Tierney—but the captain had asked for it.

Sara smiled briefly at the recollection as she seated herself in a chair facing the general's desk.

But no sense revealing any of her thoughts and emotions—and definitely not her lust—relating to Jason.

"I think it was successful, sir," she told Greg Yarrow. "At least the USFT members appeared to accept the idea of shifting, although Captain Tierney made it clear he'd like to watch a shift for verification."

"What do you think about that?" His wide brow furrowed as he regarded her from behind his desk. He looked tired, and Sara wondered what had gone on during his interaction with General Myars while the joint mission between Alpha Force and USFT members played out.

"I'm aware that's against the protocol established by Alpha Force—that only unit members are supposed to have access while someone is shifting. I also know there have been some exceptions now and then, like me. And—"

"You're not an exception."

"Well, I'm not really a member of Alpha Force." Yet she felt now as if she had become one. She believed in, had seen, shifting. Wanted to learn more about how Alpha Force would be used in actual military deployments.

Especially the one being considered in conjunction with USFT.

The general smiled. "Sure you are, just as much as I am. You're my right arm, and though I'm not a shifter or aide, I'm close enough. That gives you standing with the unit, too."

She couldn't help grinning back. "Guess so, sir." She hesitated, then added, "Thanks, Greg."

"Oh, you'll pay for it, Sara. In fact, I'd like you to set up a lunch tomorrow for both units together—thirty people or so. In Mary Glen. Everyone'll be sleeping in tomorrow since it's so late now, so lunch will be better than breakfast. There's a restaurant there—I don't remember the name—but it should be able to accommodate us, even on short notice. Ask one of the local Alpha Force members. They'll know. In fact, your shifting charge Jason Connell should be a good resource for that."

"I'll check with him first, sir." Sara hoped that the blush she felt creeping up her cheeks wasn't visible in the daylight of the general's office. "But just to clarify. We still have no intention of allowing any USFT members to actually watch a shift occur, right?"

"Did any of them doubt the reality of it after your exercise?"

"No one seemed to, especially after the human cognition of the shifted animals was verified." She described how Jason had stuck the rat up Tierney's leg.

The general laughed. "I might get chided about that from Myars, so it's a good thing you told me. But was that the only thing that gave them an indication shifting was real?"

"No, sir. Even though we didn't let them watch any shifting, they checked to make sure that the cover animals remained in the kennel areas when the shifted wolves appeared."

That caused the general to frown again. "And someone went with them? No one got down into the lab area?"

"That's right, sir. And afterward, they watched animals go into closed rooms with their aides, and only people exit from them after shifting." Sara hesitated. "You don't really trust those USFT personnel, do you, sir?" She didn't—not after what had happened to the general and his car. And the scratches on the door down to the lab. A break-in attempt? Not that anyone in USFT had been proven involved. Not yet.

"I trust them to do an excellent job doing what they do best—perfect vision and marksmanship to assist in the joint assignment we'll have with them if all goes well." The general was standing now. "But I really don't understand their attitude toward Alpha Force. Skepticism about shifting? That might have made sense before, but now they've seen enough to buy into its reality. And there appears to be ongoing antagonism that I've not been able to nail down any answers about. Maybe this latest exercise will help dispel it. I certainly hope so." He turned and looked down at the computer on his desk, shifting the mouse. "It's time. We'd better get off to our meeting."

Sara couldn't help it. She scanned the crowd in the assembly room as she entered with the general, looking for Jason.

She had an important question to ask him, she reminded herself. She glanced at her wristwatch. She needed to find out what restaurant the general had been talking about to ensure she could line up a place for the units to have a joint lunch the next day.

Once again, Alpha Force seemed to have taken over

the first few rows, with the USFT members planted in the rear. One good thing Sara noted, though, was that there were at least a few conversations in which members of both units participated. Those folks banded together along the side of the assembly room.

In fact, she was able to join one of the groups, since Jason was standing with Vera Swainey, Cal Brown, Colleen Hodell and others. They all appeared to be chatting amicably. Some held bottles of water from a case that had been left near the door.

Maybe the night's exercises really did turn the page on their attitudes.

Sara wended her way along the crowded aisle, overhearing brief snatches of conversations including jokes from USFT members about renting an old version of *The Wolf Man* movie, and promises to teach Alpha Force members some tricks of the USFT shooting abilities if they'd teach them how to shapeshift.

Sara had heard that request before occasionally coming from some nonshifting aides of Alpha Force, but she'd also heard it wasn't possible.

She finally reached Jason's group but stood on its periphery, listening. Jason was describing some of the most unusual and fun things he claimed to have done while shifted. He looked amazingly good, his dark, silver-flecked hair slightly longer than when she'd first met him, his strong hands waving in punctuation while he talked…and his amazingly sexy body moving in emphasis, too. Sara listened to what he said, interested in his description of howling at an outdoor sign not far from Ft. Lukman that depicted a full moon to advertise some kind of beer, and playing tug-of-war while shifted, with Shadow, using as a toy a car rug he'd taken out of a military vehicle he was fixing.

"You mean sticking a rat up our CO's leg wasn't the most fun and unusual thing you've done?" Cal asked. The muscular guy stood straight and looked serious, as if he was attempting not to scowl at Jason. But then he broke into a large grin. "Never seen anything like that before."

"Well, I admit it was creative." Jason nodded. "But now I'll have to think of something to top that. Anyone want to volunteer for me to experiment on?"

"Hey, how about us?" demanded Samantha, a smile on her face. "I've heard rumors that the secret formula you shifters drink could turn us into shifters, too."

"Where did you hear that?" Jason demanded.

But Samantha just continued to grin, raising her brows. She had a bottle of water in her hand and she raised it, as if in a toast. "Here's to giving it a try someday."

"No," said Jason with as cold a voice as Sara had ever heard from him. "You won't. That's against orders, and whatever you've heard is wrong."

It was time for Sara to break in. "Hey, sorry to interrupt, but I have a question for you, Jason." As the others looked at her, she said, "Not sure yet if I'm supposed to let everyone know, but we're all getting together for a group lunch tomorrow. Assuming I get the info I need."

At the edge of the crowd, Sara explained. "General Yarrow said you could tell me the name of a restaurant in Mary Glen that can accommodate a group this size on short notice." She looked into Jason's golden eyes as she spoke and felt drawn in. She would get lost in them if she allowed herself to.

She looked down, drawing her smartphone from her pocket as both a diversion and a way to find contact information and location of whatever eatery Jason mentioned.

"I've only eaten there once, since everyone's favorite place is the Mary Glen Diner, but try Danny's Delicious Café," he said. "They're open twenty-four hours so you should be able to make the reservation now."

"Isn't that a new chain out of Baltimore?"

"Yeah, I think so. They're expanding."

The conversation was so mundane that Sara longed to say something to Jason to remind him she'd been there for him earlier, watched him shift, watched his mesmerizing, naked body...

What was she doing? He was acting completely professional while her mind exploded with everything she didn't dare think, didn't dare feel, ever again.

"Thank you," she said formally, moving her finger on her phone screen to locate the restaurant's listing. "I'll call them now." But she couldn't help asking, as Jason turned to walk toward the front of the room, "I don't suppose those rumors about the elixir are true, are they?" Not that she wanted to try to become a shifter.

"Of course not. And those rumors have to stop. I'll make sure Drew's aware of this nonsense."

She hesitated. "Will you be joining the group for lunch?"

She'd asked for it. Even so, a shiver went through her as he turned, said, "Oh, you can count on it," then winked. Again. The usual, carefree Jason back in charge.

Her insides turned momentarily to hot, flowing lava.

She made herself stare back at her phone and quickly exit the room to make the reservation.

Praying that no one else had noticed that damnably sexy wink.

Chapter 16

The meeting was fairly uneventful, but Jason understood why General Yarrow wanted to hold it, even this late at night. It allowed members of both units to suck up to their commanding generals and show how well they'd followed orders earlier and were now the best of friends.

Jason wondered if anyone was dumb enough to believe that. On the other hand, there seemed to be a bit more camaraderie between them now.

He himself was getting along well with some of the USFT members, now that he had managed, in an excusable way, to humiliate their captain.

He remained in the crowded room listening to the generals congratulate themselves and their subordinates, as if all ill will had now evaporated like steam from a hot spring. But he knew the heat between the two groups could rise again at any moment.

He still wasn't sure why.

He'd glanced often toward the door where Sara had gone to make her phone call. Was she using the lunch reservation for tomorrow as an excuse to stay away indefinitely tonight?

No. There she was. She slipped inside and stood near the door. The meeting was wrapping up, anyway. Both generals had gotten in their thanks and made it clear to their troops that what had been started tonight would be continued. That was an order.

As they were all dismissed, everyone stood and streamed toward the door. Sara moved out of the way.

He only wanted to say good-night. That was what he told himself. She'd have plenty of takers wanting to walk her to the BOQ, and it wouldn't be right to join them.

But she was apparently waiting for General Yarrow. The two top guys were among the last to leave, and Sara was still standing there when they, and Jason, approached.

"Did that place work out?" Jason asked before the generals reached her.

"Yes, it did. Thanks." As Yarrow and Myars joined her, Sara told them about the reservations she'd made for lunch tomorrow. Both gave her formal military kudos, and the three left the auditorium.

Jason followed. The generals were wrapped up in conversation as they walked through the building's lobby and out the door.

Good. That gave Jason the opportunity he wanted to say a friendly good-night to Sara.

"Same to you." She smiled, then looked beyond the generals where some of the USFT members stood in a group, talking.

"I'd like your help tomorrow morning, before lunch," Jason heard himself blurt, his voice low.

She turned back, surprise on her lovely face. "Are you shifting in daylight?"

"Oh, no, not that kind of help. Not about cars, either."

She smiled, and he suspected that would have been her next question.

"No," he continued, "I'm planning on a training session with Shadow and a couple other cover dogs. You worked well with us before, and I'd like to have you join us. Okay?"

"Sure," she said. "What time?"

It probably was a bad idea, Sara thought as she turned her back on Jason and joined the nearby USFT members to walk to the BOQ with them. Had they been waiting for her? Unlikely.

Drat, she thought a minute later. Cal Brown had probably gotten them to hang around for her. At least the way the large guy joined her immediately, as if claiming her company, suggested he'd wanted to talk to her.

Flirt with her?

Fortunately, Colleen joined them when they reached the main sidewalk. She started talking animatedly to

Cal and Manning Breman, asking what they now thought of shapeshifting, and didn't they prefer cougars to wolves?

They all just laughed. Sara hung back a little, letting Colleen handle the requisite camaraderie.

She wondered how far behind them Jason was.

She knew better than to look.

She did, however, hesitate for a moment, pulling her phone from her pocket as if checking something. She surreptitiously glanced behind them—only to see one person not far behind.

Walking alone.

When he stepped beneath one of the lights along the walkway she confirmed what she already knew. It was Jason.

She felt a surge of warmth. Of knowing she was protected without needing protection.

She looked forward to that dog training session tomorrow.

When Sara finally got to bed that night, she figured she would sleep well. And probably would have if her phone hadn't rung.

"Sara? Sorry to call so late, but it's Colleen. Can I ask a favor?"

"Sure," Sara replied hesitantly. What could she possibly want at this hour?

But five minutes later, Sara had put her uniform back on and hurried down the dimly lit hall. Colleen opened the door to her apartment almost before Sara knocked.

"I really appreciate this," she said. "But Rainey has an upset stomach—maybe too much excitement today. And even though I just shifted back a short while ago after our exercise—well, I'm just so restless I need to do it again. Since my usual aide can't help, I hope you don't mind my bothering you."

The cat Puka came out to greet Sara but didn't stay in Colleen's small living room very long. She disappeared back into the bedroom.

Near the door, Colleen had set one of the backpacks that had become so familiar to Sara since she had begun working with Alpha Force. It probably contained a vial of the all-important elixir, plus a special light.

"I just need for you to come outside with me while I shift. I won't stay in cougar form long and I can shift back by myself, but I've never shifted with the elixir on my own."

"No problem." Sara figured it would be similar to watching Jason shift. Interesting, too, but in a very different way.

Sure enough, she found Colleen's shift fascinating.

Colleen stripped first and hid her clothes behind a rock in the part of the forest within Ft. Lukman where they'd gone. "I'll be able to find these here myself when I shift back," Colleen told Sara.

She'd already drunk some elixir. Now Sara shone the special moonlike light on her and watched as the woman began to writhe and grow tawny hair all over as she shifted into cougar form.

She soon gave a nod of her wild feline head toward Sara, then ran off into the woods.

As they'd discussed, Sara also left the backpack with Colleen's clothes. Had she really been needed here to help Colleen?

Maybe not, but the feline Alpha Force member apparently felt better having someone assisting with the shift.

And it gave Sara yet another perspective on shape-shifting.

Tired that night, Jason had fallen asleep in his tiny quarters nearly immediately. It had been late, so he hadn't even gone to the kennel to bring Shadow back. Of course, he'd be with the dog in the morning.

When he woke, he nearly sprang from bed in anticipation of the day. And it wasn't only because he'd have Shadow with him.

Hell, yesterday had had some pretty fine moments. Like shifting again in front of Sara.

And sticking a rat up a superior officer's leg with impunity. What a kick!

Now he would spend more time with Sara in a place that lent itself to having fun.

Maybe even get her sexuality stoked again.

He showered then dressed in yet another camo uniform. He was getting damned tired of looking like everyone else.

Welcome to the military.

On the other hand, Sara didn't seem to mind what he wore.

Although if he wasn't mistaken, she much preferred when he didn't wear anything.

Well, someday he'd go back to fixing cars for civilians and wear what he wanted. But how could he give up the Alpha Force shifting elixir with all its benefits?

Could he do it if it meant more time with Sara?

Yeah, like she'd pay any attention to him if he left the military.

Now it was still early. He met no one else on his quick walk to the cafeteria. There, he grabbed a steak and egg sandwich and coffee to go—after sharing a quick, meaningless, but enjoyable session of sexual innuendo with the female cashier.

He had something to do before going to meet Sara.

He headed first to the base's main garage. There, he checked the computer to make sure he wasn't falling behind on work on the rest of the base's vehicles. He had some oil changes to accomplish within the next couple of days, but the car washes and other trivial matters could wait.

Next he went to check on the remains of General Yarrow's Jeep—again. Some feds were finally scheduled to come to conduct an official investigation, so he wanted to make sure he'd done all he wanted to first.

The hulk was still locked in a secure area, although guards were no longer assigned 24/7. In fact, no one was here now.

And when Jason tried the door before inserting his copy of the key, it was already unlocked.

He froze momentarily, listening, in case someone

had just preceded him inside. Even with his acute hearing, he heard nothing, so he slammed open the door and flicked on the lights.

No movement inside, no scent of an intruder. The remains of the general's car were still there, perched on the same spot on the floor, a sorry-looking sight to someone who revered automobiles as much as Jason did.

But there was more: a hint of an odor similar to whatever had started Jason coughing during his attempt to search for clues. It wasn't strong, but it still repelled him. Even so, he wouldn't let it control him.

He strode into the room. Approached the metallic remains still decorated with black ashes.

And was surprised to see that someone had set up an AK-47 aimed challengingly at the car, as if adding a new threat—or taunting and ridiculing the sorry attempt at an investigation that had already been conducted.

He checked. The weapon was even loaded.

Where had it come from? Was this a statement that one of the people Alpha Force already suspected actually had been the perpetrator—a member of USFT?

That was absurd. Then was it an attempt to frame the USFT?

If so, by whom?

Or was this actually a ploy by members of that unit to make it appear they were being framed…an attempt to further hide the fact that they truly had done something to set the general's car on fire?

Jason didn't know.

But what Jason did know was that it made no sense. And that he had to notify his cuz. Immediately.

Though tired, Sara got up on time and reached the Ft. Lukman kennels at exactly 0900, the time Jason had said to meet him.

Jason, however, wasn't there.

Noel Chuma was, though. The sergeant who acted as aide to a couple of Alpha Force shifters seemed right at home with the dogs. He was already working with Zarlon, Marshall Vincenzo's cover dog, in a paved inside courtyard area, not far from the lush kennel areas where the dogs lived inside the building.

"Good morning," Sara called to Noel, who was using treats to encourage Zarlon to walk on his hind legs as a human would. Probably a good skill for a cover dog to know, Sara thought.

"Hi, Sara." Noel gave a signal with his right hand to Zarlon, and the shepherdlike dog lay down and rolled over. "Are you just visiting, or is there something I can do for you?"

"Neither—but I'd like to join you with Shadow." Jason had told her he hadn't come for his dog last night.

Sara went to the kennel run, said hi to all the cover dogs present and patted a few heads. She then snapped a leash onto Shadow's collar. He seemed happy to see her, nuzzling her in greeting then ready to run.

"I don't know what all Shadow can do," Sara said after rejoining Noel. "And though I've seen one training session, I don't want to get the signals wrong."

"Here, let's trade." Noel handed Sara Zarlon's leash

and said, "Sit," giving a hand signal that looked familiar to Sara. Then he started putting Shadow through his paces—including getting him to walk on his hind legs the way Zarlon had done.

"Hey, that's me over there," said a voice near Sara. She had her back toward the wall of the courtyard and had been watching the training so intently that she hadn't noticed it when Jason edged his way in.

She suspected, by the way he showed up practically behind her, that he'd planned it that way.

"You mean that dog who happens to resemble what you sometimes look like?" she said without looking toward him. "Nope, I don't buy it. He's much better behaved than you are in either form."

Jason laughed briefly, then paused. "Sorry I'm late," he said. "Something came up."

The sudden hardness in his tone startled her and she turned to look at him. There was an expression on his handsome face that she couldn't read.

"What's wrong?" she asked.

"I'll tell you when we're finished here. In fact, maybe you can help me figure out how to play it when we're all together with our USFT buddies at lunch. One of them, at least, may owe me an explanation—not to mention Drew and General Yarrow. I just had a brief, unplanned meeting with both of them."

"Really?" But Sara couldn't ask more questions then. Noel approached with Shadow and challenged Jason to a doggy duel—Zarlon against Jason's cover dog. Which, in the hands of the right trainer, performed best?

Jason accepted the challenge, leaving Sara damned curious about what he'd been talking about.

But she had to admit—only to herself—that she liked his moves while working with the dogs. The two men looked as if they were training the canines for agility in the high-ceilinged internal courtyard, weaving their own forms between the obedient, nimble dogs.

Surprisingly, a few other people joined Sara's observation, including Colleen—who didn't look at all tired after her busy night—and Jock of Alpha Force, and Rynton, Vera and Cal of the USFT. They clapped and cheered along with her as Jason and Noel put the dogs through their paces.

Presumably the USFT members were welcome here, even when joint exercises weren't being conducted, as long as they were in the presence of Alpha Force members—upstairs, at least. But not in the highly classified Alpha Force laboratories below.

Cal stood close to Sara. Too close.

"Do you like dogs?" she asked brightly, taking a step away. "Aren't they wonderful?"

"I'd like to see those shifters do the same kinds of tricks." Cal sounded condescending, strange coming from a man who always resembled a simian. Apparently, he hadn't decided to obey the orders requiring camaraderie. Or maybe he'd be friendly without sincerity.

In either event, Sara moved toward Colleen. "How are you this morning?" she asked to make conversation.

For an instant, Colleen looked startled, her feline eyes narrow in her pale face. Then glancing toward Sara, she smiled. "Just fine, despite not having a good night's sleep. I got some rest, though, and it was enough."

Soon the exercise ended. "Okay," Jason said, approaching Sara. "Shadow's telling me in canine-ese that it's time for a walk. Care to join us? Oh, in case you're wondering, I can communicate with other canines while shifted but not in any language. I teach them to follow commands in English. Gestures, too, just like everyone else does."

Feeling glad to get away from the others for a while, Sara agreed to go along. Aloud she said, though, to make it clear that the walk fit within the parameters of her job, "We have some plans to discuss for General Yarrow. This'll be a good time."

"Yes, ma'am," Jason said, and she half expected him to salute.

Once they had left the kennel building, they strolled along the sidewalk in one of the more remote areas of the base. Jason held Shadow's lead.

"So tell me," Sara said. She was horrified to hear what he described about the latest issue regarding General Yarrow's vehicle. "Can we go look at it? I want to see what you're talking about."

"Sure. I told Drew and General Yarrow before. The sentries are going to be back again, although I don't know what good they can do."

"They can at least make sure that no one uses those guns and ammo," Sara said.

"Or brings any more."

They walked in silence, taking their time as Shadow

sniffed their path and occasionally stopped to lift his leg.

After one such occurrence, Sara stopped and found herself smiling into Jason's twinkling golden eyes. "No need to ask. Yes, I do such things while shifted. I've got enough of my human consciousness, though, to do it in private."

She laughed. And felt drawn in by the intensity of Jason's gaze as it turned serious. And hot.

Hot enough for her to consider tearing her clothes off on this cool Maryland morning. There were no other people around.

But that was absurd. And Sara quickly reminded herself of the silent promise she had made. She looked away, but not as fast as she'd have liked.

"Jason, I'm sorry," she said softly. "I just can't—"

"I get it. Me, neither. It's too unmilitary, and I've made my choice to stick this out for now, at least. So... let's talk about cars."

They had reached the garage where General Yarrow's damaged vehicle was housed. On their way to that area, Sara half heard Jason's description of which kinds of parked cars they passed that he knew, from working on them, were the best.

But Sara couldn't help thinking about what else they had done, in Jason's own car, in that parking facility.

Chapter 17

Danny's Delicious Café was a family-oriented restaurant with a variety of foods. Its theme was deliciousness, and its walls were covered with posters of close-ups of all kinds of food served there—from soups to desserts.

Those posters included entrées, too—and Sara was glad to note, for the sake of the Alpha Force shifters, that some were delicious-looking steaks.

She was glad she'd called the night before, since there was a separate dining room at the rear that had been reserved just for the military group. It was lunchtime, and the rest of the place was crowded.

As Sara walked in with General Yarrow, others from Ft. Lukman behind them—all in camo uniforms—she felt some curious gazes on them. She also saw some people—patrons and servers alike—stop talking to one another, then start up again quickly.

Drew, behind Sara and the general, whispered, "There are still a lot of rumors around this town about werewolves and their supposed connection with Ft. Lukman."

"I heard something about that," Sara responded softly, dropping back to talk to Drew. "But I thought it was the result of some bad guys who were caught, and the town was set straight about the…false origin of those rumors."

"Not exactly," Drew said drolly.

No one had to mention that those rumors, though supposedly dispelled by the capture of someone who'd been using them for his own benefit, just happened to be true. And Sara continued to recognize that a person from Mary Glen could be causing the turmoil at Ft. Lukman…although getting onto the base, with all its security, would be problematic.

Sara had already had a few minutes to speak with the general and Drew, along with Jason—who followed them—about what had most recently occurred with General Yarrow's destroyed car.

The federal investigators were now finally rescheduled for a day or two away. Drew had previously dispatched some trusted Alpha Force members who wouldn't join them for lunch to photograph the newly besieged vehicle then collect the weapons and ammo to be checked for fingerprints.

Not that anyone believed whoever put them there would be so careless.

Since General Yarrow had arranged for this lunch, he got to determine who would sit where. "Join up with the people on your teams from yesterday," he said. "Since these tables seat eight, each should accommodate two of those teams."

Sara consequently sat at Jason's table, seated beside him. She kept her gaze averted most of the time. But she couldn't help looking at him now and then, enjoying the view, when he ran the conversation at their table.

He started, not unexpectedly, with his teasing demeanor. "Hey, all. Did you notice that bunch of civilians gossiping about us? What if we prove to them that all those Mary Glen werewolf rumors are true?"

A collective gasp circulated through their fortunately closed-off room. Not even any servers were with them yet.

Drew, at the same table, stood as if to do something dire to silence his cousin. "Look, Jason," he said. "You—"

"You didn't let me finish, cuz—er, sir." Jason went on to elaborate in a completely joking manner. "Too bad we didn't think to bring along wolf costumes we've collected to provide cover now and then. If we did, our USFT members could wear them as they pounce on the civilian tables next door."

Outrageous. Way over the top, Sara thought. Yet it was interesting to watch the reactions. Almost everyone, from both units, laughed and bought into the fun Jason suggested so whimsically. General Yarrow scolded Jason, but General Myars guffawed over the idea—because, he said, he'd heard about those ridiculous rumors even before the Ultra Special Forces Team was deployed to Ft. Lukman, and thought the townsfolk must be the most gullible folks anywhere.

And so the discussion went.

At their own table, the ice had been broken by Jason's silliness. Jonas Truro was the other Alpha Force member. Also seated with them were Rynton Tierney, Vera Swainey, Manning Breman and Samantha Everly. The next table over accommodated both generals, Colleen Hodell, Jock Larabey and some USFT members including Cal Brown. Sara noticed that Rainey Jessop was absent and wondered if she was still ill.

Sara saw Cal glaring daggers toward Jason. Obviously, he chose not to get the Alpha Force's humor. But every once in a while that gaze went toward her. Was he resentful she hadn't joined his attempts at flirtation?

Maybe he had been attempting to hide, all along, that camaraderie with Alpha Force members was not his preference.

Did he hate the shapeshifting unit enough to try to kill its CO by setting Greg Yarrow's car on fire?

Did he exacerbate even that by planting the weapon and aiming it at the car's remains when they were supposedly secure and out of the way?

Sara chose not to act as disturbed as she felt. Instead, she made it a point to keep talking with everyone at her table. Crack jokes designed to outdo Jason's.

Suggest that maybe she'd like to trade places with him someday—and describe to everyone that she actually had, in a way, done so that morning as she had helped to train Jason's cover dog Shadow.

Servers came and went. The conversation was edited when they were around to ensure that any eavesdropping, which would obviously be easy, wouldn't yield anything to stoke the rumors that might be circulating in the outer restaurant area.

The idea of grabbing a glass of wine intrigued Sara, but it was only lunchtime and this was, in effect, a military exercise. Instead, she chose a diet soft drink, then a Cobb salad. She also helped Jason goad the USFT members into ordering hamburgers or steaks like the shifters did—keeping the terms light and only alluding to any reason why some of the people at this luncheon might want to select meat dishes over salads.

Even so, the servers occasionally exchanged glances. Sara now felt certain they'd share their experience, and possibly their suspicions, with the restaurant's other guests and employees.

All the more reason to make it appear that they were only cracking jokes.

Sara enjoyed her salad. The others all appeared to find their meals tasty, too.

And the discussion? It turned military. Each person at the table described prior assignments and deployments—making it absolutely clear that no one described any parts of their former assignments that were classified.

Eventually, most everyone had finished. General Yarrow stood. "Okay, let's turn this into an abbreviated game of musical chairs. I want all USFT members to stay where you are, and Alpha Force, each of you replace someone else in your unit at a different table. On the count of three—one, two, three…"

The room became suddenly, and briefly, chaotic, as the Alpha Force personnel rose and complied with General Yarrow's orders.

That included Sara. And Jason. They wound up at different tables—and Sara wasn't happy with her own feelings of regret at their separation.

Given her preference, she wouldn't have sat with him in the first place, she reminded herself.

This time, Sara sat with Colleen Hodell as well as some USFT members she hadn't met before.

The cougar shifter seemed at home, asking right away for the others at the table to tell why they had decided to enlist in the military in the first place, and then why they had gravitated to an elite, demanding—and highly regarded—unit like the Ultra Special Forces Team. They all seemed pleased to talk, proud of their highly classified and uniquely skilled sight and marksmanship abilities.

Colleen herself mentioned how thrilled she had been to discover the existence of Alpha Force, and how it had made such a big difference in her life. She didn't go into detail, but Sara recalled their discussion at Colleen's apartment where she'd admitted to a difficult childhood as a shifter. Now in Alpha Force, her shifting abilities were accepted. She seemed happy to Sara.

Alpha Force looked like a good fit for a lot of people—especially shifters.

But Sara hoped that no one would turn that kind

of question on her. She'd have no problem discussing why she had joined the military. It had been her goal for years. Yet she would have to be careful in the rest of her response.

She had mostly been thrilled to have been selected by General Yarrow to become his aide. But she would never be able to tell strangers, even those she was ordered to get along with, what she had originally thought of the strange yet compelling abilities of Alpha Force.

Especially some of its members…

Jason now sat at a table that included Captain Samantha Everly—again. How did that happen? Sara thought they were all supposed to find different members of the other unit from those they'd already talked to.

But she hadn't really kept track of who was with whom. The thing was…well, the usually haughty and commanding captain seemed to listen to every word Jason said. Maybe even leaning her curvaceous body toward the man that Sara was fighting her own attraction to.

If she couldn't fraternize, neither could Samantha.

But as Sara excused herself, ostensibly for a restroom break but intending first to stop at the table where Samantha flirted with Jason, she found herself confronted by Cal Brown.

"So what do you think, Sara?" he said. "Are our two units finally getting it—becoming colleagues that get along?"

"Looks that way, Cal," she responded, not liking the fact that he was blocking her progress. She was between two tables filled with gabbing troops. The only way around was to turn and wend her way in a different direction.

Cal was a large blockade.

Before she decided how best to handle this, Drew rose from the table where he now sat—which again included both generals. So maybe Samantha hadn't been completely out of line, despite General Yarrow's orders to mingle.

By then, everyone had finished their meals and had their plates bussed. It was time for coffee, iced tea and for some of them, desserts. But not Sara.

"We have something to go over before you're all dismissed," Drew said. "I wanted to let each of you know about something that was just brought to my attention before we sat down here. I don't know the origin—although my suspicions suggest that some of you particularly excellent marksmen in the USFT might have some ideas. But has anyone recently lost some weaponry and ammunition?" He described the AK-47 that had been loaded and aimed at General Yarrow's destroyed car. It certainly wasn't the kind of equipment that Alpha Force members used most often. Nor was it what the USFT shooters had used the other day. But it was undoubtedly accessible to them.

Sara heard whisperings and looked around. Most of the quiet conversations were between members of USFT.

Which suggested that Drew's question might have the effect of erasing whatever progress had been made here in the joining of forces.

But it was entirely proper, Sara thought. Get everyone off guard, then press for answers.

"What the hell are you doing, Major?" General Myars had risen, hands on his broad hips, and addressed Drew, his round face red and furious.

"Just looking for a few answers, sir," Drew said calmly. "I don't suppose you could address them?"

"If you're accusing me, or anyone reporting to me, Major, you had better retract it. Now."

Sara saw Drew exchange glances with General Yarrow, who gave a nearly imperceptible nod. "I'm sorry, sir, if you thought that was what I was doing. I would just like to find out any way I can where that weapon came from. If anyone here, from either unit, has any answers or suggestions, please let either General Yarrow or me know."

The entire group started to disperse then. Most people seemed to get back together with others in their own units.

The supposed camaraderie had been temporary, anyway, Sara figured, and Drew's comments at the end only precipitated the separation once more.

Sara didn't plan it, but she found herself walking out the door with Jason.

"So, are you best buddies now with some of those USFT guys?" he asked. "I had fun with them, myself. Although I'm not sure any of them will talk to any of us again after my cousin's comments at the end. I really liked how he did that. We're all still under orders to get along, so it'll be interesting to see how that works now, with them knowing they're each under suspicion by a bunch of—" he lowered his head to whisper into her ear. A shiver ran through her at his proximity, even though there was nothing sensual about it. Or shouldn't have been. "—a bunch of werewolves," he finished quietly. Good thing, too, since they were outside by then, in the restaurant's parking lot, and it wasn't just military members who surrounded them.

They'd come in a number of vehicles from the base, and Jason had used the opportunity of visiting town to finally exchange the tow truck for his own classic red Mustang.

"I just hope this doesn't backfire on Drew, or on General Yarrow," Sara said. She'd have loved to ride with Jason—to listen to him make light of what Drew had said, and that was all, she told herself.

But discretion was in order. Instead, she stood there with some of the others who had dined with them.

And watched as Jason drove off first.

Jason understood what Drew had done.

There would be a lot of follow-up conversation, he was certain. He wished he was in a larger vehicle— one where he could invite USFT people on board and eavesdrop on them.

He figured that all shifting Alpha Force members who'd come in vans from the base were using their acute senses of hearing to do that.

Things were tense now. As they should be.

Until whoever had tried to harm General Yarrow, and still made silent threats, was found and stopped.

He wished he had a further opportunity to talk it

over with Sara. To get the general's take on it, he told himself, but that was just an excuse.

He simply wanted to talk to her.

Oh, and if he found some way to seduce her, caress her hot body, kiss those sweet lips…well, that would be fine, too.

Maybe he'd even suggest he needed her help shifting that night.

He hadn't actually considered doing so before…but what if he hung out in wolf form near that parking garage in case whoever left those weapons decided that, now that a new threat had been discovered, it was time to do more?

And Jason, in wolf form, would be in a perfect position to catch whoever it was.

Especially with Sara as his backup.

It couldn't fail.

Chapter 18

Sara waited at the curb patiently with Greg Yarrow until the car that had brought them to Mary Glen arrived—a black military sedan driven by one of the Ft. Lukman privates.

Probably one that Jason worked on. It was shiny and had purred on their way downtown before.

She quickly moved her thoughts away from car care—and Jason.

She hadn't previously considered what she'd be doing that afternoon after lunch. But as usual, she was on call with General Yarrow.

"We're going to my office," he said as he held the rear car door open for her. "I've already invited Myars and the officers reporting to him. Contact Drew Connell and make sure he's there, too. We'll be discussing his tactics."

Sara used her cell phone to call Drew as they rode toward the base. She'd seen him get into the car that Jason drove. "We're on our way," she told him. "General Yarrow wants us to meet at his office as soon as possible."

"Got it," Drew said.

Sara hung up. She felt certain that Jason would learn about the meeting, too. But he wasn't one of those whom the general wanted to see there.

Just as well that Sara wouldn't see him, either.

The meeting took longer than Sara had anticipated. She'd figured, from what General Yarrow had said, that it would be a quick recap of what had gone on at lunch—including an explanation of why Drew had decided to push the envelope with the USFT and what, if anything, had been gained by it.

But the representatives of the USFT had a lot more to say than Sara had figured on.

They sat in General Yarrow's quaint, antiques-filled office, everyone facing the mahogany desk with Greg holding court behind it. Present were the general, Drew and her from Alpha Force, and General Myars and Captain Rynton Tierney from USFT.

Sara knew that General Yarrow intended to run the meeting. But almost as quickly as she shut the door, General Myars began a tirade.

"What the hell makes you think one of my men ambushed your Jeep, Yarrow?" demanded the tall yet flabby officer. "Why would they? And then to think any one or more of them would be stupid enough afterward to point to the USFT by leaving some of our own gear there—especially a weapon that makes them what they are—ridiculous! Someone's obviously trying to mess not only with you, but with your mind, too—and they've succeeded."

"I asked the questions I did to see the reaction." Drew was at the end of the row of ornate chairs facing General Yarrow's desk. Now he stood. "Indignation was what I expected—and mostly what I got. There were a couple of your people, though, whose expressions—and scents, by the way—were a bit off. Fear, maybe. Although one, at least, also looked smug."

"Who was that?" Tierney demanded.

"You." Drew's bland expression looked to Sara as if he tried to hide his own smugness.

Tierney denied everything. His face was flushed and his hands were fisted enough to make his muscular arms fill out his uniform sleeves. He did, however, admit to pride in his unit. He wouldn't protect anyone who resorted to attempted murder to upgrade the USFT's status at Ft. Lukman, though, if that was what had happened. And if the later game with the AK-47 was to underscore the USFT's involvement, that was sheer stupidity.

"You know what I think?" Tierney said. "Not only is someone trying to frame us, they're trying to make sure our two units never get along enough to accomplish a vital mission together."

"And who would do that?" General Yarrow was a lot calmer than Sara.

"If I knew that, it'd have been stopped by now."

Sara would have liked to believe Tierney committed the dangerous mischief they were discussing. But she doubted it.

She decided to throw out the other possibility they'd all considered, no matter how unlikely. "Who says it's someone here on base who's trying to discredit the USFT and antagonize Alpha Force? I know we've kind of eliminated that as a possibility, but what if it is, after all, one of the civilians from Mary Glen?" She looked at Drew, who'd had his own issues with some Mary Glen residents a while ago. "Could it be because you caught whoever was after Alpha Force before? Or because there are others who want the military here at Ft. Lukman to go away?"

"That's something we need to consider further," General Yarrow said. "And it's why I wanted us to have our lunch there today."

The rest of the discussion that afternoon speculated even more about who might be conducting the nasty shenanigans to distract the military at Ft. Lukman, and how to follow up with the security staff on possibilities.

Of course they reached no conclusions.

Then General Yarrow brought up the main reason for this meeting. "Our exercises the other day came out all right, though not perfect. What I want next is to ramp them up. Perform exercises where the two units don't just show off their talents to one another, but have to work together—the way they'll need to if the mission the commander in chief has in mind for our combined troops goes forward."

Discussion on methodology and how it could be accomplished filled the rest of the afternoon. General Yarrow even had Sara call the cafeteria and get them to deliver the equivalent of a fast-food dinner as the planning continued.

Eventually, the members of both units sounded satisfied with the maneuvers to be held in two days.

The USFT members finally departed the general's office, leaving Sara there with Drew and Greg.

"What do you really think?" Greg Yarrow asked Drew a minute after the door had closed behind their visitors.

"We have to work with them, even if we're still not sure we can trust them." Drew shook his head.

Sara once more absorbed the resemblance between the major in charge of Alpha Force and his cousin, Jason. Their coloration—dark hair with silver highlights, their golden eyes—and even their muscular physiques were similar.

Why was she even thinking about Jason at that moment, in his absence? She felt irritated that Drew Connell brought Jason back into her thoughts.

She had to stop. As the two men in the room continued to discuss strategy for a while, she reminded herself that there was no way someone like Jason could have participated with them.

Eventually, General Yarrow said, "Let's meet again tomorrow—for less than an hour, I promise. Before that, Sara, please enter our proposed plans onto the computer and print them out so we can go over them one more time before the final exercise."

"Yes, sir." And then Sara said good-night and left the general's office.

Sara felt stifled. It wasn't that she didn't love what she did. And the meeting in the general's office, being his confidante and assistant—well, that was who she was these days, and she wouldn't trade it for any other post in the world.

But attacks on the general, disagreements between the two units, other issues she'd had to face lately—including her unwanted attraction to a noncommissioned officer who also happened to be a shapeshifter—she thought about these too intensely. Too often.

She needed a break.

A short one would be fine. And so, after leaving the office, Sara headed not for the BOQ but for the small open-air parking lot nearby where she had left her car.

She was off duty for now. She'd hidden a civilian outfit in the trunk. She could change clothes inside the vehicle and head back to Mary Glen—for a smoothie. Or a mocha. Or something else sweet to perk up her mood.

It was sunset and only a faint glow of sunlight's residue illuminated the base. Soon artificial lights would flick on.

A few other people were on the sidewalks mostly across the street from her. She saluted or smiled, as appropriate, and kept going.

Nearby she saw the building where noncommissioned officers were housed. Was Jason inside? Or was he off somewhere getting dinner, meeting with other Alpha Force members or doing something she didn't even imagine?

Like shapeshifting? Tonight?

She wouldn't be there as his aide, though plenty of others could help. But why would he?

Making notes on a computer was far different— a lot more boring—than handing a shifter a vial of elixir, aiming a light on his naked body and watching him change from the most gorgeous specimen of male human to an amazing, feral yet somewhat tame wolf.

She closed her eyes for a moment at the recollection she tried so hard not to think of. Or to consider Colleen Hodell's shift from a female human's body to a cougar's.

Sara knew full well the old axiom: the more you don't want to think about something, the more it'll pound at your mind.

Sighing, she opened her eyes—a good thing since a car, a huge SUV, was driving out of the lot. Cal Brown was the driver. He saw her, too. He grinned and waved and stopped, rolling down his window. "Need a ride?"

"Thanks, no. I've got it covered. Have a good evening." And then she walked on.

Too bad he didn't attract her in the slightest. If she wanted to take up with someone at Ft. Lukman, Cal, at least, was also a lieutenant. A more or less by-the-book commissioned officer, unlike Jason. She allowed her thoughts to return not to Jason, but to her old college boyfriend who'd gone rogue and tried to get her to take drugs with him, too. And how fast she had dropped him.

By the book was the only way for her.

She reached the last row of cars parked along the curb in the nearly full lot and turned to walk toward hers.

And stopped—as soon as she noticed the broken glass on its far side, near the wall of the adjoining parking garage.

She walked around. On the side of her gold hybrid, deep scratches etched the side.

Some seemed random—but others formed words. Nasty words: *Die bitch. Your CO is still alive but you won't be for long.*

The headlight and taillight on that side had been smashed.

Sara bit her lips. Who could have done this?

The obvious answer was that the perpetrator had been whoever had set General Yarrow's car on fire.

Who'd also aimed the weapon at the remains of the general's Jeep?

Maybe.

But why target her, too? Because she worked with the general?

She wanted to scream. Instead, she looked around the parking lot, then stopped.

Even if she saw someone, whom could she trust?

The answer came to her immediately. There were several people here to trust.

But only one was committed to taking care of cars.

She pulled her smartphone from her pocket and

pressed the buttons for the number that somehow had gotten programmed in—because she had called it before.

Jason's.

But the call went into his voice mail before he answered.

He had gotten shifting assistance from Noel Chuma.

Now Jason prowled in his wolf form.

He had first headed to the garage where the general's car slept, its remains further violated.

People around here might look for a shifter, but it was still easier for a wolfen creature to crawl low to the floor, hide in smaller crevices, be less obvious.

The place was empty except for cars.

Plus, the guard remained there.

If anyone came to further bother the Jeep, it would not likely be now.

And so, restless and not wanting to shift back yet, Jason now roamed the periphery of the base.

Spotting what—who—he wanted to, he'd stayed hidden as he watched Sara McLinder leave the office building and head toward the parking lot.

Communicate with that ass, Lieutenant Cal Brown.

Then continue toward her car.

Time for Jason to creep away, back to the garage before shifting back.

But he watched Sara a few minutes more.

Good thing he did.

For in moments, he had joined her at the far side of the car.

Even in wolfen form, he understood the desecration that had occurred.

And smelled a hint of whatever had sickened him before while investigating the destruction of the general's car.

Resisting a howl, he joined Sara at her side and rubbed his furry body against her uniform-clad legs in sympathy.

Chapter 19

Sara knelt to hug the wolf that was Jason. She needed his presence, his comfort. She would prefer it if he were in human form, but his being there for her, no matter what presence he was in, helped her deal with the horror.

"Thanks for being here, Jason," she whispered. Those tall wolf ears moved at the sound. He nuzzled her cheek, and she sighed. "Who could have done this?"

Her mind roiled, especially after the day's events—hearing about the weapon aimed at what was left of the general's Jeep. Lunch, and then the meeting. She'd sensed possible animosity from the USFT personnel toward Alpha Force.

Not against her, too…or was it?

The damage to her car couldn't have been done by a civilian from Mary Glen—could it? If the whispering and glares she had seen there translated into genuine hatred, why her? Even if someone knew who she was and hated her position as General Yarrow's aide, how could they have gotten onto the base unnoticed?

How would they know which car was hers?

In any event, how could the damage have been wreaked and not noticed while it was happening, even by someone stationed here?

She realized then that she was vocalizing some of her thoughts.

Jason's golden wolf eyes were locked on to her. He understood.

"Can you shift back?" she asked. "You know cars. Maybe you can see some clue here that I won't recognize."

He bent his head as if nodding, then turned it slightly, as if telling her to follow.

"Okay," she whispered.

As she stood, she looked around the parking lot again. It was late enough that it remained devoid of people, thank heavens. Not that most people here would be surprised to see an Alpha Force member with a wolf, or perhaps a cover dog, even if the timing seemed off.

Even so…she didn't want to talk to anyone else about shifters or her car, just now.

Instead, she followed Jason's sleek, wolfen form as he crossed the street and entered the woods at the edge of Ft. Lukman.

* * *

Maybe he shouldn't have shifted that night.

Maybe he shouldn't have assumed that any nastiness at Ft. Lukman would only center around the remains of General Yarrow's car.

But shifted or not, he couldn't have been everywhere on base. Seeing everything.

Watching everyone.

Consequently, he had missed the one thing he had needed to see: someone vandalizing Sara's car.

Now at a clearing in the woods, he was back in human form.

Naked. With Sara's eyes trying so hard not to look at him—and failing.

Under other circumstances, he'd have laughed. Teased her.

She had offered her shirt for him to tie around his waist and drape strategically, but it would have left her clad above in only her bra. Intriguing, but he wouldn't embarrass her that way.

"Sorry," he said. "I'd intended to return to the lab area before I shifted back. I left my clothes there."

"I… We're not far from your quarters," she said. He enjoyed the flush on her face, visible even in the faint glow from the base's artificial lights. "I could go inside and get you something—if I could get in, that is."

"Maybe." But his keys remained in his uniform pants, and they were still at the lab. "Look, I shifted back now because I didn't want you to be alone. Why don't you just accompany me back to the lab? We can stay in the woods for most of the walk."

"All right." Her next words surprised him. "Or maybe we should just go deeper into the woods first."

He looked at her. Her lovely, full lips were raised into a teasing smile.

She was teasing him for a change. And he loved it.

"Like the thought behind it," he said. "But I don't think either of us would do well rolling on the ground there. Scratchy leaves, nasty bugs, the works. At the lab, though, I just happen to know where some nice, clean and unused bedding for the dogs upstairs are kept."

Her expression turned speculative. And hot. Especially when she glanced down at his exposed genital area. All the talk had spurred his interest—enough that his cock had grown hard. Really hard.

"Sounds promising," Sara said huskily. "If I can hold out that long." She was suddenly in his arms, her body pressed hard against his, especially down below.

"This isn't just because you're scared, is it?" he managed to ask. He wouldn't want her to regret what they surely were about to do—at least not for the wrong reasons.

He already figured she sometimes regretted having made love with him before.

"Yes, I'm scared," she said, "but no, that's not the reason."

He groaned with need before pressing his mouth on hers. She tasted salty, seasoned by her tears of anger and fear upon finding her car.

The thought spurred him to hold her closer. Deepen the kiss—partly out of an urge to protect her. To make her feel safe and cared for. To replace the thoughts of her car with thoughts of him…and the sex they soon would be sharing. That they now had to share.

He'd want to get back to that car soon, to check it out. To move it inside near the general's, to ensure it wasn't damaged further, especially not until he had a chance to examine it.

But the hour was late enough, the car's position in the parking lot distant enough, that it could wait.

It had to wait.

He had other things on his mind.

He ended that kiss, pulling his searching tongue from her welcoming mouth then placed one more hard kiss on her lips.

"Let's hurry." He grabbed her hand and began to lope with her through the trees.

"Sure," she said, matching his pace. "But…why not go even faster?" She started to dart ahead, still holding his hand. Now it was his turn to keep up—which he did, gladly. Grinning in anticipation.

Sara knew that Jason was aware of all aspects of the kennel and lab building, certainly a lot more than she was.

As they reached the rear entry to the low-slung building and eased into the shadows beyond its exterior lights, she asked softly, "Are you sure no one will be here at this hour?"

"Can't be sure of anything, but it's unlikely. I'd already told Noel, who helped with my shift, that I wouldn't need his help on the other end. We just arranged to leave my clothes downstairs where I changed. I'm supposed to call him later. If we see anyone else, you've already aided in my shifting before. We'll just say you helped again—and can even mention what happened to your car. That'll keep them from suspecting what we're really up to."

She shouldn't be so drawn to his teasing ways, his sexy smile. But she was. Especially now, when she needed a distraction from reality.

And what a distraction, with his hard, muscular body so close. So bare. So enticing, with his penis thick and jutting and daring her to partake in mind-blowing sex with him.

She doubted they'd be able to voice their way out of anyone's noticing that. But heck, maybe they wouldn't run into anyone.

She hoped not.

But as they entered the building, after going in through a seldom-used rear door that was left unlocked for Jason while shifted, the dogs inevitably sensed their presence and began to bark.

Sara laughed nervously. "So much for trying to sneak in here."

"It's soundproofed enough that, unless someone's already inside, no one will come to check why they're barking."

They headed for the door to the narrow stairway that led downstairs to the lab area. Sara noticed that the scratches on the door were still there.

"The general got me my own key cards for this building," Sara told Jason, but he'd already gone down the hall and into an unlocked room, where he emerged with a key card of his own. "Was that one hidden, too?" she asked.

"Yeah, but not all Alpha Force members would know where to look for it—only those with a need to get to the lab. Or their cousins." He grinned.

"But you'd have returned as a wolf," Sara reminded him. "How would you have gotten the key and gone downstairs then?"

"If I didn't have an aide with a card around, I'd have shifted first if necessary," he told her. He zipped the card along the track that opened the door.

Then Jason flicked on the lights and held her hand as they walked down the steep flight.

She held on as if she were frail and needed his help. On the contrary, she felt strong. Jazzed. Ready, really ready, for what she was anticipating below.

Jason turned on the hallway lights once they exited the stairwell. The area looked sterile—like a laboratory should, Sara figured. The doors were all closed. Each had a small window, and no lights into the lab rooms were on.

Jason led her to the last door on their right. "Here we are," he said.

Sara wondered for a moment what the room would be like inside. She'd seen some of the labs before—and they all had easily cleanable tile flooring and plenty of laboratory cabinets and surfaces.

Not the kind of place she hoped they would wind up in each other's arms.

She'd also seen the small office that Drew Connell used here.

She really didn't want to think about Drew now.

Still clasping her hand, Jason turned the knob and pushed the unlocked door open. He turned on the light.

Sara followed him inside.

And smiled.

This was an unexpected lounge area. Jason's clothes—she assumed the camo uniform that lay there—were resting on a plush, if well-worn sofa.

This must be where those hanging out in the lab went to veg out while their concoctions were brewing—or whatever.

In any event…well, given her choice Sara would have chosen something more comfortable than that sofa for what they had in mind. But it was better than so many other alternatives.

She opened her mouth to say so as Jason turned—and his erection, still taut and enticing, waved slightly in the air. She saw that before he took her into his arms and kissed her again.

And more. His hands didn't rest. She felt him immediately start to unbutton her shirt. "I'll—" she began against his mouth, but he didn't let her talk. Instead, he stripped her shirt off her, then stuck his hand immediately beneath her bra, clasping one breast gently, then the other, pushing the bra upward so he could more easily reach them—which made her moan.

Without waiting for him, she moved one of her hands from behind his back downward to push her pants off. She had to kneel to finish the act, and he moved with her. Helping her.

Then using his hand to move slowly, teasingly, sexily up the inside of her leg.

She moved so he could reach her. Touch her. Plunge a finger inside her, even as she grasped his cock and began pumping it gently.

Enjoying his deep moan of pleasure.

In moments—she wasn't sure how—she was on her back on top of that sofa. Its texture scratched at her back, but she didn't care. Her sense of touch, everywhere, was heightened by her sensual awareness of Jason.

She wanted him inside her. Instead, he kissed her once more, then moved down her body, tasting her with his lips, sucking her nipples, then farther down until his tongue lapped at her intimately and nearly made her scream. She caught herself, not wanting even the dogs to hear. "Please, Jason," she whispered huskily.

He moved away from her altogether for what seemed like eternity, but when he returned from behind her, near the end of the sofa, he had apparently fished a condom from his pocket.

He carried one all the time?

She didn't want to consider what that meant. Not now. For the moment, it only meant he was prepared, and she loved that.

And then, after he was shielded, he fulfilled her desire, plunging his hot and hard cock deep inside her. She was ready, bucking upward at his every thrust.

She didn't know how long it took, but all too soon

she reached a crescendo and he levered her over the top into an orgasm unlike any she had ever experienced before, ameliorated by his own gasp of pleasure as he, too, climaxed.

Jason lay there, out of breath, on top of Sara. Lord, had that been magnificent. Earth-shaking.

And even though he had not a shred of energy left, he knew he wanted—needed—even more.

He would never get enough of this woman.

But this was not the right place.

Neither was his car.

He wanted to take her somewhere special the next time.

There had to be a next time.

But at the moment, there was only now.

She was breathing just as heavily below him. He moved a bit, wishing the sofa was a little wider. He didn't want to crush her.

"You okay?" he asked.

"Oh, yes."

He smiled. Those words… They surely weren't the biggest turn-on in the whole world. But they were enough, that and her body still up against his, to lure him into touching her again. More. And as she gasped his name, in a way that suggested she, too, was ready for more, he started in once more to touch her. Everywhere.

Sara had no idea what time it was. She just lay there on the couch, Jason pushed up against her, facing her.

His arm over her, just as hers twisted around him, since she had no other place to put it.

If she hadn't felt so sated, his body so close and so hot would turn her on again.

His breathing had eased up a bit, as had hers.

They couldn't stay here all night, though it was tempting. But someone might come in. Even if no one did until morning, staying here was really no option.

A thought struck her and she wound up smiling.

"What?" Jason asked in a lazy tone. His eyes had opened and now studied her face.

"I thought we were here for you to get dressed, not for me to get undressed." Despite how her respiration had quieted, she still felt her nipples touch his hard chest with each breath. It felt damned sexy—but with all that she had just experienced, she couldn't do it again...could she?

"Both," he said, and she realized he was speaking in only single syllables at a time. He must feel as exhausted as she did.

"Let's do the other part, then," she said with determination she didn't really feel. But then she considered how, and why, they had gotten together in the first place that night. "I want to get back to my car. I'd like for you to examine it while you're not shifted. And... should we move it into the same place as the general's till it's been examined? Maybe there'll be fingerprints or some other way of figuring out who vandalized it."

His body grew tense against hers. "You're right. We can't leave it there like that. Not till we at least make an attempt to figure out who did it."

He drew away and stood, and she almost sighed at the loss.

He disappeared from her view in the dim light, but she heard him beyond the end of the couch. He was undoubtedly getting dressed.

Time for her to do the same.

Odd for her to feel a little shy standing and searching the floor for her clothing. She didn't even look toward Jason—even though she felt certain she would enjoy watching him put his uniform back on.

She definitely had the other times she had seen him perform that action. Even more so when he took it off.

The light in that room remained dim, but it was bright enough for Sara to follow the brief trail they'd taken while Jason helped her remove her clothes. She took it in reverse now, picking things up. She wished there was someplace private to go to get dressed, but of course that was silly.

Even so, she drew everything back on quickly, looking down at the floor as if not watching Jason would keep him from watching her.

Which was ridiculous. And wrong. When she finished and looked up, he was back near the couch, fully dressed, his gaze on her. Smiling.

She knew she was flushing again. She felt shy suddenly. But that was silly. "Are you ready to go?" She attempted to sound businesslike, a soldier prepared to jump back into battle.

With herself.

The fact that she had just made love with Jason—

again—remained wrong, no matter how good it had felt.

But she would scold herself for it later.

Right now she needed his assistance with her car.

And she especially liked the idea that her car would give her a good reason to remain in his presence. For now.

Chapter 20

The walk back to Sara's car helped to wake Jason. No, it did more than that. It stoked the anger that he'd felt even while shifted, when he had seen the vandalism.

He liked cars. He liked them in pristine form. No one should harm them intentionally, for any reason.

Mostly, he wanted to strangle whoever had done this, since it was Sara's car. More than anything, he wanted to protect her.

Well…maybe have sex with her again. But that would come later. He hoped.

For now he just stood there with her, in the dimly lighted parking lot, staring at what someone had dared to do to her nice hybrid. Scratches were bad enough. So was the damage to her headlights and taillights.

But that threat: *Die bitch. Your CO is still alive*

but you won't be for long. That begged to be avenged. Maybe even doing to the perpetrator what he had dared to suggest would happen to Sara.

And that wasn't just the wild, shifter side of him talking. No, even as a human he craved some kind of retribution.

He didn't tell Sara, though. She had waited till they got there but was now on her cell phone. "Yes, General," she said. "I know it's late but I wanted you to know what happened. I'm going to take some photos, then drive my car to store it, for now, with yours, where there's at least some security." She paused to listen. "No, sir. I'm not here alone. I called Jason Connell first since he works with cars. He came as soon as he could, and he's here with me now."

She tossed a glance at Jason, as if asking him to back her up—that he had just arrived. He nodded as if hearing her request aloud. Far as he knew, no one had seen him here before, in shifted form, when he'd first reconnoitered with Sara near her car.

Sara looked away again, staring at the car. She appeared pale in the soft light, all military in her camo uniform, all woman in the way she hunched over her phone, her short, blond hair framing her face, her blue-green eyes even more luminous than usual as she seemed to hold back tears. The outdoor parking lot remained full of cars. Sara and he stood off to the side of her car, squeezed in near the wall that had obscured the damage at first.

"Yes, sir," Sara said. "I will." She hung up and looked at Jason. "He's calling base security. We're to wait here until they arrive." Her smile was wan. "I guess till then you're under orders to help to keep me safe, notwithstanding what's written now on my car."

"Yes, ma'am." Jason saluted her, hoping his sorry attempt at levity would cheer her, even just a little.

He thought—hoped—maybe a reminder of what they'd just shared would do that, too.

He considered taking her into his arms, just for a minute, to comfort her. But he'd no idea how long security would take to get here so he stayed back.

Instead, he told her about the awful added smell that hid from him the scent of whoever had done this.

It didn't take long for a couple of guys in a marked sedan to arrive. They wore the same kind of uniforms and insignias as the guys who guarded the front gate— who hadn't been much help when General Yarrow's car had caught fire.

They exited their car and approached where Sara and Jason stood. "This the car?" one asked, the tall, skinny private named Kerry.

"Yes," Sara said.

They looked at the damage, took some pictures then said to Jason, "General Yarrow said it was okay for you to drive it to the area where his Jeep is now being stored, sir. But you're to use gloves and not touch anywhere outside the car, in case there are fingerprints."

"Fine," Jason said. "Thanks."

He was not about to let Sara stay with them. Donning the rubber gloves proffered by the guards, he gingerly opened the passenger door—careful not to touch anything other than the handle since that was the side that had been damaged.

At the guards' attempt to voice an objection, he said, "I want Lieutenant McLinder to stay with the car until I get it parked. This is the best way to let her accompany me. Her fingerprints will be on it and inside anyway, if that's what you're worried about." Then he got into the driver's seat and they drove off.

Sara had remained quiet. She didn't say anything as he drove, either. He wondered what she was thinking.

The parking garage was nearby, and they reached it quickly despite having to maneuver a bit along the roads inside the base. Jason drove Sara's hybrid to the enclosed area, behind which the remains of General Yarrow's car still sat. A lone guard stood outside. After a peek to see who they were, he opened the door and allowed Jason to drive in.

He had barely parked before he saw, in the rearview mirror, the general approaching.

"Look who's here," he told Sara. With him were the security guards they'd left behind in the outdoor lot.

She turned, then leaped out of the car. She stood beside it, waiting for the general to reach them. "I didn't realize you were coming here, too, sir."

"I wanted to see the damage." He turned to look at it then got closer. Shaking his head, he said, "This damn thing is escalating. Guess whoever it was isn't pleased I wasn't killed so he's issuing more threats—including to my personal staff. We have to catch whoever it is. Fast." He turned to the guards and began asking procedure questions.

Jason saw how Sara hung back, not offering suggestions or taking notes or acting the way she did in full general's aide mode. Instead, she seemed to just watch and listen. And study first the scratches on her car, then the ground.

He hated to see her this way. It was as though she had turned into a different person. Quiet. Sad.

As if she had also forgotten what they had just shared.

Maybe this time it had just been a respite for her. An interlude to take her mind off what was troubling her.

Something she wouldn't want to think about, let alone experience again.

That made him want to punch something—like whoever had done this to her car.

He had already determined to figure out who it was. That person had been crafty enough to spread some of whatever had make Jason ill at the site where the general's car had been sabotaged, so he hadn't been able to find the perpetrator's scent.

He'd have to think of something else…like making the person believe that little trick hadn't completely worked.

So far, though, he wasn't sure how.

While the general talked to the others, he edged closer to Sara. "I'm working on some ideas," he told her. "We can talk about them. We'll find the guy. Count on it. For now, though, we need to make sure you stay safe." He turned away before she could say anything.

He decided to present his idea to General Yarrow. As soon as the CO was done talking to the guards about how they'd better ensure things in this garage remained under scrutiny, he approached him.

"Sir," he said, "I would like to volunteer to help protect Lieutenant McLinder."

He heard a soft gasp from behind him—Sara.

"Thank you, Sergeant," she said, "but that won't be necessary."

Jason saw the frozen look on General Yarrow's aging face and groaned inwardly.

Had he made a mistake just by suggesting it?

He meant well, Sara knew. Under other circumstances she might have appreciated Jason's protective nature.

But she had already been around while he had shifted. General Yarrow knew that, and that she had seen Jason with no clothes on.

He didn't know the rest, at least. Even so, Sara worried about her position as the general's trusted aide.

She moved away from Jason, close to where Greg Yarrow stood with the base's security personnel. "I'd like to request that some members of your group be posted around the BOQ," she said to the guards. "To keep both General Yarrow and me under your protection."

"I've already got a guard contingent," the general said. "I'll have them keep an eye on your quarters, as well."

"Thank you, sir." Sara looked at her CO. She knew him well enough to recognize that he wasn't as blasé as he acted. Not with that slight lift of his dark brows, the interest shown in his unyielding light brown eyes.

"I'd like to speak with you in private, Lieutenant," he said, and those words made Sara tremble deep inside.

"Of course, sir."

She accompanied him to the area beside his car's remains.

"Sara," he began, "I don't have to tell you that I'm quite concerned about a lot of things going on here at Ft. Lukman. If I don't assign you to further TDY here—and I'm inclined not to now—then we'll be able to leave here in a few days, after the exercise the day after tomorrow where members of both units show their stuff together. But when we do, we're likely to leave some questions unanswered—like who's threatened both of us."

"That's true," she said. "Unless…well, maybe we can get further information before we go."

"Do you think Sergeant Connell can help with those answers?" He didn't let her respond before continuing, "He seems very protective of you, Sara. Maybe too protective. I don't think I have to remind you that he is a noncommissioned officer, and you're a lieutenant who in any event is here only on temporary duty."

Sara felt as if he was giving her advice, not only as her commanding officer but as a father figure. And friend.

She cared about Greg's opinion. Always wanted to stay in his good graces. Intended to keep her military career spotless so she could rise someday in rank.

"I understand, sir," she said. "And though it really wasn't necessary, I appreciate the reminder."

They returned to her car, where Drew Connell had just arrived, too, to survey the damage.

"I've called my investigative contacts again," Drew told them. "I doubt they'll be much help now but assured me they'll arrive soon to look into both cars."

While the general and Drew were talking, Sara edged her way toward Jason. "Thank you again for all your help, Sergeant," she said. "But it won't be necessary again."

And then she walked off to stand beside the two officers in charge.

When she dared a defiant glance toward Jason, she saw him staring at her. The expression in his eyes was far different from the sexual interest he'd shown before. Or even his protective look.

Instead, he appeared disgusted and remote.

At least he apparently understood what she wasn't saying.

And Sara suddenly felt glad…yet bereft. And alone.

They all left—except for the guards stationed to watch the cars.

As if whoever had damaged them would return in the middle of the night to do more. Or gloat.

Jason felt certain that whoever it was felt delighted to cause such concern at Ft. Lukman.

And was undoubtedly planning something else.

That's why he stayed in the garage for a little longer. Or at least part of the reason.

Even more important was that he didn't want to be anywhere near Sara. He wasn't certain what General Yarrow had said to her, but her attitude, which wasn't great with everyone around previously, had gone to crap.

It was time to move on. Or go back to being who and what he'd been before she arrived here: a guy who'd joined the military because he had to, to salvage the rest of his life.

"Hey, guys," he said to the two guards on duty. "Just wanted to let you know I'll hang around a little longer. You know I work on cars for Alpha Force?"

Both sentries nodded. One appeared to reposition his rifle a bit, but not in a threatening way.

"I'll be looking over this latest damaged vehicle. Maybe I'll recognize someone's handwriting. What do you think?"

He grinned, and both guys grinned back.

Good. He still had the ability to jostle people's sense of humor.

Now if only he could feel a bit humorous, too.

Sara felt furious with herself.

She should have checked before to make sure she hadn't left anything behind in the lab, when her clothes had been strewn all over the floor.

But her keys, including those to get into her quarters in the BOQ, weren't in her pocket.

Fortunately, she'd walked back there with the general, who'd swiped his key card to get into the building then headed for his own more elite wing without walking her to her apartment. He'd obviously not been concerned, despite the threat on her car, that someone would be stupid enough to attack her here.

Neither was she.

But when she got to her unit, neither her keys nor her cell phone were in her pocket.

She could have awakened some maintenance person and gotten inside her unit. But how would she ever explain losing the keys—and her phone? She knew where they had to be: on the floor in the lab, having fallen out of her pocket in the frenzy of stripping to make love with Jason.

She didn't want anyone else to find them. Consequently, she decided to retrace her steps, return to the lab to retrieve them.

She doubted Jason would be there. He was probably a lot more sensible than she was and had headed back to his quarters to sleep for what was left of the night.

If she did happen to run into him…well, she'd made it clear to him that whatever they'd shared was over.

For now she stayed in shadows as she maneuvered toward the far end of the base, where the lab building and kennel were.

At least no living quarters were nearby, so even if she disturbed the dogs no one would be awakened by their barks.

She worried, though. Among what she was missing were her own key cards into the building and lab that the general had gotten for her. She'd seen that an upstairs door had been left unlocked so a shifted Jason could get into the building, but that was before. And she didn't know where the key card to the downstairs lab was hidden—if Jason had even left it again.

If she'd had her phone, she could call him so he could let her in.

He might misinterpret that, though. No, she'd check first to see if she could somehow get inside—no matter how unlikely that was.

In the meantime, she'd stay alert. And careful.

It was late enough that she saw no one as she returned to the low, secluded building and started walking around it, testing doors.

Fortunately, a remote door to the kennel floor—not the one Jason and she had entered—was unlocked.

Which seemed strange. But maybe upstairs security was never that good.

Downstairs was a different matter.

Sara went inside. As anticipated, the dogs heard her and began to bark.

A dim security light illuminated the area, so she could see well enough without flicking any switches. She approached the nearest lush kennel areas and began talking to the dogs, including Shadow. Presumably, most Alpha Force members on duty at Ft. Lukman had brought their dogs into their quarters for the night.

So why was Shadow still here?

Sara had to hurry. Maybe Jason hadn't yet gone to bed. If he'd left Shadow here he might return for him.

"Good night," she said to the dogs then walked rapidly to the narrow door at the top of the stairs leading down to the lab.

Unsurprisingly, it was locked.

She closed her eyes in frustration. Where had Jason gotten the hidden key card?

She doubted there was another, easier entrance but she had to look. She walked farther along the short hallway and tried additional doors. One led into an unlocked closet that contained animal supplies. Another was also locked.

Damn.

Should she contact Jason?

But how—without her phone?

The dogs started barking again. She hadn't said anything aloud. Maybe they were just frustrated.

She headed back to calm them while considering ways to contact Jason—and saw the reason the dogs were noisy once more: Jason was there.

He spotted her at the same time as she saw him. "What are you doing here?" he demanded, loud enough to be heard over the barks.

She approached and explained about her missing phone and keys. "A door to the kennel was already unlocked," she finished, describing its remote location. "The door to the lab was locked, though."

"Strange," Jason said. "And definitely against general policy. I locked the door that had been left open for me under the unusual circumstances of a shifter having to get back inside alone. No other door in this building is ever to be left unlocked."

He looked concerned as he pushed past her to the door down to the lab.

It again wouldn't open—not without his key card.

He had to use it twice, though, before it worked. "Did you try to force it?" he asked her.

"Of course not."

But the skepticism on his face alarmed her. And made her feel even sadder that what they'd shared so briefly was definitely over.

He finally opened the door and they went downstairs. Sure enough, her card keys and phone had fallen beneath the sofa—the one that she would never be able to look at again without being bombarded by delightful, and now bittersweet, memories.

They left soon after. He'd gotten Shadow from his kennel, and they walked together across the base in the dark toward her quarters.

She only hoped that no one saw them and assumed they were fraternizing.

Because they weren't. Not now. Jason was just her champion. Her guard.

And this was likely to be the last time they'd ever be alone together.

Chapter 21

The designated night had arrived. Both of the major units at Ft. Lukman were to conduct a joint final exercise to ensure they could be deployed together on the anticipated mission in sync, without conflict between them.

No matter how individual members might feel about one another.

All those to take part in the exercise had met first in the assembly room. Sara stood off to the side while the two generals greeted their respective troops as they filed in. She watched intently. As she'd figured, members of the two units acted cordial yet sometimes remote toward one another. At least she saw no overt antagonism. All seemed well.

Except that, as Jason entered with Noel Chuma, he acted as if he didn't see her.

Which was probably best...although even the USFT members seemed friendlier to the Alpha Force members that evening than Jason acted toward her.

"Everyone take your seats, please," Sara called at General Yarrow's nod. Compliance seemed instantaneous.

General Myars deferred to Greg Yarrow. The Alpha Force general described, at last, what their real mission was to be: to work together to rescue some U.S. government civilians who'd been taken hostage months ago by terrorists in one of the many Middle East countries once again threatened with civil war.

Interesting, Sara thought—and probably a good assignment for such a unique, combined group of elite soldiers, since it appeared that all else had already failed. She had heard of the kidnapping, and the news was periodically full of updates about attempts to save the captives. Diplomacy had failed. Military saber rattling and even attacks had been to no avail, except that one of the hostages had been killed in retaliation. Negotiations were at a stalemate. The options for saving them had become nil—almost.

The situation clearly called for something more covert and absolutely effective. Like a combined mission using the extraordinary senses and unanticipated stealth of the shifters of Alpha Force and the lethal, perfect weaponry of the Ultra Special Forces Team.

And that, apparently, was what would happen—assuming these two units truly did find their rhythm of working in harmony.

General Yarrow explained the rationale and the current status. General Myars then described how the exercises tonight would be conducted.

Then they were all ordered to go outside to their assigned areas to get ready.

The Alpha Force shifters would all change into their animal forms, with the backup of their respective aides. They would sneak into the area on base where mock civilians were being secluded in similar conditions to the real ones overseas.

They would be followed by the USFT members who would wait until military members designated to act like the bad guys were confronted by the wild animals. In the ensuing chaos, they would shoot unloaded weapons until the pseudo-civilians were rescued.

Sounded easy. Sara was completely fascinated by the process—and hoped it worked out problem-free. Of course if it was less than perfect in this exercise, the flaws could still be dealt with.

First to leave the auditorium was the Alpha Force team. The shifters included Jason, Drew, Seth Ambers, Colleen Hodell and Jock Larabey. Their aides accompanied them, including Rainey Jessop, who'd apparently recovered from her illness.

Would five shifters be enough to stoke the distraction needed for the real mission?

Of course foreign forces confronted by wolves and a cougar would at least be unnerved—and hopefully scared enough to allow the creatures to reposition them away from their hostages…until all were rescued by the lethal, armed human forces of the USFT.

This exercise was being conducted at night, when it was easiest to hide the shifters.

Sara was there as General Yarrow's aide, extra pair of eyes and backup. And as an enthralled observer.

At the general's nod, she followed the Alpha Force members outside. They headed from the main office building into the wooded area at the periphery of Ft. Lukman.

There, in a clearing, aides removed vials of elixir and light from their respective backpacks.

After drinking elixir, the shifters repositioned themselves. One of them, Colleen, the only female, was sent off by herself for a little privacy, along with her aide.

And then the shifting began.

He felt free! Even though it hadn't been long since his last shift, Jason had been aching to prowl again.

Besides, this exercise would be vital to the United States, and he would be a part of it.

Would its success provide him the ultimate redemption in the eyes of his cousin? His country?

He hoped so.

But for now, he would just revel in his ability to leap into a staged situation and help rescue pretend hostages…and wait until he could accomplish the real thing.

And the fact that Sara would be watching this exercise? Possibly watching him?

Irrelevant.
For now.

The exercise went smoothly. Almost.

There was a bit of chaos when the USFT members arrived after the shifted Alpha Force team had done a great job of scaring the pretend kidnappers. Sara knew that the supposed victims and their captors hadn't been informed of all the details of how the rescue would be staged, so they didn't realize that many wolves and a cougar would be scaring the bad guys off till they were captured by the armed and dangerous USFT members.

But it all worked—though, for a while, the shifters in animal form were dispersed by the pseudo-captors' own use of unloaded weaponry. Sara watched them run off, glad about their caution.

She recognized, of course, which wolf was Jason. He moved away but stayed close enough to slink around to watch what was happening. So did the other wolves.

Poor Colleen, though. The cougar that was her must have been more unnerved. Sara didn't see where she went, at least not at first.

But in the end, it all worked. The "kidnappers" were all rounded up and locked in an area of the base that had been fitted out to act like a surrogate jail.

All the shifters, including Colleen, regrouped along with the USFT members after changing back to human form. The "rescued" hostages reconvened at the "jail" area, where those who'd played kidnappers were also released. All participants soon got together to congratulate themselves. The generals, too, celebrated.

Sara saw how pleased Jason appeared. How he seemed to joke and enjoy the party. His cousin Drew patted him on the back for how well he'd done. Sara hadn't been watching at the time, but apparently one of the "captors" hadn't been fazed by the shifted animals until Jason virtually attacked him, knocking him to the floor as might happen in the real situation and keeping him under control till the human marksmen could take charge.

He was in his glory.

Sara was happy for him, but she didn't want to stay there. Not then.

She slipped away.

She considered returning to her quarters but decided she needed face time with some of the dogs in the kennel, who hadn't been invited to participate in this exercise with their humans.

She could take one for a walk. Maybe even Shadow. No problem getting inside; she'd brought her card keys along in case she was needed to help the shifters.

When she reached the building, she stopped and stared. The door was wide open.

She ran inside. The dogs remained in their kennels and started barking at her.

Sara knew that Jason had reported to Drew the other day about her having found this kennel door unlocked when no one had intentionally left it like that to help a shifter. Everyone was under orders to take special care not to allow that to happen again.

But this was even worse.

Worried, Sara went down the hallway to the door that led down to the lab.

It, too, was open.

She needed to report this. Not touch anything. Not go inside herself.

She could call the general. Or Drew. In fact, Drew was the one she probably should notify.

But Jason had been with her here the other night. They'd both talked to the major. She'd thought security would be beefed up—but on this night, with the exercise that had involved nearly everyone at Ft. Luk-man, someone had either been completely careless… or had taken advantage.

Sara pulled her phone from her pocket. "Drew? It's Sara. I'm at the lab. It looks like someone else has been here, too."

"Like the other night?" he demanded.

"Maybe worse."

"Wait there. I'll join you right away."

"Please bring Jason," she said. "He also saw what went on here the other night."

"Fine," he said. "Oh, and Sara?"

"Yes?"

His words conformed with the sternness of his tone. "I hope you're armed."

Damn the woman.

Soldier or not, she shouldn't put herself into danger-ous situations without backup.

Jason was furious as he accompanied Drew back to the kennel/lab building.

At least she was waiting outside—with Shadow on a leash beside her. For company? For protection?

Though they stood near the building, away from the door and in an area near the back that was sheltered, neither would be protected from being shot from a distance—particularly if the attacker was one of the highly skilled marksmen of USFT.

That was where he and Drew found them—partly thanks to their enhanced sensory abilities. At least Sara and Shadow weren't easily visible, but Jason quickly smelled the woman's citrusy scent as well as the dog's light canine odor.

"You okay?" Jason asked Sara immediately. Bending to give Shadow a pat, he watched Drew hustle around the building toward the open door to the kennel area and slip inside.

"Yes, I'm fine." She looked better than fine—except for the paleness of her smooth skin. But there was anger in her blue-green eyes and a determined set to her mouth that told him she wasn't lying. "But this attempt to get in was more successful than the other. There was even an intrusion into the lab area. The stairway door was unlocked. But the doors along the hallway downstairs that lead into the actual laboratories were still locked. I checked."

Jason wanted to throttle her. Better yet, kiss her in relief to find that she was unharmed.

But even if he chanced Drew seeing them, Sara wouldn't appreciate his touch or even his concern. Instead, he merely snapped, "You checked? Before you called us?"

"No, after. But I wanted to—"

"What if whoever broke in was still there?"

"I'm a trained member of the military," she said slowly, as if she needed to remind him. "I also had a weapon in my pocket."

"Good." Drew was back with them. "Show me the unlocked door then we'll go downstairs."

They did. All was as Sara had described.

After locking everything again, Drew called in the base's security force to plant sentries outside.

When the security detail arrived, Sara, Drew and Jason again began walking, in the dark, toward the area where they'd left the participants in that night's exercise.

"So who was it?" Sara asked. "Like before, with the cars, it's unlikely to be a stranger from town who snuck onto the base. With all the activity here tonight, they'd have been noticed."

"Unless they dressed like some of the others," Drew reminded her. "A lot of the people stationed here were in disguise for the roles they played tonight—pseudo-hostages, tangos who were the false enemy terrorists. Not to mention the USFT members."

"And even Alpha Force members, although a lot of us were shifted most of the time," Jason said.

Sara shot a look at him that suggested she'd seen him shifted. Maybe even shifting. But any heat in her gaze dissipated immediately into the chill of the night-time air.

"I still think it's got to be someone in USFT," Drew said.

"Yeah," Jason agreed.

They walked on in the darkness, the silence broken by noises from the distance, including voices and cheers. Everyone was still celebrating this night's activities.

Everyone but them.

"We need to figure out—" Jason began.

At the same time, Sara said, "Let's see if we can trap whoever it is."

Drew's pace slowed as he laughed. "Great minds think alike," he said. "I was trying to come up with a plan, too, to bring this to a close—and figure out who's trying so hard, and getting so close to, breaking into the lab."

"I have an idea," Sara said as the three stood on a sidewalk facing each other under the dimness of a base streetlight. She looked gorgeous to Jason, despite the way the faint illumination cast shadows onto her face. "As you said, Drew, the most logical scenario is that it's someone from the USFT trying to get in. Are those rumors still going around that the elixir can help regular people become shifters? If so, why don't we add to them? Suggest they're true, but because of the attempts to break into the lab, all the premixed stuff will be moved the day after tomorrow since you need time to figure out a safe enough place to take it. And then we'll watch and wait for what should be the final break-in."

Jason couldn't help it. He grinned at her. "Hey, Drew and I are the ones with the woo-woo powers around here. Are you some kind of mind reader?"

"What, you want to claim my idea as yours?" Sara demanded. Though her tone was sharp, there was a twinkle in her eyes.

Damn, but he really wanted to kiss her.

Even more, he wanted to do exactly as she'd suggested—but find a way to keep her far from the site of their trap.

Though he couldn't be near her anymore, he still wanted to keep her safe.

But he had a feeling that trying to prevent her participation would be as impossible as making love with her again...no matter how hard he strove for either.

Sara kept Shadow leashed beside her as she walked back along the darkened sidewalks of the base. Her goal was the area where she'd left the participants in that night's exercises. Then, she had departed because she didn't feel part of what had been accomplished.

Now she had another mission to accomplish.

With Jason, of course. He stayed with her on the walk. Even tried to take possession of Shadow's leash and tell Sara to disappear.

A far cry from the times they had made love, and the last thing he'd wanted—either of them wanted— was for one of them to go away.

Drew was with them, too. As he should be. He'd need to be the primary one to start—actually, add to— the rumors that would hopefully result in ending the attempts at breaking into the lab once and for all.

Because the perpetrator would be caught and appropriately dealt with.

"So how will we handle this, cuz?" Jason had walked ahead to join Drew while Sara lagged behind as Shadow did usual dog things like sniffing the ground and lifting his leg.

"I'll keep as close to the truth as seems logical," Drew said.

Sara enjoyed watching both men from behind. They were of similar height and build. They strutted in their camo uniforms as if proud of who they were and what they represented.

They looked all military, even if Jason was just pretending because he had to.

And the fact that both men—dark haired with silver highlights that glowed now and then as they walked beneath streetlights—happened to be shapeshifters? That wasn't obvious at the moment, but Sara was well aware of it.

Everyone they eventually met up with would know it, too.

"I'll tell them you went to get your cover dog Shadow to take him back to your quarters for the night, and you found evidence of an attempted break-in at the kennel. Since the lab is below, you checked there, too, and found there was an apparent attempt to break in to the refrigeration storage unit."

"Will you mention that it wasn't the first time an Alpha Force member became aware of possible tampering?" Sara had moved up, urging Shadow forward, so she wouldn't have to speak loudly to be heard.

"That's not necessary now," Drew said. "We'll hold

it back, use the knowledge when and if it makes sense for trapping our bad guy."

Jason had stayed quiet all this time. That wasn't like him. Sara expected a quip of some sort.

When he did speak, it was to Drew. "I think it's important, cuz, to make it clear I was the one who noticed the attempted break-in. If we do get our bad guy to make himself visible, he may not be happy. It'll be better if I'm the one who has the fun of fighting back."

He didn't even look at Sara, damn him. He ignored her. Pretended she wasn't even with them. What, was Shadow walking himself?

"I appreciate your attempt to protect me, Jason, if that's what you're doing," Sara said coldly. "But as you know full well by now, I can take care of myself. I'll definitely be prepared."

"Maybe so," Jason retorted, "but since when have you become a shapeshifter? Or maybe you want to buy into those rumors we're about to exaggerate—that all you gotta do is take some of the elixir. One of us is a lot more likely to be able to—"

"Enough," Drew cut in. They had reached the exterior of the sham jail area of the base. There were still a lot of voices emanating from inside, so clearly the party wasn't over. "We need to present a unified front. My orders, for now, are that Sara will be our lead since she'll represent not only Alpha Force but also the general. I'll start things off by making the announcement that hopefully will result in our capturing whoever's doing this."

"Fine," Jason snapped, but Sara was glad to see

he was addressing Drew's back. She followed with
Shadow. Jason was left to follow them into the concrete
building usually used for storage that now represented
triumph and unity in the two units' working together.

Yet they were about to be torn apart again, Sara
thought.

Temporarily. But when the thief was caught, everyone else, in both units and otherwise at Ft. Lukman,
would be able to cheer.

Chapter 22

"Everyone, listen up," Drew called from the front of the crowd.

If Jason had been in charge, he'd have let out a loud whistle to get the crowd's attention. But his cuz was a major in a crowd of mostly subordinates, except for the generals. So everyone listened up.

Jason did, too, although he kept a sideward gaze on Sara and Shadow, who stood just behind Drew. Like it or not, and notwithstanding Drew's outranking him, Jason would do what was needed to keep Sara out of whatever was about to explode.

Sure, she was one fine military officer, trained and all that. But despite her skills, this wasn't her war.

It was Alpha Force's, since it involved someone attempting to undermine it by stealing its best underlying weapon: the elixir.

"You all need to know what's going on," Drew continued loudly. "We've just uncovered an incident at our laboratory where apparently someone tried to break in and possibly steal some elixir. Right now we've set some guards there. We need to move the premixed elixir to a safer location, though. We'll figure out where first thing tomorrow morning, then get it done."

General Yarrow joined him at the front of the throng. Good, Jason figured. That would give even more authority to what Drew was saying.

And most of it was true.

Except maybe the part about moving the elixir. That was just a ruse to smoke out whoever would attack the formula in motion and try to take it then.

If that didn't do it—well, they'd use wherever the stuff was theoretically taken to keep the trap set. Whoever it was would undoubtedly move soon.

Maybe thinking that all he had to do was steal some of the elixir, drink it and turn into a wolf who could be vicious enough to ward off all who would stop his theft.

Not gonna happen, you goon, Jason thought.

"If whoever tried to steal the elixir would come forward and confess, we'll make sure things go a lot easier on him," the general said calmly. "We'll need to take precautions that the elixir, and the secrecy of Alpha Force, haven't been compromised, but that person might even be able to help us. Advise us on why you did it and how we can better protect our people and our Alpha Force supplies and objectives."

That, too, wasn't reality, but Jason still felt admiration for the general. Something like that just might make the bad guy step forward to protect his own butt.

No one in the large crowd remained in disguise after the exercise. All stood watching as if they gave a damn. None leaped up and confessed.

No matter.

The bars would be lowered tomorrow. Whoever it was would be caught, confession or not.

And Jason, on behalf of Alpha Force, would be there to lay his paws all over the guy.

Sara felt exhausted.

Though she had only been part of the Ft. Lukman exercises as an observer, that had still been tiring—to make sure all seemed to go well.

And then there'd been all that had happened since.

She was back in the BOQ now. After the meeting Drew had presided over, she'd wandered through the crowd, using Shadow as her ostensible reason for walking around.

She had eavesdropped on a lot of conversations.

Some Alpha Force members sounded outraged that someone had used their primo exercise as a cover for trying to steal the elixir.

"What a jerk," Jock Larabey proclaimed. The muscular lieutenant shook his head and gritted his teeth as if he'd have liked being in wolf form to go for the perpetrator's jugular.

"The fool probably wants to become like us," Colleen Hodell said, running a hand sharply through her layered, tawny hair as if she wished it belonged to the bad guy. "Can you blame whoever it is?"

"Maybe not." Rainey Jessop sucked in her lips grimly as she looked at her Alpha Force boss. "But that isn't going to happen."

Sara had listened just as avidly to some USFT members. Captain Rynton Tierney was his nasty, confrontational self as he told his subordinates, "You'd think after a successful exercise like we had, those damned conceited Alpha Forcers would suck it up and not assume the whole world wants to be them. We don't. We just have to work with them."

Other members of that team were not as blunt, but neither did anyone she heard admit to believing the rumors that they, too, could become shapeshifters on the swig of a bottle—nor did any say they wanted to. No indication from this who'd been trying to steal the stuff.

Afterward, Jason took Shadow back with him. "He's going to stay with me in my apartment tonight," he told Sara. "I'll enjoy his company. No need for both of us to be on our own. And you should be safe as long as you're in your own quarters—so head back there with other Alpha Forcers who're your neighbors then stay inside your apartment." He'd turned his back on Sara then and walked off with his cover dog.

Leaving her feeling hurt. And bereft.

But she made herself snap out of it—after watching Jason's sexy backside for a minute more than she should have. They were both doing what they should: staying away from one another.

But even if Jason hadn't made that jibe, Sara would have felt envious of Shadow and the fact the dog could stay, unquestioned, in the same apartment as Jason.

If Sara could have…well, she wouldn't get any sleep that way.

She might not, anyway, despite how tired she felt. Her mind might not leave her alone after all this.

She had hung around that busy area until some Alpha Force members were ready to head back to the BOQ. She'd said goodbye to them inside the main entry hall and headed toward the door to the stairs leading to her unit.

As she started walking up the steps, though, Colleen came into the stairwell behind her. "Hey, Sara?" she said. "Got a minute?"

Sara turned and looked down. Colleen had a perplexed expression on her face. "Sure," Sara said. Did she want Sara to help her shift again? But Rainey had looked fine that evening.

"Come on outside with me, would you? I thought I heard something that might help to figure out what's going on with that attempt to steal some of the elixir."

"Really?" Sara perked up slightly. That might be worth staying out of bed for a few minutes—especially if she learned something that could help catch the thief even before the planned ruse for tomorrow.

She'd love to do that, particularly if she could then show Jason she was more than just the general's assistant.

She followed Colleen back outside. Together, they stood in the shadow of the BOQ.

"I don't know if it'll help or not, but there's something I need to see in the lab before I tell you what I suspect. I know it's late, but what I heard is just so odd, and yet it might make sense. But I want to look and see if all the pieces fit together."

"I'd rather wait till morning," Sara said. "I'm tired. Aren't you? You were right there in the middle of the exercise."

"And that's why… Okay. If you don't want to come, I'll do it on my own. I can tell Drew tomorrow, or the general, if I'm right."

Sara pondered that, but only for a minute.

She wasn't about to tell anyone, even Colleen, about the ruse they would be conducting tomorrow—or about what had really happened that night with the attempt to steal the elixir.

But if she could learn something useful just by going back there…

She recalled Jason's warning, of course. He'd said she should stay in her quarters. But this was Colleen. A member of Alpha Force. Even if they weren't good friends, they were at least close enough acquaintances that Sara had helped the feline shifter before. Had no reason not to trust her. And she would stay wary.

Besides, she still had a military issue weapon in her pocket as she had earlier that evening.

"Let's hurry," she told Colleen. "I'd really like to get to bed soon."

But as it turned out, Sara realized about twenty minutes later, she wasn't going to get to see her bed that night at all.

Maybe it was exhaustion, or her belief she could solve the main Alpha Force problem before Jason or anyone else could, but despite her earlier determination to remain wary, she wasn't as careful as she should have been.

After Colleen had slipped her card for the two of them to pass through the kennel with the barking dogs, they headed for the door downstairs to the lab area.

"I just need to check my recollections about something down there," Colleen said.

She had a key card for that, which somewhat surprised Sara since not all Alpha Force members were given ready access to the labs. Maybe Colleen was working on the elixir formula without Sara knowing about it.

But when they reached the bottom of the stairway, Colleen stopped, moved swiftly behind Sara and grabbed her around the neck, jabbing the barrel of a small gun against her cheek.

"Hold very still while I pat you down," Colleen said, slightly loosening her grip around Sara's neck as she ran her hands along her sides—and pulled Sara's weapon from her pocket. "Ah, here it is. Now we're going to go into that dumb little office of Drew's down here and you're going to call him."

Sara felt dumbfounded. "It's you?" she demanded, although her words came out as a croak since Colleen once more held her neck as she propelled Sara down the hall. "But why?"

"Shut up," Colleen demanded and kicked Sara's side.

"You don't need to know anything. You just need to obey me, you damned nonshifter bitch."

What the hell was she doing?

Jason had been outside giving Shadow a final walk of the night when he saw Sara leaving the BOQ with Colleen Hodell.

Staying in deep shadows, he followed.

He realized, after they passed through most of the base, that they were heading toward the kennel/lab building. Why? Especially at this hour.

He decided it was a good thing he had Shadow with him as cover. He could say he needed to leave his dog in the kennel tonight—which wasn't true. He liked having Shadow's company whenever possible and had planned to have him around overnight.

Now, though, he drew nearer, watching as Sara and Colleen walked into the upstairs area of the kennel—causing all the dogs inside to bark. He waited for a minute, then entered with Shadow before the noise died down. Were they just going to see the dogs?

Colleen's cover feline was in her own quarters, wasn't she? This probably wasn't a middle-of-the-night visit to wish the small cougar look-alike sweet dreams.

So…were they going downstairs into the lab?

If so, why? Was Sara taking Colleen there? She had an access key. But what was this all about?

Using his own card key, Jason walked inside with Shadow and waited while his dog traded nose sniffs through the wire mesh entries to the kennels—also using his own enhanced senses to try to hear voices through the barks.

He couldn't make out any words, but he did hear something from downstairs, or so he thought.

He tied Shadow's leash to a kennel door then headed toward the stairway, where he carefully opened the door.

And listened some more.

And froze. If he had been shifted, he knew his hackles would rise.

"I don't understand," Sara was saying. She sounded as if something was choking her. "Colleen, if there's something we should—"

"I told you to shut up, bitch! Oh, and if you're wondering what you're doing here, you're bait. And my ticket to get out of here with everything I want. Come on, we're going to see the guard who's now outside the refrigerator unit…again."

There was a gagging sound, and the shuffling of feet.

Jason almost bolted down there. Instead, he made himself wait patiently, but only for a minute.

He was glad the dogs kept barking—and that Colleen was not a wolf shifter.

He knew what he had to do. And he had to do it fast.

He drew his weapon, in case he ran into the two women, but he prayed that wouldn't happen. Colleen would undoubtedly use Sara as a shield.

No, Jason knew he needed the element of surprise to save Sara.

Slowly, but with utter determination, he sneaked his way downstairs and into the nearest lab.

"What the hell—" Kerry began. The sentry had been sitting on a chair while guarding the door to the refrigeration unit, but now he stood.

When she realized where they were heading, Sara had hoped that the guard would be able to help her.

Instead, she realized, she had become a bargaining chip.

"I know you're buddies with Lieutenant McLinder," Colleen oozed smoothly from behind her. "If you don't let me into the refrigerator this time, I'll kill her slowly in front of you, and then it'll be your turn."

"But I can't..." the guard said. "You'll be caught, anyway. Why don't you—"

Sara felt Colleen's arm tightening around her neck and tried not to gag. Instead, she realized how light-headed she had become. She was going to pass out.

"Do it!" Colleen snapped. She aimed the weapon she held now in her free hand at Kerry, waving it back and forth between Sara and him, even as she kept Sara close.

This time, Kerry closed his eyes briefly then nodded. He used the electronic release and soon the door snapped open.

"This way," Colleen said. "Both of you."

Sara was too weak to resist. She knew she was going to die, anyway now. How could she have been so stupid? She hadn't suspected Colleen.

She should have suspected everyone.

Now…she would at least try to save Kerry.

And if only she could see Jason just one more time…

"He's right," she managed to say to Colleen. "You'll be caught. You think I just went with you like an obedient dog? I let people know—"

"You bitch! You told someone, signaled them, whatever?" Colleen's fury spewed out—and so did the force at Sara's throat. She saw Colleen wave Kerry into the large refrigeration room, even as she was dragged inside.

She was suddenly released, and she stumbled to the floor. That was when Colleen, still holding the gun on them, pulled free a large cloth bag she'd used as a belt around her waist and started, with her free hand, to carefully stick vials of elixir from the many shelves of the unit into it. Because of their usual potentially rough handling in the backpacks of shifters' aides, Sara knew that the thick glass of the storage vials was fairly unbreakable, and the seals were secure and tight.

Shifting Alpha Force members were generally issued only enough of the elixir to help with their next change or two to keep in their possession. How much was Colleen taking? All of it that was currently being stored, apparently—enough to trigger hundreds of shifts.

"I thank you, and my family thanks you," Colleen said. "Not that you'll be around to enjoy their gratitude. But now there's something I'd better do so I can…" Her voice tapered off as she moved away from them.

Sara had no idea what Colleen meant by her family and its thanks, but she couldn't be allowed to get away with this. As Colleen backed toward the door, Sara, weak as she felt, aimed a careful glance toward Kerry. The look in his dark eyes seemed terrified, but she thought she detected a small nod.

"Now!" she cried as Colleen moved to open the door, the bulging sack attached at her shoulder.

But the distraction didn't help.

"You're going to die in here," Colleen said. "I don't even need to use this." She waved the gun toward both of them, making Kerry hesitate, Sara saw from the corner of her eye.

She didn't hesitate, though—but her strength had ebbed because of the choking she'd undergone.

She didn't reach the door before it slammed shut—leaving Kerry and her inside.

Should he have taken the time to shift?

No matter now. Jason figured that he would be better able to slink around the lab facilities—and subdue Colleen—while in wolf form.

He had stopped within the main lab and set things up for himself, drinking elixir and using the light to ensure he could shift quickly.

But not before he had used his phone to notify his cousin what was going on, and where.

Now, easing his shifted form against the wall, he moved down the hallway toward where he heard voices—clearly, now that he was in wolf form, despite the fact they radiated from behind apparently closed doors.

Sara was in trouble.

He had to get there in time....

Suddenly, a form jumped out of a door just in front of him.

A growling cougar.

It leaped upon him—its fangs going for his neck.

Sara stopped talking to Kerry, who, shivering, had ceased arguing with her and headed toward the control panel within the refrigeration unit.

He'd been certain that Colleen would be waiting outside to shoot them. She knew better.

Especially now, with the roaring sounds of animals fighting to the death outside, the sound muffled by the thickness of the door.

Jason, shifted? Some other werewolf?

And Colleen? A few minutes had passed since she had locked them inside. Had it been a mistake to lie and claim Sara had the foresight to secretly notify someone she was going to the lab with Colleen?

At last, Kerry was successful. The door burst open, allowing heat to pour into the area that was just above freezing. Sara no longer had her gun. Colleen had taken it. But even if she'd had it, aiming it would have been difficult.

She had to stop shivering.

She first needed a weapon.

The best thing she could find at the moment was one of the substantial shelves that was now emptied of elixir. She grabbed one, wresting it away from the wall.

"You take one, too," she demanded of Kerry.

Then she hurried outside into the hall.

And stopped, horrified to see the fighting wolf and cougar. Was the cougar winning? Both were covered in blood.

Her wooden weapon was unlikely to help, but she ran forward, anyway, hoping she could get a good aim at the feline's head.

Before she could, the cougar saw her, bared its teeth and leaped away from the wolf and onto her. Sara felt its fangs on her throat—but only for an instant.

The wolf had not only knocked it off her, it shoved the cougar onto its back on the floor and stood on its chest, its own fangs sinking into the feline's neck.

The creature roared and moved—but only for a minute.

"Freeze!" shouted a human voice, and suddenly a cadre of armed military men, led by Major Drew Connell, stood down the hall, aiming their weapons at the cougar.

The wolf moved off it and loped toward Sara. It soon sat at her side, bloody but looking up at her with caring golden eyes.

"Thank you, Jason," Sara whispered throatily, bending to give the wolf a hug.

Chapter 23

It was over.

Sara sat in General Yarrow's office once again, eager to hear everything that had gone on since Lieutenant Colleen Hodell was taken into custody yesterday.

From what Sara had heard, Colleen was being flown to Fort Leavenworth, Kansas, where she would be incarcerated in a highly classified facility within the U.S. Disciplinary Barracks there, pending her court-martial trial for treason and more.

"So here's what we've learned, sir," Drew Connell was saying to General Yarrow, who scowled from behind his desk. Drew sat in a chair on Sara's left.

"One thing I hope you learned, Drew, is that your

vetting process for Alpha Force members had better be beefed up." Greg leaned forward with his arms crossed.

"Yeah, like getting more shapeshifting car thieves to enlist." That was Jason, who sat at Sara's right. That comment brought a smile to the general's face and lightened the atmosphere, just a little.

"Yeah, car thieves do a good job of protecting the rest of us," Greg Yarrow agreed. "Or at least one does."

Jason's face lit up in a proud grin that managed to enhance his rugged, handsome features.

Sara felt herself begin to smile, too, but she stopped herself. She still had a lot of questions.

She also knew that her time here, around Alpha Force and Jason, was limited.

Not much to smile about…despite Jason's teasing bad-boy way breaking through the otherwise heavy atmosphere here.

"What do you mean, sir?" she asked, addressing the general. "I take it that there were things about Lieutenant Hodell that weren't known before?"

She made it a question, since she didn't want to accuse Drew, or his other Alpha Forcers, of incompetence. They had their procedures that had to be followed before a shifter could be invited to enlist and join their unit. She had to presume that those procedures were used with Colleen Hodell, too—even if they failed.

"That's right," Drew acknowledged. "She was one hell of a liar. She convinced not only me but our whole enlistment committee, too, that she was a solid shifting citizen despite an upbringing in the wilds of South Dakota that left a lot to be desired."

Hadn't she said she'd come from the Midwest? That part of what she'd said, at least, wasn't a lie—although she hadn't been specific about the state with Sara.

He described what they'd heard from Colleen about her childhood attempts to hide out from hunters and others who tried to kill them.

"She said that her family had had to fight back, and that some of her relatives had actually become more feral, even attacking humans and claiming it was self-defense. She didn't believe in what they were doing, so she fled as soon as she reached college age. We felt sorry for her."

She'd told Sara about her family and having to hide, not that they'd fought back—nor that she had supposedly run away from them because of their actions.

"So what's the truth?" General Yarrow demanded, which was exactly what Sara was wondering.

Drew sighed. "Well, she's admitted now that she remained part of that family. Close to them. Hated non-shifting humans and vowed revenge on them. So when she heard rumors of Alpha Force and its elixir…well, she made up a story that had us believing she was one of the good guys and deserved a chance. She's been with Alpha Force for almost a year now, and we had no reason to doubt her, or consider her anything but what she claimed…till now."

The major looked ashen, his golden eyes, usually so much like Jason's, haunted and flat.

"That'll teach you to try to help someone, cuz,"

Jason interjected. Sara felt horrified at the criticism and prepared to chastise Jason, but then he continued, "Like me. I'll blame it on my family that I became such a loser, like them. I mean, I even had a loser of a cousin who developed an elixir that helped all shifters choose when they change and keep their human awareness. What could be worse? And—"

"That's enough," Drew snapped.

"Nope, it's not," Jason said. "I want to hear more about dear Colleen, but you've got to stop blaming yourself, cuz. She's the loser. Not you. Bad family or good, we make our own choices."

Drew stood suddenly and turned his back on the rest of them, looking out the window of the general's antiques-filled office. "She could have killed General Yarrow," he said, so low that Sara had to strain to hear him. Greg probably did, too, since neither had a shifter's enhanced hearing.

She rose and put a comforting hand on Drew's camo-clad shoulder. "Did she admit that?"

"Yeah. You know, she shoved stones into the road to slow the general's car. Then she shot a wooden arrow that she'd set fire to, one she'd doused with an incendiary liquid that enhanced the flames but burned up so it was unidentifiable. She'd already checked out the general's Jeep and figured it would work. Hopefully kill him, or at least warn him to stay away from Ft. Lukman."

"Why did she want that?" Sara felt confused.

"She was angry that the general had brought the USFT unit here for exercises. She wanted the base to stay remote—so she could steal as much of the elixir as had already been formulated before running back to her family. But then she decided to use the USFT presence, frame its members, so she could get away with what she wanted."

"Which was?" Jason was now standing at his cousin's other side. He was touching Drew's other shoulder in sympathy, and Sara adored him for that.

"Okay, let's sit down again," Drew said. "I'll tell you what we know, or think we know, so far. Some Colleen has admitted, some is just speculation, but here goes."

They all resumed their seats. Drew explained that Colleen, instead of hating her family and its destructive attitude toward nonshifting humans, felt part of them. Wanted to help them.

Her intent, in joining Alpha Force, was to steal both the formula for the elixir and as much of the brewed formulation as she could. She'd take it all home to her family—they'd already acquired some property in the Canadian wilderness—and they'd all learn how to make elixir. They planned to take turns drinking it then going places where they could attack people while shifted and kill as many as they could.

"They surely didn't think they'd be able to destroy all regular humans that way, did they?" Sara demanded.

Drew's face looked bleak. "No, but apparently they hated people enough to kill as many as they could possibly get away with."

"Strange. And damned nasty." General Yarrow stood behind his desk, shaking his head. "Did she manage to steal the formula? Any of the elixir?"

"No, I do keep the formula well protected in a safe down in the lab area," Drew said. "And the amount of elixir kept in the refrigerator at any time wouldn't have let her succeed in her horrible plan, either. I think that's one reason she was so frustrated. She'd stolen a little, whenever she could get her hands on it, but not much. But she did make good use of having the USFT group here."

"How?" Jason asked. Where he sat, at Drew's other side, made it harder for Sara to see him. Just as well. She needed to wean herself away from what she now considered an addiction to him.

"She started the rumor that the elixir, taken by non-shifters, would turn them into shapeshifters. She swore the few she told to secrecy, which of course meant they blabbed it to one another. She'd also 'revealed' it to her aide Rainey so she, too, would pass the lie around. The thing was, Rainey decided to try it herself."

"Oh, my," Sara exclaimed. "Is that what gave her the stomach problems she's been experiencing?"

"Exactly," Drew said.

"But did it—" General Yarrow began.

"Turn her into a shifter?" finished Drew. "Of course not."

Colleen had additionally planted the AK-47 aimed at General Yarrow's car out of anger that things weren't going exactly as she'd planned, and she blamed the Alpha Force CO.

"She also resented your attempts to protect the general and chase down what was happening here," Drew said to Sara.

"So she was the one to deface my car, too," Sara said.

"Right," Drew agreed.

"Anyone contacted her family?" General Yarrow asked.

"We've tried, but they've disappeared."

"Into the wilds of Canada?" Jason asked.

"Maybe," Drew said. "Just in case, we've notified the Royal Canadian Mounted Police. And we're still trying to figure out how she finally got a copy of the card key that let her downstairs into the lab. Like all Alpha Forcers, she had a card key to get into the upstairs kennel area, but since she wasn't working on the formula she didn't have a way to open the door to the lab stairway. She'd been the one to scratch that door out of frustration that she couldn't open it."

"I wonder..." Sara said. She told them about how she had helped Colleen shift that one night when Rainey was ill. "I don't know how she did it, but there probably wasn't anyone else around the lab building that night. Maybe she found a hidden card key then."

"She's stopped talking," Drew said, "so we may never know."

Their meeting was finally over, but Jason wished that it had gone on all day, not just the morning.

"You going to drop over to the area where the general's car and Sara's are finally being examined by the military investigating team?" Drew asked him.

"Yeah," Jason said. From the corner of his eye, he watched Sara as she conversed with her boss, the general. Drew had already said that a couple more exercises would be held here at Ft. Lukman with the USFT gang, and then both they and Alpha Force would be deployed to handle the overseas rescue of the kidnapped government civilians.

The general was apparently heading back to the Pentagon.

So, then, would Sara. Jason knew that, and it made him feel like someone had run over him with that big car-mover tow truck he'd rented. Or worse.

Well, he'd already known that things couldn't stay as they'd been. At least he'd been able to have mind-blowing sex with Sara. Twice.

He'd have to be content with the memory.

Yeah. Right.

"I think I'll head there now, in fact," he told Drew. "Are the feds there yet?"

"Yes, they arrived early this morning and I met them at the gate to the base then took them where they needed to go."

"Great. I'll be interested to hear what they have to say."

"And you can do a little prompting, if you want. See if any of the detritus found in the ashes could be remains of the arrow or ignition stuff."

"Oh, and what the hell did that bitch Colleen use to mess up my breathing, make me cough when I found where she'd been hiding to shoot her arrow?"

"That's still an unknown, too," Drew said. "She only grinned when we asked. But see if the feds can draw some samples from the earth and run tests."

Jason had become enough of a military peon to salute goodbye to General Yarrow and mention that Drew had given him the assignment of helping the fed investigation team. He nodded briefly toward Sara, whose stare, with those gorgeous blue-green eyes, remained unreadable.

And then he left.

Sara sat in the general's office for a long time after Drew and Jason walked out.

Greg and she had talked. About the situation with Colleen Hodell and Alpha Force. And the harm the angry shapeshifter had inflicted on the unit.

As well as relief it hadn't been any worse.

They also discussed Sara. And her future in the military. As Greg's aide.

So much depended on things that weren't entirely within her control. Like shapeshifters.

And yet.…

Afterward, she walked into the part of the base garage where the general's Jeep, and her car, were still being stored.

"Hi," she said to Kerry, the sentry. Sweet, young guy, he flushed and saluted and waved her into the secured area.

Four guys in suits were there, wandering around the site and apparently poking here and there into the remains of General Yarrow's car. They wore rubber gloves and carried a bunch of plastic bags with ashes and more potential evidence inside them.

And there was Jason, with them. Scowling.

"How are they doing?" Sara said after reaching Jason's side.

"Fine. Probably confirming all the stuff we already know now."

"Well, that should be a good thing." She paused. "When you're done here, would you call me? There are a few things I'd like to discuss with you."

"Sure." He looked at her then. Was that a shred of hope she saw in his gold-flecked eyes? If so, it disappeared almost immediately.

"Promise you'll call," she added.

"Sure," he said again, and only then did she leave the suits to their work.

Jason watched Sara depart. How could she look so sexy in the same old shirt and pants with camo print and work shoes as everyone else around here?

Everyone but these guys he was watching. Listening to their chatter. Finding them exceedingly annoying.

So far, he had not heard anything that he hadn't suspected before.

He'd told them about the bow-and-arrow scenario. The flame accelerant. The stuff that had sickened him outside—of which they still needed to collect samples.

They'd taken pictures of these ruins and the damage to Sara's car.

Nothing new.

Now he wished they'd hurry.

He had a phone call to make.

Would he hear anything good from Sara? Maybe

she just wanted to talk over more about Colleen Hodell and her treachery around here.

Sara had seemed excited. Maybe even eager to talk to him.

More debriefing about what had happened around here could excite her that way. But not him.

So could her obtaining orders from the general to return to D.C. and their usual posting. Maybe she just wanted to say goodbye.

Hell, all this speculation was doing him no good. But as much as he tried, he couldn't keep his mind off Sara.

Sara was in the cafeteria, drinking coffee with Rainey Jessop when her smartphone rang.

Poor Rainey was distraught. The pretty, young brunette with the curly hair said she'd loved being a shapeshifter's aide.

She hated that the shapeshifter she'd been assigned to was a liar and a potential killer.

She hated that she had been a fool.

"I really believed her," she had wailed a while ago. "I thought it would be so cool to drink something and turn into a shifter. Instead—" She'd groaned and clutched her stomach. "It still hurts just thinking about it."

"I'm sorry," Sara had lied. Oh, she felt bad that the young woman had suffered, but she had brought it on herself.

Not that the truth about shapeshifters was easily available on the internet. But if Rainey had just asked someone around here—someone other than the bitch whose aide she had been—she'd have had it verified that shapeshifting was strictly hereditary. Not something she could just opt into by swigging a drink.

Now she was delighted that her phone rang, a good excuse to say bye to Rainey.

And she was even more delighted to see who it was: Jason.

"Hey," she said. "Those guys through?"

"Yes," he said.

"Great. Then please meet me outside the BOQ in five minutes. There's something inside my apartment I'd like you to see."

"Aren't you afraid that'll look like fraternizing?" His tone over the phone sounded jaded and skeptical.

"No. Come on over and let me explain."

Five minutes later she was outside the BOQ door she preferred as an entrance, where she could open the door and walk up the stairs to the floor where her unit was.

She saw Jason strolling down the sidewalk toward her.

She tried not to smile but didn't succeed.

Nor did she succeed in keeping herself from melting down below from the heat she couldn't suppress at just seeing him.

"Hi," she said as he reached her side. She looked up into his eyes, watching his gaze heat up as he observed her, too.

He was the one to pull away. "What's up?"

"Come to my apartment and I'll explain."

She could hardly keep herself from grasping his hand and pulling him up the stairs at twice his pace.

No one was around in the hall to observe their entry. Probably a good thing. But at this point…

He walked behind her into her small apartment. She shut the door behind him—then reached up and pulled him down for one torrid kiss.

"Hey," he said against her mouth. "This feels like fraternizing to me. Not my problem, but you're the officer."

"Yeah, I am. But my next assignment…well, that's what I want to discuss with you."

She adjourned into the kitchenette, where she pulled a high-end beer from the fridge—a bottle for each of them. Then she led him into her living room and pointed to the small sofa.

"Please, sit down."

When he complied, she joined him, putting her beer bottle onto the coffee table.

"So…what's up?" The remote expression on his gorgeous masculine face nearly made her cry. But she understood where it came from. He probably thought she'd invited him here to beg him to fix her car.

She might do that—but not now.

"Well, I have a decision to make, and I wanted your input." She felt her throat close with emotion and took a quick swig of beer to open it again.

"Yeah?" He still sounded skeptical. Where was that teasing bad boy that she had fallen in love with?

Love? Was she willing to admit that even to herself?

Hell, yes. Wasn't that why she had brought him here?

She held her beer bottle toward her lap and watched

it, not his face, as she said, "General Yarrow told me he's leaving for the Pentagon in a few days, after another exercise is held here between the two units. Both groups should be deployed for their joint mission next week, if all goes well, as it should."

She looked up to see Jason nodding. "Yeah, without the shenanigans of Colleen Hodell getting in the way." She opened her mouth to continue, but he beat her to it. "So…does that mean you're leaving, too?" There was a choking note in his voice. Dared she hope that he wanted her to stay?

"That depends," she said quietly. "Jason, do you know Lieutenant Quinn Parran and Staff Sergeant Kristine Norwood?"

"Sure. They're Alpha Force, stationed here. They're off on vacation now, but they helped to save Simon and Grace—Quinn's brother and sister-in-law—from some pretty bad stuff that happened on their honeymoon."

"That's right." Sara nodded. "They're on vacation… together. A lieutenant and a staff sergeant."

"Guess they're fraternizing," Jason said.

"Guess they are—but since they're members of Alpha Force, and things around here aren't as formal as the rest of the military, it's okay."

At that, Jason's tight expression seemed to change into something else. That hint of hope was back. So was his cocky attitude, the way he gave a half grin. "So I've heard."

"General Yarrow said he needs eyes and ears right here. Oh, he thinks your cousin and the others are doing a fine job running Alpha Force, but he suggested that I stay here on a long-term assignment and observe what's going on. Report to him often. Even offer suggestions for keeping Alpha Force running well and interacting with other units like the USFT."

"So you might stay here?"

"Yes, but that depends on you. If you think—"

She didn't get a chance to finish. Suddenly, both bottles of beer were on the table, and she was on her back on the narrow sofa, Jason on top of her. His lips were on hers. His hands were exploring her body, first on top of her uniform, then beneath it.

"Hey, Lieutenant," Jason whispered against her mouth. "I'm all for informality around here. Aren't you?"

"Yes," she said breathlessly. "But Jason, for how long—"

She didn't get to finish before he pulled back. "If you're asking how long I'd like to fraternize, how about forever? I love you, Sara."

His tone was so serious that it brought tears to her eyes. "I love you, too, Jason."

"And if you think you could stand hanging around a mechanic, former thief and wolf shapeshifter—"

"Stand it? I'd love it!"

He kissed her again. And again. And soon his hands were tearing off her clothes.

"Can I watch you shift again tonight?" she gasped between kisses and her own efforts at undressing him.

"Count on it, Lieutenant," he said, and then he entered her.

Epilogue

Just over a month had passed since the last exercise at Ft. Lukman between Alpha Force and the USFT—and the capturing of Colleen Hodell for her attempts on the general's life as well as Sara's and others.

A lot had happened in that month, Sara thought as she sat once more at the front of the assembly room. It was filled again with people from both military units, only now there was a true camaraderie between them.

As there should be. They had joined together in the mission to rescue the government workers held captive in the Middle East—and had succeeded in liberating them.

The rumbling of voices around her sounded pleased. An aura of excitement enveloped the audience members.

This was a special event. The USFT members would

be redeployed to another base as of tomorrow, their mission here accomplished.

That was why today had been chosen for the awarding of medals for bravery.

And more.

Sara sat between Melanie Harding-Connell, Drew's wife, on one side, and Captain Rynton Tierney on the other. Melanie had always been friendly, thanks to her close ties to Alpha Force. Rynton not so much—before. Now he was chatting with her on and off as though they were best friends.

"I still wish I'd been more than an on-site observer during the rescue," he was telling her. "Things happened so fast—and all to the good."

"Your real-time reports back here were definitely appreciated," Sara assured him. She had been on the radio with him a lot of the time, giving up-to-the-moment updates to General Yarrow and General Myars, who had remained here.

"You've heard, haven't you, that the terrorists we rounded up in the raid—those who survived—are being sneered at by their fellow countrymen for claiming that they were attacked by a bunch of dogs as well as snipers."

Sara laughed. "Yes, I heard that."

A hush suddenly befell the room. Sara quickly looked up. Speaking of the generals… There they were. Behind them stood the members of Alpha Force and the Ultra Special Forces Team who had been deployed on this mission.

That included Jason. Sara couldn't help smiling at

how proud he looked, all smiles up there in his camo uniform just like all the rest—but somehow he stood out.

"Thank you all for coming," General Yarrow said to the crowd. "This is a very special day."

"It sure is. For all of us." That was General Myars who, for once, didn't appear to be playing one-upmanship with the CO of Alpha Force.

They told everyone to stand, and the entire room pledged allegiance to the American flag.

And then it was time.

More than a dozen troops had been sent to perform the overseas mission, most of them from the units stationed here.

"I want to read the commendation from the commander in chief first," General Yarrow said, and he did. The president of the United States expressed his pride in the soldiers who had participated and those who had helped to train them.

Next both generals pulled out the medals of bravery and each awarded them to the members of their units who had performed so honorably in rescuing the captive American citizens.

That was when Sara couldn't help really smiling. Oh, it felt good to see the commendations given to Alpha Force members Drew Connell, Seth Ambers, Jock Larabey, Marshall Vincenzo and Simon Parran.

Their shifting aides, too, were commended.

She even appreciated the medals given to the USFT members: Cal Brown, Samantha Everly, Manning Breman and Vera Swainey.

But mostly she waited.

And then it was time. "We've saved the best for last," Greg Yarrow said. "Sergeant Jason Connell, please step forward."

Jason did, approaching the general.

"Jason, thanks to our camera equipment used on this mission, we both heard and saw your actions in combat, when two tangos attempted to flee with a couple of the hostages. You were in wolf form then, and despite the gunfire around you, you attacked the enemy, brought them both down and maintained domination over them until the USFT members were able to approach and take control. I hereby award you this medal for your bravery." The general took a box from the table near him, pulled out a medal and pinned it onto Jason's uniform."

"Thank you, sir," Jason said.

"And in addition," the general continued, "that special bravery both then and here at Ft. Lukman during our recent issues has earned you more, Sergeant. You have earned the right to be equals with the other shifters in Alpha Force. You are hereby promoted to Second Lieutenant." And General Yarrow pinned those bars onto Jason's uniform, as well.

Jason beamed. "I really appreciate this, sir." He saluted the general, then turned and saluted General Myars and the others. "We all did a damned good job, didn't we?" he asked his fellow soldiers.

They mostly laughed and shook his hand.

Sara couldn't get close to him. Not just then. But she would congratulate him later.

* * *

Damn it all, Jason thought a while later. Who'd have thought that he'd actually be proud to be in the military?

But heck, he was a real officer now.

Which meant…

The crowd was dispersing.

And there she was. Sara.

She hurried up to him. Saluted. "Good afternoon, Lieutenant," she said.

"Good afternoon, Lieutenant," he repeated.

They had been told of his promotion in advance, and she had already expressed her pride to him. But now…

"Hey. Come here. I want to show you my new… stuff. And prove to you how brave I really am."

She laughed. "I already know how brave you are. But I do want to see that medal more closely."

Lord, was she beautiful. And she looked at him so proudly that he couldn't help grinning back.

He hurried with her into Drew's office and closed the door behind them. His cuz had been primed to stay away for now.

"What's—" Sara began, and then she gasped. He saw the tears in her gorgeous blue-green eyes as she watched him go down on one knee.

He was about to do something he'd never have dared—before this moment.

"Lieutenant Sara McLinder, would you do me the honor of fraternizing with me for the rest of your life— I mean, becoming my wife?"

"Oh, Jason. Oh, yes, yes, yes."

He pulled out the box containing the ring he'd bought a few days earlier on a trip to D.C. He'd kept it in the glove compartment of his Mustang until a short while ago, just before the awards ceremony was to begin.

He stood and slipped the ring onto Sara's finger.

And this time, when they kissed, he knew it would be the first of forever.

* * * * *

ALEXIS MORGAN

USA TODAY bestselling author Alexis Morgan grew up in St. Louis, Missouri, graduating from the University of Missouri, St. Louis, with a B.A. in English, cum laude. She met her future husband sitting outside one of her classes in her freshman year. Eventually her husband's job took them to the Pacific Northwest where they've now lived for close to thirty years. Author of more than nineteen full-length books, short stories and novellas, Alexis began her career writing contemporary romances and then moved on to Western historicals. However, beginning in 2006, she crossed over to the dark side. She really loves writing paranormal romances, finding world-building and developing her own mythology for characters especially satisfying. She loves to hear from fans and can be reached at www.alexismorgan.com.

IMMORTAL COWBOY

Alexis Morgan

I want to dedicate this story to the memory of one of my favorite uncles, who shared his love of Zane Grey with me. I blame him for my lifelong love of stories about gamblers, cowboys, lawmen and gunslingers with hearts of gold.

Prologue

No one was ever alone on the mountain. Sometimes voices whispered in the mists, uttering words too faint to be understood. Eyes watched from the shadows, the weight of their gaze sitting heavily on those few brave enough to venture far up the slopes. The most sensitive of the visitors might feel the fleeting touch of hands without substance, leaving a chill on their soul. Smart folks didn't linger for long.

Chapter 1

Rayanne charged into the dappled shadows under the trees, following the narrow path that led toward town, the dense growth making it impossible to see more than a few feet ahead.

Where was he?

Her breath came in fits and jerks as she broke into a run down the game trail. A few feet in, her shoe caught on a root, sending her sprawling forward to land on her hands and knees. Ignoring the warm trickle of blood down her shin, Rayanne lurched back to her feet, wishing she'd taken the time to exchange her flip-flops for running shoes. But there hadn't been time for practical matters, not when Uncle Ray needed her.

The trees thinned out ahead, affording her a better view of the town. There wasn't much left of Blessing, but that was no surprise. The last residents had abandoned the place over a hundred years ago, leaving behind only the few buildings too stubborn to fall down.

No sign of her uncle in any direction. What would she do if he didn't come back soon? At thirteen, she could take care of herself for a while, but the mountain was a scary place to be all alone. She yelled Ray's name several times with no answer except the soft rustle of leaves.

Should she go back to the cabin and call the authorities for help in finding him? No, he'd never forgive her. Uncle Ray wanted nothing at all to do with the government that had taught him how to kill and then did nothing to repair the damage it had done to his soul.

So that left it up to her. As his namesake, she took her uncle's well-being very seriously.

Ignoring the pain in her side, she sprinted toward the old church, the one place that would give her the best vantage point. It sat right smack in the middle of Blessing, directly across from the saloon. Inside the sanctuary, she waited a few seconds for her eyes to adjust to the dim interior before making her way to the staircase that led up to the belfry. Out of habit, she avoided the missing second step, using the banister to pull herself up directly to the third. The rest of the stairs were sound enough, allowing her to reach the roof quickly.

The hinges on the door creaked in protest when she pushed it open and stepped out onto the narrow confines of the belfry. She carefully skirted the hole where a bell used to hang. It had probably been sold off for scrap metal by one of the former residents, but that was old history. Right now, all Rayanne cared about was finding her uncle.

She hated heights, and each step across the rough wood floor took all the courage she could muster. Dread made her feet heavy as she crossed the short distance to the front edge of the roof. She latched on to the worn wooden railing in relief. But the second she touched it, the air around her rippled and blurred. Her stomach heaved as she clutched the railing and waited for the world to quit rocking.

When the floor beneath her feet finally steadied, she risked a quick peek at the street below. She blinked twice and looked again.

"What the heck?" she asked, not expecting an answer.

The town below was no longer a skeleton of what it used to be. Instead, the street was lined with buildings that hadn't been there only minutes before, all constructed out of fresh-hewn lumber.

And there were people—men, women and children—going about their business as if they strolled through Blessing every day, all wearing clothes straight out of a history museum. Were they reenactors? She couldn't imagine Uncle Ray tolerating such an intrusion on his privacy.

Besides, how could she have missed seeing them on her way through town? As she scanned the faces to see if Uncle Ray was among the throng of people, a shout went up, drawing everyone's attention to the far end of town. A group of men on horseback appeared in the distance, riding hard for the center of town, sending everyone on the street scurrying for cover. Something was dreadfully wrong. Rayanne ducked down even though the railing wouldn't provide much cover.

Just as the last child was dragged inside the old store and the door slammed shut, a solitary man appeared in the doorway of the saloon, carrying a rifle in his right hand. He paused long enough to inhale deeply on his cigarette before tossing it on the wooden sidewalk and grinding it out with the heel of his boot.

He stepped out into the street and the bright sunshine, moving with a lethal grace. Just like the others, he wore an authentic-looking costume: a cowboy hat, boots and a duster that had seen a lot of hard miles. His hat sat tipped back slightly, giving her a glimpse of coal-black hair. From the faded blue of his shirt to the scuffs on his boots, whoever had designed his costume had an amazing eye for detail.

Her pulse tripped and stumbled as the stranger turned to face the oncoming riders. He pushed his duster open, revealing a lethal-looking pair of revolvers. The holsters rode low on his hips, looking all too comfortable there as if he'd been born wearing them. There was a deadly stillness about him that she could feel even from her perch two stories above the street.

A few daring people in town peeked out of windows and through cracks of open doors. Playacting was one thing, but the scene unfolding in front of her felt too real, dangerous. If Rayanne could've run away, she would have. But her feet ignored her orders and remained right where they were.

The riders slowed their horses to a walk and fanned

out across the narrow confines of the street. If the man was nervous about being badly outnumbered, he gave no sign of it. Instead, he planted his feet in a wide stance, as if hurricane winds couldn't have budged him.

Was she witnessing an actual gunfight straight out of the Old West? The tension radiating from everyone in sight certainly seemed real enough. She should go back to hunting for Uncle Ray, but at that moment nothing could've dragged her away from the drama unfolding before her. When the riders started forward again, time stopped and the seconds stretched to the breaking point.

The hinges creaked behind her, warning her that she was no longer alone. Thinking it had to be her uncle, Rayanne smiled in relief and turned to scold him for worrying her so. Instead, a man she'd never seen before stepped through the narrow doorway, ducking to avoid the church bell.

Before she could wonder much about its sudden reappearance, she saw that he, too, was heavily armed. She shrank back into the corner, hoping that he wouldn't notice her even though she huddled in plain sight.

He ignored Rayanne completely as he crouched down to peer over the railing. When he brought his rifle up to his shoulder, there was no doubt in her mind that he had his sights centered on the lone man below and meant to do him serious harm. When he pulled back on the hammer, preparing to shoot, her voice finally broke loose. Her terrified warning echoed down the street.

The man on the street spun to face the church. For a long heartbeat, his pale blue eyes met Rayanne's just before he fired his own rifle. The man beside her jerked and stumbled. He had a puzzled look on his face as he slowly sank to the wooden floor, his fingers trying to hold back the red stain spreading over the front of his shirt.

For a few seconds, silence reigned. Then blood, hot and bright, rained down on Rayanne's face and hands. At first she only whimpered as she frantically tried to scrub her hands clean on her clothes. But when Rayanne saw the man's eyes staring up at her, dull and lifeless, she screamed and kept on screaming until her throat was raw and her face burned with the hot acid of tears and fresh blood.

Her uncle finally appeared and pulled her into the solid warmth of his arms. He stroked her back, murmuring words of comfort in that awkward way of his. After a few moments, he stepped back.

How odd. Ray no longer towered over her. Either he'd grown shorter or she was taller. He'd also aged, the gray streaks in his red-gold hair more pronounced. All of that was strange enough, but it was the sadness in his smile that caused her heart to stutter.

"I've always loved you, Rayanne. I always will. I'm so proud of the woman you've become."

Woman? She was barely a teenager.

Ray brushed her hair back from her face. His eyes, so like her own, looked at her with such serious intent. "You have the gift, same as me. The mountain and

Blessing need your special touch. Don't let anyone tell you different. Promise me that much."

She had no idea what he was talking about, but she nodded, anyway. "I promise."

"That's real good, sweetheart." Then he looked around. "It's time for me to go."

He smiled one last time as he slowly faded into shadow with no substance, leaving her alone on the rooftop bereft and still splattered with blood.

Rayanne bolted from her bed and went stumbling across to the bathroom, barely making it to the toilet in time. Kneeling on the floor, she heaved and retched until there was nothing left to come up. After a bit, she pushed herself back to her feet, waiting for another wave of nausea to pass before stepping closer to the sink.

It had been years since the nightmare had been so vivid, and she needed her mirror's reassurance that she was twenty-eight, not thirteen. Even with her face pale and her hair a tangled mess, it helped to calm her nerves a little.

She grabbed the robe hanging on the back of the bathroom door, an old flannel one Uncle Ray had loaned her one summer. Having that little piece of him close by always comforted her. Her next stop was the kitchen to brew a cup of chamomile tea. Along the way, she turned on every light she passed.

Anything to keep the shadows at bay.

After putting the kettle on the stove, she sank down on the nearest chair and waited for her heart to stop pounding. Dawn was still an hour away, but she wouldn't risk going back to bed for fear the dream would play itself out again. She'd had as much terror as she could handle in a night, thank you very much.

Things might be different if she had someone there to help ward off the fear, but she didn't. Bright lights, hot tea and a warm robe would have to suffice.

Just as the kettle started to whistle, the phone rang. Rayanne stared at it for several seconds before reaching for the receiver, her hand trembling hard enough she almost dropped it.

"Hello?"

"Rayanne? I'm sorry if I woke you up, but I thought you'd want to know. Uncle Ray passed away during the night. It was his heart."

Her mother's stark words stole the oxygen in the room, leaving Rayanne struggling to breathe around the lump of grief in her chest. Had Ray really come into her dream to say goodbye? She wouldn't put it past him.

"Rayanne? Did you hear what I said? Ray's gone."

She forced herself to answer. "Yes, I did, and I'm really sorry, Mom. I'll call you later about the arrangements."

Then she hung up and let the tears come.

One week later

Rayanne taped up the box and set it down on the floor by her office door. She had more packing to do, but right now a break was definitely in order. Dropping into her chair, she popped the top on a bottle of water and then picked up the book that had come in the morning mail. Flipping through it distracted her from the quagmire of her own thoughts.

The past seven days had been hell, plain and simple. They'd honored her uncle's request that they not make a fuss over his passing. In truth, he'd had few friends, and they weren't the kind to stand on ceremony.

Two days later, a lawyer had contacted her about Ray's estate. Her mother had been with her when the call came in and insisted on accompanying Rayanne to the appointment. What a disaster that had been. She'd spent the ensuing days either berating her late brother for forcing Rayanne to move up to his mountain cabin to claim her inheritance or demanding that Rayanne contest the will. The attorney had repeatedly emphasized the terms of the will were rock solid, but her mother had a habit of hearing only what she wanted.

Rayanne had finally quit answering her mother's calls. Eventually, she'd have to deal with her, but right now she had other priorities.

Lost in her thoughts, a knock on her office door startled her. Who could it be? Surely her mother wouldn't have tracked her down here. Setting her book aside, she unlocked the door. When she saw who it was, relief had her smiling.

"Hi, Shawn, I'm glad it's you. I was afraid my mom had decided to drop in for a visit." She looked around at the surrounding chaos in her office. "Sorry about the mess. I was just taking a short breather before I finish packing."

She pointed toward the stack of boxes she'd yet to fill in hopes he'd take the hint. He didn't. Instead, he shoved a pile of papers aside to make room for himself on the corner of her desk. He picked up the book she'd been reading.

"Still studying up on dead towns, I see."

"The correct term is ghost towns, not dead ones."

She let a little of her irritation show. Even though he was teasing, she wasn't in the mood. She took her research seriously. Normally, Shawn respected that, but he'd been in a strange mood lately.

She took the book from him and set it aside. "What's up?"

"When were you going to tell me that you'd asked for a leave of absence from the university?" His voice was a shade too cool for the question to be completely casual.

Oh, that. Whoops. "I only got the approval late yesterday afternoon, and I asked the dean to make an announcement this morning at the staff meeting."

Shawn's eyebrows snapped down tight over his eyes. "That's not the same as you telling me yourself."

She'd been dreading this moment. "I left you a voice mail this morning."

His expression lightened up a little. Good. She really hadn't meant to hurt his feelings, but she'd already faced off against her mother over her acceptance of the terms of Uncle Ray's will. She didn't want to have to defend her decision to anyone else.

"It's just that all of this is so sudden, and I'm feeling a bit overwhelmed."

He looked marginally happier. "Are you sure putting your life on hold is a good idea?"

Was that what she was doing? Maybe, but then what choice did she have?

"I'm simply following the dictates of my uncle's will. He didn't leave me any wiggle room on this."

Shawn drew a deep breath. "Somehow I doubt you would've fought the terms regardless."

He was right. "I'm sorry, Shawn. I haven't been myself since all of this happened. Ray's death hit me hard. The semester is almost over, so the dean was pretty understanding about me leaving early. One of the grad students will cover the last few classes for me and give the final."

"That's good. I'd hate to see you jeopardize your career here at the university on a whim."

That wasn't what this was, but Shawn clearly had something on his mind. "Just spit it out, Shawn."

Her comment startled him, his smile a bit rueful. "Okay, here's the thing. I was hoping the two of us could go somewhere together this summer for a few days, maybe a week."

He shifted to look at her more directly. "I'm not picky about where. Heck, we can even go explore some of those dusty, old ghost towns you love so much. I just thought some time away from all of this—" he waved his hand to indicate more than just the clutter in her office "—would be good for *us*."

The emphasis on the last word wasn't lost on her, and perhaps he was right. Some time spent away from their normal surroundings would definitely answer some questions for both of them. They'd had dinner a few times, but she'd been reluctant to take the relationship to the next level.

Obviously, he wasn't.

Part of the problem was the recent resurgence of her nightmares. She'd never shared the story with Shawn and didn't intend to anytime soon. It was the main reason that she'd never invited him to spend the night at her place. Until she could be sure that she wouldn't wake up screaming, that couldn't change.

On the other hand, she had to wonder that if she'd been convinced that there was something special possible between the two of them, would she have trusted him with her secrets? Their friendship was familiar and comfortable. If it was ever going to be more, she needed to resolve the questions that had plagued her for years once and for all.

For now, she had to offer Shawn an answer that he could understand, a version of the truth that he could accept without revealing her real reasons for going back to Blessing alone. Once she'd made peace with her past, maybe she'd know if there was a place for Shawn in her future.

"I plan to spend the time I'm at the cabin on my research. Things are too up in the air right now for me to make any other commitments."

"Will you at least think about it?"

He wasn't going to give up unless she conceded at least that much. "Yes, I'll think about it, but no promises."

Her effort at a reassuring smile must have succeeded

because he gave her an approving nod. "Great. Now I'd better get back to my office. We've both got work to do."

As a fellow college instructor, he knew the constant pressure to publish. She let him think that was what was driving her research, a far more acceptable explanation for her almost obsessive need to study the past.

In truth, the dream that had haunted her for years was the real reason she scoured bookstores and the internet for new primary sources of information on the lost towns of the West, and specifically about Blessing, Colorado.

It didn't help that all she felt when Shawn left was relief. Her mother would be the first one to tell her that she was being foolish. Shawn was educated, handsome and financially secure; in short, everything Rayanne should want in a man. She liked him; she really did. What did it say about her that she'd rather focus her energy on research than on building a relationship?

This wasn't getting her anywhere. A few more minutes of reading and then back to work. As she opened the book, a dank, musty smell wafted up from the pages, but she didn't mind. Books as old as this one were rarely in pristine condition. Besides, it was the words on the pages that were important.

The passage she'd been reading made her smile. It was like having a private conversation with someone who had lived and breathed more than a century ago. The author, Jubal Lane, had clearly shared her interest in the boom and bust of the towns that dotted the landscape in the late 1800s. The only difference was that he'd seen them firsthand.

Jealousy was pointless, but at least she could see those same towns through his eyes. She read slowly to savor Jubal's thoughts and descriptions, pausing periodically to make notes. When she was about to stop, a word at the bottom of the page caught her attention: Blessing.

With her pulse racing, she quickly scanned the remaining few lines. Jubal Lane had actually visited Blessing, the town that had formed the backdrop of the nightmares that had haunted her since she was thirteen years old.

Before that summer, she'd played in the deserted buildings as a child, loving every minute of her visits with Uncle Ray. But that last trip, everything had changed and she hadn't been back since. The memories flooded through her mind.

How ironic that she'd run across a reference to Blessing now when it was too late to share it with Ray.

Rather than letting herself get dragged back into the past, she closed the book and put it in her bag. For now, she had to finish before the shipping company arrived. Most of her things were headed for storage; the remaining few would be shipped to the cabin up on the mountain where she'd need them for her research.

As she sealed the last box, she paused to look around her office. Odd that it felt as if she were leaving for good rather than for the summer. That was ridiculous. Of course she'd be back in the fall. The terms of Uncle

Ray's will had only dictated she had to live on the mountain through August, not the rest of her life.

By the end of summer, hopefully, she will have laid the past to rest once and for all. She'd return rested and ready to pick up the pieces of her life here at the university. That was her plan, and she was sticking to it.

Later that night, Rayanne curled up in her favorite chair, ready to learn what Jubal had to say about Blessing. Since no one in her family had ever answered her questions about the town, perhaps she'd finally find them for herself.

Did she really even want to?

As a rule, she did her best not to think about the solitary man who wore a black duster and carried a rifle. After all, he and the others only existed in her imagination. But if that were true, why had she continued to be plagued by such vivid, horrifying dreams about them?

Worse yet, why had she secretly compared every man she'd met to a nameless man with black hair and blue eyes?

She'd spent years searching for even a mention of Blessing with no luck until now. With a mixture of trepidation and excitement, she opened the book to the last page she'd read and started over at the top.

When she reached the lines where Jubal mentioned his next stop was to be Blessing, she took a deep breath and turned the page. His words drew her back into the past. He described the valley where the town sat with near-perfect detail, enough to convince her he was talking about the one on Uncle Ray's mountain.

Jubal said most of the townspeople had moved on to greener pastures after some tragedy had occurred. He also alluded to a gunslinger who had met his fate in the street outside the saloon, his tone implying the man had gotten no less than he'd deserved.

Rayanne stopped right there to give herself time to process what she'd just read: there really had been a gunfight in Blessing. Did Jubal have more to say on the subject? With her pulse pounding in her head, she drew a deep breath and turned another page.

"Whoa, this can't be!"

But it was. Not only had Jubal written more about the shootout, but he'd also included a picture. As the reality sank in, her hands shook so badly she dropped the book. She picked it up again.

Nothing had changed. Even in the faded tintype, it was easy enough to recognize the man who'd haunted her dreams for fifteen years. He wasn't wearing a hat, but the hair was the same. So were the intense, pale eyes that stared up at her from the page. She bet they were blue. In fact, she knew they were.

The gunslinger had a name—Wyatt McCain.

He was real.

He'd lived and died right there in the dusty streets of Blessing.

For years, her family and the shrink they'd dragged her to had insisted that she'd made it all up. Her mother had blamed her father for filling Rayanne's head with stories about the Old West. In return, her father had blamed her mother for leaving their impressionable young daughter alone with her nutcase brother. The shrink had blamed it all on her parents' constant bickering and its effect on their daughter. Idiots.

None of them had even considered the possibility that it had all been real—the people, the gunfire, the blood and, most of all, Wyatt McCain.

Had Uncle Ray known? Was that why he'd come to her in the dream to say goodbye? He'd mentioned a gift they'd shared. What had that been about?

Now that she had a few facts to go on, she wouldn't rest until she'd learned everything she could. Once she had her arsenal of evidence, the facts would free her of the nightmares from her past. Even if no one else ever knew the truth, she would.

A real man had died that day in the streets of Blessing, one who haunted her dreams a hundred years after his passing. She would tell his story—her story, too. Her purpose clear, she set the book aside and started a list of what she needed to take care of before she left for the mountain.

Chapter 2

The road leading up to Ray's cabin was in far better condition than she'd remembered, but otherwise it all looked the same. Funny, it felt as if the cabin had been patiently waiting all these years for her return, but this time as owner rather than guest.

Rayanne eased her car around a slow bend to the right, her pulse picking up speed even if the car didn't. After fifteen years, she was about to catch her first glimpse of the chimney that marked the location of her new home. The trees had grown taller, but she could just make out a glimpse of gray stone.

Tension had been riding her hard ever since she'd learned of Ray's death. All the arguments about her decision to take a last-minute leave of absence from her job and move to the mountain hadn't helped. But as she neared the cabin and the freedom it had always represented, the muscles in her shoulders and neck eased, and her mood lightened.

"Well, Uncle Ray, we're almost there."

Wouldn't her mother freak out to hear Rayanne carrying on a one-sided conversation with her uncle? Well, not him, exactly, but the pewter urn that contained his last remains. One of the sidebars in his will was a request that Rayanne scatter his ashes on the mountain. He'd left it up to Rayanne to pick the time and place.

But until she carried out his wishes, she found comfort in the notion that her uncle was riding shotgun and could actually hear her. Maybe she was losing her mind just like her mother had said when she learned Rayanne had willingly accepted the terms of the will without a court fight.

Not that her mom's opinion mattered. The mountain and the town that had haunted Rayanne for years was now hers, lock, stock and belfry. That is, provided she moved there and stayed through the entire summer. Come September, she was free to stay on or move back to the city. But if she didn't follow the dictates of her uncle's will to the letter, the entire estate would pass to a distant cousin. She couldn't bear the thought of that happening.

It hadn't been a surprise that Shawn had agreed with her parents. However, if there was any hope of a future for the two of them, she needed to find the answers she'd been looking for.

"I'm sorry to have to tell you this, Uncle Ray, but I don't plan to live up here for the rest of my life."

A stab of guilt had her giving the urn a remorseful glance. "But I will stay long enough to find answers to questions that my folks would never let me ask. And with luck, I can find enough information about the short history of Blessing itself to write a paper."

Her mouth curved in a wide smile as she considered the possibilities. If she didn't have enough information for a scholarly paper, there was another option. She loved historical romances, and she already knew the time period inside and out. Surely she could come up with a story line that fit the few facts about Blessing that she'd been able to uncover.

The ideas twirled and danced through her head. A beautiful schoolteacher for the heroine would be just the ticket. And the hero would be the sheriff, strong and valiant and handsome. She could picture Shawn in the role, his arm around her waist as together they defied the bad guys.

But then a vision of a gunslinger dressed in black shoved that picture aside, replacing it instead with a man who moved with predatory grace and had a killer's ice-colored stare. Wyatt McCain. Rayanne flushed hot and then cold. A woman would have to be a fool to think a man like that could be anyone's hero.

The excitement died just that quickly.

Finally, the last of the trees faded into an open meadow. Her breath caught in her throat as the cabin came into sight. She hit the brakes, bringing her car to an abrupt halt, needing time to adjust to the onslaught of emotions threatening to overwhelm her. It was almost impossible to sort them all out—relief, trepidation, remembered joy and a great deal of pain that Uncle Ray would never be waiting there to greet her again.

She put the car back into gear and slowly pulled up in front of the cabin. The sun was already sliding down the far side of the sky. If she didn't hurry, she'd be unpacking in the dark. The idea worried her more than she'd expected it to.

She pulled out the ring of keys that the attorney had given her at their last visit. Each one was carefully labeled in Uncle Ray's familiar scrawl. She picked up the urn and stepped up on the porch.

As the door swung open, Rayanne stepped back through time. Her uncle hadn't changed a thing since she'd left all those years ago. Maybe there were a few more books stuffed in the shelves and the sofa was a bit more worn, but that was all. She set the urn down on a small table in the corner and got busy settling in.

Bedtime always came early on the mountain. As Rayanne brushed her teeth, she studied her image in the mirror. Uncle Ray's hair had been a little curlier than hers, but the color had been the same, a shade somewhere between blond and red. They'd also shared a tendency to freckle during the summer and the same bright green eyes. In a lot of ways, she'd resembled her favorite relative more than she had either one of her parents. Once again, the thought of him had her eyes stinging with the threat of tears.

It was definitely time to crawl into bed. Would coming here intensify her nightmares? She sure hoped not.

The past several nights she'd slept without incident, a huge relief. She stepped across the threshold into her bedroom, happy that her childhood sanctuary had remained unchanged.

She turned down the quilt that had covered the bed for longer than either she or Ray had been alive. Trailing her fingers over the familiar patches of fabric, she wondered again about the people who had worn the various bits and pieces of cloth in shirts and dresses.

Had they been happy in their lives? She closed her eyes as she caressed the cloth, worn smooth and soft by the years. Maybe another girl had slept under this very same quilt, tucked in by loving hands with a kiss and a wish for sweet dreams or maybe the quilt had been a wedding gift for a bride about to start her new life as a wife.

She doubted she would ever know the real answers, but it didn't matter. The warmth of the quilt gave her a connection to the past, one that appealed to her deep interest in history. Stretching out on the narrow bed felt like heaven. A huge yawn surprised a giggle out of her as she turned onto her back to watch the sweep of the stars and moon through the skylight overhead. Just as she had as a small girl, she fell asleep counting the stars twinkling in the night sky.

A new energy had arrived on the mountain, altering the patterns and drawing his attention toward the cabin. Ray's niece was back. He recognized her even though she'd grown into a woman with long legs and ridiculously short hair.

Drifting closer to the porch, he stared up at the open window high up near the peak of the roof. The man's room had been on the other side. He'd always kept his window closed and the doors locked against the perils of the darkness, real and imagined.

But the girl had her window open to the night. Would she continue to keep it that way if she found out about him and the others? A grim smile crossed his face briefly. Hell, even the others knew to steer clear of him. They certainly recognized bad news when they saw it; maybe the girl would, too.

The light in the window winked out. He lost interest in his vigil and moved away, back toward town. Folks still called it Blessing. What a joke that was, one he doubted the others appreciated. But then he didn't give a damn what they thought, any more than they cared about him.

He passed through the trees, startling a doe and her fawn. As quietly as he moved, he was surprised they even noticed him. But after one look in his direction, the wary beasts bounded away, covering a lot of distance with each graceful leap. He paused to watch them disappear into the shadows, enjoying the sight. God knew there was little enough that he took pleasure in these days.

His thoughts drifted back toward the cabin and its sole occupant. The redhead had been there before. It had been a long while since she'd last visited the man, although time had become too fluid over the years for him to be sure how long it had been. An uneasy feeling churned in his stomach as vague memories stirred about this girl, now a woman. Used to be, she'd come and run wild through the woods and the town, only to leave right before it all unfolded.

All except that last time.

Damn it to hell and back, how many months had slipped past him unnoticed? If she was on the mountain, it could be almost time. Again. No wonder the deer had fled his presence. He didn't blame them one bit for running. Canny creatures that they were, they knew when death roamed free on the mountain. He turned his back on the cabin and faded into the shadows, alone and wishing he could stay that way.

A cool breeze drifted through the open window, carrying a fresh, woodsy scent with it. Rayanne drew a deep breath and smiled without opening her eyes, still caught up in the fading memory of a dream, a good one this time. Instead of fearing Blessing, she'd been walking through the town hand in hand with a handsome man.

That he bore a striking resemblance to Wyatt Mc-Cain came as no surprise. After all, he'd dominated her thoughts ever since she'd discovered his picture. Only in her dream world, he seemed less grim, younger and more carefree. She woke up smiling with the sound of his laughter echoing in her mind.

What an interesting start to her day!

The telephone started ringing. Cell phones couldn't get reception this high up, so Ray had run a telephone line to the cabin. No doubt it was her mother calling to check on her.

Rayanne sat up, hoping if she moved slowly enough the woman would give up. No such luck. As soon as the phone quit ringing, it started right up again in the time it took for her mother to hit redial.

Rayanne reached for the receiver. Figuring on a long call, she stretched out and made herself comfortable.

"Hello, Mother."

"Well, I guess you made it safely since you're able to talk on the phone."

Nothing like a snide remark from a parent to start the day off on a low note. Why couldn't the woman just admit that she'd been worried?

"By the time I got settled in last night, it was too late to call."

A small exaggeration perhaps, but it would've been rude to admit to the truth, that she'd never even considered calling.

"I can't believe that you're really up there." Rayanne could picture her mother leaning against the kitchen counter, with a nonfat double latte in her hand.

"Of course, I never understood the appeal of the great outdoors. Seriously, Rayanne, I know you loved my brother, but you don't have to exile yourself up there just to prove it. I should've put my foot down about this."

As if that would've done any good. Maybe someday the woman would accept the fact that Rayanne had grown up and could make her own decisions, even ones her mother didn't approve of.

Especially ones she didn't approve of.

"I'm fine, Mom. I'm safe. I'm happy."

Please let it go at that. She really didn't want to start the day off rehashing old arguments.

"That's good for you. But what about Shawn? Is he happy?" Her voice clearly indicated she was playing her trump card.

She was wrong. "My relationship with Shawn is not open for discussion."

Mainly because she wasn't all that sure they still had one. He hadn't spoken more than a dozen words to her after she'd announced her decision to leave school early and move to the mountain.

"Your father isn't pleased to hear that you're back up there."

Okay, that got Rayanne's attention. "Since when are you and Dad on speaking terms?"

Her mother's voice turned frosty. "He deserved to know what you were up to, especially when your last visit ended up such a disaster."

"Mom, that was years ago. I'm here to do research, nothing more. You shouldn't have gotten Dad all worried for nothing."

She'd give her mother another thirty seconds and then pretend that her reception was failing.

"If I don't hear from you every day, I will be calling the authorities to report you missing or something. Whatever it takes to get someone up there to check on you."

Oh, brother. Rayanne counteroffered. "I'll call you once a week and no more than that."

Rayanne's hand ached from gripping the phone so hard.

"That's not enough." Her mom was going into full martyr mode now. Tears wouldn't be far behind.

"It's my best offer, Mom." And just to make sure her mother got it straight, she repeated it. "Once a week or not at all."

After a long, painful silence, her mother conceded defeat. "Fine, Rayanne. Be selfish. Once a week will have to do."

"I love you, Mom." She did, really, even if the woman drove her crazy most of the time. "I'll call you on Saturday. Bye."

She disconnected the call before her mother could think of something else to argue about. With that behind her, Rayanne headed for the shower, anxious for the day to begin. It was going to be a good one; she could just tell.

Chapter 3

He wasn't sure why he'd returned to the clearing. Curiosity wasn't something he normally indulged in anymore, but it had drawn him back to the cabin. There was no smoke coming out of the chimney. Either the woman must not mind the morning chill or else she wasn't up yet.

When he reached the door of the cabin, he sneered at the lock. As if that flimsy bit of steel could keep him out. Once inside, he looked around. Had he been in the cabin recently? He couldn't remember. Most of the time he'd watched the man from the cover of the woods or where the shadows deepened to near black by the porch at night.

Ray had usually sensed his presence, even though he'd rarely said anything. Maybe it was because what

Ray had seen in the war had been so much worse. Either way, there had been real strength in the man right up to the end. The former soldier had always been silent but content in his own skin.

Unless his demons were riding him hard. Then Ray would stalk the woods, muttering under his breath. Sometimes he stood at the edge of a cliff and screamed out the names of men who'd never set foot on the mountain except in his mind.

But Ray was gone now. They'd come with flashing lights and carried his body back down the mountain. Now someone else, the woman, had come to the mountain to live. He hated having his routine disturbed, but he'd have no choice but to adjust to her presence.

She'd seen him once. Did she remember?

A noise from overhead caught his attention. She was talking to someone, even though he knew full well that she was alone. No one passed through his territory unnoticed. A few minutes later, the shower came on, warning him that his time was limited. He needed to leave before she walked down those steps, although it was tempting to linger long enough to get a closer look at her.

But for the moment, he had time to poke around a bit. He moved toward the kitchen where she'd dumped a few things on the table the night before. He studied the clutter, trying to make sense of the stuff. It wasn't worth the energy it would take to dump the bag out. Besides, he wasn't there to drive her away, just to learn more about the woman who would be sharing his mountain and town.

A paper caught his attention. Careful not to disturb anything, he gently reached out to touch it. Would she remember if she'd left it faceup or facedown? He didn't care. Hell, what was life without a few risks?

Laughing at his own joke, he turned the paper over. Shock rolled through him as soon as he got a good look at the picture staring up at him, leaving him unable to do anything but stand and stare down at the image.

Where the hell had she gotten that?

So caught up in the memories that came flooding back, he failed to notice the silence from upstairs. The shower was no longer running. Before he could react, one of the steps behind him creaked. Hellfire and damnation, the woman was coming down the stairs.

The hot steam had washed away the last bit of tension from talking to her mother. Eventually, maybe she'd long for the company at the other end of the phone line but definitely not today.

About halfway down the stairs, a weird shiver started at the base of her spine and danced its way right up to her head. Even the hair on her arms stood up, as if lightning were about to strike. Had the late spring weather taken a sudden turn for the worse?

No, sunshine was streaming in through the skylights overhead.

Rayanne couldn't shrug off the feeling that something wasn't right. As a city girl born and bred, maybe she wasn't ready to face life alone on the mountain. However, she wasn't about to admit that her mother had been right all along. No, it was only a matter of adjusting to the quiet murmurs of nature outside the window rather than the jarring cacophony of city noise.

That was when she heard a sound that had nothing to do with any four-legged beast that lived on the mountain: human footsteps. She swallowed, trying to get her heart out of her throat so she could breathe. The silence felt frozen now, as if in anticipation of the next sweep of cloth against cloth. It wasn't long in coming.

"Who's there?" Her voice echoed hollowly.

No answer. To her surprise, that made her mad. She came down two more stairs, hoping to find evidence that it was only her imagination running wild. This time the steps were more definite and headed right for the door. Should she remain cowering on the stairs forever or take control of the situation?

This was her home; she would not be a prisoner of her own fear. Besides, if the intruder had meant her harm, he'd had ample opportunity.

Bracing herself for the worst, she charged down the last few steps, determined to give someone a piece of her mind. The bottom few stairs curved down into the kitchen near the door. One glance told her that the door was still bolted but that didn't mean much. If someone had broken in, it could have been through a window, instead. But if so, why hadn't she heard anything?

Nothing in the kitchen looked disturbed, but then she sensed a movement off to her right. Time slowed as her mind scrambled to make sense of what she was seeing. She made a grab for the wall as her knees gave way. Surely this was some kind of joke.

"Who are you?"

Her question was little more than a whisper, but the man heard it all right. There was no mistaking the temper in those ice-blue eyes, not that she really needed him to answer her. His outfit matched the one he'd worn in the picture he held clutched in his fist: scuffed boots, a faded shirt, dark trousers and a worn duster. It couldn't really be him, but every cell in her body screamed that it was.

"Wyatt McCain?"

His name was the last thing she said as the floor rushed up to meet her.

Cool. Smooth. Hard.

Slowly, the fog in Rayanne's mind faded and awareness of her surroundings returned. Right now, her cheek was pressed against something flat and cool to the touch. Her eyes refused to open; instead, she concentrated on moving her right hand and then her left.

Her fingertips felt just the slightest grittiness to the surface, like a hardwood floor that hadn't been swept recently. She slowly processed all the data, because the side of her face was pounding. Finally, she arrived at the obvious conclusion that she was sprawled on the floor, most likely in the kitchen.

Why?

Flashes of memory played out in her head. Shower. Brushing her teeth. Sweats rather than jeans. All of that made sense. What next? She'd started downstairs to fix her breakfast. Halfway down she'd heard something.

No. Someone. Wyatt McCain. Well, not him, but someone who looked just like him, down to the faded blue shirt and scuffed boots. Thanks to her dream, his image had been the first one she thought of.

Her eyes popped open, and she found the strength to push herself up to a sitting position. Ignoring the fresh wave of dizziness, she scooted back until she bumped up against the nearest wall. It offered support but no comfort as she surveyed her surroundings.

From where she sat, she could see the entire ground floor of the A-frame cabin. She was alone. Gradually, her pulse slowed to somewhere near normal, and the pain on the right side of her face eased up enough to allow her to think straight.

The deadbolt on the front door was still firmly in place. No broken windows. No back door, so no other exit. Adding up all the facts, she had to think that she'd imagined the whole thing. Whatever she'd heard had to have been just the wind or a tree limb brushing against the cabin in the wind.

The side of her face was tender to the touch. Obviously, she'd tripped and fallen, landing hard enough to bruise. Nothing that a bag of ice and some aspirin wouldn't cure. She slowly pushed herself to her feet, taking care not to move too quickly.

She rooted around in the cabinets until she found a small plastic bag and filled it with ice. After zipping it shut, she wrapped it in a thin dish towel and pressed it to her cheek. The cold burn stung but gradually numbed the pain. Next up, the painkillers.

She always carried some in her purse, which she thought she'd left here in the kitchen. Where was it?

Hadn't she set it down on the counter when she'd first come in last night?

It wasn't there now. She was sure she hadn't taken it upstairs with her, so that left the living room. Before she'd gone two steps, she spotted the strap of her purse sticking out from underneath the microwave cart. She bent down to pick it up, wincing as the motion exacerbated the throbbing in her face.

How had her purse gotten down there? It wasn't anywhere close to where she'd landed on the floor, so she hadn't knocked it off the counter. Another mystery with no answer. Rather than dwell on it, she dug out the small bottle at the bottom of the purse and took out two pills. She swallowed them with a drink of water.

Next up, caffeine and lots of it. The few minutes that it took to set the coffee to brewing kept her too busy to think about the things that didn't quite add up.

Such as the noise she'd heard, and how her purse came to be under the cart. While she waited for the coffee to perk, she leaned against the counter and studied the room to see if anything else was out of place.

Her computer pack sat right where she'd left it on the kitchen counter. She frowned. Something was different, though. Last night, one of the last things she'd done was look at the picture of Wyatt McCain that she'd printed out. She smiled. Uncle Ray would've gotten such a kick out of what she'd learned about Blessing when the town had been alive.

But now the picture wasn't where she'd left it.

She searched her pack in case she'd put it back. No dice. Nor was it in the living room or anywhere in plain sight. She'd found her purse under the cart. Had the picture fallen there, too?

Only one way to find out. She tugged on the cart, wheeling it out of its usual position. The only thing she uncovered was a wadded-up piece of paper, obviously not the picture of Wyatt. Uncle Ray must have missed the trash can with it.

She bent down to pick it up. Before throwing the paper away, she'd make sure it wasn't something important. As she smoothed it out on the counter, her pulse kicked right back into overdrive. Okay, so she'd been wrong. Uncle Ray hadn't thrown this paper away. He couldn't have for one important reason: he'd never seen it. Wyatt McCain's piercing pale eyes glared up at her, the wrinkled paper doing nothing to dilute the intensity of his gaze.

This was the picture she'd brought with her, but she hadn't been the one to crumple it up. Chills washed through her as she looked around the room. She had proof positive right there in her hands that she hadn't imagined the sound of someone moving around in the kitchen earlier.

She dropped the paper on the counter and hurried to double-check the lock on the door and the windows. It didn't take long to verify that everything was locked up tight. Even if someone had the key to the deadbolt, they couldn't have fastened the chain from the outside. There was no obvious sign that the cabin walls had been breached.

Surely she would've heard someone climbing to the second floor? Had she left her window open when she came downstairs? She grabbed the nearest weapon she could find, her uncle's rolling pin, and charged upstairs. Sure enough, her window was still open. She knelt on the bed to close it and throw the latch.

She paused long enough to survey the clearing surrounding the cabin. Her past visits had taught her that anyone walking across the meadow while the dew was still on the grass left a visible trail. From what she could see, there was no sign that anyone had passed that way.

She checked the tree line, too. No movement there except for a few birds flittering among the leaves. So it was just her, the bright morning sunshine and the mountain.

From there, she went into the bathroom, but the window in there was too narrow for anyone but a small child to squeeze through.

That left Uncle Ray's room. She hesitated before opening the door. Eventually, she'd have to cross that threshold, but she hadn't planned on doing it so soon. It was Uncle Ray's most private space, his sanctuary from the world outside. Even when she'd visited him, she'd never been allowed inside.

She turned the doorknob but still hesitated before pushing the door open. This was silly. What did she expect to find? She gave the door a soft shove and took a single step forward into the space that her uncle had kept private.

Tears stung her eyes as she realized how much the room looked like her uncle—solid, comfortable, plain. The queen-size bed filled up most of the space. Made from pine, the design was simple, which matched the patchwork quilt and utilitarian blue curtains. The haphazard pile of books on the bedside table came as no surprise. Nor did the closet full of flannel shirts and T-shirts featuring the names of old rock bands.

"Uncle Ray, you sure loved your books and music."

Something else they'd both shared besides their love for his mountain home. She pulled one of the flannel shirts off its hanger and slipped it on. Maybe it was whimsical of her, but wearing the soft cotton felt like one of Uncle Ray's hugs. For the first time since waking up on the kitchen floor, she felt safe.

Eventually, she'd figure out what had happened downstairs. Maybe she'd walked in her sleep; not exactly a comforting thought. And even if it were true, why would she have crumpled Wyatt McCain's picture? Too many questions she had no answers for.

But now that she'd reassured herself that she was alone in the cabin, it was time to do something useful. At some point, she'd have to go through Ray's things and dispose of them. Surely there was a homeless shelter in one of the nearby towns that could make good use of his clothing. Maybe some of his books, too. His extensive music collection, though, she'd keep.

As she walked back out of the room, she rolled the sleeves of the flannel shirt up several turns. Despite being a couple sizes too big for her, the black-and-white-plaid fit her just fine.

At the bottom of the steps, she hesitated briefly. Nothing but silence this time. Good. Where to start? The attorney had gone over the terms of Uncle Ray's will with her in great detail, some of which were odd to say the least. To start with, he'd made the attorney include a message from him saying that he'd loved Rayanne and had known that she'd loved him right back.

Bless the man, those few words had melted away her guilt over not visiting him up here on the mountain. He'd known how she felt about him and that's all that mattered.

Next on the list was the requirement that she had to move to the cabin immediately. If she stayed until Labor Day, the property and everything on it was hers to take care of for her lifetime. She couldn't sell it, rent it, or give it away. Failure to comply would result in the place being left to a distant cousin, and Rayanne and her parents would be banned from ever setting foot on the property again.

He'd also set aside enough money to see her through the summer. Once September rolled around, the rest of Ray's surprisingly substantial estate would also be hers. With care, she wouldn't have to work again.

Meanwhile, the attorney had suggested that she begin by doing a room-by-room inventory of the cabin. The only question was where to start?

The kitchen would be the simplest. Before starting, she picked out some CDs from Ray's collection and put them on to play. His taste was eclectic, but this morning some red-dirt rock and country fit her mood.

With the sound of fiddle and guitar filling the empty silence, she got out her spiral notebook and favorite pen and started to work.

* * *

Wyatt drifted closer to the edge of the woods to listen. With the doors and windows closed up tight, he couldn't make out the lyrics. The singer had a smoky voice, the kind that had a man thinking of a pair of lovers breathing hard as they tangled up together in between soft sheets.

After all this time, he had only vague memories of what it had been like to coax a woman into sharing his bed for the night. Closing his eyes, he tried to remember the scent of his last lover's perfume. Something flowery, maybe. He had better luck remembering how silky smooth her skin had been, but nothing at all about what she looked like. Could have been a blonde or a brunette, not that it mattered. She was long dead and buried.

Lucky her.

Rather than continue down that dusty road, he dragged his thoughts back to the moment at hand. The man had always played music, too. Wyatt hadn't realized how silent the mountain had been since Ray's passing. It seemed odd to know he was gone but that his music would play on beyond his death. It was truly a gift of the modern world, one of the few things Wyatt enjoyed.

Where he'd grown up, music had been a rarity. Sometimes a passing stranger with an old fiddle or guitar would offer an exchange of music for a meal or two. Ma had always thought that was a fair deal.

What was the woman doing now? He hadn't meant to scare her earlier, but then he hadn't expected her to be able to see him at all. When she'd crumpled to the floor, he'd stuck around long enough to make sure she'd wake up on her own. He wasn't sure what he would've done if she hadn't. He'd used up all his energy when he'd wadded up that picture of himself in a fit of anger.

Where had she found that? Why had she brought it with her? Did she remember that long-ago summer? Too many unanswered questions. He'd spent many an hour thinking about her and why she'd been able to see him at all. No one else ever had, not that he knew of.

She'd screamed back then, too, but to warn him about the shooter on the roof. That was the only time he'd shot the bastard instead of taking one in the shoulder himself. It hadn't changed the outcome, just the bullet count. He caught himself rubbing the scar, easing an ache that had nothing to do with the actual shooting.

But music or not, he wanted the woman gone. She'd already disturbed his peace enough. These were his woods and Blessing was his town, even if only by squatter's rights. The law didn't count for much out here. Rules and regulations only held sway when there was authority around to enforce them.

And this morning's encounter was proof enough which one of them belonged here. She had no business intruding on his solitude, especially when he had no way of knowing if she'd be able see him all of the time or if this morning was a fluke. How could he find out without risking scaring her into a fit again?

He hated change almost as much as he hated that nothing ever really changed up here on the mountain.

Time to move on. Maybe see if anyone else was

stirring back in town. It was doubtful. Too early in the summer yet. Soon, though. And when the good folks of Blessing put in their appearance, would the woman see them again?

Only time would tell.

For now, he'd check on the town and then rest. Normally, he could hold on to his form most of the time once the days started growing longer. But the encounter with the woman had burned up a great deal of his energy. Even now he couldn't see his feet or feel his hat on his head. If he waited much longer, he'd fade completely. Hating the feeling that he was nothing more than a shadow with no real substance, he preferred to disappear at a time and place of his own choosing.

So for now, he'd just let go. Tomorrow would be soon enough to check in on the woman and see if he could learn when she planned to leave. She wouldn't stay. There wasn't anything up here to hold a woman like her—all modern and independent.

The song faded away, so he did the same.

Chapter 4

Morning dawned sunshine bright and warm. Wyatt preferred the shadows under the aspen trees, but he'd been drawn back to the edge of the meadow. It had been a day since he'd faded out. He rarely paid much attention to the passage of time, but things were different right now. She was still there, for one.

As he'd drifted on the breeze, he'd sensed her movements. He wasn't sure what she was doing, but she'd spent most of the day before banging around in the kitchen. If she'd been hunting for something, he hoped she'd found it. He was tired of the noise, not to mention it disturbed the other residents in the woods.

The deer had moved farther off, the birds were quiet and even the squirrels and chipmunks were nowhere to be seen. Eventually, they'd adjust to the woman's presence, but for now they were being cautious.

Probably good advice if he was in the mood to listen to it, but curiosity won out over caution. Since he'd yet to regain form, it should be safe enough to peek into the kitchen window. One glance and he'd be gone.

He caught a breeze that carried him toward the front porch, the only sign of his presence a faint shadow on the ground below. Nothing a rational person wouldn't put off to a random cloud passing overhead. At the edge of the porch he drifted up next to the wall, keeping well below the level of the window. Once he was settled in place, he rose up slowly.

The kitchen looked as if it had been ransacked by a bunch of wranglers just coming in off a long trail drive with nothing but dust and cows for company. Every inch of counter space was covered with pots, pans and dishes. In all the years Ray had lived there, he'd never once left a mess like that. In fact, the man was obsessively neat, always doing things in the same way on the same days.

Wyatt suspected the habit had given the man some sense of control. When that failed to calm his demons, Ray had walked the game trails for long hours at a time, especially at night. Often Wyatt had followed along, glad for the company, even if Ray had only rarely acknowledged his presence. He'd been too busy trying to outdistance the ghosts of his own past, not the ones who actually shared his mountain home.

Sometimes Ray had also wandered through what was left of Blessing. Each year more of the old town fell victim to the passing years. Dry rot had left most of the remaining buildings unsafe for humans to explore. Sometimes Ray did small repairs, like when he'd replaced that missing step in the church.

Had he hoped the girl would come back to visit again? Well, she hadn't. Not until it was too late to do her uncle any good.

A movement inside caught his attention. She was headed for the door, holding one of those little things Ray used to talk into. A telephone, Wyatt knew. He had no idea how it worked, but then he didn't understand a lot of things these days.

He flattened himself against the cabin wall as she stomped out onto the porch. Her voice rang out over the meadow, loud and full of frustration. Her free hand waved around in the air to emphasize whatever point she was trying to make, not that the person she was talking to could see it. Or maybe he could. In this ever-changing world, anything was possible.

Eavesdropping was rude, but it was one of the few pleasures Wyatt had anymore. He settled in to listen.

"No, Dad, I won't be leaving here until the first week of September. I told Mom that before I came up here, and nothing's changed."

She listened a few seconds, rolling those expressive green eyes and biting her lower lip, probably trying to hold back her temper. He didn't know what her father said next, but she immediately cut in.

"Dad, don't *Now, Rayanne* me. I'm an adult, even if you and Mom have a hard time remembering that. I'm using the time up here to do research. I can work here just as well as I could from my apartment. Which, I might add, I've already sublet to a grad student for the summer semester."

She listened some more, her fair skin flushing with frustration.

"Look, I understand why you're worried, but I'm doing fine. Don't show up here without calling first because I don't like being interrupted when I'm working."

Wyatt grinned. In the bright sunshine, her hair looked more red than blond, and she sure enough had a redhead's temper. He almost felt sorry for her father, but maybe the man deserved the sharp edge of her tongue.

Her voice softened. "I do love you, Dad. Talk to you soon."

She disappeared inside with the phone but immediately returned to lift her face up to the sun as if needing its warmth. He could still see the gawky girl she'd been the last time she'd come to the mountain, but she'd matured into a beautiful woman. Were those waves of red-gold framing her face as soft as they looked?

He drifted closer, careful to make sure the breeze wouldn't push him into her. She might not notice anything other than a brief chill, but she'd already surprised him with her ability to sense his presence. Even in his current scattered state, it was hard to resist the sweet warmth of her life force. She positively glowed with it.

Hellfire, he wanted a taste of that. What he wouldn't give to kiss his way across that scattering of freckles on her cheeks. He bet she hated them, but he'd always had a weakness for freckles. Did she have them anywhere else? No way to tell with what she had on.

That old flannel shirt of Ray's did little to hide the female curves underneath. He preferred a woman to dress like a woman with lace and petticoats. He'd always loved the challenge of peeling off one layer at a time before he reached all that silken skin underneath. On the other hand, her dungarees certainly showed off the sweet curve of her backside in enticing detail. She certainly didn't need a bustle to draw a man's eye.

Suddenly, she shook her head and smiled. He didn't know what she was thinking about, but he had to wonder if that lush mouth would taste as tart as her words had sounded. And why did he care? It wasn't as if he'd ever know. He wanted her gone. That's all that mattered.

After a few seconds, her smile faded, and she drew a deep breath that she let out in a soft sigh.

"Uncle Ray, I don't know if you can hear me, but thank you for this gift. I need this time up here on the mountain, even if Mom and Dad don't get that."

Her smile was back and she laughed. "Well, Rayanne, you've only just gotten here, and already you're talking to yourself. Time to get busy."

Rather than heading back inside, she stalked off toward the woods. So now he knew her name—Rayanne. Seemed only fair since she knew his, even if she didn't realize he was around. After all, no matter how he felt about it, it appeared they were destined to be neighbors for a while.

He waited until she reached the edge of the trees before following her. Where was she headed? And why did he care? He couldn't remember the last time he felt curious about much of anything, but he wanted to see for himself where she ended up. He was betting on the old church belfry.

Besides, he had nothing better to do.

No matter how determined she was to not let anyone ruin her time on the mountain for her, it was hard. Why couldn't they just leave her alone? Yeah, like that was going to happen. Her parents meant well, but it freaked her out to have them joining forces against her. It was the first time they'd put up a united front since their divorce.

She understood their concern. As her father had rudely pointed out, they'd spent a lot of time and a ton of money dealing with the aftermath of her last trip to Blessing. Not that it had helped. After months of counseling and arguments, she'd simply given up and spouted whatever the shrink wanted to hear. He'd marked her down as another success on his scorecard, and her parents' guilt had eased. Whoopee, everyone won except her. All she'd done was learn to keep the nightmares to herself.

Even Shawn hadn't bothered to disguise his own displeasure in her decision to accept Uncle Ray's legacy. Did they really think she didn't know her own mind?

Well, she wasn't going to let them ruin her good mood. She was proud of what she'd accomplished so far, even if she'd made a total wreck of the kitchen.

She'd washed out all the drawers and cabinets. After she walked off her frustration, she'd replace the shelf paper and put everything back. Tomorrow she'd start on another room. Or not.

Her decision. No one else's.

She stepped into the shadows of the trees. The old game trail looked unchanged from her last visit. At least this time she was wearing the right kind of shoes for hiking over the uneven ground. The faded scar on her shin was just one other reminder of that fateful day.

Here under the trees and out of the direct light of the sun, the day wasn't as warm as she'd thought. Even with Ray's flannel shirt, there was a bit of a chill in the air. As long as she kept moving, she'd be fine. If memory served her right, the far side of these woods was less than half a mile away, at best a ten-minute walk. From there, it was only a short distance to where Blessing sat nestled in a small valley.

She'd keep today's visit short, just a quick trip to reacquaint herself with the general layout of the town. Her plan was to do a complete survey of Blessing, measuring each of the remaining buildings and marking them on a map. When that was complete, she'd follow up with a photo survey.

Once she finished that much, she'd make a trip to the county courthouse and see if there were any records of the town still on file. Maybe one of the local newspapers would have archives that went back far enough to tell her something. Who knew? Wyatt McCain's death might have warranted a column or two.

Slowly, step by step, she hoped to complete the picture. By then, she should have a feel for whether her work would justify a book on the subject or if she'd submit a paper to one of the professional journals. Either of those choices would be the sensible thing to do.

Or she could just say the heck with being sensible and try her hand at writing a historical romance based on what had happened there in Blessing. She grinned up at a squirrel, which was chattering at her for disturbing his afternoon.

"Sorry, guy. Didn't mean to encroach on your territory. I promise I'm just passing through."

She laughed and kept walking. The trees came to an abrupt end just past the next bend in the trail, giving way to the valley below. The bright green of the grass sprinkled with early-blooming wildflowers stole her breath away. How could she have forgotten how pretty it was?

Somehow the beauty had been overwhelmed by the darkness in her nightmares. No wonder Uncle Ray had found some peace of mind living up here. She'd often wished there had been some magical way she could have known the man he'd been before the war had changed him. It was clear that Ray had come back from Vietnam a different man, one far different from the older brother her mother had grown up with.

Rather than dwell on the past, Rayanne started down the slope toward the edge of town. She'd like to think her pulse was picking up speed because of the workout she was getting from the walk, but there was no use fooling herself. This first trip back to Blessing was bound to stir up a few bad memories.

Keeping to a slow pace, she walked through the middle of town. In its heyday, Blessing had boasted a population of nearly two hundred people, but there was little evidence left of most of the houses. At least the old church looked much the same, as did the saloon. It was ironic that those two polar opposites survived.

It didn't take long to reach the far end of town. Turning back, she had the oddest sensation that she was being watched. She did a slow turn, looking in all directions, but the only movement came from the breeze brushing across the grass and wildflowers. Obviously, her imagination was running hot.

There wasn't much left of Blessing except faded boards and failed dreams. But maybe, just maybe, with hard work and the right words she could bring the town back to life. Through her, others could get a real glimpse of what life had been like here. She liked that idea. Maybe she could figure out a way to lay out the bare-bone facts of the town's history and then make them come alive through the eyes of a fictional resident. The wife of one of the miners might be fun.

As she considered the possibilities, a glimpse of the town alive and thriving suddenly superimposed itself over the deserted street. She stared in horror at a scene straight out of her nightmares. That the vision had no more substance than did her dreams made it no less frightening. She had the awful suspicion if she were to look behind her, she'd see those gunmen riding into town with death in their eyes.

She rubbed her eyes and looked again. Everything was back to normal. The experience was disconcerting, but perhaps her ability to see what had been would stand her in good stead when it came time to write her book.

She'd already been gone longer than she'd planned, but she had one more stop before she left. If she was going to face her personal demons, it had to start with where it had all happened. She'd climb the steps to the church belfry, take a quick peek around and then head back to the cabin.

She entered the church through the front door just as she had before. The first thing she noticed was that Uncle Ray had replaced the missing step. Since she was the only other person who ever visited the church, he'd done it for her. She brushed her fingers over the unfinished board and smiled. He'd always done his best to take care of her.

She put her full weight on the step, enjoying its solid feel beneath her feet. Then one by one, she climbed the rest of the way up the stairs, noticing he'd also reinforced a few more of the cracked and worn boards while he was at it. The door to the roof swung open on well-oiled hinges. No more loud creaking to warn her if someone followed her out onto the roof like the gunman in her dream. She shivered, but shoved that thought out of her mind.

A few short steps carried her across to the railing. She kept her eyes firmly focused on her feet, telling herself she was keeping an eye out for rotted boards that could give way beneath her weight. The truth was she wasn't quite ready to risk looking down at the street below.

Would she see weeds growing up between the wooden sidewalks or the townspeople going about their daily routine? There was only one way to find out. She latched on to the faded railing with both hands, locked her knees to make sure they'd support her, took a deep breath and cast her gaze outward.

Her relief at seeing nothing but a ghost town was palpable. Another major hurdle cleared. As she started to turn back toward the door, a movement below caught her eye. How odd. The batwing doors on the old saloon were swaying as if someone had just passed through them.

She glanced around, realizing for the first time that the breeze had picked up and white puffs of clouds she'd noticed earlier now covered most of the sky overhead in an angry gray blanket. One of the first things Uncle Ray had taught her was that storms could roll in with little notice. Getting soaked in an early-summer rain wouldn't kill her.

A lightning strike might.

A deep rumble of thunder echoed down the valley, sending a shiver through her. Time to get the heck off the roof of the tallest building in town. Ignoring the grumble of a few of the boards, she hustled back to the door and breathed a little easier when she was back inside. She wasn't out of the woods yet.

She smiled at the image. Actually, she had to reach the woods first. They'd shelter her from the storm well enough. Once the worst of it was past, she could make the final run for the cabin. At least the day was still warm enough that she didn't have to worry about hypothermia setting in if she did get soaked along the way.

She cursed herself a fool for setting off so ill prepared. She knew better or at least she used to. Ray had laid out the rules for her the very first time she'd come to visit. He'd written them out in big block letters so she could read them on her own. Then he'd ordered her to study the rules until she knew them backward and forward.

When she'd recited them to him, he'd handed her a pen. Once she'd scrawled her name on the paper, Uncle Ray had presented her with her very own backpack filled with emergency supplies: granola bars, bottled water, a first-aid kit and even a rain poncho. It had been one of the proudest days of her life.

"Sorry, Uncle Ray. Guess I need a refresher course."

She wouldn't make the same mistake again. On her next trip to Blessing, she'd bring emergency supplies and stash them inside one of the buildings. For now, though, she had a long way to go to reach the slope leading up to the timberline. The dust kicked up by the wind stung her eyes, and another crash of thunder warned her that the storm was moving faster than she was.

Okay, so maybe she'd be better off waiting out the storm back in town. She reversed course and took off running for the nearest building. The church might be sturdier, but right now she couldn't afford to be picky. The saloon would have to do.

The darkening sky flashed bright with another bolt of lightning. The resulting thunder followed right on its heels, warning her the storm was now centered right over the valley. Big, fat drops of rain splashed down on the dusty road as Rayanne ran. She kept a wary eye on the ground in front of her to avoid stepping in one of the wagon-wheel ruts still visible after all these years. The last thing she needed was to twist an ankle.

After another crack of thunder, the rain poured down even harder, instantly turning the dust into mud so that her shoes made a sucking noise as she ran. It was too late to worry about staying dry. Finding shelter was paramount. The wooden sidewalk outside the saloon creaked in protest when she put her full weight on it, but it held. After shoving through the swinging doors to the dim interior, she bent over, hands on her knees as she waited for her lungs to catch up on oxygen.

When she could breathe, she slipped off her flannel shirt and wrung it out as best she could. She reached for the hem of her T-shirt, planning to do the same with it, when the memory of watching the saloon door swaying in the breeze popped into her head. She froze and looked around to make sure she was alone.

What was she thinking? No one ever came up here uninvited. Of course the room was empty. She peeled off her T-shirt and twisted it until the rainwater dripped down onto the dusty floor. When it was as dry as she could make it, she slipped it back on, figuring her body heat would dry it out eventually. She hadn't bothered with a bra, so at least she didn't have to deal with the discomfort of wet lace and elastic while she was stuck here.

One of the old chairs looked sound enough to sit on,

so she dragged it over toward the front window and made herself comfortable. The weather would change for the better soon, and then she'd head back to the cabin where a mug of hot chocolate with her name on it would be waiting.

Hellfire and damnation, did that woman have to follow him around?

Earlier, Wyatt had drifted into the saloon out of habit, not because he remembered the place where he'd had his last drink with any particular fondness. All those years ago, knowing full well he might die, he'd tossed back one last shot of good whiskey, kissed Tennessee Sue full on the mouth and walked out the door.

Nope, he didn't have any good memories of this place, even back when it was in its heyday. But thanks to what he was witnessing at the moment, old Bert's saloon had just become Wyatt's favorite place in the whole damn world.

With the thunder crackling overhead, the woman had bolted through the doors, already stripping off her flannel shirt. Thanks to the rain, the white shirt underneath stuck to her like a second skin, outlining her curves in considerable detail. One thing for sure, Rayanne was a damn sight more appealing than Tennessee Sue had been.

It would've taken a lot nobler man than Wyatt to look away, especially when he realized Rayanne wasn't wearing anything underneath the shirt. Her plentiful breasts swayed gently with each move she made, their dark tips faintly visible through the clingy cloth.

What he wouldn't give to test their weight with the palms of his hands. And damned if she wasn't reaching for the hem of that shirt, too. Surely she wasn't going to— No, she stopped and looked around suspiciously.

Had she sensed his presence? He wasn't visible; he knew that much. But even her late uncle had an uncanny knack for realizing when Wyatt came near. He'd nod in Wyatt's direction and then go about his business. Maybe his niece had inherited the same talent.

But then she went ahead and stripped her shirt right off in front of him. The storm outside had nothing on the one raging inside him right now. He moaned. Her skin was all peaches and cream. He loved the sprinkle of freckles across her shoulders and the dusky peach of her nipples. He sure enough wanted to kiss those freckles and suckle her pert nipples and watch them pebble up. Hell, he just plain *wanted*.

Incredible. He hadn't felt anything this powerful since the day he died. No hunger, no pain. Dread, yeah. Fear, even knowing how things would play out again. But no joy, no peace, no thirst, no hunger.

But by gosh, he hungered now. Unable to help himself, he drifted closer to where Rayanne stood, trying to squeeze some of the rainwater out of her clothes. If she didn't cover herself soon, he wasn't sure what would happen. In this state, his ability to interact with his surroundings was extremely limited. If he brushed against her bare skin, she might feel a chill or a buzz. He might not feel a damn thing.

If she was aware of him, he might have tried it. But a man didn't sneak up on an unsuspecting female. He was no hero, but he had enough black marks on his soul. With that in mind, he needed to put more distance between himself and temptation before he weakened and reached out to her.

He directed his focus toward the back wall to give her a chance to cover herself decently. The white shirt still left too little to the imagination, but it was better than all that peach-toned skin screaming out to be tasted and touched. Once the storm passed, he was sure she'd make her way back to the cabin. Good. He wished she was already gone, back to where she belonged, preferably off his mountain.

Taking her peaches-and-cream complexion and all that temptation with her.

Frustration with the whole situation left him wanting to break something. But if he let his temper slip its leash, he'd do something stupid. Like materializing right here in Bert's place to start breaking up the few pieces of furniture still left intact.

How would she react? She'd already fainted once at finding him in her kitchen. He bet she'd already twisted and turned the facts of yesterday morning to convince herself that she'd only imagined the whole incident. If for one second she'd believed he'd really been there, she wouldn't still be up here on the mountain by herself. He tried to imagine her pelting down that switchback road back to wherever she came from. The picture wouldn't come into focus.

Most folks would cower in a corner while nature raged outside. Instead, she'd dragged a chair right over to the window to watch. Even now, she sat forward, trying to see better through the filthy glass. She sure had gumption; he gave her that much.

If he'd been solid, he realized he would've been smiling. Even in his present state, he felt lighter, more buoyant. That realization scared him. He didn't want to feel lighter, didn't want to *feel* anything.

He needed to get out of there. There was plenty of energy to be had right outside the door. If he was careful, he could absorb enough to let him resume standing guard in the woods. The time was coming when others started prowling the mountain, gathering close. He'd need to make sure they kept their distance from the woman.

He wasn't sure how much harm they could do, but they all grew stronger as the time grew near. He drifted closer again, this time feeling protective rather than lustful. He might not want her there, but neither did he want her hurt or scared.

Damn, why did she have to be there at all?

For now, she was safe enough. She could find her own way back to the cabin once the storm passed. Far better that their paths crossed as rarely as possible.

Better for him, anyway.

With that, he slipped through the doors and out into the street. The storm had weakened considerably already, the dark clouds having dumped most of their rain before moving on wherever the wind would carry them. The air felt clean as he drew on the natural energy it carried.

Slowly, he moved on out of town, growing more solid as he neared the timberline. By the time Rayanne followed him into the woods, he stood hidden in the shadows, solid from his hat to the soles of his boots.

The rain had brought out more curl in her hair, framing her pretty face and drawing attention to how young she was. But Rayanne moved with the kind of strength and purpose as another woman in his life had. He was surprised he hadn't noticed it sooner.

It wasn't as if he could forget about Amanda, the one woman he'd tried to be a better man for. The one he died trying to protect and succeeded only in destroying them both. He'd always wondered if they would have gone beyond simple friendship if things had played out differently for the two of them. No way to know now.

He followed after Rayanne, preferring her unknowing company to the darkness of his memories. For a second, she hesitated, stopping to look around. She frowned and rubbed her hands up and down her arms, clearly feeling a chill. Whether it was from his presence or from the dampness of her clothes didn't matter.

It was tempting to step out into a small circle of sun to see if she could see him at all and how she would react. But no, that wouldn't be smart. Besides, it was too late now. She was already back in motion, quickening her pace now that the cabin was almost in sight. He didn't blame her. Dark and dangerous things prowled these woods.

He should know. He was one of them.

Chapter 5

Rayanne was finished in the kitchen. Everything was stowed away, and she'd put a fresh shine on the counters, appliances and even the floor. She wasn't ready to face the living room yet.

It had soaked up so much of Uncle Ray's essence, for the lack of a better word. The wear on cushions of his favorite chair showed the outline of his body and carried the scent of his aftershave. The shelves lining the walls were filled with his favorite books, most dogeared from multiple readings. Bits and pieces of the man, but not the whole.

She missed him so much. Had been missing him since long before he'd actually died.

No, she wasn't ready to sort through all those memories. Not yet. Cowardly, maybe, but she couldn't help but feel that she was intruding on Ray's privacy. Instead, she'd get started on her work in Blessing. The day was sunny and clear, perfect for taking pictures.

She'd made a list of the things she'd need for her survey as well as the emergency supplies she wanted to stash inside the church. That would require a trip down to the small combination grocery store, gas station and post office located at the base of the mountain.

She wanted to get back in time to start on measuring out the streets of Blessing, so she grabbed her purse and stepped out on the porch. Locking the door seemed a bit silly considering she was the only one around, but city habits died hard.

Besides, she never quite lost the feeling that she wasn't alone here on the mountain. Crazy, she knew, and the last thing she'd admit to anyone, but it felt as if someone was out there watching over her. She liked to think that some part of Uncle Ray had remained tethered to the mountain after all the years he'd spent taking care of it.

Her parents would never understand why she'd find that thought comforting, but she did. She stared in the direction of the trail to Blessing, fighting the whimsical urge to roll down the window to yell that she'd be right back.

Then she cranked up the stereo and sang along with the music all the way down the mountain.

"Where's she off to now?"

Not that it mattered. Rayanne would be back because she hadn't taken anything with her other than her purse. Probably going after supplies. Too bad. It would be better for both of them if she'd packed her suitcase and left the mountain.

He'd been spending way too much time lurking near the cabin, hoping to catch even a glimpse of her. All he could think about was the color of her skin, the fullness of her breasts and the way she would have smelled of rain and woman. He'd felt guiltier about that, but it wasn't his fault that she'd revealed all the creamy skin right in front of him.

What would she do if he were to return the favor, even fully clothed? She'd seen him twice before, once as a young girl and on her first morning back. He took off his hat and ran his fingers through his hair in frustration. Would she faint again or finally realize that he was more than a figment of her imagination? Thanks to that god-awful picture she had of him, she had to know he'd been real at one time.

No one in the hundred-plus years he'd been stuck here, straddled between life and death, had ever done more than caught a glimpse of him, except when he lay dying in the dusty street of Blessing. He suspected it was like catching a movement out of the corner of your eye, just a hint of something being there but just out of sight.

A sound deeper in the woods drew his attention away from the clearing and back toward town. Something was stirring or maybe someone. By his reckoning, it was far too early in the summer for most of the townspeople to put in an appearance. That left two people most likely causing the disturbance, the ones responsible for his being in Blessing at all.

Sometimes Amanda, the schoolteacher, and her son, Billy, showed up early with no warning. They never stuck around for long, leastwise not until later in August, right before the whole nightmare started up again. Even when they were there, they only rarely acknowledged his presence. For some unknown reason, he was the only one who truly haunted the mountain year after year. Maybe because it was all his fault.

But even if Amanda and Billy didn't speak to him, he'd seek them out, anyway. Even just a glimpse of Amanda gave him a sense of belonging, a belief that he wasn't truly alone. Her boy, Billy, served as a reminder of the price paid for innocence lost.

Wyatt watched as Rayanne drove out of sight before making his way back toward Blessing.

On the way, he stared up at the sky and muttered, "Someone up there has a hell of a sense of humor. I've got one woman who shouldn't be able to see me but can, and another who should be able to, but can't. Where's the sense in that?"

He paused for a second, tilting his head to the side, hoping against hope this time would be different and someone would answer. Instead, he got the same response he'd always gotten whenever he begged, pleaded or just plain asked for some kind of explanation for this ongoing hell he lived in: absolute silence.

The old general store hadn't changed much since the last time Rayanne had been there. A few different brands on the shelves, but the same old, faded sign out front advertising gas, groceries and postage stamps.

She grabbed a basket on the way in and made her way up and down the three aisles, picking up the items on her list and a few impulse purchases, as well. For the moment, she was alone in the store. If Phil, the proprietor and postmaster, didn't make an appearance by the time she was done, she'd ring the buzzer by the register to summon him from the small apartment attached to the back of the building.

More than once she and Uncle Ray had been invited back there for a lunch of grilled cheese sandwiches and root beer floats. Ray enjoyed the occasional game of chess with his old friend and hadn't minded her hovering over his shoulder while they played.

She smiled, grateful for another happy memory of her time on the mountain.

The shuffle of feet announced Phil's arrival. She snagged an extra pack of gum off the shelf and tossed it into the basket before making her way to the register. The passage of fifteen years had added a few wrinkles to Phil's face, and his hairline had receded a bit more, but she would've known him anywhere.

She coasted to a stop just short of the counter, waiting to see if he recognized her. It didn't take long. His welcoming smile brightened considerably as his faded blue eyes crinkled at the corners, leaving little doubt about her welcome. He charged back around the counter to sweep her up in a huge hug.

"Rayanne, girl, it has been too damn long. We've missed your pretty face up here on the mountain."

Tears stung her eyes as she hugged her uncle's old friend back. "I should have been here for him, Phil."

Phil held her out at arm's length. "Now, listen here, missy. Your uncle understood that your life was down in the city. He knew you loved him just like he loved you. If you don't believe anything else, believe that."

His words, spoken with such quiet authority, eased the knot in her chest enough so that she could breathe again.

"I'd like to think so, Phil. Thanks for saying so."

"It's no less than the truth." His own eyes looked a bit shiny as he held out his hand for her basket. "Let's get this stuff rung up for you. Have you had lunch?"

"Not yet." And realized she hadn't eaten already because she'd been subconsciously hoping Phil would make that offer.

"Great! We'll have cheese sandwiches and root beer floats, just like old times."

A shaft of sharp grief shot through her chest. Just like old times except that Uncle Ray wouldn't be there. But his memory would be, and that would suffice.

Phil was still talking. "Don't let me forget that I've got a package I've been holding for you. If you hadn't come in today, I would've brought it to you on Sunday when the store's closed."

Really? Her local post office had said it could take a week or more for her mail to catch up with her. She wasn't expecting any more book deliveries, either. She knew better than to rush Phil. He did things in his own way and at his own speed.

At least he made quick work of her groceries. He

added the last can of soup to the bag and then hit the total button on his old-fashioned cash register. "That'll be fifty-five dollars and forty-seven cents."

She handed him the cash and then took the bag with her perishables and stuck them in the cooler at the back of the store. Another habit she'd learned from Ray. With that done, she followed Phil into his apartment.

Two hours flew by as he caught her up on all the changes in the area since her last visit. A few old-timers had passed on; some new folks had moved in. All the usual gossip, only the names changed. She didn't mind hearing about people she didn't know, not if it made Phil happy to talk about them.

Finally, she finished the last of her float, enjoying the combined flavors of vanilla ice cream and root beer. She'd have to live on lettuce for a few days to make up for the calories, but the guilty pleasure of the sweet treat was worth the penance.

"Thank you for lunch, Phil. That really hit the spot. Nobody makes a root beer float like you do."

His smile was tinged with sadness. "It wasn't anything special, Rayanne. Nothing fancy like what you probably have all the time down there in the city."

She reached across the table to put her hand on his, noticing for the first time how knobby his knuckles had gotten. Her friend wasn't getting any younger. Who would run the store when he was gone? She didn't want to think about it.

"Fancy doesn't make it special, Phil. Having lunch

with you and Uncle Ray right here at this same table are some of the best memories I have."

He blushed a bit but looked decidedly happier. "I'll get that package for you. Ray brought it down to me about the time the doctors told him his heart was plumb worn out. He asked me to keep it until you moved into the cabin."

Interesting.

"So he was sure I'd come?"

Phil stared up at the ceiling for a second before answering. "I was sure. He hoped."

Okay. Before she could ask Phil to explain, he was up and heading for his bedroom. She could hear him rummaging around and muttering under his breath. Finally, he returned with a shoebox sealed shut with duct tape. Whatever was inside, Uncle Ray had wanted to make sure it was safe from prying eyes.

Phil handed it to her. "No idea what's in there, but I figure it had to be important because he made a special trip down to bring it to me."

Wow, a special trip. Ray had been a man of habit. He only came down to Phil's on the first and fifteenth of every month to pick up his mail and supplies. Only the worst of weather kept him from his appointed rounds.

"I wonder why he didn't just leave it in the cabin for me to find."

"He didn't say." Phil shook his head. "Who knows, maybe he just wanted to make sure it didn't fall into the wrong hands. You know how he was about protecting his privacy."

The box felt heavier somehow, as if knowing Ray

had driven all the way down to entrust it to Phil's care gave it more weight. She was tempted to rip the tape off now instead of waiting until she got back to the cabin, but that didn't feel right.

No, she'd wait until after dinner and curl up in Ray's favorite chair to open it. For now, she needed to get moving. She had work to do up on the mountain.

She set the box down long enough to give Phil another hug. "Thanks for lunch, Phil, and for keeping Ray's package safe for me. I'll let you know what's in it next time I come in."

He shook his head. "No need. If Ray wanted me to know, he'd have told me himself."

Phil pointed to the mountain that dominated the view from his living room window. "I chose to live here because I like things quiet and simple. Your uncle, though, he needed to be up there on the mountain. Ray never talked about what it was that held him there all these years. He was a man who kept his secrets, that's for sure. Years ago I asked him one time why he didn't move down here where he could be around other people instead of living up there with that ghost town."

Then he nodded toward the box she held in a white-knuckled grip. "I figure the answer to that question is in that there box."

There wasn't much she could say to that. She had her own special reasons for spending time in Blessing.

Driving back to the cabin, she kept glancing at the box sitting in the passenger seat. It sat there like a homemade time bomb ready to explode the minute she peeled back the tape.

An uncomfortable thought, but that didn't make it any less true. Somehow she just *knew* that the secret truths it would reveal were going to change her life forever.

Rayanne was back. Even if Wyatt hadn't been watching for her, he'd have figured it out from all the racket she'd been making. It had started with her slamming the door of her car and then doing the same thing with the door of the cabin, both going and coming out again a few minutes later.

From the way she was marching along on a straight line toward the trail through the woods, something sure enough had her worked up. He grinned as she stubbed a toe on a root and turned the air blue with an impressive string of cuss words. That temper of hers was something to behold, that was for damn sure.

He drifted after her, making sure to stay far enough away so she wouldn't pick up on the fact she wasn't alone. Not really, anyway.

As soon as that thought crossed his mind, she froze and slowly looked back in his general direction. Her eyes narrowed, leaving no doubt that she was staring right at him. Actually, considering he was currently nothing more than a cloud of energy, she was staring right through him.

What had he done to draw her attention? Most likely nothing. Obviously, she'd inherited more than her uncle's eye color. Rayanne clearly sensed him on some level. He hovered right where he was, waiting for her to move on. In the future, he'd need to maintain more distance if he was going to follow her around.

Finally, she hobbled on down the trail, her gait smoothing out as her foot quit hurting. When she was out of sight, he cut straight through to the far side of the woods, moving far faster than Rayanne's human legs could carry her. Then he skirted the edge of the woods to approach Blessing from the other side of town.

First things first. He made a quick trip up and down both sides of the street, reaching out to see if there was anyone else around. Earlier, Amanda and her son had passed through. He'd called out their names, waved his hands and even stomped his feet, but failed to draw their attention. All he'd done was use up all of his power for the day, leaving him nothing but a mist on the wind.

Even if it was too early in the summer for them to really be there, he hated to be ignored. He might not feel the heat of the summer sun or the bitter cold of the winter snow, but he could feel lonely.

But not right now. Rayanne had finally caught up with him. She came around the far end of town headed toward the church as usual. At the last minute, she surprised him by veering off course into the saloon, instead. Interesting. What was she doing in there?

Only one way to find out. He drifted close to the door, keeping low and moving slowly to avoid drawing her attention again. She'd already dragged an old table over beside the chair she'd left by the window. When she had it right where she wanted it, she tested its strength. Thanks to one leg being shorter than the others, it wobbled like crazy. Resourceful woman that she was, she used a scrap of wood from another broken table to shim it up.

Satisfied with her efforts, she unloaded one of the packs she'd carried with her. Paper. Pencils. Ruler. Those things he recognized. She pulled out another item, something shiny and new-looking. What was that? There were so many things in the world that he knew nothing about. Then she pulled on a small tab and ran out a short strip of metal as she looked around.

"Might as well start in here."

The device's purpose became clear as she used it to mark off distances in the room and jotted them down on paper. Why was she measuring the room? Who would care how big a saloon was, especially one that hadn't served a single drink in a hundred years?

He edged through the door, moving slowly. She was so intent on her ciphering to take note of his presence. Inside, he drifted up toward the ceiling to stay out of her way. She'd finished marking down the size of the floor and had moved on to the old bar and even the table she was working on.

It made him tired just watching her.

On the other hand, he wasn't about to complain about the view. Right after she'd started working, she'd stripped off her oversize flannel shirt, another one of Ray's old castoffs. The shirt she wore underneath would've scandalized the good folks of Blessing back in his day. It was dark blue with no sleeves and a neckline that plunged low enough to offer a tantalizing glimpse of those freckles he liked so much. Memories of yesterday's storm had him smiling.

He didn't know when women took to wearing trousers, but he had to admit he could get used to how that well-worn denim hugged her feminine charms. She'd been bent over, checking the number on that measuring device when she abruptly straightened up. Her hand moved up to rub the back of her neck as she slowly glanced around the room. After a few seconds, she walked over to the door to look outside. Finally, she turned back to face the bar and slowly lifted her eyes up to the corner where he was.

"Okay, so I'm imagining things."

No, she wasn't, but he'd just as soon hope she didn't figure that out. The last thing he needed was a hysterical female on his hands. He drifted back outside. On his way, though, he used a small spurt of energy to set the doors swinging. His efforts were rewarded when Rayanne charged out onto the sidewalk right behind him, her hands on her hips as she glared up and down the street. He couldn't help but laugh at her frustration.

Besides, why bother haunting the place if he couldn't have a little fun with it?

Chapter 6

Dinner was done, and the few dishes Rayanne had used were washed and put away. She'd run out of excuses for avoiding the shoebox she'd left sitting on the coffee table in the living room. Right now she was heating water for a pot of tea. She'd picked a blend that was supposed to soothe the nerves.

She hoped it worked because she'd been jumpy as heck ever since she'd left Phil's place. She'd never minded being alone; most of the time she preferred it. No parents and no would-be boyfriends questioning her every decision.

What she didn't like was the creepy-crawly feeling that someone had been staring at her both in the woods and a little while later in the saloon. Silly, probably, but then there was that swinging door. Not exactly a smoking gun, but it was the second time it had started swinging while she was in town.

Granted, the first time was when the storm was moving in, and she'd written that time off to the wind. However, today when she'd been plotting out the saloon, there hadn't been even a hint of a breeze.

Her uncle had told her often enough that people didn't stick around long when they came to visit him because they weren't welcome. Lord knew her mother and father had hated the place. She'd always thought what he'd really meant was that she was one of the few he didn't mind sharing his space.

Now she had to wonder. Was it possible that it was the mountain itself that didn't like intruders? As soon as that thought crossed her mind, she shook her head and laughed. Maybe she should write a fantasy story with a sentient mountain complete with a ghost town. She even had the perfect dark hero, the same one who'd haunted her dreams last night.

She studied the picture of Wyatt McCain that she'd smoothed out and stuck on the fridge with a magnet. Those pale eyes followed her wherever she went. Had that straight slash of a mouth ever softened into a smile? And why did it matter? He'd been dead and buried a hundred years before she was born.

Enough about Wyatt. He'd already claimed too much of her thoughts lately. Time to open the box. She put the old teapot on a tray along with her favorite mug and the cookies she'd picked up at the store. Then she added a box of tissues.

Just in case.

Ray's favorite chair was the perfect spot for the great unveiling. She dug out the old pocketknife he kept in the drawer of the end table and used it to loosen one edge of the sticky, gray tape. When she had enough to grab hold of, she stripped off the first layer of tape. It took her a solid ten minutes of careful work to finally get down to the cardboard.

Before lifting the lid, she took time to drink a cup of tea and nibble on one of the cookies. Maybe some music would help. She reached for her iPod and turned it on. Better. Out of excuses, she removed the lid and set it aside.

Inside, a stack of leather-bound books were nestled in a bed of wadded-up newspaper. A white envelope was stuck inside the top one with her name on it written in Uncle Ray's handwriting.

She left the books in the box and set it aside for the moment. Using the same knife, she slit open the sealed envelope and pulled out folded papers. They had ragged edges, looking as if they'd been torn out of a spiral notebook.

As she spread them out, she closed her eyes and took a deep breath.

Dear Rayanne,
If you're reading this, well, we both know why. Even before the war, I was never much good with words, spoken or otherwise, but I'm going to give this my best shot. I knew you'd accept the terms of my will although I figure your mom and dad

probably gave you hell about it. Sorry about that, but they never did understand the mountain and how it called to you just as it did me.

There's a reason for that, Rayanne. This is no ordinary mountain, and Blessing is no ordinary town. I regret like hell how things went down on your last trip up here. I hope you can find it in your heart to forgive me for letting you get caught up in something you were too young to handle. I tried to tell your folks, but they wouldn't listen. No surprise there.

But not all of the story is mine to tell. When Great-Aunt Hattie left the place to me, she gave me the bottom two books to read. The next one is mine. Read them in order, starting with the one with a brown cover, then the black one, and finally the blue one. I bought the green one for you.

All that I would ask is that you not tell anyone about what you've read. First off, they'll think you're crazy. Secondly, the mountain likes to keep its secrets. You don't want a bunch of crazy outsiders up here trying to prove you right or even wrong.

Remember that I love you. Even if you decide to live down below, keep an eye on the place for me. When it comes time for you to pass the place on to the next generation, choose your successor well. I know I did.

Love,

Ray

Okay, that was strange. But when she lifted the four books out of the box, she could have sworn she felt a jolt of energy that left her fingertips tingling. She set all but the brown one aside and opened to the first page. The lines were covered with a decidedly feminine handwriting that gradually grew more shaky toward the end of the old journal.

Feeling as if she were about to take a step off a precipice, she turned the lamp up a notch and began reading aloud, her voice echoing through the cabin.

"My name is Amanda Green, and I live here in Blessing in the state of Colorado. There's not much left of the town now, but I have nowhere else to go. This is my home, and the people I love are buried here, my husband, William, and my son, Billy. The mine took William, and Billy died the day of the Great Incident. Someday I will sleep beside them out there on the side of the valley."

Rayanne read aloud until her voice grew hoarse; then she read on in silence. Even though Amanda had thought to live out her life alone, eventually she did remarry and start a second family.

As interesting as that was, it was Amanda's vague references to the Great Incident that kept Rayanne turning pages long after she should have been in bed. Details. She needed details even if she wasn't sure how she felt about finding out that her great-great-grandmother had actually known Wyatt McCain.

For sure, it was a relief to find out he'd been real, but she was also just a little jealous of Amanda's relationship with the man. And wasn't that a little bit crazy?

Even so, for the first time she felt a real connection with the woman, who until then had only been a fading name in the family Bible.

Finally, Rayanne set the book aside, her eyes too tired to make sense of the spidery handwriting. The lack of detail about the day Amanda's son died was frustrating. Wouldn't a day that significant warrant more than a handful of vague references? The passage in Amanda's journal made it sound as if Billy might have been another casualty in the streets of Blessing the day Wyatt McCain had died.

Tomorrow she'd pick up where she'd left off and see if the rest of Amanda's journal held the answers to Rayanne's questions. If not, perhaps Great-Aunt Hattie had been more forthcoming.

Upstairs, Rayanne climbed onto her bed and opened the window to let in the night air. She stared up at the stars overhead. Reading the journal had left her both exhausted and yet too wired to immediately fall asleep. Sometimes making mental lists helped her to relax.

She'd start off with the normal routine—shower, breakfast and getting dressed. Next, she'd head back to Blessing to map out another building. The old mining office should keep her busy for a good part of the day. Maybe she'd take the journals to read when she needed a break.

Perfect. Having everything planned out, she snuggled down under the quilt and drifted off to sleep, secretly hoping she'd dream of a certain gunslinger with those startling blue eyes.

* * *

Rayanne was in town again. Evidently, she was done in the saloon because she'd spent the past hour or more poking around in the old mining office. Measuring out the saloon was a waste of time, but the mining office was even more so. Hell, the mine had been pretty much played out shortly after Wyatt had breathed his last. What possible use was it to her?

Wyatt would be better off wandering in the woods than watching her from across the street. All it did was aggravate him, and he didn't need that. From the way she kept wiping her forehead with the back of her hand, the weather must be hot. He couldn't tell one way or another. No matter what the temperature was, winter or summer, he felt the same. Good thing, too, considering he'd been wearing his duster that last day.

Rayanne stepped out on the porch and stared up at the sun. Once again, her attire had him wondering how modern men managed to keep their hands to themselves. She was wearing another one of those formfitting shirts with no sleeves and no modesty. But today, instead of her usual dungarees, she had on short pants. Very short pants.

Were her shapely legs as smooth to the touch as they looked? Wouldn't do him much good if they were, but a man had the right to wonder about such things when they were put on display like that.

Now what was she up to? She'd dragged her pack outside and then sat down on the porch, leaning up against the side of the building. She pulled out a bottle of water and a sandwich, obviously her lunch.

After the first couple of bites, she reached back into the bag and brought out a book. He frowned. It looked familiar. Before he could figure why, Rayanne opened it to somewhere near the back and read a short passage out loud as if to make better sense of it.

"I hear voices sometimes. See shadows that should not be there. They move through the trees as if blown about by the wind, even though the leaves hang still on the branches above. Today I swear I heard my Billy calling for me.

"That's when I realized that it was that time of year again. I used to love the heat of the summer sun. Now it only reminds me of all that I lost on that hot August day. Does a mother's love carry on beyond the grave? I think it must. That's the only reason I can think of that would allow me to hear Billy's laughter on the breeze.

"I've learned to keep to myself in the safety of my cabin. Too many strange things happen here when summer draws to a close. I won't speak of them here. Not yet. Not until I come to terms with what it all means. Could it be that they were all trapped here, just as I am even if I yet live and they don't? For years my grief has consumed my every breath. Only now, with Billy's laughter echoing in the woods, have I started looking beyond my own selfish pain and wondering about theirs. Is there nothing to be done to ease their burden and let them find peace at last? Could it be that my grief keeps them anchored here? I shudder to think that could even be possible."

Rayanne's voice carried well in the quiet, but then she went back to eating her sandwich and reading silently. That was all right. She'd read enough for him to realize who had written those words—Amanda. It had to be her journal, and the reason it looked so familiar was because he'd spent a lot of nights watching her write in it. He'd never wanted to pry enough to see what words she'd written on all those pages.

Had she mentioned him? If so, it was doubtful that it had been anything good, and he was right sorry about that. Amanda had good reason to hate him, though, so he could hardly blame her. He ought to go wander around somewhere else but couldn't resist trying to get a glimpse of Amanda's words.

But before he managed to slip close enough to peek over Rayanne's shoulder, she closed the book. Damn. Now he'd never know what the book contained.

She stuck it back in her pack and pulled out another book. It was probably Hattie's. She'd been the first one to live on the mountain after the town had dried up completely. She'd gone about her daily chores without paying much attention to him. If she'd known he was around, she'd never said.

On the other hand, after her first summer on the mountain, she'd packed up and left the mountain for two weeks every August. He had to think she'd known more about what went on in Blessing than she'd let on. Cantankerous old biddy, he'd missed her when she'd passed on.

He settled against the wall and listened as Rayanne started reading aloud again.

"My kin thinks me addled for living up here by myself. If I ever told them I was never really alone because

a certain handsome man haunts these woods, they'd come drag me down to see some city doctor. But Wyatt's here. I know it even if they don't."

Well, damn, so Hattie had known he was there. Did she know about the others? The next sentence answered that question.

"I know it's cowardly of me to leave in August, but I watched Wyatt die once. I have no desire to do so again, not when I can't do a thing to change what happened to him or Aunt Amanda's first son. There are others around, but I don't know their stories or why they're still here."

The words hung heavy in the hot summer air. Rayanne slammed the book closed and scrambled to her feet, staring up and down the street, looking as if she'd seen a ghost. But then, she had. She'd probably convinced herself that the gunfight had all been a dream, a nightmare, something she'd conjured out of the clear mountain air. Then there was that first morning in the cabin.

It had to shake her up some finding out that she wasn't the only one in her family who'd seen that day play out again and again over the years. She thought it was scary seeing ghosts. How did she think it would be to feel your body torn apart by a hail of bullets only to wake up trapped in a never-ending hell?

Disgusted with the whole situation and even more so with himself, he had to get away from Rayanne. Right now. Before he did something stupid like pulling himself together out here in the bright sunshine just to see if she'd see him this time.

And what she'd do if she did.

He didn't really want to scare her again, not like he'd done before when she'd hollered out a warning at him from the belfry. She'd done her best to save his worthless life. Even though it hadn't worked, he owed her for trying.

As he moved off, she whispered something, a hopeful note in her voice. He tried to tell himself he'd misheard her, but then she whispered it again.

"Wyatt? Are you here?"

Should he answer? Even if he did, would she hear him? Before he could make up his mind, she laughed and walked back inside the mining office, shaking her head and muttering something about an overactive imagination and crazy talk.

Rather than prove her wrong, he decided it was time to make himself scarce. More scarce, actually.

He'd barely crossed the street, heading for the saloon, when he heard a crash followed by a scream.

"Rayanne!" he hollered and charged back to the mining office, latching on to the blazing heat of the summer sun overhead to pull himself back together. By the time Wyatt hit the front porch, his body was rock solid and the sound of his boots landing on the old wood rang in the air.

Old habits die hard, so he drew his gun as he charged inside to see what kind of trouble Rayanne had gotten herself into.

Chapter 7

Rayanne scrambled for something to hold on to, anything to avoid slipping any farther into the hole that had opened up in the floor. One of the old boards had shattered with no warning when she'd put her weight on it, sending her lurching to the side. Her foot slipped down the old wood to get wedged in the tangle of broken timbers and the floor joist below. If the ground was only a couple of feet down, she wouldn't be worried, but there was a good eight-foot drop down into an old cellar.

And something was stirring down there. She didn't want to know what. At best, it was a varmint of some kind. At worst, rattlesnakes were known to seek out cool, shady places.

Right now every move she made only made mat-

ters worse. Trying hard not to panic, she supported her
weight with her arms as she considered her options,
none of which were good. Finally, using her other foot,
she kicked the broken board as hard as she could to
loosen its hold on her ankle. Her first attempt failed,
but the second one did the job and then some. Not
only did that board give way, but so did the one she
was sitting on.

She yelped again as the floor beneath her collapsed,
sending her slip-sliding down toward the jagged timbers below. As she toppled off the edge, her trapped
foot came free, and she managed to brace herself long
enough to stop her fall. Fear tasted bitter, and her pulse
was running hot.

What now?

"Son of a bitch, woman!"

A pair of strong hands grabbed hold of her arms just
before another piece of the floor cracked wide open.
With her heart banging around in her chest, she was
left dangling over the gaping hole in the floor.

The same deep voice growled. "Are your feet hung
up on anything?"

She wiggled them slightly to make sure. "No."

No sooner had she answered when the mystery man
heaved her up and out of the hole, carrying her toward the edge of the room. From there, he dragged her
through the door into the other room and then straight
out onto the porch where he dumped her in an undig-
nified heap. Not that she was complaining. Without
his help, she could've been badly hurt or even killed.

The mountain was unforgiving when it came to the

careless or the unlucky. Her mysterious savior disappeared back into the mining office, returning a few seconds later to drop her things on the sidewalk beside her. He'd left her sitting, facing the street, and even now he stood in the doorway out of her line of sight.

"Are you hurt?"

She'd already done a quick survey. A few bumps, a bruise or two and a scrape on her knee. "Nothing serious. My ankle hurts, but all things considered, I'm not complaining."

He snorted in disgust. "That's what you get for poking around where you don't belong."

Okay, she was willing to cut the guy some slack for coming to her rescue, but who did he think he was to tell her she didn't belong here in Blessing? She owned the place and had the paperwork to prove it. The land had been in her family for four generations now. Feeling decidedly at a disadvantage sitting on the ground, she gingerly pushed herself back up to her feet.

When she turned around, the doorway was empty. Where had he gone? She hobbled a couple of steps to peek in, but the room was empty. She wasn't about to go any farther inside, not with the floor as rotten as it was.

"Mister? It's not safe in there."

"Not for you," he said in the same deep voice.

She jumped when he answered from behind her. How had he gotten past her? She got her answer when she spun around to face him. For a brief second, her stomach lurched as if the sidewalk had just done a roller-coaster dive. Rayanne stumbled backward until her back was pressed against the side of the building. Locking her knees kept her upright, but just barely.

"Who? You? How?"

Okay, her babbling only made her rescuer even angrier. Rather than continue, she stared down at her feet and concentrated on taking a slow, deep breath and then a second one. Finally, when she thought she could string together a coherent statement, she looked up again and tried to put all the puzzle pieces together.

There he stood, still wearing that same blue shirt, hat and duster he'd had on fifteen years ago. His steel-blue eyes stared right back at her, his mouth set in an angry snarl. Maybe if she hadn't spent much of the past twenty-four hours reading Amanda's and Hattie's journals, she might have convinced herself that she'd knocked her head hard enough to scramble her brains.

But if she hadn't, though, then this was really happening. What had Hattie said? Something about once she let herself accept that it was possible, then it was. Once she believed Wyatt McCain haunted the mountain, he'd become real to her. Rayanne got that now as all the pieces of the puzzle finally fell into place. The why or how didn't matter.

It was easier to fall back on good manners than it was to ask for explanations. Especially when she wasn't sure there were any.

Rayanne drew a deep breath and stepped toward him on legs that still wobbled. She thrust her hand out toward him. "Mr. McCain, thank you for saving me."

He immediately backed away, his eyes flicking

briefly to her hand and then back up to her face. Then the air crackled and shimmered as he faded from sight.

"Wyatt?" she whispered.

Silence again. She looked up and down the street, looking for some evidence that she hadn't just imagined the whole thing. That was stupid, though. If he hadn't just rescued her, how had she ended up out here on the sidewalk instead of the cellar floor? Who else would've left those boot prints in the dust?

She took a tentative step forward and thrust her hand into the spot where he'd been standing. Nothing of substance although the air felt several degrees cooler. Did that mean he was still there? Just in case, she jerked her hand back.

"Sorry. I didn't mean to..." To what? Touch him?

Suddenly, it was all too much—the near disaster and the even more shocking rescue. She grabbed up her pack and started for the far end of town and the trail back to her cabin. Maybe there would be something in either Aunt Hattie's journal or Uncle Ray's that would help her make some sense of things.

Walking as fast as her sore ankle would allow, she made her way back toward the woods. It was a constant battle to keep from glancing back over her shoulder, but she needed to watch where she was going. She allowed herself one look when she reached the trail through the trees. Staring back to where Blessing sat baking in the summer sun, she shivered.

"Well, that gives a whole new meaning to the term *ghost town*."

It was a poor joke, but she laughed, anyway. She'd

come to the mountain to find answers to the questions she'd been living with all too long, and today she'd definitely made progress. But staring down at the twin sets of bruises forming on her upper arms where Wyatt had grabbed her, she had to wonder if the truth might not be even scarier than her worst nightmares.

With that worrisome thought, she stepped into the shade of the trees and followed the narrow trail back to the cabin. Before she went inside, she hesitated in the doorway. Had he followed her? Had his efforts to rescue her hurt him in some way? Was that why he'd disappeared right there in front of her? God, she hoped not.

But just in case he could in fact hear her, she called out, "Thank you again, Mr. McCain. I hope to see you soon."

She meant that, but not right now. Not until she could get her mind around what had just happened. Looking back to that first morning at the cabin, it was obvious now that a locked door wouldn't keep Wyatt McCain out if he was of a mind to come inside. Even so, she set the deadbolt and fastened the chain.

And if she laced her tea with a medicinal shot of Uncle Ray's favorite brandy, who was to know?

Wyatt hurt. It didn't make sense, but it felt as if he was coming down off a three-day drunk that had involved a fistfight or two. He wasn't sure how he'd managed to haul Rayanne to safety, but he had. A good deed. Who would've thought it possible?

All he could remember was hearing her scream and

reaching out for every drop of power he could grab. For a few minutes, he'd been rock solid, almost human again. For the first time in a hundred-plus years, he'd felt the heat of the sun, the pull of air into his lungs and the sour taste of fear.

Not for himself. For Rayanne.

Hellfire, that woman needed someone to shake some sense into her. What did she think she was doing, risking her life like that? If he hadn't been there, hadn't been able to pull off that miracle… No, it didn't bear thinking about. The mountain had already claimed enough lives.

An even bigger surprise was the connection he'd felt when she'd looked him straight in the eye, recognizing both who and what he was. Rather than run screaming down the road or fainting as she had when she'd seen him in her kitchen, she'd stood her ground.

He hadn't expected that. It had been almost a relief when his last bit of energy had burned up, leaving him fading back into oblivion. He couldn't believe that she actually stuck her hand out again to see if she could find him that way. He grinned or would have if he'd been solid again. From the way she'd jerked her hand back, she must have felt the chill that he'd heard Ray and Hattie complain about once in a while.

What was there about Rayanne that affected him so strongly? This was the second—no, make that the third time she'd seen him clearly. Even when she couldn't, she obviously sensed his presence. She'd looked straight at him in the woods that time and again in the saloon when she'd been caught in the rain. That had him wanting to grin a second time. Would she eventually figure out that he'd been watching when she'd stripped off her wet clothes?

He bet she'd pitch a fit if she did. He'd sure enough gotten an eyeful, but that wasn't his fault. After all, he'd been there first. If he floated on this mountain for another hundred years, he wouldn't forget how she'd looked. He should be ashamed of himself for thinking about it so much, but too bad. What else did he have to do?

At least she'd had the good sense to pack up her stuff and hightail it back to the cabin. He had little doubt that she'd had a big enough scare to keep her barricaded inside for the rest of the day. He hoped so, because he was in no shape to ride to her rescue a second time.

He was so scattered right now that a good breeze might tear him apart for good. Probably not, but he sure enough felt like hell. Slowly, he gathered himself back together piece by piece, although it did little to ease the pain. When he'd patched himself together enough to move, he drifted out into the sun, hoping the combination of heat and light would seal the rifts that had been ripped in his ghostly hide.

Ah, yes, the warmth gradually soothed the aching until once again he felt…nothing. Back to normal.

Rather than drift aimlessly around town, he headed straight for the cabin. Once he knew the woman had made it back safely, he'd prowl the woods. Come sunrise, though, he might just show up at her door and see what happened.

* * *

Rayanne sipped her morning coffee and skimmed a few more pages of Hattie's journal. Eventually, she'd go back and read it more carefully and take notes. Much of the time Hattie had written about her day-to-day activities: gardening, knitting, mending, cleaning. Interesting to Rayanne as a historian, but right now her focus was on something else. Actually, someone else.

She ran her finger down the page, searching for even the vaguest reference to Wyatt McCain, Blessing and the events of August 23, 1883. More and more, she was convinced she'd witnessed a replay of the gunfight on the anniversary of the original events.

She marked the passage where Hattie talked about believing making it real. Right now it was the only proof Rayanne had that she wasn't just imagining things. After reading over it one more time, she moved on.

A few pages later, she found another passage that had her pulse racing.

He was watching me today. I sensed his presence even though I couldn't see anything but shadows under the trees. I suppose I should simply ignore him, but that seems rude. I'd wave at any other neighbor. Why not him?

No response, but then I didn't really expect one. I went back to hoeing the garden. At the end of the row, I stopped to rest. Enough weeding for the day. Before I could quit, though, I needed to haul water for the potato plants.

When I started toward the well, something knocked

*me stumbling backward. I didn't fall, but it was a close
call. What had just happened? Then I saw a movement in the grass right where I'd been about to step.
A snake. Most were harmless, but that one sure wasn't.*

*I froze, unable to move. Despite the heat of the sun,
I shivered from the close brush with death. Against
all logic, I knew who had just saved my life. Looking around, I finally spotted a bit of shadow that was
darker than the others. Maybe I was imagining things,
but I swear that shadow had substance. I could just
make out the shape of a man's hat and maybe a hint
of broad shoulders.*

"Thank you, Wyatt. Much obliged."

*The shadow faded away, but I know he heard me.
There were those who never had a good word to say
about Wyatt McCain. But I figure if he was such a
coldhearted bastard, he wouldn't have lifted a finger
to help me.*

*I waved one last time and headed for the cabin.
The potatoes would just have to wait until tomorrow
for that water.*

When Rayanne reached the last page, she closed
Hattie's journal and ran her fingers over the cracked
leather cover. What an amazing story! So she wasn't
the only one who'd been rescued by their phantom
neighbor. She set the book aside and reached for the
next volume in her family's history of life up here on
the mountain.

She found herself reluctant to read Uncle Ray's
story. He'd been such a private man, and she hated intruding. On the other hand, he wouldn't have entrusted

the three journals to her care if he didn't want her to learn what was in them.

But rather than delving into his, maybe it was time to start her own. She poured herself another cup of coffee before taking the journal and one of her spiral notebooks out onto the front porch. She settled into one of the old Adirondack chairs and set her coffee on the table. Chewing on the top of her favorite pen, she tried to decide where to start.

At the beginning seemed to be the logical choice, which for her was fifteen years ago. Yeah, that felt right. Rather than start writing in the leather-bound journal, she'd take notes first in the spiral notebook. That felt less scary, less serious. If she was going to hand her journal down to another generation, it was important to get it all right.

Closing her eyes, she thought back to that summer and how awful the tension had been at home. Her parents had been too caught up in the downward spiral of their marriage to pay much attention to how it was affecting their daughter.

It had been such a relief to leave all of that tension and anger behind to come visit her uncle. The memories came so fast and furious that it was hard to get it all down on paper.

After about ten minutes of writing, she stopped to stare out into the distance, her thoughts turned inward, lost in the past. Gradually, she realized that she was rubbing the back of her neck again. That same eerie feeling of being watched was back. She sat up straighter and studied her surroundings.

The meadow was empty except for a few butterflies making the rounds of the wildflowers. She cocked her head to the side as she listened. Nothing. No cars coming up the drive, no voices. That left the woods. She scanned the shadows under the closest trees and worked her way outward.

After the first pass, she started back across again, going more slowly this time. There, off to her right, next to the trunk of one of the bigger pines. It was almost, but not quite big enough to disguise the man standing behind it.

She rose to her feet, panic nipping at her nerves. She didn't want to think Wyatt McCain was any kind of threat. From this distance, she couldn't even be sure it was him. Did she even want it to be? It was rare than anyone happened to pass through Blessing and the meadow, but it wasn't unheard of.

She stepped down off the porch, unwilling to go any farther until she knew more about the intruder. Whoever he was, he had to realize he'd been spotted. Should she go inside and get Ray's old twenty-two? He'd made sure she knew how to use it, but she had no desire to shoot at anyone.

Her mysterious guest stepped out from behind the tree, leaving little doubt it was Wyatt McCain. Even from a distance, she recognized his profile, although he was too far away for her to make out his facial features. Besides, how many men would be wandering around this area wearing that exact style of duster?

Finally, he started toward her. Her pulse kicked it up a notch, and she felt an odd rush of heat watching him walk with such predatory grace. Breathing became difficult as if the air around her were too thick to breathe.

Even as she struggled for control, she wished she had her camera or even her cell phone. Anything to snap a picture of the man now skirting the edge of the woods but definitely heading her way.

Doing her best to act casual, she returned to her chair, grateful for its solid support. Keeping one eye on the approach of her reluctant visitor, she picked up her pen and scrawled a note, this one about her current situation.

He's coming toward me, his hat pulled low, making it impossible to read the expression on his face. He looks unchanged by yesterday's events. Where did he go? Will he speak this time? If I touch him, will my hand go through him? If he's able to talk, will he answer my questions? Should I offer him a cup of coffee?

She waited until he was within a few feet to look up again. As soon as she did, he stopped. Unsure of the etiquette, she stood up, nervously wiping her sweaty palms on the seat of her jeans. There was a stillness about the man that gave her the courage to abandon the high-ground position the porch afforded her.

"Mr. McCain?" she asked with a tight smile as she walked down the steps.

His lips moved, but no sound came out. She thought he had tried to say his first name, but she couldn't be sure.

"I'm sorry, I didn't quite catch that. Did you say I could call you Wyatt?"

Her smile felt more genuine when he nodded. "I'm Rayanne Allen, Ray's niece. You know that he died."

She winced. Dying might be a touchy subject given Wyatt's current situation. She plunged on. "He left me this place in his will. I'll be here until after the first of September."

Okay, the one-sided conversation was definitely awkward. She didn't know about him, but she needed to sit down again. "Would you like to come up on the porch and sit for a while?"

Without waiting for him to respond, she led the way back to the two chairs. She assumed he wasn't interested when she only heard her own footsteps crossing the porch. When she turned around to see what the hang-up was, he was right there behind her. She squeaked in surprise and dropped back down in her chair.

"Don't creep up behind me like that!" she snapped, more embarrassed than angry.

Wyatt stepped past her to settle in the other seat. He wasn't exactly smiling, but his expression had softened just enough to let her know he'd found her reaction amusing. She was amazed how silently he moved, especially for such a big man. The old wooden chair didn't protest at all as he sat down.

She picked up her coffee again. It had grown cold, but her mouth was cotton dry.

"I'm going to get more coffee. Would you like a cup?"

There was a definite twinkle in his eyes as he reached out to touch her coffee cup. His hand went straight through it. She stared at him, her mouth moving but with no words coming out.

Finally, she sputtered, "Right. I'll be back."

Inside the house with a stout door between them, she grabbed on to the counter with both hands as her world shifted on its axis as she struggled to come to terms with a new reality. Not only had she seen a ghost, he was sitting out on her porch, his boots propped up on the railing as if he'd settled into staying awhile.

Right now another shot of brandy sounded pretty appealing, but she needed her wits about her. She poured a fresh cup of coffee and headed back outside to entertain her very special guest.

Chapter 8

Wyatt couldn't remember the last time he'd actually laughed. But, by damn, it was pretty entertaining to watch Rayanne Allen act like having a ghost come calling was an everyday occurrence. Especially after the way he'd spooked her when she hadn't noticed him standing right next to her.

Spooked. Exactly the right word for it. He chuckled again. Maybe he shouldn't take such pleasure in her discomfort, especially because she was the first person he'd actually spoken with in over a hundred years. At least the first live one. The others who'd taken note of his presence had mostly done their best to ignore him, pretending he wasn't real or that they didn't know him.

Rayanne was definitely different, though. Yeah, she'd fainted that first day, but since then she'd dug in her heels and refused to cower. She'd not only sensed him watching her from the woods, she'd stood her ground when he'd come strolling right up to her front porch.

Amazing. For such a little bit of a thing, she had courage.

What was taking her so long with that coffee? Had the reality of what was going on finally hit her? He started to get up to peek in the window when he heard the turn of the doorknob. As she stepped back out on the porch she had her cup in one hand and the telephone in her other hand, its cord stretching back into the kitchen.

When she stepped closer to him, she jerked the receiver away from her ear. Even from where he sat, he could hear the loud crackling that came from it. The noise lessened as soon as she backed away a few steps. Smiling now that the mystery was solved, she kept her distance. Obviously, something about him interfered with the stupid thing.

"Mom, it hasn't been a week since we last talked. I told you that's how often I would call, so you're jumping the gun. I'm doing fine, just busy."

Wyatt shook his head and tried to look shocked that she would lie to her mother. Rayanne's mouth quirked up in an unrepentant grin, and she stuck her tongue out at him. He gave up the pretense of disapproval and grinned back at her.

As soon as he did, she backed up another step, an odd look in her eyes as she stared at him. What was going on in that pretty head of hers that put that extra sparkle in those spring-green eyes? He wasn't sure he wanted to find out.

"Look, Mom, I promised I'd keep in touch. I'm sorry I've missed your calls, but I must have been down at the grocery store visiting with Phil. Uncle Ray didn't have an answering machine, but I'll try to remember to pick one up next time I go down the mountain."

After listening for another few seconds, Rayanne was looking a bit ragged around the edges. She turned her back, probably to keep him from seeing how the call was affecting her. Whatever her mother was saying had to be truly awful to upset Rayanne so badly. Judging by how she handled yesterday's near disaster in the mining office, she didn't rattle easily.

Maybe her mother would give up if he got close enough to the phone to cause it to crackle again. He'd have to be careful, though. If he destroyed the phone altogether, her mother might come charging up the mountain to confront Rayanne in person. Before he could decide, she took care of the problem herself.

"That's enough, Mother. I'll tell you everything when I see you at the end of the summer. I promise I'll call you in a few days."

Then she pushed a button and calmly walked back inside. Well, maybe not so calmly. If he wasn't mistaken, that was the sound of something being knocked over, accompanied by a few words that ladies in his day weren't supposed to say. He liked her all the better for it.

She came back out and stood staring off at the

trees for a few seconds before resuming her seat with a heavy sigh. "I'm sorry you had to hear all that."

She glanced in his direction and asked, "You can hear me, can't you?"

He nodded, wishing she could hear him in return, but he wasn't solid enough. Not like he was yesterday. He'd spent much of the night puzzling over that whole event. For those few minutes, he'd been there, all of him. Not just the shadow of the man he used to be except for one day a year.

She clutched her coffee with both hands, maybe drawing some comfort from its heat. "You probably figured out that was my mother. She's not happy about me being up here. Nobody is."

Who else was included in that disapproving group besides her parents? He watched Rayanne out of the corner of his eye. He couldn't be the only man who liked the combination of red-gold hair and freckles. Did she have a beau waiting for her down below? If so, he couldn't be much of a man to let his woman go wandering off by herself.

Hell, she'd come damn close to being badly hurt or even killed yesterday. The mountain was unforgiving. There were more ways to die up here than being torn apart by bullets. He should know.

"You're looking pretty angry there, Mr. McCain."

He glared at her. "It's Wyatt."

She stared at his mouth and then repeated herself. "Fine. You're looking pretty angry there, Wyatt."

He spoke slowly, hoping she could make out what

he was trying to tell her. "Your mother is right. Dangerous."

Rayanne's efforts to lighten up the moment faded away. "Yes, it is, and I don't need you to tell me that any more than I need my mother's rantings on the subject."

She picked up her pen and paper. "Tell me, Wyatt, do you remember me visiting my uncle when I was a little girl?"

Where was she going with this? He nodded and held out his hand to indicate how little she'd been when he'd first seen her. She couldn't have been more than five or six, all pigtails and no front teeth.

"I came for the same two weeks every summer."

Not exactly, and they both knew it. He waited to see what she had to say next.

"Except for the summer when my parents split up. Dad thought Mom would come back for me, and she thought he would. Dad called to say he'd been delayed, and I'd have to stay a few days longer."

Her voice sounded more distant, as if they were both being dragged back to that hot summer day. He didn't want to go there, not with her, not now. But she kept right on talking, totally oblivious to his growing agitation.

"I was fine with it." She lifted her face up to the sun, its warm light bathing her creamy skin. "I knew Uncle Ray was unhappy, but not why. I thought he was tired of my company or something. He got so agitated. I was scared, too. Not of him, but for him."

Her silence was telling; her pain obviously still raw after all these years. After all, why would a mere uncle want her if her own parents couldn't be bothered to come back for her on time? Wyatt wanted to take a bullwhip to the lot of them. Instead of taking care of the one person who had needed them the most, they'd left her up here on the mountain to get caught up in his nightmare.

"Do you remember seeing me that summer?"

It was time to go. Even if she could hear him, he had no interest in rehashing the past, not when he had to relive it again in a few weeks. He stood up, planning on walking away. But Rayanne leaped to her feet to plant herself right in front of him. She stood close enough that he could have counted the freckles scattered across her nose and cheeks.

"Move," he mouthed, making sure she could understand his order.

She didn't budge. "I asked you a question, Wyatt."

That didn't mean he had to answer. He arched a brow and said, "So?"

She not only saw him, she saw too much. "You do, don't you? Remember me and what happened? On that day when I was up in the belfry?"

She kept her eyes pinned right on his mouth to read his response. It was clear she wasn't going to give ground until he answered. Instead of giving her what she wanted, he stared down into her upturned face, at her lips, liking the way the lower one was a bit too full. Damn, he bet she'd taste sweet. Before he realized what he was doing, he'd leaned down far enough that all that separated them was his ability to resist temptation.

What would happen if he actually kissed her? Would she be able to feel the press of his lips against hers?

He had no business even thinking such thoughts. She'd quit demanding answers and stared up at him in silence. He got lost in her eyes and the possibilities, imagining the slight sizzle and burn if her lips were to actually touch his.

Then they did. Had he closed that gap or had she? He didn't know. Didn't care.

The tingle he'd expected surged hot and hard, as her mouth softened beneath his. He canted his head to the side, to find the perfect fit between them, as he slowly lifted his hands to tangle his fingers in the soft silk of her hair.

It was the first good thing that had happened to him in a lifetime of loneliness spent on this godforsaken mountain. But then it all went to hell when Rayanne's eyes flew open and instantly filled with fear or maybe it was horror. She staggered backward, putting the full width of the porch between them, rubbing her lips with her fingertips. Was she trying to erase his taste, his kiss? Her whole body shook far worse than it had the day before when the floor had caved in beneath her feet.

What had he done wrong? She'd been right there with him, kissing him back. He might have been a century out of practice, but he knew when a woman was enjoying a kiss. Her head whipped back and forth. What was she looking for?

"What's wrong?"

She turned to stare out at the woods. "Wyatt, where did you go?"

"Damn it, I'm right here."

Fury and frustration had him reaching out to her, but when his hand passed right through Rayanne's body, he jerked it back to his side. Hellfire and damnation, he'd poured everything into that kiss and now there was not enough left of him to be seen or even felt. Maybe he was wrong about that last part because she was rubbing her arms again, which were covered in goose bumps.

She stared right at his chest, although he knew she couldn't see him. "Wyatt? What happened? Are you all right?"

"Hell, no, I'm not all right. I'm dead," he bellowed right in her face, even though she clearly couldn't hear him.

Unable to answer her with words, he resisted the urge to touch her again, not when all he had to offer was the cold chill of the grave. He'd always thought being caught up in this never-ending cycle of death and more death had been bad. But knowing what he was missing, how Rayanne felt in his arms, how she tasted and not being able to act on it, was hell itself.

He had to get away, back to the darkest shadows where he belonged. Wyatt floated past her, careful to keep his distance, and on across the meadow without stopping, even though she called his name twice more.

When he reached the sanctuary of the trees, he looked back one last time. The porch was empty, and Rayanne was gone.

Rayanne paced the length of the kitchen and back. Okay, what was she going to do about what had just happened? What could she do?

She'd kissed a ghost. What could be crazier than that? Well, enjoying it that much also ranked pretty high on the crazy charts. Was he still out there watching? As she peeked outside, she brushed her fingertip across her lips, remembering that last millisecond before Wyatt's mouth had claimed hers. It wasn't just her mouth that had been left aching, needing far more than a simple kiss.

Who was she fooling? There had been nothing simple about the whole incident. From the second he'd touched her, she had melted, craving the press of his hard body against hers. If he'd been human, their embrace wouldn't have ended out there on the porch, but upstairs in her bed. Her wayward mind tried to imagine what it would be like to have his ice-blue eyes staring down into hers as he surged over her, in her.

Enough of that. There were other things to think about. God knew the metaphysical and scientific implications alone were mind-boggling. She lived in the here and now while Wyatt existed trapped somewhere between this world and the next. Even so, there was no denying the very real connection between the two of them.

Over the short time she'd been dating Shawn, how many times had she kissed him? A half a dozen times? And never, not once, had she experienced anything like the burn of desire that she'd felt kissing Wyatt McCain.

What did it say about her? She didn't want to think about it, but she could imagine what her parents and that idiot shrink they used to drag her to would have to say on the matter. She'd be lucky if they didn't have her court ordered into a hospital for a psych evaluation.

Maybe the only good thing that had come out of the experience was that she now knew she had to tell Shawn that things were over for them. It was only fair to let him go. He deserved better than a woman who preferred a ghost from the past to a real-live man.

This one-sided discussion was getting her nowhere, and she had work to do. She wanted to snap a few more pictures from the front door of the mining office and then move on to the old mercantile. Building by building, she'd learn everything Blessing had to teach her. She packed up her gear and headed to town.

The woods were quiet and cool as she passed through them. She paused more than once to simply listen to the breeze and the rustle of leaves overhead. So far, she didn't sense anyone watching her. She was too new at all of this to know whether that meant Wyatt wasn't around or if she simply wasn't picking up on his presence.

Maybe he'd returned to Blessing. When she reached the road through town, she headed straight for the saloon where she'd set up her makeshift office. Inside, she looked around. Again no sense that she was anything but alone. Ignoring her disappointment, she pocketed her tape measure, camera, pencil and notebook.

"I'm going back to the mining office, but I won't go inside."

She pitched her voice loud enough to carry some distance, refusing to be embarrassed that she might be only talking to the mountain. Photographing the mining office went without incident. Moving on from there, she headed toward the building that had served the town as general store and post office. Inside, she took a few cautious steps, testing the feel of the floor beneath her feet.

The whole building was in much better condition than the mining office, maybe because it had been built better to begin with. It was pretty much intact with only the faded gray color of the wooden walls and the floor showing the building's true age.

There were still a few glass jars on the counter. Had they held candy? Crackers? No way to know for certain, but it didn't matter. She picked one up to study it. Maybe she'd take them back to the cabin and wash them clean of the cobwebs and dust. They'd make a nice souvenir from her time here in Blessing. Or not. There was so little of the town left now. She didn't want to contribute to its disappearance.

She started with her usual rough sketch of the room's layout. Once she was done, she measured the floor and then the windows, jotting the numbers down on the sketch. Next, the remaining counter and shelves.

Behind the counter she found several rows of cubbyholes, obviously designed for sorting the mail. Had Phil ever been up here to see this? She'd have to ask him because she thought he might like seeing the similarities between this old place and the store he ran today.

She snapped a few close-ups from different angles for her study but also to show him on her next trip down the mountain. Meanwhile, she was done with the interior of the store. If the light was good, she'd take a few outside shots before heading back to the saloon for lunch.

The day had grown warm enough to take off her chambray shirt. Did she want to eat inside or out on the porch? She studied the saloon, sensing it was empty except for her. That made the decision for her.

She carried her chair outside and made herself comfortable in the shade of the overhang. Propping her feet up on the railing, she slowly ate her sandwich and apple. Anything to linger here awhile longer.

Where was Wyatt? Was he all right? She hoped so. She let her eyes drift closed, trying not to think about their heated encounter, concentrating instead on the details of the man himself. On impulse, she made a trip back into the saloon and grabbed her sketch pad and pencil.

She pictured how he'd looked as he'd strolled across the meadow toward the porch. He was a shade under six feet tall and built along lean lines, all muscle and sinew without an ounce of extra fat on him anywhere. The calluses on his hands came from a time when men worked with their hands, his skin weathered and tan.

What had he done besides use those guns he wore with such casual ease? So many questions and no way to get answers. Instead, her pencil flew across the paper as she struggled to get the shape of his cheekbones and mouth just right. Next, she filled in the details of his clothing. His shirt had a double row of buttons down the front, his trousers were black and a bit faded. And thanks to that duster, he'd cause a heck of a stir in the female population at the university if he were to go strolling through the center of campus. The thought made her smile.

When that picture was done to her satisfaction, she started another one, this time just of his face and how angry he'd looked the day before when he'd rescued her. Next, she drew him in Uncle Ray's kitchen. And finally, how he'd looked right before he'd kissed her. She'd come full circle.

Sighing, she looked up and realized her lighting wasn't quite as bright and the temperature had dropped a few degrees. Where had the day gone? It was definitely time to be heading back home.

No, not home. She couldn't let herself think of it that way. All of this was temporary, a chance to do some firsthand field research. Come fall, she'd return to her life down below, picking up where she'd left off. Well, sans Shawn and most definitely sans Wyatt McCain.

Only one of those last two things hurt.

There was no use in hauling everything back to the cabin every time, so she left it all spread out on the table in the saloon. She'd be back early in the morning to pick up where she left off.

As she started out of town, she stopped and looked back one last time. "Wyatt, I hope you're all right. Stop by anytime."

The breeze kicked up a small dirt devil, the only movement anywhere. Feeling a bit foolish, she turned her back on the town and walked away.

Chapter 9

Wyatt rolled his shoulders and stretched his arms out to the side. A tentative step forward and then another went without mishap. Everything was back in working order, such as it was. He patrolled the town, checking every building as he made his way down one side of the street and then the other. No changes. No new gaping holes in floors. No broken and bleeding bodies anywhere.

If he still breathed, he would've sighed in relief. Rayanne had managed to avoid any new disasters while he'd been wherever the hell he'd been. The same thing happened to him every year when the bullets tore into him. He felt the pain, tasted his own blood in his throat and then nothing. Gradually, he would become more aware of his surroundings, and then he'd find himself standing back in front of the saloon right where he'd died.

As he headed for the saloon, the last spot on his tour, he skirted the patch of dust where he always spent his last few seconds before it all went down. How many quarts of his blood had soaked into the ground there over the years? Too damn many. How many days had passed by since that morning on Rayanne's front porch?

Several, if he had to guess, but no more than that. Most times he lost the rest of the summer after the gunfight, reappearing when the trees were dressed in their fall colors. He didn't know how all of this stuff worked, but with the gunfight looming on the horizon, it was doubtful he'd been gone long.

Had Rayanne missed him? He smiled at the thought.

He wandered into the saloon and looked around. Rayanne had cobbled together another couple of tables out of the bits and pieces of furniture left in town. Judging by the piles of papers scattered on their surfaces, she'd been busy.

Curious, he studied the ones on the top of the pile. He recognized the layouts of the mercantile and the mining office. So that's what she was doing. Another was only a rough sketch, clearly a work in progress. Cocking his head to the side, he decided it was the shipping office.

The next table was covered in photographs, all done in exquisite color. Obviously, cameras were another device that had come a long way since his time. He'd only had his picture taken once. He couldn't even remember the occasion or who the photographer had been, but the picture was the same one he'd found in Rayanne's kitchen that first morning.

The third table was covered in pencil drawings. All things considered, he liked them better than the actual photographs. Rayanne had a real talent. Somehow she'd looked at the town and seen past the scars and damage to the way Blessing had been in its prime. She'd even included a few of the old places that had been torn down and scavenged for their wood. The only thing missing in her sketches were the people.

Or maybe not. There was a boot and a bit of a leg showing on a piece of paper sticking out from underneath the top layer of sketches. He tried to pull it out from the stack, but his fingers slipped right through the paper. On a good day, he could sometimes move something a little, like when he'd made the saloon door swing.

Considering he'd only just pulled himself back together again, he shouldn't risk trying any harder to dislodge the paper. He couldn't bring himself to walk away, though, not when there was something about that boot that stirred his curiosity. Finally, he decided to risk it.

Concentrating all of his energy into his right hand took longer than usual. Using the tips of his thumb and forefinger, he grasped the paper and tugged and then tugged again. At first the paper stubbornly stayed right where it was, but then it gave way and flew out of the stack, scattering papers all over the place.

He let it drift back down to the table and waited to see if he'd overextended himself again. His fingertips faded out of view for a few seconds but then snapped back into focus. Good. No real harm done.

Now that he knew he wasn't headed for oblivion again, he moved around to get a better look at the paper. What the hell? She'd drawn him, not just once, but half a dozen times. No wonder that boot looked familiar. He'd been wearing the damn thing for longer than he'd been dead.

He leaned in closer, wishing he could hold the picture up in better light. If that's how she saw him, it was a wonder she'd let him get within spitting distance of her. He'd spent much of his adult life earning his livelihood with his guns. That amount of killing showed in a man's eyes, and he recognized the look in his own. He should. He'd crossed paths with enough killers in his time.

But then he looked at the last picture she'd drawn. It was different than the others, although at first he couldn't quite put his finger on the reason. Then it hit him. In the others he looked angry, cold, determined. In this last one, he looked hungry, his eyes reflecting his desire for Rayanne. This was what she'd seen in his face right before they'd kissed.

Memory of that moment wrapped him in warmth, making him smile, something he'd rarely done even in life and almost never since he'd started dying on a regular basis.

"Wyatt?"

His hand automatically went for his guns, but he managed to stop short of drawing them.

He yanked off his hat and slapped it against his leg

in frustration. "Damn it, woman, don't sneak up on a man like that!"

Rayanne hovered in the doorway, neither in nor out. He waited for her to make up her mind which way she was going to go. When she stepped inside, he suspected what he was feeling was relief.

She nodded toward his guns. "Would the bullets have hurt me?"

An image of her stumbling backward, a circle of red blooming on her chest, filled his head. Even the idea of something hurting her that badly made him want to howl. His voice felt like gravel when he spoke. "I don't know, but do you really want to find out the hard way if they can?"

She'd started out watching his mouth, but then she looked up in surprise. What was wrong now?

"What?" he mouthed slowly so she'd understand.

"I can hear you." She took a cautious step toward him. "Why? What's different?"

How the hell was he supposed to know? It's not like anyone ever gave him a book of rules that explained how any of this stuff worked. She could see him when no one else did. That she could also hear him at times was just more mystery.

"I don't know. I wouldn't count on it lasting."

The bright green eyes studied him for the longest time before she finally spoke again. "I've been worried about you. Where have you been?"

He didn't know how to deal with her first statement so he focused on the second. "Something else I don't know. One minute I was there by the porch and then

I was gone. Not sure where I go when—" he waved his hand around to indicate the town "—I leave here. Nowhere, maybe. Eventually, I'm back with no idea how I got here."

She nodded, chewing on that full lower lip. "So what we did shorted you out somehow."

What did that mean? "I'm no shorter. I'm always the same."

A bit of humor sparked in her eyes. "Sorry, I forgot they didn't use electricity much in your day. What I mean was that when we, uh…"

Her cheeks turned a bit rosy. Cute. He finished her sentence for her. "When we kissed?"

Looking exasperated, she rolled her eyes. "Yes, that. Maybe somehow it was like dumping boiling water into a cold glass jar, making it shatter. Everything inside pours out, leaving it empty."

He shrugged, although it was as good a description as any. "That's sounds about right."

"So we should avoid physical contact, not if there's a chance you wouldn't make it back next time."

Was that disappointment in her voice? He hoped so, because he wasn't all that happy about the idea himself. They'd been in the same room for less than five minutes, and she already had him thinking about how it had felt to touch her. For those precious few seconds, he'd been a man again, not this shadow who haunted a dead town.

What choice did he have? "Agreed."

There was a sadness in her pretty face that hadn't been there before. Could one kiss have meant that much to her? If so, either modern men were idiots or she was picky about who she kissed. He liked both of those possibilities.

Time to move on. "You've gotten a lot done while I was gone."

"I've had a week without interruptions to concentrate on my work."

Okay, he wasn't sure he liked being referred to as an interruption. A distraction, maybe, but it was enough to know that he bothered her as much as she did him. He nodded in the direction of the tables.

"What is all of this for, anyway?"

She moved past him and picked up the sketch she'd started of the shipping office. "I'm doing a detailed survey of the town, starting with how it is now. Once I've finished with the existing buildings, I'm going to look for evidence of the ones that are gone. I figure there might be corner posts left in the ground, bits and pieces of dishes and things."

"You want to look for trash? Why would you waste your time doing something like that?"

Rayanne lowered the paper she'd been studying to frown at him. "It's not trash, Wyatt. It's evidence of how people lived. I'm a history professor with a specialty in the American West. If I can gather enough information, I'm hoping to write the history of Blessing."

He understood that she was excited by the prospect, even though he didn't understand why. From what he could see, modern people had it so much better than people had back in his day. But if helping her find what she was looking for meant spending more time in her company, he'd do it even if the last thing he wanted to do was relive his past.

It hadn't been that good the first time around, and now it just reminded him of everything that had gone wrong. Even so, for the first time he had someone who could see and hear him. Talking about the past wasn't nearly as painful as drifting through the hours and days alone.

"I didn't live here in Blessing, not for long, anyway. But I can share what I remember about the place."

His begrudging offer was rewarded with a huge smile. "I was hoping you'd say that."

"You might not always be able to hear me or even see me, but I'll try to let you know when I'm around."

"Sounds great."

She picked up the sketch of the shipping office. "Well, I should get started."

Then she frowned. "What happened over here?"

Rayanne bent down to gather up the papers he'd accidentally sent flying when he got curious about the sketch of the boot. His boot.

"Maybe a breeze caught them. I noticed them on the floor but couldn't pick them up."

Luckily, she was too busy straightening her artwork to question his explanation. Those sketches were on the table farthest from the door, so it would be unlikely a breeze would send them flying and leave the other two tables undisturbed. When she picked up the sketches of him, she blushed again and shoved them to the bottom of the stack.

He pretended an interest in the floor plans she'd

drawn out. What would her family think of her work? It was clear that her mother had disapproved of Rayanne's decision to spend the summer in Blessing. He could only imagine what the woman would say if Rayanne ever told her about him.

"That smile is a tad scary, Mr. McCain."

He toned it down. "I was just thinking about that history you're planning to write. How would people down below react if they found out you'd gotten some of your facts from the likes of me?"

She picked up her pack and headed for the door, making sure not to brush against him on her way out. "Let's just say that I'm going to make darn sure they don't find out."

"That's what I figured."

He followed her out into the sunshine. Stirring up old memories wasn't going to be any fun, but he couldn't find it in him to walk away.

Three more weeks had flown by. Other than a quick trip down to Phil's for supplies and the answering machine she'd promised to buy, Rayanne had spent every possible minute with Wyatt McCain. They'd wandered the streets of Blessing together as he pointed out everything he could remember about the town. With his help, she'd been able to fill in a lot of the empty spaces on her hand-drawn map.

She wasn't sure how she was going to explain to anyone else how she knew where the schoolteacher lived and that some of the miners had lived in tents pitched outside the edge of town. She also had a list of names to research, ones she had no way of knowing other than that Wyatt had told her.

Wyatt stayed with her as much as he could, but there were times that he simply melted out of sight with no warning. The first few times had startled her. One minute they'd be having a conversation, and the next she was talking to herself. Evidently he only had so much energy to expend, and maintaining visibility ate it up pretty quickly.

Right now, he was nowhere to be found. She shivered despite the heat of the day. Common sense said she should be a bit scared to be up there alone with no one but a ghost for company, but she wasn't. But then Wyatt was more real to her than any other man she'd ever known.

She lived for the odd moments when he found something amusing, and the rough sound of his laughter would ring out over the streets of Blessing. From the little he'd told her about his past, the man hadn't had much to laugh about. The one thing they never talked about was the gunfight that had claimed his life.

She couldn't blame him, but his story was an integral part of the history of Blessing. Her work wouldn't be complete without it. But anytime her questions skirted anywhere near the subject, he'd fade right out of view.

"Good morning."

His deep voice slid over her skin like warm honey, making her think about things she shouldn't. The trouble was, that particular subject was never far from her mind since that single kiss they'd shared. For both their sakes, she hadn't mentioned it since the day he'd reappeared. That didn't mean her days, and especially her nights, weren't filled with dreams of how things might have progressed beyond that first kiss.

And a few of those moments had been incredibly intense and real, as if somehow the two of them were connecting in her dreams in a way they couldn't in the real world. It was unsettling, to say the least.

For a lot of reasons, it would be far smarter to keep herself firmly grounded in the present, her focus on her work. Although she appreciated Wyatt's companionship, if even the slightest touch damaged him, they needed to keep some distance between them.

Which was easier said than done, especially when she seemed to be hyperaware of him at all times.

She loved the way he moved, all power and confidence. It was hard not to stop and stare when he appeared at the end of the street and walked toward her. Maybe she could get past it and see him just as a friend, but it was obvious the attraction ran both ways.

He might not think she noticed the way he stared at her backside whenever she bent down to take measurements. Then there was the day she'd worn a halter top to town. He'd been unable to tear his eyes away from her chest for the longest time, his pale eyes glittering with a delicious hunger. That the weight of his gaze had left her nipples pebbled up hard and achy hadn't helped the situation.

"Are you all right?"

His question sounded amused rather than worried, a clear sign that he'd picked up on the direction her thoughts had taken again. She'd also failed to answer his greeting.

"I'm fine. I was just thinking about what I want to do next."

Wyatt didn't even try to hide his smirk, but at least he didn't push it. "You still haven't surveyed the church."

No, she hadn't. What's more, she had no explanation for her reluctance to do so. Right now, it was just a blank square on her map of the town, and she hadn't set foot in the place since her first day back on the mountain. No photos. No diagram. All because she associated it with Wyatt's death. Not going into the building wouldn't change anything, but—

Wyatt was no longer looking at her. Instead, he was staring off in the direction of the woods, his expression dark.

"What's wrong?"

His eyes were chilling as he shoved his duster back to rest his hands on his guns. "Someone is coming up the mountain."

She didn't doubt him for a minute, but still she had to ask, "How do you know?"

He'd also moved to stand between her and the perceived threat. "The energy changes."

It was unlikely that whoever was making the long drive up the mountain had done so by mistake. That narrowed the field of possibilities to a handful of people. Best-case scenario, Phil had taken her up on her invitation to come for lunch sometime, but she wasn't holding out much hope for that. He'd said he'd call first.

None of the other options were good, but she'd never find out standing here in Blessing.

"Well, there goes my morning's work."

She shouldered her pack. "I'll be back after I deal with this."

Wyatt still radiated a whole lot of tension. "I'm coming with you."

"That's not necessary."

He just stared at her, clearly unwilling to budge on the issue.

Heck, if it was her mother who'd decided to drop in, Rayanne would need all the moral support she could get. "Fine, but it's your funeral."

As soon as the words slipped out, her hand flew up to cover her mouth. "Oh, Wyatt, I can't believe I said that. It's just a saying. I didn't mean anything by it."

His expression softened a little. "Rayanne, you don't have to watch what you say around me. I know I'm dead. Nothing's going to change that."

She started to reach out to touch his arm, but stopped herself just in time. "I know, but I'm the one who forgets sometimes. Don't you?"

The sadness in his handsome face hurt her heart. "I wish I could."

He stared past her, toward the far end of town. "We need to get moving. That car will be here soon."

The two of them walked through the woods in silence. The closer they got to the cabin, the bigger the knot in her stomach grew. She was in no mood to fight with her mother, and confronting her father wouldn't be any picnic, either. Together, well, she'd rather bang her head on the wall.

But then it wasn't her mother's car rolling into sight. Oh, no, nothing that simple. She coasted to a stop.

"Well, rats. What's he doing here?"

Especially uninvited and unannounced. Her temper flared hot. Yeah, Shawn had mentioned wanting to visit her and to see the town that was holding her captive for the summer. His words, not hers. She hadn't wanted to hurt his feelings by telling him that he wasn't welcome up here on the mountain, but she'd made it clear that she was too busy to entertain guests.

Wyatt stared at the man climbing out of the SUV parked next to hers. "Who is he?"

The deep rumble of Wyatt's voice startled her, not that she'd forgotten he was standing there. "His name is Dr. Shawn Randolph. He teaches at the same college that I do."

"Somehow I doubt he drove all the way up here just to check on a colleague." Wyatt's eyes were ice cold as he moved up to stand between her and the clearing. Doubt dripped from his every word. "I'm guessing he's more than that. Is he your lover?"

Honesty had her saying, "No, but he wants to be."

With that, she stepped around Wyatt and marched off to greet Shawn, already counting the minutes until he left.

Chapter 10

"Shawn."

Her smile felt brittle, but her guest didn't appear to notice that Rayanne's greeting lacked something in the enthusiasm department. Maybe that was a good thing. He set his overnight bag down at his feet and started right for her, his smile bright and his arms held out for a hug.

She let him enfold her and reluctantly hugged him back. After all, they'd been friends long before they'd started dating. It would be a shame if they couldn't find their way back to that. At this point, she wished they hadn't taken their relationship in that other direction at all. With Wyatt around somewhere, she was relieved that Shawn didn't try to kiss her.

Instead, he held her at arm's length and smiled approvingly. "You're looking good, Rayanne. The mountain air must agree with you, and I like the tan. You're obviously spending a lot of time outdoors."

How else did he think she'd be studying a ghost town? She bit back the snark and aimed for pleasant. "Pretty much. I work in Blessing all day and type up my notes at night."

Wyatt picked that moment to move up beside them, standing where she could see him out of the corner of her eye. He was staring at Shawn with what she called his gunslinger game face on. Clearly he wasn't happy about Shawn being there, but then neither was she. She especially wasn't happy about his showing up, suitcase in hand. The question was, what spurred Shawn to make the trip in the first place?

Time to play hostess. "Why don't you come on inside and tell me why you're here."

As if she couldn't guess. While they made their way to the porch, she glanced back to check on Wyatt, but he'd disappeared. Somehow she doubted it was one of those times when his energy had run out or whatever it was that caused him to blink out of existence for a while. Where the heck was he?

She unlocked the door and stepped back to let Shawn walk inside. "Set your bag down anywhere and have a seat in the living room. I'll fix us a couple of cold drinks and join you in a second."

He dropped his suitcase on the steps that led to the bedrooms upstairs. "Sounds good."

She filled glasses with ice and grabbed a couple of soft drinks from the refrigerator. Shawn stood in front of the picture window, staring out at the meadow and the trees beyond. He turned to face her just as she set his drink down on the coffee table.

"That was lucky timing that you happened to be coming back to the cabin right when I drove up."

"Yes, it was. I usually stay gone most of the day."

She sipped her drink, stalling until she came up with a good reason why she would've needed to return just then. Somehow she didn't think Shawn would believe her if she told him the truth, that her friendly neighborhood ghost had sensed him approaching.

"I've been taking measurements of all the buildings left standing in Blessing, but I forgot my tape measure this morning."

She automatically headed for Ray's favorite chair, leaving Shawn no choice but to take the sofa. An odd look crossed his face, but it was gone before she could read it accurately—maybe disappointment or even frustration. Did he expect her to cuddle up next to him?

If so, too bad. She wouldn't have felt very comfortable doing that before she'd left to come up on the mountain. Now that they've been apart for a while without her calling him even once, she felt the distance even if he didn't. She didn't want to hurt him, but she felt nothing for him beyond the ordinary friendship between two colleagues.

When the silence dragged on too long for comfort, she asked, "So, what brings you up here?"

Shawn immediately sat up straighter and set his glass down hard enough to cause the pop to slosh over the top. Obviously, she'd hit the wrong button with that question.

His expression went completely flat, yet his barely controlled anger was obvious. "You promised to consider spending some time together, Rayanne, but obviously you're set on spending the whole damn summer up here. That left me no choice but to surprise you. I thought maybe we could take off for a few days, do some sightseeing and stay at a nice hotel somewhere."

She hated to disappoint him. "I really wish you'd called first, Shawn. You do know that I'm working up here, not vacationing. I've made good progress, but I still have a lot left to do. Once I get my survey done, I want to get a good start on writing. I also need to finish going through my uncle's things. I've barely started on that."

If he was aiming for charming her into giving in, he failed miserably. "Oh, come on, Rayanne. You can afford to take a day or two off. It's not like that ghost town is going anywhere."

She prayed for patience. "You're welcome to stay for dinner and spend the night. I'll even show you around Blessing this afternoon if you're interested in seeing it before you go."

"Fine, then," Shawn snapped, not backing down. "I'd love to see what it is about this place that's kept you fixated on it since you were thirteen."

Okay, that did it. "And who told you about that? Never mind, don't answer that. It had to be my mother. When did you two become so friendly? As far as I knew, you two had only met that one time she stopped by my office last semester."

He flushed guiltily. "Uh, yeah, the subject might have come up when she called me at the college to see if I had heard from you recently. She was concerned about you being up here all by yourself and suggested I surprise you with a visit."

Before she could decide how to respond, a wave of cool air washed through the room. Great, Wyatt listening in on the conversation was just what she needed right now. She took a slow look around. No sign of him, but he was there. She'd bet money on it.

Finally, she set her drink aside. "Shawn, I'm sorry you made the trip up here for nothing. I appreciate your concern, but I'm doing fine. I've waited my whole professional life to work on a project like this, and, thanks to my uncle, now I've got the chance. As I said, you're welcome to spend the night so you don't have to risk driving down the mountain in the dark, but it would be better for both of us if you left in the morning. The offer for a tour still stands."

She stood up. "I ate breakfast really early this morning, and lunch is sounding good to me. How about I make us each a sandwich?"

"If you're sure it's not too much trouble."

She ignored the sarcasm. "Not at all."

As she gathered the makings for a quick lunch, she struggled to regain control of her temper. Maybe Shawn did have the right to assume she'd be glad to see him. It wasn't as if they'd parted on bad terms.

He followed her back into the kitchen. "So tell me how your work is going. Have you decided what the focus of your paper will be?"

Slowly, the tension between them faded away, and it felt like old times as she described what she'd accomplished. Over the past couple of years, they'd often spent hours discussing each other's research projects, colleagues supporting each other. The whole time they talked, she remained all too aware they might not be alone. But if Wyatt was still in the cabin, she couldn't feel him.

As she and Shawn carried their lunch out onto the porch, she studied the trees. Finally, she spotted her ghostly companion standing deep in the shadows. He raised his hand to acknowledge her and then faded out of sight. Her own hand automatically raised to wave back. Realizing what she'd been about to do, she acted as if she were brushing away an insect. At least Shawn didn't appear to have noticed.

For the next few minutes, the two of them concentrated on finishing their lunch. Once they were done, she'd show Shawn around Blessing that afternoon so that he could get an early start in the morning. She didn't want to hurt Shawn's feelings, but she wanted him gone so she could get back to work.

But if she was going to be honest about it, that wasn't the real reason. Sitting here with Shawn felt like she was cheating on the other man in her life—Wyatt McCain.

If that made her crazy, so be it.

* * *

Wyatt headed back to where he belonged, leaving Rayanne to entertain her gentleman caller. After all, Blessing was his home, such as it was. He let himself fade out of sight and made his way back to town. Where to next?

He had no interest in hanging out in the church. Right now the saloon held no real appeal, but it was better than drifting up and down the street with no purpose. He pushed through the doors, deliberately setting them to swinging, a reminder to himself that he had substance, that he was a little bit real. Inside the saloon, he automatically drifted toward the work Rayanne had spread out all over the place.

Her handwriting was neat and precise. She found even the smallest bit of information he could share interesting. When they'd unearthed an old pitcher underneath a pile of old lumber, she'd cradled it in her hands with a look of utter wonder on her face. He loved the way she took pleasure in such simple things.

She'd covered the wall with sketches of the individual buildings and then of the town as a whole. She had a real eye for detail. It spoke to how strongly that day in the belfry fifteen years ago had affected her that she could draw the missing buildings with uncanny accuracy. He hated that for her. Getting drawn into his world was the last thing he wanted for anyone, but especially her.

The only pictures missing were the sketches she'd done of him. What had she done with them? He smiled, remembering how she'd blushed when she'd picked them up and shoved them under a stack of files. He didn't expect her to spend any more time here on the mountain after she finished her research, but he hoped that she kept the picture of him.

It would be nice to be remembered by someone.

He froze, listening to what the wind was whispering. People were coming his way. It had to be Rayanne, which was fine. The question was why she was dragging her unwanted guest, Shawn, along with her. He doubted the man had any real interest in Blessing. No, it was the heat in Shawn's eyes whenever he looked at Rayanne that was the driving force behind his feigned interest in her research.

Wyatt had disliked Shawn on sight, and he didn't want the man anywhere near Blessing or Rayanne. What kind of man showed up at a woman's home, dragging his luggage on the assumption he'd be welcome to spend the night? Maybe things were different in the world beyond this mountain, but Wyatt thought he should be horsewhipped for such an outrage.

It was a damned shame that Wyatt's guns only worked reliably one day a year. With lightning-fast reflexes, he drew both of his revolvers, taking aim, pretending Shawn was in his sights. Yeah, he'd love to run that son of a bitch right off the mountain. For Rayanne's sake, he'd refrain from hurting him, but he'd make damn sure the cad didn't come sneaking back up to her cabin again anytime soon.

The temptation to shoot off a few rounds was strong. If he were alone in town, he might have tried it. But Rayanne was only down the street. If he'd become so real to her, would his bullets always be real, as well? While he wouldn't mind putting a scare into Shawn, he wouldn't risk frightening her. Not again.

They were almost to the saloon. Should he fade away and allow them some privacy?

Hell, no.

He hurried across the room to stand behind the old bar where it would be unlikely that Shawn would run into him. He might not be able to see Wyatt, but he would likely feel the cold that surrounded him. For Rayanne's sake, he'd do his best to avoid direct contact with her friend.

That is, unless Shawn made any kind of move toward Rayanne. It had been hard enough to watch him hug her earlier. Anything beyond that and he'd— No, he stopped right there. The truth was, he couldn't do anything at all. Besides, Shawn could give her everything that Wyatt couldn't. If he weren't such a selfish bastard, he would even encourage her to spend time with the man. With that happy thought, he faded to invisible.

Rayanne came through the door first. Before inviting her companion inside, she glanced all around the room with a worried expression on her face. As she panned the saloon, her eyes swept past him but then snapped right back to where he stood. She stared at him for a second, her eyes narrowed in suspicion.

So much for hiding. He gave up and pulled himself back together. Shawn wouldn't be able to see him, anyway, and obviously there was no hiding from Rayanne. It would be interesting to see if she could ignore him while she showed her friend around. He crossed his arms over his chest and leaned back against the counter behind the bar, meeting her frown with a smile.

"Come on in, Shawn. You can see what I've been working on and then I'll show you the rest of the town."

Her companion followed her inside. Shawn removed his dark glasses and blinked several times to adjust his eyes to the dim interior. Rayanne led him over to the cluster of tables and explained what he was looking at. Wyatt hated the way Rayanne chewed on her lower lip as she waited for her friend to pronounce judgment on her work.

After studying her line drawings of the interior of the buildings still standing, Shawn wandered over to study her side-by-side sketches of the exteriors now and how they would've looked a hundred years ago.

"I sometimes forget what a talented artist you are. You've definitely taken the skeletons of the buildings and brought them back to life in these."

Finally, he moved on to the pictures she'd drawn from memory along with Wyatt's assistance. After a few seconds, Shawn frowned. "I know I haven't seen the whole town, but it didn't look as if there were this many buildings left standing."

"There aren't. I drew those from memory."

Rayanne obviously regretted letting that slip out when Shawn shot her a questioning look. "From memory? When would you have seen them?"

She jammed her hands in the front pockets of her jeans and shot Wyatt a quick look. "I should have said memories. I pieced them together from descriptions in books where Blessing was mentioned and from photographs of similar buildings in other towns. My uncle also left me journals written by a couple of relatives who actually lived here in Blessing."

Shawn looked surprised. "I didn't know you'd found any family journals. I'd love to read them sometime."

Wyatt frowned. Why hadn't Rayanne talked about what she'd learned from Hattie's and Amanda's journals with him? She'd had plenty of opportunity during the hours they'd spent together roaming through town.

Hattie had been a young girl when the town died out. By that time, a good part of Blessing had already been torn down, so it must have been Amanda who'd described the town in her journal.

He had to wonder what horror stories she'd recorded in the pages of that book. He wasn't sure he wanted to know. His name had come up, though, or else why would Rayanne have kept the stories to herself? He'd have to decide whether to press her for answers. Right now, he planned on sticking close as she showed Shawn the rest of the town.

She shuffled her friend out the door, pausing in the doorway to shoot one last look in Wyatt's direction. Clearly, she wasn't happy about him eavesdropping on their conversation. He waited long enough for them to put some distance between them and the saloon before joining them out in the warmth of the afternoon sun.

As they walked along ahead of him, Shawn put his arm around her shoulders, pulling her close to his side. The casual familiarity had Wyatt gritting his teeth and wanting to reach for his guns again. But within only a few steps, Rayanne did a sidestep that took her out of Shawn's reach to point out something of interest. Wyatt smiled at the other man's frustrated expression, but Shawn was quick to paste a smile back on his face.

Wyatt moved closer to keep an eye on the situation. It was obvious that Shawn wanted far more from Rayanne than mere friendship. That was fine. It showed that the man had good taste. But if he tried to press the issue in a manner that upset Rayanne, Wyatt would do his damnedest to intervene. With that in mind, he checked the slide of his guns in their holsters and followed his lady down the street.

Rayanne's jaw ached from grinding her teeth. It was bad enough she was having to fend off Shawn's clumsy attempts to reassert himself as her boyfriend. She didn't need Wyatt following their every move as if he were some ghostly chaperone. She was an adult, perfectly capable of taking care of her own problems.

She shot Wyatt a dirty look when Shawn wasn't looking, but Wyatt didn't back off. If he thought that innocent look on his face was working, he was sorely mistaken. Finally, he brushed past her to join Shawn on the porch outside of the mercantile. The jerk! He knew she couldn't even say anything without confirming her mother's worst fears, and Rayanne had little doubt that Shawn would carry tales right back to her parents.

Rather than let Wyatt know how mad she was, she carefully schooled her features to look interested in Shawn's impressions of Blessing. But as the two men stood nearly side by side, it was difficult not to draw comparisons and note that one came out the clear winner—Wyatt McCain.

Although close in height, their builds were noticeably different. Shawn prided himself on his efforts to keep fit, but he lacked the rock-hard muscles built from years of hard labor. There was a softness about Shawn that didn't fare well standing next to Wyatt's lean strength.

Both men were good-looking. Shawn's blond hair and dark eyes combined with an engaging smile attracted women of all ages. Charm came easily to him, maybe too easily. Wyatt's face was more sculpted, all hard edges with the story of his life etched there in harsh lines. Rayanne's inner woman was definitely drawn to the classic alpha male, but that wasn't the deciding factor.

It came down to how each of the two men viewed her. Wyatt's starkly blue eyes saw too much, but Shawn only saw what he wanted. In the end, it was no contest.

Wyatt might not understand her passion for studying the past, but he'd done everything he could to help her. Shawn seemed to be jealous of her work, as if she should put it on the back burner to pay more attention to him. Maybe she was wrong to resent Shawn's intrusion, especially if he really did have strong feelings for her.

But what if those feelings were only for the woman he wanted her to be? It bothered her a lot that he was such a perfect fit for her mother's vision of the kind of man Rayanne should want in her life. She might have been able to get past that, but his unexpected alliance with her mother didn't help his cause.

The creak of wood snapped her out of her reverie. While she'd been lost in her thoughts, the two men had moved on. Realizing Shawn was about to walk into the mining office, she took off running, yelling his name.

"Shawn! Stop! That building isn't safe."

He froze and quickly backed out of the doorway. "Thanks for the warning."

She joined him on the porch, all too aware of Wyatt standing only inches away. "Didn't mean to startle you, but the floor inside this particular building is rotten."

Shawn held on to the door frame and leaned inside to get a better look. "Whoa, the whole back half is caved in. Pity the poor sucker who found out the hard way that it wasn't safe."

"Wait a minute." He took a cautious step forward. "Those breaks look fresh."

They were. She just wished he hadn't noticed. "Yes, I discovered the boards were weak. I haven't been back inside since. I haven't decided yet whether to hire someone to patch the hole and reinforce the support from underneath. There's a cellar under the building that would give easy access for any repair work."

When Shawn turned to face her, it was clear he wasn't buying her matter-of-fact description of the incident. His eyebrows snapped down to frame the anger in his eyes.

"Let me get this straight. You walked in there and fell through the floor?"

He moved closer, crowding her into backing up. He

followed her step for step, using his superior height to intimidate her. That so wasn't going to work. She stopped retreating and planted her feet, her hands clenched in fists at her side.

"No, I did not fall through."

Her stomach lurched at the memory of how close she'd come to doing exactly that. She carefully schooled her expression and went on. "A couple of boards broke when I stepped on them, but I caught myself in time to avoid falling through. No harm, no foul. End of story."

His response was one note lower than an all-out bellow, his alarm over the situation all too clear. "Damn it, Rayanne, you could've been badly hurt in that death trap. What if you'd broken something? You would've lain there for hours or even days! You could have died!"

One of them needed to remain calm to ramp down the tension, especially with Wyatt standing right next to them, his right hand on his gun. She took a long, slow breath before speaking.

"Come on, Shawn. Clearly, I wasn't hurt." She did a slow spin, holding her arms out to prove her claim. "I now make a habit of checking to see if any of the other buildings I enter have a cellar or if they're built right on the ground."

He wasn't backing down. "Your mother is right. This whole place is a death trap. You can't stay here alone."

Okay, that did it.

"I hate to sound like a four-year-old, but you're not the boss of me and neither is she. I'm an adult and a professional historian. Thanks to Uncle Ray, this property and the town itself both belong to me. I can and will stay here as long as I darn well want to. If you don't like it, that's too damn bad."

He jerked back as if she'd slapped him. "Be reasonable, Rayanne. You've got to admit this place is nothing but a disaster waiting to happen. You've got plenty of pictures and measurements. There's no reason you can't complete your research and write up your findings from your condo or your office at the college."

"No, I can't." She spaced the words carefully, injecting as much conviction into each one as she could. "Not that it's any of your business, but the terms of my uncle's will dictate that I live here until the first of September to finalize the transfer of the deed to my name. If I leave before then, I forfeit my inheritance. I'm not going to let that happen. Blessing belongs to me."

He looked thoroughly disgusted. "Your mom told me about your uncle's crazy stipulations. No wonder she's been talking to an attorney to see what it would take to break the will. He thinks she has a good shot at it."

"On what basis? She's not the heir. I am."

Shawn's mouth snapped shut, as if he realized just how far out on a shaky limb he was. She waited him out, making it clear she wasn't going anywhere until he spit it out.

"On what basis?" she repeated.

Finally, he caved. "On the basis her brother was mentally unstable."

Well, that certainly came as no shock. She didn't know if her mother was really worried about Rayanne or if she was jealous because her brother had skipped over his sister to leave his home and money to his niece, instead.

"That's a crock. He had post-traumatic stress disorder as a younger man, but he was doing fine. Besides, his attorney, who is now mine, as well, assures me that the will is ironclad. Uncle Ray clearly expected my parents would have issues with me inheriting Blessing because he took the precaution of having one of the top law firms in the state draw up his will to make sure the documents were airtight. They even included two different psych evaluations, stating that he was of sound mind when he signed the paperwork."

She looked past him at the town she'd come to love and the ghost who had his own space in her heart. "I'm sorry my mother put you in the middle of this, Shawn. I know you're trying to be a good friend to me, but I'm staying."

Then she turned on her heel and marched off, not caring if Shawn followed or not. He could find his own way back to the cabin. About halfway to the end of the street, she stopped and turned back. No matter how mad she was at the whole situation, she wouldn't leave him standing in Blessing, especially with a pissed-off ghost hovering right behind him.

"I'll tell you what," she said, forcing a small smile. "I don't want to fight on your only evening here. Let's go back to the cabin. It's been a long day already, and I'm ready for some downtime. I've got lasagna in the freezer that I can heat up for dinner, and then we can watch a movie if you'd like."

His charming smile was firmly back in place. "That sounds great, Rayanne, and then tomorrow maybe we can—"

"No, Shawn, don't go there. Come morning, you need to leave."

When he started to say something, she held up her hand to stop him. "Alone, Shawn. I'm staying here."

This time, when she walked away, he followed her. With his longer legs, he could have caught up with her easily. That he didn't spoke volumes.

Chapter 11

The lights blinked out, leaving Rayanne's cabin bathed in moonlight. Lucky for Wyatt, he was at home in the darkness, his vision as sharp in the shadows as it was in sunlight. But right now, none of his senses were telling him anything.

He hated questions without answers. Always had. But when those unanswered questions were about Rayanne, they left him edgy and trigger-happy. Maybe he should head back into the woods to do some target practice but rejected the idea. He wasn't sure if Rayanne would hear his gunfire if they weren't in close proximity. More and more often, he felt solid and real when she was right beside him, but not always. Either way, if she was asleep, he didn't want to disturb her.

He stared up at her bedroom window hoping like

hell she was sleeping alone there. It was none of his business if she'd decided to forgive Shawn's attempts to bully her into leaving the mountain. Their relationship was a puzzle, that was for damn sure. The man acted as if he'd staked a claim on her, but one that Rayanne didn't accept.

On the other hand, it clearly pained her to fight with the fool. Had they been more than friends down below? When they weren't striking sparks of temper, it was clear they knew each other well and even enjoyed each other's company.

Which brought him back to the question he'd been pondering. Where in that cabin had the city man bedded down for the night? Ray had never minded Wyatt wandering inside once in a while. Sometimes he'd lurk in the corner while Ray watched that box with moving pictures in it. Rayanne's uncle had a fondness for what he called Westerns even though most only had a nodding acquaintance to reality.

Wyatt had never ventured upstairs in the cabin, but knew Rayanne's bedroom was at the front of the house overlooking the meadow. Ray's was at the back, looking toward the woods. No light had come on in Ray's old room all evening. So either someone was sleeping on the couch downstairs or else Rayanne had invited Shawn into her bed.

And damned if the very thought didn't give Wyatt an even stronger urge to chase the bastard down off the mountain.

The not knowing was driving him crazy. He'd be better off wandering the woods and town looking to see if any of the others who came to life in Blessing had shown up yet. Most only flickered in and out of existence, gradually staying longer as the time grew closer.

He hadn't mentioned anything to Rayanne, but he'd already spotted half a dozen or so of the townspeople over the past few days. Considering she could see him, would she also be able to sense whether others were around? Old Hattie certainly could. She'd pack up and leave for most of August because she didn't like being bombarded by ghostly images. She'd told him so once.

Rayanne, stubborn thing that she was, wouldn't budge a step off the mountain between now and the day it all played out again. He knew that without asking. It was too important for the adult she'd become to face down the demons from her past.

But with Shawn planning on carrying tales back down the mountain to Rayanne's mother, she'd be lucky if they didn't come boiling right back up to drag her back down to their world. If he had any decency left in him, he'd do whatever he could to make sure that she left with them.

She didn't need to watch him die, cut down in a hailstorm of bullets. What's more, he didn't want her to learn what he'd done there right at the end—something so terrible that he was still paying the price after more than a century of penance.

He cared what she thought of him. Considering how he'd lived his life, he wasn't sure what to make of that. True, he'd tried to do the right thing by Amanda and her boy, but look how that turned out.

It was time to go. Not knowing about Shawn's role

in Rayanne's life had him too wound up to simply stand there. He studied her window one last time, ready to retreat. Before he turned away, though, he caught a movement in the kitchen window. He moved closer to get a clearer look.

It was Rayanne. He took two slow steps toward the cabin, hoping to draw her attention. She raised her hand in a small wave and pointed toward the cabin door. If his lungs still worked, he would've held his breath in anticipation. A few seconds later, she stepped out onto the porch.

She didn't stop there but headed straight for him. He wanted to hold out his arms, to pull her close to his chest, to kiss her long and hard. Anything to mark her as his. None of that was going to happen. It couldn't.

Rayanne had that sweet look a woman had when she was fresh out of bed with her hair all tousled and her eyes sleepy. She had on a white shirt over plaid short pants that barely covered her backside. Not at all proper attire for a lady, but he wasn't about to complain, not when they allowed him to admire those long, tanned legs.

"What's the matter? Couldn't you sleep?" he asked, despite never knowing when she'd be able to hear him or not.

She nodded as she stretched her arms over her head and yawned. The movement drew the soft, white fabric tight across her chest, drawing his attention to the soft curve of her breasts. From the way they moved, it was clear that they were once again unbound.

He'd give anything to be able to cup them in his

palms, to feel their weight, to coax them into stiff peaks right before he took them in his mouth. Right before he took her, hard and slow. Had he ever wanted to bed any other woman this much in his life? He didn't think so. Yes, he'd been attracted to Amanda, but nothing had ever come of it. She'd still been in mourning for her late husband, and then there was her young son underfoot all the time.

"I'm sorry you had to hear all of that between Shawn and me earlier."

Even in the dim light of the moon, Wyatt could see the echo of anger mixed with pain in her eyes. All the more reason for her houseguest to depart at first light.

"I wanted to punch him." He softened the comment with a small smile.

Rayanne tipped her head to the side and grinned up at him. "Me, too."

They both laughed, savoring the moment. He couldn't remember ever enjoying a woman's company so much. Or anyone's, for that matter. He could've spent all night standing in that one spot and staring down into her pretty face.

She shivered, a reminder that she was standing out there wearing next to nothing.

Rubbing her arms, she said, "I forget that even in summer the nights are chilly."

"I'd lend you my coat if I could. You'd better get inside and try to get some sleep." He walked her back to the cabin.

She climbed the steps to the porch and turned to look back down at him. "What do you do all night?"

Watch her cabin and wonder what it would be like to share her bed up there. That wasn't something a man said to a lady, especially when he had no right to want her that way.

"Wyatt?"

He realized he'd never answered her. "I wait for you."

She drew in a sharp breath and took a half step forward, her hand lifting as if to touch the side of his face.

Before she could do so, the door behind her opened and Shawn stepped out on the porch. "Rayanne, what are you doing out here? I thought I heard you talking to someone."

Wyatt retreated. He'd said enough. Too much. He'd wait to make sure she didn't run into any problems with her houseguest and then go. She kept her back to her friend when she spoke.

"Sometimes I come out here at night to look at the stars. You can see so many more than back down in the city." Then she smiled. "I like that there's always something special waiting for me."

Wyatt couldn't find the words, so he simply nodded. Message received. Then he faded into the night.

Rayanne reluctantly followed Shawn back inside. She poured herself a glass of milk. She held up the carton. "Want some?"

Shawn leaned against the kitchen counter. "I'm good."

She sipped her drink and waited to see what Shawn had to say. It was obvious he had something on his mind. She just wished he'd picked a more convenient time to decide he wanted to chat.

Finally, he drew a deep breath. "Rayanne, I've been lying awake upstairs and thinking about how badly I've handled this whole situation. I should've called first, but honestly, I was afraid you'd say no. I also shouldn't have let your mother's concerns blind me to how important all of this is to you."

For the first time since his arrival, Shawn sounded like the man she both liked and respected. "Thank you for that, Shawn. I appreciate it."

He sidled close enough to tug the glass from her hand and slid his arm around her shoulders. "I still think we could share something special if you'd give us a chance. I know I sprang this visit on you, and I'll leave in the morning if you still want me to. But how about this? Why don't I come back in a few days, even a week from now so you have time to get your ducks in order so you can leave Blessing for a few days. We'll go somewhere nice, just the two of us, and then I'll bring you back up here."

No, that wasn't happening. He'd heard what she'd said earlier, but he hadn't really listened. She tried to step away, to put some distance between them again. "I don't think that's a good idea."

"Why not? At least give us a fighting chance."

If his tone had been an accusation, she would've walked away. Instead, he was trying to coax her into letting him try to convince her that there was a spark, a possibility of something more than what they'd shared so far. He leaned closer, going slowly but obviously still determined to kiss her. She didn't fight him, her own curiosity kicking in.

His lips brushed across hers and then settled more firmly against her mouth. She had to give Shawn credit for giving it his best shot; it was a far more impressive kiss than they'd previously shared.

Then he broke it off, his dark eyes staring down into hers for a second. Then he shook his head and leaned his forehead against her, his smile rueful.

"This really isn't going to work, is it?"

When he stepped away, she should have felt regret. All she felt was relief. "I'm sorry, Shawn. I know it sounds clichéd, but I hope we can still be friends."

His laugh had little to do with happiness, but at least he didn't press the issue. "The jury is still out on that, Rayanne. Right now all I can promise is that we can try. Tell me, though, is there someone else or is it just me?"

What could she say to that? Telling him she preferred a dead gunslinger to a live college professor wasn't going to help. Even so, she couldn't help glancing toward the picture of Wyatt still hanging on the refrigerator door.

It was too much to hope that Shawn wouldn't notice. A brief flash of temper in his expression. "A phantom from the past won't keep you warm on cold nights. I hope you realize that before it's too late, Rayanne."

As if to prove his point, a cold blast of air shot through the room and sent Shawn stumbling backward into the opposite wall of the kitchen. He looked around as if hunting for the source of the draft.

"What the hell was that?"

Rayanne knew full well that it wasn't a *what* but a *who*. However, she wasn't about to tell him that it was the very phantom he'd just mentioned, a man who'd died a century before Shawn had even been born. She ignored her other uninvited guest, hoping he'd behave.

"So you'll be leaving in the morning?"

"Yes," he said, "I guess I should."

As he spoke, another chill rippled through the room. Shawn's hair fluttered as if someone had just run their fingers through it. He shivered as he looked all over the room for the source of the cold touch.

His eyes were a bit wild when he looked back toward Rayanne. "Did you feel that?"

"Feel what?" she asked, trying to sound innocent but failing miserably. "You know how drafty these old cabins can be. Of course, maybe it's haunted. Uncle Ray died here, you know."

"That's not funny, Rayanne. I've never felt anything like it."

Of that she had no doubt. Right now she wanted to kick a certain ghost. She knew he was feeling protective, but she didn't need him fighting her battles for her.

"It's almost sunrise. Why don't I fix us both breakfast while you get packed up and ready to go?"

Shawn finally conceded defeat. "Fine, but I'm guessing your mother's going to want a report. What should I tell her?"

So be it. "Tell her the same thing I do. I'm happy and doing fine up here."

"I'm not sure she'll believe me."

Rayanne had to laugh. "Don't take it personally.

She doesn't believe me, either. Now, how do you like your eggs?"

"Scrambled."

"Perfect."

When he started up the stairs, Rayanne waited until she heard the door to her room close before speaking. She'd let Shawn have her room while she'd slept on the couch downstairs. Eventually, she'd have to deal with Ray's room, but she still wasn't ready to cross that threshold.

"Wyatt, are you still here?"

He shimmered into visibility briefly, barely long enough for her to locate him in the room. "Thank you for defending me, but you'd better disappear until he's gone. I can't afford for him to carry tales back to my family."

A cool touch brushed across her skin, sending a delicious shiver coursing through her veins.

"See you later," she whispered, crossing her fingers that was true.

For now, she put the coffee on to brew and started Shawn's farewell meal.

Chapter 12

Rayanne was noticeably absent as her unwelcome guest tossed his valise in the back of his car and slammed the lid shut. A few seconds later the car roared to life. Shawn rolled down his window and stared at the cabin, his expression flat. Not that Wyatt cared what the man was thinking. He clearly wasn't the right man for Rayanne. The car pulled away from the cabin in a cloud of dust.

Good riddance.

Earlier, Wyatt had reached the edge of the woods on his way to Blessing when he'd abruptly turned back. A mix of curiosity and jealousy had made him slip inside the cabin, determined to see what was going on between Rayanne and her would-be beau.

Watching the bastard kiss her had been like being

dragged behind a horse across rocky ground. The only comfort was in knowing that Rayanne didn't welcome his advances. Even so, there had been a hint of guilt in her eyes after Shawn retreated upstairs to pack. What was that about?

Hell, if he had her best interests at heart, he would've encouraged her to give the guy a chance. After all, Shawn could offer her everything Wyatt couldn't, including a future.

Now wasn't the time to press her for answers. He'd brushed against her on his way out, but it hadn't been enough. He wished he could wrap her in his arms and hold her, to offer at least the comfort of his touch. On the other hand, he doubted being enfolded in a wave of cold would improve her mood. If only he could find a way to be with her. He could still sense her sadness.

Should he check on her?

Yes.

He drifted back toward the cabin. In his present form, he couldn't knock. He passed through the door, stopping inside the kitchen to listen. Rayanne wasn't there or in the living room. That left the upstairs, the one part of the cabin he'd never been before.

He paused, hovering at the foot of the steps. If he waited for an invitation, hell could freeze over before he got to see where Rayanne slept. Maybe it was wrong of him to want to intrude on her privacy, but it wasn't only lust that had him wanting to see her in bed. He was worried about her.

He drifted upward, still considering his options. If she appeared to be fine, he'd leave, and she'd be none the wiser. But if she wasn't, well, he'd do whatever he could to comfort her.

At the landing, he stopped to listen. The bathroom door was open, so he knew she wasn't in there. The door to the room that had belonged to Ray was closed with nothing but silence on the other side. That left Rayanne's bedroom.

A true gentleman wouldn't cross the threshold into a lady's room uninvited. Good thing he'd never been accused of being one. Her door was open. She stood by the bed, still wearing those skimpy shorts and shirt. In a burst of action, she peeled the sheets off the bed and heaved them toward the far corner. Okay, so Shawn had indeed spent the night in Rayanne's bed, but from her behavior earlier, he'd slept there alone.

The odd thing was that even though Wyatt had never been in this room before, it somehow felt incredibly familiar. He knew without looking that there was a painting of a mountain scene on the far wall and that a matching one hung behind the open door where he couldn't see it.

There'd been long hours during the night where he'd stared up at the window from the meadow below and wondered what it would be like to hold Rayanne in his arms. At times, those moments had been so real to him that he could have sworn her hands had touched his bare skin as he'd made love to her. Probably just wishful thinking on his part. With her usual quick efficiency, she made up the bed with fresh linens. When she finished fluffing the pillows, she tossed them on the mattress.

"Wyatt, I know you're there. The question is why?"

He pulled himself together. The incident with Shawn had burned up a lot of his energy, but he managed to solidify enough that he could be seen.

"I needed to know you were all right."

Rayanne frowned and sat down on the edge of the bed. "Sorry. I didn't quite catch that. I'm guessing that whole mess downstairs took a lot out of both of us."

He nodded.

"Shawn is a nice guy. We've dated a few times. I enjoyed his company, but..."

She stopped for several seconds, staring down at the floor. "I knew he wanted more than I was willing to give. I didn't want to hurt his feelings, but I should have broken it off as soon as I realized all I wanted was a dinner companion while he wanted a wife."

For the first time, Wyatt felt a glimmer of sympathy for the other man. After all, he wanted the same things from Rayanne and was just as unable to satisfy her needs. He wanted to punch something and curse the gods who had condemned him to this nonlife.

He waited until she looked up again and slowly mouthed. "Are you all right?"

This time she understood him. "I will be. Right now I'm tired, so I'm going to go back to bed for a while. Maybe I'll feel like working later, but I'm thinking I'll probably take the day off."

Her smile was anything but happy. "I'll need all my strength to deal with my mother once she hears from Shawn. She won't be happy that I let him leave without me."

Her voice caught on a sob. "I came up here to lay the past to rest. Why can't they understand that?"

Damn, he wished those people would leave her alone. It didn't help that instead of laying the past to rest, she'd gotten tangled up with him. He edged closer, unsure what he could do to make her feel better. Touching her might use up the last bit of strength he had, but it was worth the risk.

She tracked his movement as he came toward her but made no attempt to dissuade him. When he stood right in front of her, he slowly raised his hand, bringing it ever closer to the soft curve of her cheek. The warmth of her life force drew him like nothing he'd ever known before. When his fingertips came to rest on her cheek, her skin felt like living, breathing satin.

She sighed and leaned into the curve of his palm, obviously taking as much pleasure from the small contact as he did. Once again, thanks to Rayanne, he felt solid; he felt real; he felt like a man.

One who hungered.

But the last thing she needed right now was another man pushing her for something she couldn't give. He backed away.

He forced one word, hoping she'd hear him. "Rest."

Then he started to fade away, to leave her alone to recuperate from the strain of the past twenty-four hours.

Her green eyes looked at him with such sadness, the sheen of tears making them shine brighter and even more beautiful. "I wish you and I could… I mean, I feel so comfortable with you, not like when I'm around other people and have to pretend to be like them. If you weren't… But you are, and I'm not."

She swiped a hand across her cheek to catch the tears. "I'm sorry. I'm not making any sense. Go ahead and go. I'll be more myself later."

He owed her a bit of his truth, too. "I wish we could, too."

Then he dissolved into nothing at all.

Rayanne had slept like the dead. Well, all things considered, maybe that wasn't the best analogy. But at least no dreams had plagued her this time. She sat up on the edge of the mattress, her thoughts sticky with too much sleep and not enough caffeine. The light from outside was dim, meaning she'd lost most of the day.

A shower would help clear out the cobwebs. She needed to be sharp because she had no doubt that there'd be a message waiting for her downstairs from her mother. Coward that she was, she'd turned off the phone to avoid another crisis until she'd gotten some rest.

Twenty minutes later she stepped out on the porch to watch the sunset, her mood vastly improved. No message from her mother or her father. She wasn't foolish enough to think they'd finally decided to back off and let her make her own decisions, but she'd take what she could get.

Out of habit, she scanned the area, looking for Wyatt, but he was nowhere in sight. She'd learned enough about his condition, for lack of a better word, to know that the events of the early morning would have taken their toll on him, as well. For the moment, she'd fix herself some dinner and eat it out on the porch. If he didn't appear before then, she'd take a stroll into Blessing to check on him.

As she put together a salad, she glanced at the calendar and realized she'd lost track of the days. Tomorrow was Uncle Ray's birthday, the day she'd planned to scatter his ashes on the mountain that he loved. It seemed an appropriate way to celebrate his life.

The only question was where she should take him. Maybe Wyatt would have a suggestion. He knew better than she did where Uncle Ray liked to prowl when he'd walked in the woods. Some quiet spot, one off the trail where he'd find peace at last.

But that was tomorrow. Tonight, all she wanted to do was relax. Picking up her food, she headed back outside. To her surprise, Wyatt was waiting for her. Her mood brightened immediately.

"I'm glad you're here. I was going to go into town to check on you if you didn't come back."

He'd tipped his hat back and propped his boots up on the railing, looking content. "I'm fine."

His gaze was pinned on the fading light to the west. That didn't mean his real attention wasn't on her, just as hers was on him. "Thank you again for this morning, Wyatt."

He nodded, but the following silence was comfortable, two friends enjoying the evening air. When she was done with her dinner, she set the plate aside.

"Uncle Ray asked one last favor of me. He wanted me to scatter his ashes on the mountain. I was wondering if you had any suggestions where he might have had…you know, a favorite spot where he can be laid to rest."

Wyatt sat so quietly, she wondered if she'd somehow offended him. There was a sadness in his expression that she hadn't seen before. Sometimes she forgot that he'd actually died back when Blessing was a bustling town, but he'd remained trapped here on the mountain. Would he ever know peace?

"I'm sorry, Wyatt. I wasn't thinking. I forget sometimes."

He stopped her. "It's all right, Rayanne. It means a lot that you forget what I am, that you treat me like a real man and a friend."

"You are my friend, Wyatt. Never doubt that."

There was a lot of heat in his eyes when he smiled at her, the kind of heat a man felt for a woman he found attractive. She suspected that he could see the same need reflected in hers. Something dark and hungry stirred in the night air between them.

She wanted this man. And what an irony that was. She'd gotten rid of Shawn because he left her cold.

And Wyatt, who carried the chill of death with him everywhere, made her blood run hot. The gods obviously had a perverse sense of humor. The single kiss the two of them had shared had almost destroyed him. Losing him would destroy her.

Damn.

She couldn't sit still, but night had fallen. Too late to walk off her frustration. Rather than stay in one spot, she stood up and walked to the far end of the porch, well aware that Wyatt watched her every movement. When she finally lit in one spot, he joined her at the railing.

"I know a spot Ray loved. I'll take you there in the morning. Pack a lunch. It's a bit of a walk."

"I will. Thank you." She stared at him, drinking in the strength in his handsome face.

"You have something on your mind, Rayanne?"

His voice was a deep rumble that she felt all the way to her bones. She tried to put what she was feeling into words. "I was just wondering about the why of it all. Why you're still here. Why I can see you when even Amanda, Hattie and Uncle Ray only got the occasional glimpse of you and the others. Why I want—"

Oops, almost went too far with that. It's bad enough that she'd developed such an attachment to her ghostly companion without embarrassing both herself and him by admitting that she had feelings for him. Desires the likes of which she'd never known before for any man.

He stared off into the distance. "We'll need to get an early start tomorrow."

She managed a small smile. "Okay. I'll be ready at first light. Thank you for doing this for me, Wyatt."

"Anything within my power."

Once again he raised his hand to her face, but this time the cold made her flinch. He knew it, too, because he jerked his hand back down to the railing.

"I'm sorry."

"Don't be. I like it when you touch me. A lot." Feeling a little embarrassed, she admitted, "I dream of you…of us every night. It's like you're right there with me."

His eyes widened in surprise. "I think maybe I have been." He glanced up toward her bedroom window. "I'd never been in your room before, but I knew exactly how it looked."

"Maybe somehow we find each other in the one place we can be together, but it's not enough, Wyatt. I want to hold you in my arms for real."

As she spoke, she eased closer to him, but he shook his head and stepped away. "As much as I'd like to, Rayanne, we shouldn't. You deserve a man of your own time, a good one. Not someone like me. And I'm not just talking about the fact that I'm dead. If you really knew me, knew what I was capable of, you wouldn't want me."

Tears stung her eyes, but she blinked them away. "I don't believe that. I've seen the kind of man you are. I *like* the kind of man you are."

"You don't know—" he started to say, but then he hesitated. "Look, none of that matters. Nothing will change that I'm not alive. I'm just a fragment of a man caught between here and hell."

She hated the pain in those words, the despair. How had he remained sane after all this time?

But if he wouldn't defend himself, she would.

"Stop that right now. You are not just a fragment, Wyatt McCain." She faced him head-on to make sure he knew she meant business. "I don't know why you're stuck here like this, but I'm damn glad you are. You saved my life that day in the mining office. That makes you a hero in my book, and I won't let you tell me any different."

She didn't know what kind of reaction to expect, but laughter wasn't it. On the other hand, the bright smile across Wyatt's lips took years off his face, reminding her that he hadn't been much older than she was now when he died.

"What's so funny? I meant what I said."

She knew she sounded more than a bit defensive, but at least his laughter had brightened both his mood and his image. Before, the gleam of the porch light had passed right through him. Now he actually cast a faint shadow.

"I'm sorry. A gentleman should never contradict a lady."

His eyes crinkled in good humor as he held up his hands in surrender.

"See, that proves you're smart, too."

This time their shared laughter rang out across the meadow. As the last echo died away, she found herself lost in the wonder of Wyatt's gaze. She could feel the power of it calling to her, pulling her closer, right into the strength of his arms.

She whispered his name as he closed the last bit of distance between them, for once his lips warm and soft against hers. His arms held her so very carefully, as if she were something precious and fragile. She leaned into his strength, learning for the first time what it would've been like to hold this man in her arms when he'd been alive, back when he walked the streets of Blessing.

His tongue swept into her mouth, tasting, touching, exploring, driving her crazy. She shivered, this time with anticipation, not cold. The heady scent of leather and man filled her head. How could this be real?

But it was.

At that moment, Wyatt was right there, solid as a rock, kissing her, holding her, demanding as much from her as she could give. She moaned, wanting so much more.

She broke off the kiss long enough to ask, "Will you come upstairs with me?"

But as soon as she did, he faded, no longer solid, no longer there.

"Wyatt!" she cried as he stepped away from her, staring at his hands as they flickered in and out of sight.

Even so, he smiled. "That was amazing!"

Although his voice was little better than a whisper, his joy remained real. "Did you mean that? About me coming upstairs with you?"

"Yes." She put all the conviction she could into the single word.

More of him was gone now. "I'll try to come to you in your dreams again. Not sure if—"

But then he was gone.

What had he meant by coming to her in her dreams? Only one way to find out. She picked up her dinner dishes and went inside. After locking up and turning off the kitchen lights, she headed upstairs. A long bubble bath, a glass of wine and an early bedtime were definitely in order tonight.

Then maybe she'd find out if dreams could really come true.

Chapter 13

Wyatt stared up at the night sky, watching the moon rise overhead and counting the stars. As beautiful as they were, all of those countless shiny specks combined didn't compare to the bright light of Rayanne's spirit.

A hero. She thought he was a hero. Who would've thought a woman would ever look at him that way? Earlier, her unshakable belief that he'd done something special had been enough to give him substance. If it never happened again, for those few short seconds he'd held her in his arms as a man, not a ghost.

He'd always thought the gods had cursed him, but maybe this was the only way they had of letting him exist long enough to meet Rayanne. If so, he owed them an incredible debt. What a gift it was to hold her, to kiss her, to love her.

And damned if that last part wasn't true. He'd thought he'd felt something special for Amanda, but he'd never once held her in his arms or kissed her. But looking back, his feelings for Amanda paled in comparison to the connection he shared with her granddaughter, several times removed. Just knowing Rayanne soothed the anger he'd carried with him for as long as he could remember.

Amazing.

Right now she was moving around in the cabin. The lights were off downstairs, but he could hear her splashing around in that big claw-foot tub he'd seen earlier. He could imagine how she looked right now—all slick skin, her red-gold hair curling up in the steam, and that lush mouth curled up in a soft smile.

The images flashing through his mind had him hard and hurting. He wished like hell he could join her. First off, he'd work up a lather with his hands and then use them to learn every curve of her luscious body. He'd spread his legs and tuck her in between so that she'd lean back against his chest.

He loved the thought of massaging those pretty breasts while he nibbled his way along her elegant neck. But that wasn't happening. Not for real.

But maybe, just maybe, he could find Rayanne in her dreams. It wouldn't be the same, but it was as close as the two of them would ever share. Was he being selfish? Hell, yes, but after living in this nightmare for more than a hundred years, he deserved one last good dream.

Because eventually, Rayanne would return to her

real life, the one down below where she stood a chance of finding a man who could give her everything she deserved and more. Wyatt would do his best to be happy for her when that happened. Really. He'd like to think he was a good enough man to want that for her. However, if he had to spend eternity caught in this endless circle of pain, at least he'd have the memories of one night in her dreams, in her arms, to carry him through.

Now the only light in the cabin came from Rayanne's bedroom. When she stepped in front of the window, he deliberately moved farther into the shadows. Even though he was shrouded in darkness, Rayanne stared right at him and raised her hand in a brief wave. She always managed to find him. He smiled and stepped into the light.

She opened the window and called down. "I'll be waiting for you."

Then she disappeared. A few seconds later, the light winked out. How long should he wait? And where? For now, he'd make himself comfortable on the porch. Somehow he doubted she'd find it easy to go to sleep with him standing beside the bed and looming over her.

As he waited and watched, a family of deer moved into the meadow. The doe watched him with wary eyes until she was sure he presented no danger to her twin fawns. He remained still until they'd eaten their fill and moved on.

He should do the same, but he found himself reluctant to make the next move. What if this didn't work? Telling himself he could try again on another night wasn't much help. Time was running out. He could feel it slipping through his fingers as the anniversary of his death drew near. Soon, he'd be caught up in that same cycle of pain and death again. Rayanne had no part in that tragedy.

But tonight with the full moon overhead and only the two of them on the mountain, maybe they could share something special. With that thought in mind, he pressed through the door of the cabin and took that first fateful step up to the second floor.

He stopped outside Rayanne's room, although she'd left the door open.

For him? He'd like to think so.

The only sound was the soft rasp of Rayanne's breathing, slow and easy. Good. He'd been worried she wouldn't be able to sleep. Normally, his movements were totally silent because his body had no substance, but right now each step was awkward and loud to his own senses.

He froze, waiting to see if his movements had disturbed Rayanne, and then eased into her room. Inching toward the side of her bed, he was stunned by her beauty. The silvery light of the moon spilled through the window right on her pretty face. She looked peaceful with her mouth curved up in a small smile.

One hand lay flung out in his direction, as if she'd fallen asleep reaching out for him.

Her shoulders were bare, making him wonder what, if anything, she wore under that patchwork quilt. He wouldn't peek, not while she was unaware of his presence. If he were able to find her in her dreams, they'd be on equal footing. Right now, she was far too vulnerable for him to take advantage of the situation.

He stepped back and sat down on an old cedar chest and stretched his legs out, trying to get comfortable. Studying his old boots, he wished he could have cleaned up before coming to her, but that wasn't possible. Even if he'd had access to other clothes, he couldn't have worn them. Only the things that he had on, held in his hands, or carried in his pockets had made the transition to this life.

If he'd had his druthers, he'd have bathed, shaved and worn a suit. Certainly his guns had no place here, not with the taint of violence that had soaked into the very metal they were made from.

He dragged his eyes up from the floor and his mind out of the past. While he might not have a future, he had this one chance, and he'd be a fool to waste it. Anchoring himself firmly in this place and this moment, he closed his eyes and sent a tendril of thought toward the sleeping woman who called to his heart.

Gradually, he poured more and more of himself into the effort until at last he saw her. She stood at the edge of a small stream that ran along the far edge of the meadow. Her hair was twisted up in a knot at the top of her head with a few tendrils hanging loose along the back of her neck. She wore a loose-fitting dress that ended just above her shapely ankles. It left her shoulders bare, the only thing holding it up a narrow ribbon that tied at the back of her neck. The pale green suited her coloring well.

He noticed her pretty feet were bare. Funny how that one detail was the one that made him ache to touch her.

In their dream world, he spoke her name. She immediately turned to face him, her smile radiant.

"You came."

He nodded. "I promised."

She held out her hands. "Do you have to stand way over there?"

Now that the moment had arrived, he wasn't sure how to proceed, feeling like a youngster gone courting for the first time, not a full-grown man who knew what he was about. He stepped forward, slowly at first, but then faster, needing to close the distance between them.

He stopped short of where she stood. "I'm not sure what will happen when we touch."

Her smile warmed him from the inside out. "Only one way to find out, Wyatt. You look handsome, by the way. I'm really fond of that duster you always wear, but that shirt really brings out the color of your eyes."

He hadn't noticed that somewhere between sitting on the cedar chest and stepping into this meadow, he'd changed clothes. His shirt was a deep blue and his trousers a dark tan. Even his boots were new. He touched his face, relieved to find he'd shaved.

Rayanne closed the distance between them, near enough that her scent filled his head and her warmth left him edgy and hungry. Slowly, he lifted his hand to toy with a strand of her hair, twirling the curl around his finger.

"You smell like roses."

She looked a bit shy. "I took a bath in rose-scented bubble bath before I went to bed."

"I like it."

His hand found hers and gave it a gentle squeeze. It felt so normal, so perfect. Both of them let out a small sigh of relief. Here, in the dream world she'd created, they were both solid and real.

As much as he hungered for her, he didn't want to rush things or even presume that she wanted more than a simple day in the sun with him.

"Would you like to take a walk?"

Rayanne stared up at him with a temptress's smile. "That depends. How long do we have here?"

"I don't know. I've never done this before, not on purpose anyway."

"Then let's save walking for later. Right now, I'd rather sit down on the quilt I brought with me."

She tugged on his hand, leading him down toward an open area surrounded by a stand of aspens. If he wasn't mistaken, it was the same quilt that covered her bed back in the cabin.

By the time they reached the blanket, his pulse was racing and his breath was shallow, two sensations he hadn't experienced since the day he died. The combination of anticipation and nerves was a potent one. He felt young and reckless.

"May I kiss you, Miss Rayanne?"

"You may do anything you want to with me, Mr. McCain. And sooner rather than later."

She slid into his arms as if she'd always been at

home there, lifting her face to him. God, she was so beautiful.

He kissed her gently at first, thanking her without words for the gift of this moment with her.

Then he kissed her with a promise of what was to come, but making sure she'd know he would treat her with care.

And finally, he kissed her with everything he had. He claimed her mouth with lips and teeth and tongue, loving it when she gave as good as she got. It was a dance, one where their steps matched perfectly.

He broke it off as he carried them both to the ground, glad for the cushion of the soft grass and quilt. Rayanne murmured her approval as he pressed her back and kissed her again, this time letting his hands do a bit of roaming. First he traced the bare skin of her shoulder down the length of her arms and back. He trailed his fingers over her collarbone and back up to her neck. As their tongues played tag, he gave the ribbon that held her dress up a gentle tug.

She smiled against his mouth, well aware of where he was headed next. He owed her a confession.

"That first day when you got caught in the rain, I was in the saloon."

She frowned and then her eyes opened wide. "You were watching when I stripped off my shirt to wring out the water?"

He nodded, his smile feeling a bit wicked. "I did. Liked what I saw, too."

"Really?" She reached for the top of her dress and

tugged it down to reveal another inch or two of her silky skin. "Did you only want to look?"

"No, I wanted to touch," he whispered as she gave the soft fabric another tug until the top edge of her areolas showed. "And I wanted to taste."

The minx immediately pulled the fabric back up. "Fine, but take off your shirt first. It's only fair since you've already seen me without mine."

He sent a couple of buttons flying in his haste to finally feel her hands on his bare skin.

"I like what I see, too," she said as she rose up long enough to kiss his throat and run her hands across his chest and back. "Now, where were we?"

This time there were no half measures. Just that quickly, the top of her dress was gathered at her waist, at last giving him free access to the breasts that haunted his thoughts since that first day. He'd been right. They filled his hands perfectly, and their pretty tips begged to be kissed.

Rayanne tangled her fingers in his hair, pressing him closer as he captured her nipple with his lips, working it hard as he squeezed and plumped her other breast with his hand. He loved the sounds she made as he worked them both up to a fevered pitch.

When he tried to tug the hem of her skirt up, it was tangled in her legs. Damn, he wanted it out of the way along with everything else they were both wearing. In a flash, all of their clothes disappeared, leaving only the dappled shade to protect them from the bright light of the day.

His lady grinned, obviously delighted. "Nice trick, Wyatt."

"Thank you," he said as he tugged the pins out of her hair, wanting it spread out on the quilt.

For a few seconds, they both seemed content with a few touches and easy kisses. Gradually, though, they coaxed the embers of passion back into full flame. This was what he'd been looking for. This connection, this mutual hunger, this coming together of two people across time to find each other.

When at last he rose over her, seeing the welcome in her eyes and feeling the sweet way her body and his fit together, he knew he'd finally found heaven.

The grass beneath Rayanne's back was as soft as the bed she slept in. The man who'd just settled on top of her was as hard as steel. She loved the contrast, loved the way he touched her with such care, and flat-out loved him. She'd keep that last tidbit to herself.

The press of his body against hers kept her anchored in this dream, if that was what it was. It was so real, his weight too solid for her to believe it wasn't more. He rocked against her, centered right against her core, a promise of what was to come.

She wanted him to take her, to claim her in this most basic way. "Wyatt, this feels so good, but it's not enough."

He pushed himself up to support his weight on his arms and smiled down at her as he rocked against her again, this time a little harder, faster. "In a bit of a hurry?"

So he wanted to tease, did he? She reached between them to capture his cock in her hand and gave it a squeeze. He moaned and threw his head back when she did it again. She loved having this power over his pleasure; it was only fair since she'd wanted this since the day he'd rescued her and she'd first felt his touch.

He held so still, dragging out the anticipation to the breaking point. Finally, he flexed his hips enough for her to guide him as she opened her heart and her body to him. He slid in deep and hard. Her breath caught in her chest as he growled in satisfaction.

His blue eyes gleamed down at her. "Are you ready for this?"

She brought her legs up around his hips as she caressed his handsome face with her fingers. "I think I've been ready for you my whole life."

He stooped to kiss her again, his tongue mimicking the flexing of his hips as his rhythm picked up strength and speed. She held on, meeting his thrusts, taking him deep and then deeper until nothing existed except the joining of their bodies. He pulled her legs higher up his hips and dropped down on his elbows, bringing the hard planes of his chest back against her breasts. She reveled in the solid feel of their bodies coming together, moving together, saying what she had no real words for. The tension built, second by second, breath by breath, until her whole being stood poised at the brink of exploding.

It was hard to breathe, impossible to think. All she could do was feel. "Wyatt, it's too much!"

His smile was so sweet. "I've got you, honey. Just let it fly."

She dug her fingers into his back, trying to hold on, but his promise gave her the strength to quit fighting and let the climax roll through her. As soon as she did, she took Wyatt with her. He hollered, his whole body rigid as he shuddered in his own release.

She held her breath, hoping against hope that the power of what they had shared didn't throw them out of this perfect moment and back out into the real world. A few seconds passed before Wyatt rolled to the side, taking her with him, holding her close. She breathed in his scent, content to listen to his heartbeat and enjoy these few minutes of peace.

It wouldn't last, it wasn't real, but it was all they had.

Chapter 14

As much as Wyatt loved holding Rayanne in his arms, the same instincts that had saved his hide several times back in the day were telling him they should get moving. He smiled down at his woman and pressed one last kiss on her forehead.

"If we can rustle up some clothes, maybe we could take that walk I mentioned."

Rayanne was cuddled in with her head over his heart. She rose up long enough to look him in the eye as she let her hand wander down his chest and farther south. "And if I like you this way?"

He caught her hand in his and brought it to his mouth for a kiss. "I like you this way, too, and we can get back to it in a while but…"

He broke off what he was about to say to listen to

their surroundings. He'd heard a noise in the distance, but couldn't quite put his finger on what it had been.

The smile faded from Rayanne's eyes. "What's wrong, Wyatt? What are you hearing?"

"I'm not sure."

There it came again. Footsteps, and they were headed straight toward them. How could that be? This was Rayanne's dream, one meant for just the two of them. Who would dare intrude?

"We need to get up and get dressed."

He surged to his feet and then offered her a hand. Just that quickly, he was clothed in the same clothes he'd been wearing for the past century. Rayanne no longer had on the pretty green dress, but instead wore her usual jeans and shirt.

Another sign that the real world was intruding on their moment in paradise.

"Stay behind me until I figure out what's going on."

Now he could hear the murmur of voices. At least two people, maybe more, were nearby.

"There!" Rayanne whispered, pointing off to the left.

Sure enough, two people were moving through the woods on the far side of the creek. For now, they seemed unaware of Wyatt and Rayanne. It wasn't until the pair stepped out of the trees a short distance away that he recognized them.

Amanda and her son.

Son of a bitch, what were they doing there? How could they have found their way into Rayanne's dream?

"We need to go."

He slowly bent down to gather up the quilt, but it was too much to ask that young Billy wouldn't notice. That boy always did have more curiosity than good sense. He tugged on his mother's arm and pointed toward where Wyatt stood. Amanda smiled, but when she spotted Rayanne, it faded away.

Her voice carried across the babble of the water. "Wyatt? What are you doing out here? Who is she?"

How the hell was he supposed to answer that? *Amanda, meet your great-great-granddaughter. You and I never actually...but I'm standing here looking guilty because she and I just did.*

The two of them needed to leave and right now. It was bad enough that Amanda and her boy were there, but now he could see others moving toward them. Was the whole damn town headed this way? And what if Earl and his boys were drawn into this moment, too? They'd been willing to shoot up a town full of innocent people. What if they went after Rayanne?

He whirled around and grabbed her by the hand. "Rayanne, you need to wake up before they get here."

She let him lead her away, but she kept checking back over her shoulder. "But who are all those people?"

He waited to answer her until the two of them had gotten far enough from the creek that he could no longer see Amanda or the others.

"They're like me, but they shouldn't be here in your dream. You invited me in, not them. I don't know what it means or what will happen if they reach us. You need to wake up and right now."

But not before he held her one last time. Who knew

if they'd ever have another chance like this? He enfolded her in his arms, savoring her sweet warmth. Holding Rayanne against his heart plain felt so right, as if they'd been born to be together. The moment wouldn't last, though, and he'd feel nothing but the cold chill of death.

And if that wasn't just sad.

He kissed her one last time and then stepped back. "Wake up, Rayanne. I'll be waiting for you if I can."

She started to reach for him. "Wyatt, there's something you should know. I—"

Before she could finish, she shimmered and disappeared, leaving him alone with his fellow ghosts. Time to deal with them. But when he reached the edge of the creek, the woods were empty, and he was more alone than he'd ever been.

The morning sun spilled through the window, its warmth gradually coaxing Rayanne awake. She kept the quilt pulled up, reluctant to leave the comfort of her bed after the best night's sleep she'd had in years. Then she stretched and discovered she had a few twinges in unexpected places.

She bolted upright and looked around. The dream! Had it been real? Some of it must have been or else her body wouldn't be feeling the way it did. She blushed, remembering what it had been like to make love with Wyatt outside under the summer sun. Thinking about the powerful surge of his body moving over hers, moving in hers, had her legs stirring restlessly. Her breasts were tender, and there were other signs that made it clear that the hours she'd spent in Wyatt's arms had been more than her overactive subconscious.

The idea of birth control hadn't even crossed her mind. But then, why would it? Her lover was a ghost and they'd made love in a dream. And if that wasn't all mind-boggling, she didn't know what was.

But back to the problem at hand. Where was Wyatt? He'd promised to be waiting for her, especially because this was the day they were going to scatter her uncle's ashes. Not only was he nowhere to be seen but she couldn't sense his presence anywhere in the cabin.

She hoped he was all right. Everything had been so perfect right up until those other people had intruded. Odd, though, that Wyatt had known them when it was her dream. Shouldn't they have been people she knew?

Their presence definitely worried him. Had something happened after she left? Wouldn't her dream world have ended when she woke up? How was she supposed to know something like that? Only one way to get answers. She'd grab a quick shower, fix something she could eat on the go and head into Blessing. If Wyatt wasn't there, she'd decide what to do next.

Twenty minutes later, she reached the head of the path that led toward Blessing. Before she'd gone more than a handful of steps, she realized something felt off. Someone else was out there in the trees, and it wasn't Wyatt. She would've recognized him whether he could be seen or not.

She backed up to study her surroundings. There. Behind a clump of trees, a flash of dark red moved through the trees. Who was that? She remained still, waiting to get a better look at whoever it was. Finally, a woman strolled into sight, wearing a dress better suited to Wyatt's era than this one.

As she came closer, Rayanne realized the woman moved in absolute silence. What's more, when she walked through a spot of sunlight, she cast no shadow. Okay, so the obvious answer was that she belonged in Blessing of a hundred years ago. Was that what had freaked out Wyatt in her dream? That all those people belonged in his time, not hers?

The woman winked out of sight as quickly as she'd appeared. Before continuing on, Rayanne did a slow three-sixty to make sure that no one else, real or otherwise, was in the area before hurrying on down the path. Wyatt didn't scare her, but the presence of these others did.

It meant the anniversary of the gunfight that had cost Wyatt his life was drawing close. She didn't know if she'd have the courage to see it all play out again, not if it meant watching Wyatt die. There had to be something she could do to change things. Were the events of the past written in stone?

She hadn't seen everything that happened that day, and Wyatt never once spoke of the events that had led up to the gunfight. Clearly, the memories were powerful ones for him, but there had to be some reason he was caught in this endless nightmare. As soon as she found him, she'd start by making sure he was all right.

And then it was time for some long-overdue answers.

She found him sitting on an old bench outside of the saloon. His dusty boots were propped up on the railing, his hat pulled down low over his face. Was he actually asleep? She grinned. Maybe even a ghost needed a nap after the night they'd shared.

But at least he was all right. She'd been worried about the effect the night's vigorous activities would've had on his energy level. Walking as quietly as she could, she stopped in the street right in front of where he was seated. As soon as she stopped moving, he stirred.

Pushing his hat back, he studied her, his pale eyes staring right through to the heart of her.

He asked, "Are you all right?"

She brushed her hair back from her face and mustered up a smile. "I was about to ask you the same question. I thought you'd be waiting in my room when I woke up this morning."

Okay, that came out sounding worse than she meant it to. She'd been more worried than disappointed that he hadn't been there. "I was concerned about you."

His boots hit the porch hard. He stood up and leaned forward on the railing, looking up and down the street. "Sorry, but I had things to check on."

"Like those people who showed up when we were... when we'd finished?"

Okay, now she was blushing. Why was it so hard to just say that they'd made love? Maybe because right now Wyatt looked about as warm and approachable as a grizzly bear.

"Who were they?"

He finally dragged his gaze back to her. "The fine, upstanding citizens of Blessing. I didn't think you'd be able to see them at all, especially under those circumstances."

Rayanne swallowed hard. "I saw another one on the way here—a lady in the woods wearing a dark red dress. She wore her hair braided and coiled around her head."

Wyatt frowned. "Did she take note of you?"

"Not that I could tell. She was walking through the trees, but after a minute she simply disappeared."

"Damn it, I was hoping I was the only one you'd have to deal with. They'll be appearing more often now. It's always this way right before it all plays out again."

He slammed his fist down on the railing hard enough to crack it. "God, I hate this. What the hell do I have to do to make it all stop?"

Rayanne hated the pain in his voice, but all she could do was stare first at the broken wood and then up at Wyatt. "You broke the railing."

He glared at the damage he'd done. "Yeah, so? It's not like anyone hitches a horse to it anymore."

Clearly, he hadn't realized the significance of what he'd just done. She joined him on the porch. "I don't care about a piece of broken, half-rotted wood, Wyatt. I do care that you were able to break it."

She held her breath and stepped closer, slowly raising her hand to brush across the sleeve of his duster. The leather was buttery soft and just a bit gritty from the ever-present dust in Blessing. Wyatt froze, the muscles in his powerful forearm bunching up tight under her fingertips.

"I broke the railing." His eyes filled with wonder and his voice was gravel-rough as he stared down to where her hand had come to rest on his. "Rayanne, I broke the railing."

She smiled back up at him. "You sure enough did."

Slowly, he lifted his hand from the railing, turning it over to mesh his fingers with hers. She didn't blame him for moving slowly. They were treading on unknown territory here. Had the physical and emotional bond they'd forged in their dream world somehow spilled over into this one?

Better to savor the moment rather than risk shorting him out again. Wyatt's skin was warm to the touch, that of a living man, not the usual cool feel of her ghostly lover a hundred years dead. How long would it last? She didn't know the answer to that question, but she knew one thing. She wasn't going to waste a second of this amazing gift.

That didn't mean she wanted to rush things, especially when they didn't know what the rules were. With the lightest of touches, she trailed her fingertips across his lips, then down his jaw to follow the length of his neck and back. He closed his eyes and drew a deep breath as she continued her explorations.

She tested the breadth of his shoulders and the hard planes of his chest. Sliding her hands inside his duster, she basked in the warmth of his lean strength, kneading his chest like a kitten would a soft blanket.

"You feel so good, so real."

It was tempting to ask questions. What had happened that was different? But the wonder in his eyes warned her that he didn't have the answers, only the same terrified joy that they could share even this much.

"My turn," he whispered. His powerful hands were ever so gentle as they settled on her waist and pulled her closer to his body. She sighed with pleasure when he cupped the curve of her bottom and squeezed as he nuzzled the juncture of her shoulder and neck.

"You smell like lemons this time."

He smiled against her hair as he did some more exploring. His fingers trailed up the length of her back. His teasing assault on all of her senses had her body softening, melting into his. She ached in all the right places. Her breasts felt swollen and heavy, and her core had grown damp, preparing for what she prayed was about to follow.

Finally, she grabbed his hat and tossed it onto the bench behind them and tangled her fingers in the black silk of his hair. "Wyatt, kiss me. Please, while you're—"

She didn't get to finish because just that quickly, his mouth was on hers, hungry and demanding, just as it had been during the night. She rose up on her toes, trying to get closer, to hold on that much tighter.

He swept her up in his arms, lifting her legs high around his waist as he carried her inside the saloon. His actions made her giggle. Did he really think they needed privacy in a ghost town? But then he set her on the bar and reached for the tie on her drawstring shorts and tugged it loose.

Okay, the man definitely knew what he wanted. What they both needed. She put her hands on the worn surface of the bar and lifted her hips up long enough for him to peel down her shorts and panties.

"Lean back," he ordered. "And spread your knees."

She'd willingly comply with his orders but not before she issued a few of her own. "Take off the duster and your shirt."

His smile was all male hunger as he tossed the coat aside and reached for the first button on his shirt. He took his time, offering her a slow striptease that had her clenching her knees together, trying to assuage the aching hunger for this man's body.

When his shirt hit the floor, she stripped off her own and flung it in the same direction. Her bra quickly followed suit.

"Now your pants."

Wyatt hopped on one foot and then the other while he yanked off his boots, which hit the floor with a satisfying clunk, another reminder that he was all so solid and real. A heartbeat later, he was shed of his pants and drawers, revealing proof positive of how much he wanted her. On the other hand, he seemed content to stand just out of her reach, watching her with his sexy mouth quirked up in a half smile.

What was he thinking? "Why are you standing way over there?"

"Trying to decide where to start."

Starting at the top of her head, he stared at her with an intensity that felt as if he were stroking her most sensitive places with his hands or, better yet, his tongue.

"Have you figured it out yet? Because I've got some suggestions if you need them." She cupped her breasts and lifted them, hoping he'd take the hint.

He quickly spread his duster on the floor, adding to the rest of his clothing. Then he carried her over to settle her down on the makeshift bed.

He stretched out beside her. "Sorry this isn't more comfortable."

She didn't give a damn about the floor. "I'm betting you can make me forget all about that."

His smile was full of wicked intent. "I'll do my best."

"I know you will."

When his lips settled on her breast and drew her nipple into the wet warmth of his mouth, she arched up off the floor. He held her still with the weight of his leg between hers. She clamped her knees hard, pressing against the strength of his thigh. It helped, but not nearly enough.

When she tried to push Wyatt over on his back, he grinned and offered himself up to her. She straddled his hips, centering her core right over the hard length of his cock. Rocking forward and back gave them a little more of what they both needed.

She kissed that stern mouth and then nibbled her way down his chest and kept right on going. He propped his head up on his arms and simply watched. He was far too calm, especially when she was slowly going out of her mind. Well, she'd see what she could do to shake him up a bit.

Sliding farther down his legs, she stopped at just

the perfect position to lean down and kiss the tip of his cock. Wyatt didn't move an inch but he couldn't hide the hitch in his breath, especially when she did it a second time.

"Rayanne!"

He groaned when she took him in her mouth and pleasured him in every way she could think up. Oh, yeah, this was good. From the way he was straining up and murmuring encouragement, he was almost at the breaking point.

She cupped his sac and gave it an easy squeeze. "Like that, do you?"

"Yes!" His eyes glittered down at her. "But you'd better stop now."

She teased him with a little more tongue action. "What if I don't?"

What she should have remembered was that he was a man of action rather than words. Before she knew what was happening, he sat up, captured her in his arms and flipped her over onto her stomach and pulled her back up on her knees. He kept one arm wrapped around her waist as he positioned himself between her legs.

"Wyatt!"

"Hold still." He took a long, slow breath and added, "Please."

When she nodded, he found the entrance to her body and pushed slowly forward. She dropped her head down on her arms and pressed back toward him, taking more of him, asking without words for as much as he could give her.

"Brace yourself, honey. I don't think I can be gentle this time."

Then he cut loose, overwhelming her with the sheer power of the connection between them. She'd thought what they'd shared during the night had been amazing, but both of them had known it was but a dream.

This was as real as it got. The smooth leather beneath her hands and knees. The slick sweat on their skin. The slap of his body against her bottom. The calluses on his fingers feeling so delicious on her breasts and between her legs as he drove them both fast and hard.

The whole world shrank down to the two of them, their bodies joined in a dance with their own unique rhythm. The tension built until first she and then he shattered. She cried his name; he hollered hers as he held on tight as he shuddered out his release deep inside of her.

Then they both collapsed. Wyatt pulled away long enough to ease them both over onto their left side and then spooned behind her. He kissed the back of her neck and held her close.

"Was I too rough?"

She smiled back at him. "You were perfect. Better than perfect."

"Good."

After a bit, he added, "This all seems so unfair to you, Rayanne. You deserve better than a man who can't always be there for you."

The sadness in his words hurt to hear. She rolled

over to face him. "Believe me, Wyatt, if that had been any more real, I don't think I would've survived it."

"Thank you for that." He kissed her again, softly this time, offering her comfort rather than passion. "But I can't help but feel that we're running out of time. The day is almost upon us."

A fact that was never far from her mind. Now probably wasn't the best time to push him for answers, but he was the one who'd brought the subject up. She decided to ask, anyway.

"Wyatt, will you tell me what happened that day in Blessing?"

Chapter 15

He'd known this moment had been barreling toward them as much as he'd really prefer to avoid it altogether. But if anyone deserved to know the true story of Wyatt McCain, it was the woman who'd made him feel more alive than he'd been even in his own time.

"Let's get dressed first."

As if clothes would do anything to protect him from the acid-hot pain of the worst day of his life. At least the few minutes required to fasten his pants and button his shirt would give him a chance to pull together his scattered thoughts.

Rayanne quietly slipped back into her shirt and those ridiculous shorts and then went out on the porch to wait for him on the bench. When he joined her outside, she held out his hat. Rather than put it on, he sat down beside her and held it in his lap.

The damn thing had been pretty expensive back in the day, but now it looked as worn and tattered as he felt. There was no way to pretty the story up, to make himself out to be anything better than the gun-for-hire he'd been. The best he could hope for was that Rayanne wouldn't hate herself for consorting with the likes of him.

When he didn't immediately launch into the story, she scooted closer, pressing her body next to his. He put his arm around her shoulders, needing her touch to anchor him in this world.

As the silence stretched on, she started to move away. "I'm sorry, Wyatt. I shouldn't have asked. It's none of my business."

He caught her and pulled her back to his side. "No, you're wrong, Rayanne. You have every right to know, but it's going to change how you feel about me. I did a lot of things that I'm not proud of, but that day was the worst."

She stared across at the old church, reminding him that she'd once had a clear view of the beginning of the events that had condemned him to this existence.

"Wyatt, I know something went horribly wrong that day. I also know that you've spent over a century trying to figure out how to fix it."

She leaned back against his shoulder and tugged one of his hands over into her lap. "I want to help you so maybe you'll finally know some peace. Maybe we both will. The memory of that day has haunted me for fifteen years. I can't imagine living with it as long as you have."

"It should never have been your burden to bear, Rayanne, and I'm right sorry you got pulled into my world like this."

He sat in silence for a few seconds. "What makes you think you can change the outcome? What can you do what I've never been able to do for myself?"

His sharp words made her flinch, but she held her ground. "I don't know, but I know we've got to try. You need to move on, and I need to get on with my life. Besides, I was up there that day and saw what happened. When I shouted to warn you about the shooter in the belfry, you shot him. Did that ever happen before that day?"

"No, and it hasn't happened again since. Other than that one time, he shoots me in the shoulder."

The remembered pain of that rifle shot tearing into his body had him rubbing the old wound with his free hand. "What are you thinking?"

"And no one else has ever seen you as clearly or as often as I have. I've read the journals that Uncle Ray left me. He knew you were here, and so did Amanda and Aunt Hattie, but none of them saw you as often as I have."

"That's right."

She patted him on the leg. "You've never been real like this since that day, either."

All right, he could follow the trail she was laying out. "No, I haven't, which means you're the reason things are changing for me."

"What do you think it means, Wyatt?"

"I wish I knew." He stared down the street, seeing it as it had been all those years ago. "I'll start at the beginning and try to tell you everything. If it gets to be too much, say so and we'll stop."

His throat was dry, making it hard to get the words out. "There was only one thing I was ever good at and that was shooting. Ma always said I was born restless. My pa wanted me to be a churchgoing dirt farmer like him, but my younger brother Thad was better suited to that life. I rode out one night after we'd had another fight on the subject and never looked back."

Rayanne looked shocked. "You never wanted to see your family again?"

"It was the other way around. I rode through there a couple of years later. By then, I already had a reputation as a troublemaker with a talent for guns. When I stopped at the farm, I made a point of sharing some of my adventures with Thad. Pa cornered me with his rifle and yelled at me for filling the boy's head with sinful thoughts. Then he said I was straight on the road headed to hell, and that he'd give me just one chance to turn my back on Satan. If I left this time, not to bother coming back because he had no use for fornicators and drunkards."

Even after all these years, he could still hear the cold fury in his father's voice. He'd sounded like one of those old prophets in the Bible, preaching at him about hellfire and brimstone. Sometimes he wondered where he would've ended up if he'd made a different decision that night.

Rayanne sat up straight, her outrage obvious. "What kind of idiotic father would say something like that to his son?"

He loved that she would leap to his defense, but his father hadn't been wrong. "He was protecting Thad and my ma from the likes of me. He was right about me being nothing but trouble. After all, look where I ended up."

She would have none of it. "And maybe you wouldn't have if your family had reached out instead of turning their back on you. I'm the first to admit that my parents drive me crazy, but I've never doubted that they loved me."

Right now, Rayanne was upset because she thought he'd been mistreated. That was bound to change as the rest of his story unfurled, and he hated that. He needed to be up and moving, even though no matter how fast he walked or how far he went, he'd never figured out how to outdistance his past.

"Mind if we walk?"

He didn't wait for her to answer but immediately stepped off the porch and headed down the street. With the sun beating down, the day had grown uncomfortably warm. Not that he was complaining. If he could feel the heat, it meant he was still real. He stripped off his duster and tossed it on the railing outside of the mercantile. That still wasn't enough, so he rolled up his sleeves.

The sun wasn't the only source of heat right then. Rayanne stood close by staring at his arms with the same expression in her eyes that she'd had right before he'd taken her back there on the saloon floor. What had he done to fan that particular fire?

He retreated a step, not sure how to respond. "Rayanne?"

She slowly grinned. "Sorry, my mind went off track there for a minute. Just so you know, women love the look of strong forearms with rolled-up sleeves. At least this woman does."

He wasn't used to how outspoken modern women had become, but he liked it. "Anything else I should know about?"

Rayanne hooked her arm through his. "Well, that duster is pretty hot."

"I know. That's why I took it off."

Something about what he'd said set off a fit of the giggles. Then she apologized. "Sorry, I shouldn't have laughed, but we're talking about two different kinds of hot here. There's the sun," she said, pointing to the sky. "And then there's the kind of hot caused when a man rolls up his sleeves or wears a piece of clothing a woman thinks is sexy."

Well, all right, then. "And you think my old duster is sexy?"

"Don't look at me like I'm crazy. There's a reason so many men on the covers of romance stories set in the Old West are wearing coats just like yours."

"So if the books were meant to appeal to me, the woman on the cover would be wearing those shorts?"

Now she was blushing, probably remembering how easy it had been for him to get her out of them. "Maybe we should take that walk you mentioned."

That quickly, his good mood disappeared. He let her tug him along in the direction of the creek. It would be cooler in the shade of the trees, and for the first time in more than a hundred years, he was actually thirsty.

As they walked along, he kept watch for the others who'd intruded on Rayanne's dream. It occurred to him that he'd forgotten something. "I just realized this is the day I promised I'd take you to the meadow that your uncle liked. There's still time if you want to go."

She considered the suggestion. "Would you mind? How are you feeling?"

Did she think he was weak? "I'm fine, other than I'd like a drink of water. I'll tell you the rest of my story on the way back."

"We'll get some drinks at the cabin." She gave him a puzzled look. "So if you're feeling thirsty, are you hungry, too?"

It hadn't even occurred to him to wonder about it. "Come to think of it, I am."

How odd to be feeling so human again. "I don't know how long this is going to last, but I'd love an apple—and some of those cookies you keep hidden in the top shelf of the cabinet."

"It's a deal."

They were in and out of the cabin in a matter of minutes. She really wanted to honor Uncle Ray on his birthday, but it was tempting to put the whole thing off to take advantage of this time with Wyatt while he was solidly in this world. In fact, she'd like to take advantage of Wyatt period, especially with a repeat performance of the time they'd spent on the saloon floor. But as long as he was willing to share his story, she sensed it was important for her to hear it. He obviously worried what she'd think of him once she knew the truth, but she wouldn't judge him for mistakes he'd made decades before she'd even been born. She loved the man he was now.

She was following behind him on the narrow trail, enjoying the opportunity to watch him move with his usual powerful grace. Oh, yeah, when they got back, maybe she'd coax him into spending the night with her. Perhaps starting off in that big, claw-foot tub.

What did gunslingers think about taking a bubble bath by candlelight?

He happened to look back right then, looking as if he were about to speak. Something of what she was thinking must have been right there for him to see. Without a word, he tugged her close enough to press a kiss on her mouth, one filled with promise and just a hint of heat.

"We turn off this trail just ahead. From there on, I'll mark the way to make sure you can find your way back."

Why would he do that? "Won't you be with me?"

"Yes, but it's better to be safe. We don't know how all of this works, and I don't want to take a chance on you getting lost on the mountain because I'm not around to show you the way back."

"Good thinking."

His reasoning made sense; that didn't mean she liked the possibility of him disappearing. If that was in the cards, she would've thought it would have happened after they made love, not when they were simply taking a long walk. She'd fed him an apple, a sizeable ham and cheese sandwich, and a handful of those cookies he'd mentioned. Maybe that would keep him fueled until they returned to the cabin.

"How much farther?"

He pointed ahead. "Just past that pair of rocks up ahead."

When they got past the trees, her breath caught in her chest. The vista in front of her was simply beautiful. A small stream cascaded down the side of the mountain, and the sun made sparkling rainbows in the mist coming off the water. A few late-blooming lavender-and-white columbine were scattered throughout the grass. In a word, it was perfect.

"I can see why Uncle Ray loved this spot."

Her eyes filled with tears, and the words came out in a whisper. Wyatt's strong arm supported her as they made their way to a rocky outcropping that overlooked the small waterfall.

His voice was a deep rumble, the vista clearly affecting him, too. "I think your uncle came here whenever he needed to find some peace. I would watch from the woods as he stood right here, gazing at the water tumbling down. The first few times I thought he was considering jumping, but then I realized he found the sound soothing. After a while, he'd walk away looking as if he'd left a burden behind."

Grief clogged Rayanne's throat. "The war changed

Uncle Ray. My mother said it was like the man she knew never really came home."

She let the silence settle over her, seeking the same comfort Uncle Ray had taken from the beauty of the mountain. In truth, though, her real comfort came from the solid presence of the man standing beside her.

It was time to say goodbye to Ray, and so she did.

On the way back to the cabin, Wyatt started talking. Maybe he wanted to distract her. Maybe he just needed to get his story told. Either way, she held his hand and listened.

"You know that Blessing grew up around the mine. Anytime there's gold or silver involved, there's going to be trouble. Every so often, a group of hard cases would ride into Blessing and start raising hell. Most of the time, they'd drink, gamble, and…um, visit with the two ladies who worked upstairs at the saloon."

He shot her a quick look before adding that last part. Did he really think that would shock her? She grinned at him. "Wyatt, I'm a history professor who specializes in the American West. I'm familiar with the kind of work those ladies did. I also know there weren't that many choices for a woman to make a living, especially in remote areas."

He squeezed her hand. "That's true. They had a hard time of it, but Molly and Tennessee Sue were nice women."

"I believe that."

"Right before I came to town, the mining office had been robbed a couple of times."

The trail narrowed down, forcing them to walk single file. Wyatt started talking again as soon as they could walk side by side once more. "I rode with one of those gangs. I did my share of drinking and carousing in the saloon, but I didn't go after the gold."

Wyatt glanced down at her. "Don't go thinking that it was because I was too honest to steal from the fine people of Blessing. I probably would've been in the thick of it if I hadn't fallen down and broken my leg the night before the last robbery. One of the men got mad over losing at poker and was about to take his temper out on Molly. I charged up the stairs to stop him, but lost my footing and we both fell. The bastard was so drunk, he walked away without a scratch."

She noticed that Wyatt was rubbing his thigh as if it still ached. "Molly made them carry me down to your great-great-grandmother's place on a plank. A couple of those old miners sat on me while Amanda set my leg."

"So that's how you got to know her."

"Yes. Amanda was a decent woman, with all that meant back then. Her first husband died in the mine, leaving her a widow with a young son to raise on her own. She earned her living teaching the children in town how to read and write, but it was summer so school was out. She also occasionally took in boarders, so she agreed to let me stay until my leg healed."

He drifted off into a few seconds of silence. "I was pretty much confined to bed for a couple of weeks before I was strong enough to get around on crutches. Her boy Billy kept me company playing checkers. I was

also teaching him how to play chess. He was a quick
learner. Good-natured, too. He didn't complain overly
much about having to wait on me when he could have
been out playing with his friends."

Wyatt smiled. "He tried to talk me into teaching
him how to play poker. His ma threatened to tan both
our hides if we even thought about sneaking a deck of
cards into her house."

Rayanne was relieved to see that not all of Wyatt's
memories of Blessing were bad ones. How weird was
it, though, to be feeling jealous of her own ancestor? It
was obvious that Wyatt had liked Amanda. Had they
been more than friends? After all, Amanda had been
a widow with a handsome man living under her roof.

"When my leg healed, I found myself reluctant to
leave town. I owed Amanda and the others for taking
care of me. If they hadn't, I could've ended up dead
or crippled. I figured I could pay Amanda and her son
back by doing odd jobs around the house. Chopping
wood, mending the roof, weeding her garden and the
like. I even did some hunting. People get right friendly
when you bring back a deer and are willing to share."

He stopped to stare up at the sun. "Funny, they were
the same damn chores that I hated doing around my
parents' farm, but it felt good being useful. I didn't
drink or smoke from the night I broke my leg right up
until that last day."

They were almost back to the cabin, but he seemed
reluctant to resume their walk.

"Three months went by. My leg was pretty much
back to normal, but I wasn't in any hurry to leave. For

the first time since I'd ridden away from the family farm, I was content to stay in one place. People started treating me like I belonged here, like I was one of them. Then one of the men I'd been riding with came back through town. He spotted me and stopped to talk."

Did Wyatt even realize that his hands had strayed down to grip his pistols?

"Seems Earl had been sent ahead to do some scouting for the gang, to see if the mine had been producing. They'd already run through the gold they'd stolen last time. He was surprised to see me, but figured I was there for the same reason he was."

Wyatt looked pale, the memories obviously taking their toll. Maybe she shouldn't have insisted on hearing his story, but until she knew what had happened that day, she had no way of knowing how to help him.

"Why don't we go inside? I can fix us some dinner and then you can finish telling me."

"I'd rather just get this over with."

She hated seeing him looking so stressed. Some of it might stem from the fact he wasn't used to thinking about eating and drinking.

"I don't know about you, but I'm tired from all this hiking and everything. Would you mind sitting on the porch? I'll get us some cold drinks and maybe some snacks."

"That sounds good."

He followed her onto the porch, settling in the same chair he usually took. He sank into a dark silence. Not wanting to leave him alone for long, she grabbed some bottled water and crackers and cheese and hurried back outside.

He resumed talking as soon as she sat down beside him, his words coming in a rush. "I played along with him to find out as much as I could about their plans. Finally, I ran him out of town at gunpoint with orders to tell my former associates that they'd have to face me if they came back to Blessing."

"Did that work?"

"You know damn well it didn't. I should've known that I couldn't do anything right. I was better with a gun than any of them, but they had me beat in sheer numbers."

"And none of the other residents of Blessing would stand with you?"

"I wouldn't have let them if they'd offered. They were miners and storekeepers, not gunfighters." He took a long drink of water. "I think I wanted them to look at me like some kind of hero, especially Amanda and her son."

"And did she?"

For the first time in hours, Wyatt's mood lightened. "No, she railed at me for hours. Said I was a fool for thinking I could stop them. That there'd always be more gold and more men to steal it. What good would I be to anybody if I was dead?"

Then his smile faded. "Turned out she was right, but I was willing to die to protect her and the boy."

He was up and pacing now. "As long as no one ever stood up to those bastards, the attacks would never end."

"You were courageous for even trying, Wyatt."

"Don't go trying to make me out to be a hero, Rayanne. People died that day."

He stopped to stare out toward the woods. She followed his line of sight, already knowing what she'd see out there. Or rather, who. A ragged line of people, all wearing clothes right out of a history book, stood at the edge of the meadow, staring back at Wyatt. Right in the front of the bunch stood a young boy. When he raised his hand to wave, Wyatt turned his back, his face contorted in a mask of grief and shame.

"And it was the wrong people who died."

Then in a flash of light, he was gone.

Chapter 16

The sun was coming up when Rayanne sank back down in her chair on the porch. The night had not been one bit restful, her bed lonely, and her dreams empty and so damn sad. Her heart hurt for Wyatt, plain and simple. She now understood the burden of guilt that he'd carried around on his broad shoulders all these years. He'd died on the dusty streets of Blessing, gunned down by men he'd once ridden with, but he'd willingly taken that risk.

The problem was that somehow Amanda's son had died, too.

She scanned the surrounding woods. Where had Wyatt gone? How long would he stay away this time? Always questions and no answers. If he didn't show up soon, she'd head into town to see if he was back in Blessing. Even if she couldn't see him, she'd give anything to simply feel his presence, to know that he was all right.

It hadn't hit her until she'd been in bed that the last few minutes before Wyatt had disappeared, he'd been wearing his duster again, even though he'd left it hanging on the railing back in Blessing. Obviously, at some point he'd returned to his ghostly state, and she hadn't even noticed.

That was because no matter what form he took, Wyatt was real to her. A man, not merely the memory of one. And she loved him. What would he do if she told him? Would it help heal his wounds or only make them worse?

There was one way to find out. With so many other ghosts drifting through the woods, she hadn't wanted to risk running into them in the dark. Once the sun was up high enough to chase away the worst of the shadows, she'd head straight for Blessing and hunt for Wyatt.

She finished the last of her coffee and took the cup back inside, trading it for her backpack. Once she found Wyatt, she'd make it damn clear to him that she wanted to be with him regardless of the events of the past.

Maybe she was being overly optimistic, but she'd made sure to wear another pair of her drawstring shorts—just in case. Her bed might be more comfortable, but she'd happily settle for saloon-floor sex, too. She smiled at the memory of the conversation they'd had over what was hot and what was really hot.

As she stepped off the porch, she realized there was a noise in the distance, one she hadn't heard since the day Shawn had driven off in a huff. Damn it, just what she needed. Someone was coming. Her first temptation was to take off for the woods, but there'd be no hiding her trail through the dew-dampened grass. Besides, with her car parked by the cabin, they'd know she was around somewhere.

No one would drive this far without good reason. Maybe it was Phil dropping by for a visit, but she couldn't be that lucky. She sat down on the porch step and waited.

Sure enough, a few minutes later she caught sight of her mother's car. Maybe she should have run for Blessing and stayed there until her mom gave up and went home. God knew what kind of tales Shawn had told her.

The car hit a rut just as it came to a stop, causing it to lurch sideways. Her mom gunned the engine, sending up a spray of gravel. Rayanne winced, knowing how much her mom babied her car. If it got scratched, she'd never hear the end of it.

Her mom parked right in front of the cabin and climbed out of the car. She hobbled her way around to the steps, her shoes totally inappropriate for walking on rough ground.

"Mother, as usual a call would've been nice. Another five minutes, and you would've had to sit on the porch all day until I got back or give up and head back down the road."

Where she belonged. Lana had never been one for roughing it. The cabin had all of the usual amenities like running water and electricity. However, it failed to meet her mother's definition of civilization because it was more than five miles from the nearest mall.

Her mother glared at her. "If I'd have called, you would have told me not to come."

No use in arguing that one. It was true.

"So if you knew I wanted to be left alone, and you hate this place so much, why are you here?"

Lana gave her a thoroughly disgusted look. "Can't this discussion wait until we're inside? I need a cold drink and a bathroom."

"Fine. I'll let you in. Help yourself to anything you want to eat or drink. The bathroom is upstairs."

Her mother pushed a button on her key ring, which released the trunk lid. "Get my luggage out of the car for me."

Rayanne's first instinct was to refuse. If the suitcase stayed right where it was, there was always the chance her mother would head back down the road again today. Once the luggage was inside, she'd be staying for sure.

Rather than immediately fetching it, she unlocked the door and followed her mother inside. "Why are you here, Mom?"

"I was already worried about you, but then Shawn stopped by after you ran him off. I still can't believe you did that after he drove all the way up here to see you. Seriously, I don't know why he hadn't given up on you long before this."

Rayanne pulled a bottle of water out of the fridge and handed to her. "Need I remind you that Shawn also showed up uninvited? Not to mention he wanted me to blow off my work and go hang out with him, instead."

Lana picked up the water in a white-knuckled grip. "Which is exactly what you should have done. I don't have to tell you how much you hurt his feelings. Luckily, I reminded him that you'd just lost your uncle. If you make nice the next time you see him, I'm sure he'll forgive your rude behavior."

Enough was enough.

"First of all, Shawn and I have agreed that there is no future for us except as friends. Secondly, I'm a historian, Mother, and Shawn knows that. I only have so long to do my research and start writing before the summer is over. It's already getting to be late August. If I decide to return to my job, I still have a lot of work to finish before school starts."

Her mother only heard one thing. Her voice went up two octaves. "*If?* What do you mean *if* you decide to return to your job? Of course you're returning to the college. That's where your life is."

Right now Rayanne had more important things on her mind than picking up the pieces of her life down below. Things she couldn't share with her mother. Yes, eventually she'd have to return to reality, but not until some things up here on the mountain were settled.

Rather than point that out, she drew a long, deep breath and changed tactics. "Mom, you must be tired from the drive up here. Why don't you eat something and then lie down? I'll set your bag on the porch on my way out."

Lana planted herself between Rayanne and the door. "Where are you going?"

"Into town."

Her mother brightened and immediately pulled out her keys. "Great. I'll drive. We can get a hotel room and a spa treatment. My treat."

"Not that town, Mom. I'm going to spend the day working in Blessing."

Her mom didn't budge. Instead, she dug in her heels and crossed her arms over her chest. "I don't want you rambling around in that death trap by yourself. Shawn told me that you almost got killed falling through the floor of one of those old buildings."

Darn the man. "He exaggerated the danger. Now please step out of the way, Mom. I'll be back before dark."

"Fine. Do what you want. You always do." Her mother stood her ground a few seconds longer. "But understand that you're forcing my hand, Rayanne. Living up here allowed my brother to avoid dealing with his problems, and he ended up spending his whole life alone. He could've gotten help, and maybe, just maybe, he could have lived a normal life again."

She finally gave ground, but her voice cracked. "I lost my brother to this mountain. I don't want the same thing to happen to you, too. One way or another, I want you back home. Then we'll see about putting this place up for sale. It's been a burden to our family long enough."

Rayanne understood her mother's concerns, but her own connection to this mountain wasn't ever going to change. "I'm sorry you feel that way, Mom. Uncle Ray left this place to me and enough money to live on for years. It was his gift to me, and it will not be going up for sale, ever. If you can't accept that, I would prefer that you were gone when I get back."

She walked out, pausing by her mother's car long enough to slam the trunk lid shut, leaving the luggage locked inside. Not exactly a subtle hint, but right now she didn't have time for subtleties. Not with Wyatt gone missing and time growing short.

The first thing she noticed was the silence in the woods. No flutter of bird wings, no scurrying feet in the undergrowth. What were they sensing that had them all hiding? She took a cautious look around. Just as she suspected, there was movement in the trees, but the ghostly forms made no sound as they passed.

If they were aware of her, they gave no sign of it. This time it was a group of three men, miners by the look of them. One carried a pickax resting on his shoulder; the other two had shovels. When they reached a patch of sunlight, they flickered out of existence again.

She kept moving, preferring the open space of town to the close confines of the woods. So far, outside of her dream with Wyatt, none of the spirits had paid the least bit of attention to her. She hoped it stayed that way.

About halfway down the trail, another ghost appeared, this one much shorter. His shock of red hair marked him as the same boy who had waved at Wyatt. Billy, her long-dead great-uncle. She slowed down, hoping he'd disappear before their paths crossed, but no such luck.

Instead, he stopped to look directly at her. "You were with Mr. Wyatt by the creek."

Maybe she could have ignored one of the adults if they'd spoken to her, but this was a child, and family at that. He shifted from foot to foot, too full of energy to stand still. His overalls had been neatly patched, his shoes scuffed and worn. It was uncanny how much he looked so much like Uncle Ray as a young boy.

"Yes, I do know Wyatt. He's a friend of mine. You must be Billy. I hear you play a mean game of checkers."

The boy grinned at her. "Chess, too. I'm hoping Wyatt will teach me to play poker, but he can't while Ma is around to see."

She laughed. "He told me that, too."

Billy looked back over his shoulder as if watching for someone. "Are you going to town?"

"Yes, I thought I'd go check on Wyatt." If he was there.

She was sure she hadn't said that last part out loud, but Billy answered, anyway.

"He's there, all right. I saw him go in the saloon earlier. I'd take you there, but my ma would tan my hide if she caught me near the saloon. She won't be happy if she finds out Mr. Wyatt is in there, either. She done told him as long as he rented our spare room, he couldn't come home stinking like whiskey and those ladies who work there.

"I don't know why she said that last part." He scrunched his nose up in confusion. "Miss Molly smells real nice. I sniffed her when she came into the store one day."

Rayanne fought to keep a straight face. Definitely

time to change subjects. "I should get going. Want to walk with me?"

He shook his head. "No, I'd better not. Nice to meet you, Miss—" His eyes widened. "You never said your name."

"It's Rayanne, Billy."

"Nice to meet you, Miss Rayanne."

Then with a wave, he ran off. A few steps away he blinked out of sight. Goose bumps danced over her skin. Despite all the time she'd spent with Wyatt, she wasn't sure she'd ever get used to seeing people pop in and out of existence.

At least the unnatural silence had ended as the usual rustlings in the woods returned to normal. A few minutes later, she left the trees behind and the town came into sight. It looked the same—deserted and falling apart. With everything that had happened and the number of ghosts she'd seen over the past two days, she'd been afraid the missing buildings would've reappeared.

What a relief. After the confrontation with her mother and then meeting Billy in the woods, she could use a bit of normal. Well, if hunting down her ghostly lover could be considered any kind of normal.

She stopped at the end of the street and looked around. Other than a breeze stirring up some of the dust, the place was still. Empty.

Billy said Wyatt had gone into the saloon, so she'd look there first. Of course, there was no way to know if Billy meant he'd seen him today or back in the past.

She stepped onto the porch, wishing the town had come with some kind of instruction manual. It would sure be nice to know what she was doing when people's lives, or rather, their deaths were at stake. Her gut feeling was that she was here for a purpose other than cataloging the history of the town. That somehow, she was meant to play a role in ending the tragedy once and for all.

Even if it meant never seeing Wyatt again, never sharing another kiss, never making love with him again. She hated the whole idea, but the man deserved some peace. Then maybe she could get back to the life her mother had been talking about, one free of nightmares from her own past.

After setting her pack down, she stepped through the doors into the saloon and breathed a sigh of relief. He was there. Not visible, but she could feel his energy. She'd take him anyway she could get him.

"Wyatt, are you all right?"

There was a shimmer of energy over in the corner near the pictures she had tacked up on the wall. She stepped closer, hoping he would solidify, at least enough so that she could see him, maybe even hear him.

The struggle went on for several seconds with bright flickers of light fading in and out. A loud pop startled her, but then Wyatt was there. Tears of relief stung her eyes.

"You're back."

He nodded, looking reassuringly solid. She started toward him, but he held up his hand in warning. When she stopped, he swung his hand at the table. It passed straight through without a sound. The stacks of papers rippled a bit, but that was all.

"Can you talk?"

He tried, but no sound came out, at least none she could hear. His clear frustration had him fading again.

"Don't worry about it, Wyatt. I'm just glad that you're here and all right. I was worried."

That didn't seem to please him, either. Somehow she doubted he'd be any happier to find out that she'd met his friend Billy in the woods. Rather than push the issue right now, she'd finish sketching the last building she'd measured out. Even if she was only going through the motions, it might help him deal with the powerful emotions yesterday had triggered.

She pulled a chair up to the closest table and started sketching. This time she added a few people strolling in front of the store now that she'd seen what they looked like. An hour or more passed before Wyatt moved closer, looking more solid. She'd finished the first picture and started a second, this one a portrait. Drawing Billy was a risk, but it felt right.

"You've caught his likeness. You've only seen him twice, both times at a distance."

She kept her focus on the sketch as Wyatt stood behind her, watching her intently. "I met up with Billy on my way here this morning. We had a nice talk."

"He spoke to you?"

Wyatt's hand came down on her shoulder, his touch feather light. She brushed her fingers across his as she turned to look up at him. "Yes. I told him you and I were friends and asked if he'd seen you. He told me you were here in the saloon, which would make his ma mad. Something about her not wanting you to show up smelling like whiskey and Miss Molly."

He smiled a little, looking far happier than he had when he first appeared.

"He couldn't understand that last part because evidently Miss Molly smelled nice. He knew that because he sniffed her once when she came into the store."

This time she couldn't hold back a grin. The relief at finding Wyatt again coupled with the image of that little boy checking out Molly's perfume sent her off into peals of laughter.

Wyatt chuckled. "His ma would've tanned his hide if she'd found out about that."

He gave her shoulder another squeeze and stepped back. Cocking his head to the side, he studied her. "So who drove up the mountain this morning?"

She should have known he'd sense the intruder. "My mother. She wants me to leave with her. She's worried that I'm going to turn into my uncle and end up living up here all alone."

"She's right. It might have been better if you'd gone with her."

She ignored the stab of pain his words caused and focused on the one positive. "She left?"

He nodded. "A few minutes ago. Is she the type to give up easily?"

"No. She hates this place for the effect it had on my uncle and then again on me. You know, after seeing… what I saw back then."

Wyatt frowned. "You never mentioned having problems."

She hated the memory of that time. "I had nightmares for months. My parents and the idiot doctor they took me to kept insisting I had just imagined it all. That I'd gotten scared because I couldn't find Uncle Ray and blew it all out of proportion."

She'd hated the endless hours of rehashing the same things over and over again. "I didn't believe them, but they thought it was all in my imagination. But I knew deep down inside that it was all real—all those people, the gunshots."

Then she stood up and turned to face Wyatt. "Especially you. Even if somehow my mind made up all the rest, I always knew you were real."

He wrapped his arms around her, pulling her in close and wrapping her in a cocoon of leather and his strength. "I never forgot that day, either. It was the only time something changed."

Okay, maybe now was the time to talk about that.

"Why do you think that is, Wyatt? There had to be times when Amanda or Hattie or even Uncle Ray were here when everything played out again."

His voice was a quiet rumble. "I don't know. I always meant to do something different. Maybe if I could tie Billy to a tree or warn Amanda that he'd sneak out. Something. Anything to keep him from dying."

"Do you know which of the gang shoots him?"

Wyatt immediately released her, almost shoving her back out of his reach. "None of them."

"Then who did, Wyatt? I need answers if I'm going to find some way to end this nightmare for both of us."

He stared at her, his blue eyes looking faded and dull with pain. "Who the hell do you think it was, Ray-anne? The answer is obvious. I pulled the trigger. No one else. Just me. The last thing I saw before I died myself was Billy crumpling to the ground, a gaping hole in his chest, and Amanda screaming his name."

Chapter 17

Wyatt braced himself for her revulsion and rejection, not that he'd blame Rayanne one bit for feeling that way. After all, he'd hated himself for over a hundred years. He'd done some pretty questionable things in his life, but nothing—NOTHING—could be worse than killing that little boy. Even if Rayanne could forgive him for not telling her before they'd crossed the line to becoming lovers, she'd never forgive him for killing her great-uncle.

He wouldn't be surprised if she stormed out of the saloon, never to speak to him again. Hell, if she wanted to borrow one of his guns and shoot him with it, he'd stand still and let her take aim. Maybe this would all end if she torched the place and let Blessing burn to the ground.

But none of that happened. Instead, this one incredibly strong woman looked up at him with such compassion in her beautiful green eyes.

"Oh, God, Wyatt. I'd figured out that Billy died that day, but I'd never for a second thought that it was you who'd pulled the trigger."

She reached up to cradle his face with her soft hands. "I'm so sorry. How awful for you."

Wait a minute. He backed up a step as he tried to make sense of what she'd just said. Rayanne felt bad for him? His chest hurt from the force it took to spit the words out.

"Awful for me? Are you deaf, woman? I killed that boy right there in front of his mother. They were nothing but good to me, and my stupidity cost them everything. They trusted me. I promised to make the town safe for them. Instead, Billy bled to death in the street with my bullet in his chest."

He turned his back to those eyes that saw too much. Tears burned his eyes, the images in his head not just memories, but something he had lived through over and over again. Each time was fresh and horrible as when it originally happened. He closed his eyes and remembered the heat of that day, the gritty dust that had clung to his damp skin, the burn of whiskey in his throat from the one shot he'd drunk for courage only moments before stepping out into the street.

The fine citizens of Blessing had all scurried for cover, knowing death was about to stalk the streets of their small town. He drew no comfort from knowing that he'd killed enough of his former associates to keep them from coming back again. Looking back, he'd rather the bastards steal every speck of gold dust that mine ever produced if it meant that Billy could have lived a long and happy life.

He realized Rayanne was trying to get his attention, planting herself right smack in front of him again. He blinked hard, trying to focus on her, the one bright spot in his existence.

"Wyatt McCain, I heard what you said, and I understand what you did. Yes, it was a horrible tragedy, but it was a mistake, an accident. Nothing more. Even Amanda knew that. Did you know that she blamed herself for Billy's death?"

Now that made no sense. "She didn't pull that trigger. I did."

"Yes, that's true. However, she knew Billy was curious about what was going to happen, but she left him alone, anyway. If she'd stayed home like you told her to, he wouldn't have died, not like that. But who knows, maybe in the great scheme of things it was just his time."

Knowing he wasn't the only one who'd suffered because of Billy's death didn't help at all. Rayanne was still talking.

"So back to what I was saying, Wyatt. I have to think there's a reason I can see you, hear you, feel you when no one else can. Aunt Hattie said all it took was someone believing to make it all real. You and I changed things fifteen years ago. If we believe we can do it again, maybe the two of us can change things for good this time."

He wanted that more than anything. Well, almost anything. Right now he wanted Rayanne something fierce.

"Change it how?"

"I don't know, but we've got two days to figure it out."

She snuggled close again, holding on to him with such fierce strength. "You don't have to face this alone anymore, big guy. And if we don't figure it out this time, then we'll try again next year."

"No, we won't." He pressed a kiss to the top of her head. "The last thing I want is you wasting your life on me, Rayanne. You need to find a man from your own time, someone who makes you happy, and build a life with him. Not that jackass who was here, but a good man who deserves you. Promise me that if I let you watch this play out this one last time, you'll walk away no matter how it turns out."

She didn't want to do it. It was clear in the way her eyes shifted away from his face to stare at some point past his shoulder. It had to be the belfry on the old church, the one place she'd been avoiding since right after she'd shown up on the mountain.

He wanted to shake some sense into her. Instead, he gently tilted her face up toward his. "I mean it, Rayanne. I can't bear the thought of you caught up in this nightmare year after year."

"But—"

Rather than listen to all of her foolish reasons for wanting to tangle her life up with the tragedy, he hushed her the only way he could. He kissed her. He'd never been a man of many words, preferring action to get his point across. No one misunderstood the solid impact of a fist or what it meant to stare down the barrel of a gun.

If only he dared tell this beautiful woman what she'd come to mean to him. He poured everything he had into the kiss, hoping she'd understand. She sighed and settled into his arms, allowing him to deepen the kiss, to savor the sweet spice that was uniquely Rayanne's.

When he lifted her up onto the table and moved to stand between her knees, he felt her smile. He pulled back, trying to decide if he should be insulted. "You find this amusing?"

Her eyes sparked with good humor and a lot of heat. "No, I find it arousing. But I have to wonder if we'll ever actually get around to doing this in the comfort of a bed."

Leave it to her to make him laugh when only minutes ago he'd been hurting so damn bad. He stepped back and tugged her back to her feet.

To let her know he was only banking the fire, not putting it out altogether, he kissed the palm of her hand before saying, "How about we finish what you need to do here today and then go back to your cabin for the night?"

Her eyes glittered with hunger. "Sounds perfect. Even better, if we get a move on, I promise to knock off work early."

"Then by all means, let's get down to it."

She trailed her fingers down his chest and kept going. "Exactly which *it* are you talking about?"

He caught her hand in his. "Keep that up and we won't get anything else done."

She gave an exaggerated sigh and gathered up her sketch pad and walked away. He laughed and followed her out of the saloon.

Rayanne was glad that she'd managed to improve Wyatt's mood because she was about to rip all those old wounds open again. She hated to hurt him that way, but she remained convinced that the only way they'd break the awful pattern that he'd been caught up in for more than a century was to figure out how to change what happened.

Outside, she stood in the bright sunshine and stared up at the intensely blue sky above. Wyatt stood beside her, ignoring the beautiful day to watch her, instead.

"Spit whatever you have stuck in your craw, Rayanne. If I'm not going to like it, anyway, just say it."

"Fine." She did a slow turn, looking from one end of the street to the other. "I want you to walk me through that day again. Tell me everything, good and bad. All the things you did right and all those that went wrong."

He glared down at her, his hands clenched in fists. "Why the hell do you want me to do that? You already know all the important stuff. You saw most of it play out right in front of you. I walked out of that saloon to face down the men I used to ride with. When the gunfire ended, most of them were wounded or dead."

He waved his hand toward the other end of town. "They rode in from that direction, but they sent one guy around from the other end to hide out in the belfry.

He's the one you warned me about. That was the only year when I shot him instead of the other way around."

But then he stopped to stare up at the belfry, his eyebrows riding low over his eyes. "Why do you think that happened? And if it happened once, why not again?"

He strode off down the road. "People were hiding in all of the buildings. Someone had to have seen him up there, but no one said a word. Never tried to warn me."

"Maybe for fear of drawing attention to themselves?" Although as far as she was concerned, that was cowardice of the worst kind. They could have banded together to face down their attackers, not let a single man take on the whole bunch by himself.

"That and I told them to stay out of sight. I didn't want to shoot one of them by mistake." His mouth twisted up in a bitter smile. "See how well that worked out."

"Start at the beginning and go from there, Wyatt."

She flipped open her pad and prepared to take notes because she'd never get him to go through this a second time and wouldn't want to. She quickly sketched out a rough map of the town and began marking down the details as he described them. Speaking in a soul-weary monotone, he might as well have been reciting the alphabet for all the emotion he conveyed with his words.

It took them nearly an hour to go through it all before she was satisfied that she had all the details down. Start to finish, the whole gunfight had probably lasted a handful of minutes, but the memories of it seemed to play out in slow motion in Wyatt's mind. As he talked, he'd flickered in and out of existence, most of the time in that halfway state where she could see him, but he had no real substance.

He looked like hell right now. She hoped a change of scenery would let him come back to her, solid and real.

"All right, that's enough for today. Let's head back to the cabin where we can relax."

He'd just shown her where Billy had died in front of the mercantile. Wyatt knelt down, touching the faded and cracked wood as if he could still see the pool of blood and the boy's sightless eyes staring up at him from where he lay sprawled on the ground. In reality, Wyatt hadn't actually seen Billy bleed out. He'd been too busy dying himself.

She tried again. "Let's go, Wyatt. I don't know about you, but I could use a cold drink and something to eat. I'll go get my things from the saloon. I'll meet you at the edge of town."

That is, if he even noticed she'd deserted him. She wasn't sure what she'd do next. In his current state, she couldn't touch him, much less physically drag him away from Blessing to her cabin.

Inside the saloon, she gathered up her things and stuffed them all back in her pack. Outside, Wyatt stood at the edge of the porch, waiting for her. They fell into step together and made their way toward the tree line.

"That wasn't the most pleasant experience I've ever had," he said, his voice tight with emotion. "However, I have to admit that it was a relief to talk about it, especially with you."

Wyatt wrapped his arm around her shoulders, once again solid, as if she somehow grounded him in the world. "None of the others who show up every year seem to remember what happened. They think they're real with no knowledge that a hundred or more years have passed. Then on the twenty-third, all of a sudden, the town is back to exactly the way it was. Everyone says and does the same things. Even me."

Inside the cool shade of the trees, he pointed toward some vague shapes in the distance. "They get more real, hang around longer as we get closer to the anniversary. Then it all explodes again, gunshots coming from every direction. I know what is going to happen. I even know how many times I'm going to get shot before I die. It's as if I'm caught in a flooded river, getting swept along with the current and drowning in my own blood."

He stumbled to a halt. "But you're different. At least in the beginning, your uncle thought maybe he was imagining me, like I was one of those memories he brought back from the war with him. Before him, Hattie wasn't sure for a long time. I can only think of a handful of times when she tried to speak to me. But from the first, you've always treated me as if I'm more than a fragment of some nightmare."

She hurt for him. The other ghosts might not be sentient, but he was. "You are real to me and always will be."

For the first time since they'd kissed in the saloon, there was less pain in his gaze and a note of excitement in his voice. "You've seen the others, and you spoke to Billy like he was real, too."

Where was he going with this? "Actually, he spoke

to me first. But for those few minutes, he existed in this place and time, just like you do."

"So like the last time, maybe you can make yourself heard on the day of the gunfight."

His excitement had a dark edge to it as he spun her around to face him. "But this time, when you make yourself heard, it won't be me you'll try to save. It will be Billy."

His words stabbed right through to the heart of her. "But, Wyatt, I can't let you die. Not if I can stop it. I love you too much to let that happen."

Okay, she hadn't meant to let that slip out, but she wouldn't deny the truth of her words, either. He stared down at her for the longest time.

He drew a long, slow breath. "I love you, too, Ray-anne. More than you'll ever know. I'd give anything for the two of us to have a future together, but I belong in the past. If you really do love me, promise me you'll do what you can to save Billy. It's the only way I'll ever know any peace. All I'm asking is that you try this one time. No matter how it turns out, it's time for you to get on with your life down below."

Wasn't that what she wanted for him, too? A chance to stop this travesty? But if Billy didn't die in the past, how would that change everything that had happened ever since? Would none of this have happened? What if that meant she'd never met Wyatt at all? None of it made sense.

The woods closed in on her, leaving her feeling trapped and choking on the pain. She was the one to turn away this time. "This hurts so much, Wyatt."

He moved up behind her and wrapped his arms around her shoulders, holding her with such care.

"Do you want me to go back to Blessing?"

She actually considered it, but then shook her head. "No, I want you with me. We're down to less than two days, and I don't want to waste a single minute of that time."

"If you're sure." He rested his head next to hers. "I don't want to cause you any more pain than I already have."

"It only hurts because you've made my time up here so special, Wyatt. I love the way you make me feel."

Several more former residents of Blessing appeared a short distance away. Wyatt's hold on her tightened. "Let's go to the cabin and forget about all of this until tomorrow morning."

She shivered at the sheer number of ghosts she could see at the moment. It was as if they'd stolen all of the heat from the summer day.

"Good idea. We'll lock the door, pull the blinds and pretend the rest of the world doesn't exist. There's just me, you, a claw-foot tub and that bed I mentioned earlier."

He pressed a soft kiss to her temple. "Lady, I do like the way you think."

Then they ran down the narrow trail all the way to the cabin, laughing when she closed the door and threw the lock.

"Food first."

Rayanne had been trying to drag Wyatt up the stairs,

but he dug in his heels. She'd looked ashen back there
in the woods when the fine citizens of Blessing had
strayed too close to them. Although he didn't seem to
need much of anything in the way of food and water,
that wasn't true for her.

"But taking a bath first would feel so good."

The heat in her eyes made it clear just how good it
would feel. It was damned tempting to take her up on
the offer, but she hadn't been able to hide the slight
trembling in her hands when she tried once again to
coax him to follow her.

Two could play at that game. "Eat something first.
You're going to need all your strength for our—" he
studied her with all the heat he could muster "—bath."

She stopped right where she was, her mouth slowly
curving up in a smile. "Well, then, there is that. I'll fix
a quick sandwich. Do you want one?"

"No, thanks. Right now I don't appear to need anything."

Rayanne had been about to open the white cabinet
that held cold air. "Are you all right?"

He suspected what she really wanted to know was
if he were solid and was reluctant to find out for herself. He quickly stripped off his coat and hat, tossing
them on a nearby chair. Then he picked up a book off
the counter and thumbed through it, answering her
without words.

She shot him a relieved grin and returned to fixing
herself a quick meal. At the moment, he was alive or
at least solid and able to impact his surroundings. That

could change at any moment, but he hoped it wouldn't. He was really looking forward to that bath.

Rayanne slapped two pieces of bread together with a piece of cheese between them and then devoured it all in very little time. When she swallowed the last bite, she grabbed his hand and dragged him toward the steps again. He outweighed her by a lot, but he let himself get towed along.

"That's not much of a meal."

"It was enough for now."

At the top of the stairs she ducked into the bathroom and turned on the water and added some pink liquid that bubbled up when the water hit it. The scent of roses filled the damp air. Holding her hand under the stream of water, she adjusted the two knobs until she was happy. "That feels about right. Gotta love hot and cold running water."

Her hands immediately grabbed the hem of her shirt, leaving wet prints on the cloth as she tugged it up and over her head. When he didn't immediately follow suit, she tapped her foot impatiently. "Get started, mister. I need you to wash my back."

He'd taken his share of baths over the years, but he'd never once shared a tub with anyone. The possibilities left him fumble-fingered as he started working on his own buttons.

It didn't help watching his lover fling her clothes aside and slide into the steaming water without him. He slowed down, determined to savor the moments. Rayanne had settled back in the bathtub, watching his every move with hungry eyes. That was only fair. He'd been needing this moment with her ever since she'd stormed into the saloon, looking for him earlier that morning.

He wanted nothing between them except the sweet slide of her skin against his. Sex would be great, but right now he needed more than that. Her touch soothed him in ways he couldn't find the words to describe. He'd been alone for so damned long, and being with her kept those lonely shadows at bay.

Rather than rush things, he took his time folding his shirt and laying it neatly on the floor. Next he toed off his boots and set them side by side next to his shirt. Socks followed next. When he reached for the first button on his trousers, Rayanne shifted positions, leaning forward with her arms crossed on the side of the tub, her chin resting on her hands.

Clearly, she was enjoying the show. He dropped the trousers and kicked them off, giving up all pretense of being in control. She immediately moved to the end where the faucets were, giving him the end where he could lie back against the side of the tub. He made room for her between his legs, settling her against his chest, her head leaning on his shoulder. The mounds of bubbles played peek-a-boo with all of his favorite parts of her body. Her bottom sat snugged up against his shaft, offering undeniable evidence that he was enjoying himself.

In fact, if all they did was cuddle in warm water and bubbles, he could die a happy man.

But then she reached for the washcloth and soap and showed him just how much happier he could be.

Chapter 18

Rayanne lathered up the soft cloth and handed it over her shoulder to Wyatt. "If you'll wash my back, I'll return the favor."

Then she leaned forward to give him room to move. She sighed with sheer pleasure as he dragged the cloth across her skin in slow, thorough circles. He didn't limit his ministrations to the elegant length of her back. Her shoulders received their fair amount of attention, as did each of her arms.

Then he dropped the cloth into the water and gathered up a handful of the bubbles and used them to massage her aching breasts until she could no longer sit still. He tightened his hold on her with one hand and used the other to explore the slick folds at the apex of her legs.

One thick finger tested her readiness, pressing deep inside her as he nibbled along the side of her neck, moving on to trace the shell of her ear with the tip of his tongue. She tried to break free, intending to turn around and straddle his lap. He would have none of it.

"Wyatt! Please!"

"We'll get there, sweetheart, but right now I'm enjoying myself."

He showed no mercy, continuing to torment her in such wonderful ways. Finally, he loosened his hold long enough for her to turn around. She settled her knees on each side of his hips.

"My turn for some fun."

"I'm all yours."

She rose up and carefully guided his erection right to the entrance of her body and then slowly impaled herself on its rigid length. They both moaned as she settled him deep inside. Then she rocked forward and back, sending ripples of water lapping at the top edge of the tub.

This was about to get messy, and she didn't care. There'd be plenty of time later to mop up spilled water. Right now, all she cared about was stoking this hunger between them. As she came down hard, Wyatt slid farther down in the water and grabbed onto both sides of the tub with his hands. If she wasn't mistaken, his eyes had just about rolled up in his head.

She did it again, unsure which of them she was tormenting the most. When she repeated the maneuver, her lover lost all control. In a slick move, he had her pinned beneath him, but making sure her head was well above the water line as he started pumping his hips, surging in and out of her. She raised her ankles high up on the edge of the tub, taking all of him.

Wyatt's climax was building. It was there in the way he held her so tightly in his arms, in the way his breath came in short bursts as his body shuddered deep inside of hers. Her ability to make him lose control was intoxicating and drove her flying over the edge right along with him.

As he poured out his passion deep within her, she chanted the only thing that really mattered.

"I love you, I love you, I love you."

And when Wyatt finally collapsed, sinking heavily against her, he added words of his own.

"For now and for always, Rayanne, I will love you."

Life might offer very few perfect moments, but in her heart, she knew this was one of them.

She wrapped her arms around him and just breathed in the scent of sex and roses. Both of them were content to savor the moment. Eventually, the water grew too cold to be comfortable. It took all of her energy to move at all.

"Hey, big guy, want to try out the bed next?"

He lifted his head and grinned at her. "That's a bit conventional for us, don't you think?"

"I'll bet we won't find it boring, especially if we…" Then she whispered a few ideas in his ear to prove her point.

He blinked twice. "Well, I'm willing to give it my best effort."

It took him a couple of tries to start moving. Finally,

he managed to climb out of the tub and grab a pair of thick towels. They helped each other dry off. When she reached for the robe she kept on the back of the bathroom door, Wyatt stopped her.

"You're not going to need that. You have me to keep you warm."

With that happy thought, she hung the robe back up on the door and led the charge down the hall to her room. She turned back the covers and scooted all the way to the far side of the bed to make room for Wyatt. After a bit of shifting this way and that, they found a comfortable position and drifted off to sleep.

Morning came way too early. Today would be their last day together. With luck, they'd come up with a plan to break the cycle, and Wyatt would finally rest easy in his grave on the hillside outside of Blessing. If not, then he'd continue to die year after year, a man trapped in his own special hell. The only difference would be that he'd have the memory of these days and nights with Rayanne to keep him company.

He'd reminded her during the night that he fully expected her to make a life for herself without him no matter which way things turned out. She'd argued with him, but he'd held firm. When she'd cried, he'd held her close. And when they'd made love, he'd given her his best.

She'd made him feel alive, and maybe for her he was. If so, was it possible that he could have gotten her with child? Was it selfish of him to hope he had?

He stared up at the ceiling and let his thoughts drift,

imagining what their child would look like, how it would feel to share this amazing love with a third person, one they created together. It was foolish and sweet and most likely an impossibility. Besides, how was he supposed to fit into this modern world? There was so much Rayanne took for granted that was new and scary to him.

Cars were bad enough, but he'd seen those machines flying high in the sky, too. Even that bath they'd shared the previous night had been the first time he'd experienced hot water he hadn't had to heat on the stove and carry to the tub. This dream world they shared here on the mountain wouldn't exist for him down below. Blessing was his world, the one place he belonged.

Rayanne rose up to look at him. "What's wrong?"

"Nothing at all."

"Liar." She rolled on top of him. With her hands on his chest, she pushed herself up to stare down at him. "You were relaxed and cuddly. Now you're all tensed up."

Maybe he could distract her. He cupped her backside with both hands and squeezed. "I was thinking about how we should start the day."

"Nice try, but I'd hope that thinking about some hot sex in the morning wouldn't have put that particular look on your face."

She leaned down to brush her lips across his. "Don't try to protect me, Wyatt. We both know these next two days are going to get ugly."

He brushed her hair back from her face. "I was thinking if somehow I managed to survive tomorrow—really survived, not just caught up in the same old vicious circle, that I'd never fit into your world."

Damn, he hadn't meant to put even more sadness in her eyes.

"Look, forget I said anything, Rayanne. But it's true I'm not like the men in your time."

She smiled, but it was clearly a struggle. "True enough, but then I've always had a thing for gunslingers."

"Really. What kind of thing would that be?"

Before she could answer, the telephone rang. Rayanne stared at it as if it were a rattlesnake about to bite. Finally, she sighed and slid off the bed to answer it.

"Yes, Mom, I'm still here. Where else would I be?"

He couldn't hear the other half of the conversation, but it was clear that Rayanne was not enjoying anything her mother had to say.

"We've talked about this. And yes, I do know what tomorrow is."

Her lips were white with tension as she listened. "Please, Mom, don't drive a wedge between us that won't be easily mended."

Wyatt sat up on the edge of the bed and debated what to do. Whatever her mother was saying was tearing Rayanne apart. He wished she'd simply hang up. When she didn't do it herself, he gently pried it from her fingers and wrapped his arm around her, holding her close. Would her mother be able to hear him if he tried speaking to her?

"Mrs. Allen, you need to stop this now. You're hurting your daughter with these unkind words."

Success. She sputtered to a halt. "Who is this?"

How was he supposed to answer that? *I'm the ghost who haunts Blessing? I'm your daughter's lover, except I died when your grandmother was a young woman? I'm the man who is going to break your daughter's heart? I'm the man who loves her?*

There were no good options. He settled for, "I'm a friend of Rayanne's, and I can't stand seeing her hurting like this."

Then he hung up.

No doubt there would be consequences for his actions, but right now he was more worried about the woman whose tears burned against his skin. He stroked Rayanne's back, hoping it would soothe her pain. As he did so, he noticed their image reflected in the mirror over the old bureau.

They were a picture of contrasts. He was tall, his body lean and rough-hewn from years of hard riding and even harder living. His skin was dark from hours outside without his shirt on as he'd chopped wood and hauled water to Amanda's garden. His hair was longer than he liked. He'd been due for a trim and a shave when everything had gone to hell.

Rayanne, on the other hand, was everything he wasn't. Soft. Gentle. A strange mix of strong and fragile all at the same time. And so damned lovely that it hurt.

She looked up, meeting his gaze in the mirror. It wasn't their lack of clothing that left him feeling raw, exposed. No, it was their love for each other reflected there in the silvered glass. Despite the shimmer of tears in her eyes, Rayanne smiled at the man in the mirror.

"I could sit and stare at you like this all day."

Then that small bit of joy faded. "I'm sorry about that phone call. My parents can't seem to get it through their heads that I'm fine up here."

No, she wasn't. Not really. "I hope I didn't cause you more problems by talking to your mother."

The smile was back. "I'd love to have seen the look on her face when she realized I'd had an overnight guest. She's been saying I need a man in my life."

He bet he wasn't what her mother had in mind. "In my day, your father would come after me with a shotgun."

Rayanne's smile was all temptation. "Because you had your wicked, wicked way with me repeatedly and hopefully plan to again? Like right now."

It wasn't in him to refuse her, not with the clock ticking and their time running out so damned fast. They both needed something to distract them, even for a few minutes. He picked her up in his arms, lifting her legs high around his waist as he tumbled them both back down on the bed.

The real world was right outside, ready to tear them apart. But for now, for these few minutes, they could find comfort in each other's arms.

Two hours later, they finally stepped outside. As soon as the sun hit his skin, he felt a familiar tingle. Not now! It was too soon—and already too late.

"Rayanne!"

She'd been locking the door of the cabin, but looked up when he called her name. A look of horror crossed her face as she took two steps in his direction. When she reached out to him, her hands passed right through his.

They both stared at the shimmer working its way up his arms. "I'm sorry. It's time."

"Wyatt, I'll meet you in town."

He wanted her with him, but caution had him shaking his head. "Not until tomorrow. Stay here. Stay safe."

She looked distraught. "I can't hear you!"

He tried to touch her one last time and mouthed his final words to her, hoping to make himself understood. "No matter what happens, I love you, Rayanne. Never forget that."

Rayanne stood there looking fierce and determined. "I won't forget. And I love you, too, Wyatt McCain. I'll do my best to end this for you."

He nodded, knowing she would. The tingling had worsened to a burn. He could no longer feel the warmth of the sun or the ground beneath his feet. Rayanne seemed to be standing at the far end of a tunnel, growing smaller and more distant until he couldn't see her at all.

His heart broke as the darkness washed over him.

The next time Wyatt grew aware of his surroundings, aware of himself, it was late in the day, getting on toward dinnertime. He was walking down the street in Blessing on his way to the mercantile to pick up a length of fabric that Amanda had ordered to make new shirts for both him and Billy.

Before he got that far, he spotted that sneaky bastard Earl ducking into the saloon. What was he doing back in town? He veered off his intended path and followed Earl inside.

The old clock on the wall said it was after five. In less than twenty-four hours from right now, he'd be dead and buried up on the hillside. Regrets wouldn't change a thing so he ordered a beer and walked over to sit down with Earl. Even though he already knew the answers, he'd buy a few rounds to loosen up Earl's tongue and start asking questions.

Come sundown, he'd run the bastard out of town with a special message for the rest of the gang. They wouldn't listen, not when they thought the town was easy pickings. Fine. At least he'd warned them.

If this played out the way he expected it to, tomorrow they would die. Soon, the dust in the streets of Blessing would soak up their blood and their dying screams.

Chapter 19

Rayanne used to think Uncle Ray's cabin was cozy and comfortable. She'd been rattling around inside for hours now, alone and lonely. She missed Wyatt. Plain and simple. If he hadn't asked her to stay away until tomorrow, she would've headed straight for Blessing hours ago.

She considered the wisdom of digging out her uncle's old sleeping bag and camping out on the hillside overlooking the town. Anything to keep from missing a single minute of the drama about to unfold. But no, she'd promised to stay away today. For Wyatt's sake, she'd stay right where she was.

There had to be something to do. She considered stripping her bed and washing the sheets, but they carried Wyatt's scent. She wasn't ready to lose even that much of him.

That left Uncle Ray's room. She'd put off cleaning it out long enough. Bracing herself, she opened the door and took a determined step across the threshold. Listening to the silence, she realized the room now felt empty, abandoned. The memories were still there, but they were comfortable and familiar, their pain no longer fresh.

She started by emptying the closet, sorting out the clothes that were usable from those that should have been tossed in the trash years ago. When that was done, she started on the chest of drawers. One glance in the top drawer had her grinning. How many pairs of socks did one man need?

An hour later, everything was bagged up, labeled and sitting out on the deck. Eventually, she'd haul it all to town. After a quick break for lunch, she turned the mattress and made up the bed with fresh linens and another of the old quilts from the linen closet.

Already the room seemed brighter, welcoming. Maybe it was time for her to leave her childhood room behind and move into this one. She'd think more about that later. Right now, she needed to go through the bedside table and the bookshelves, which didn't take long. She set aside a few photographs that her mother might want along with some of Ray's favorite books. By the time she was finished, the sun was setting.

She'd worked herself into a pleasant exhaustion. Maybe she'd be able to sleep, after all. Food held little appeal, but as Wyatt had told her yesterday, she'd need all her strength to get through the next day—and all those days afterward.

Thinking of Wyatt made her chest ache. She stared at the grainy photograph she'd kept pinned to the wall. He looked so grim in the picture, as if he'd forgotten how to smile. She knew better.

She'd made it through twenty-four hours without him. The prospect of an entire future of such days weighed her down until it was hard to keep moving. After putting soup on to heat, she walked out onto the porch to watch the sun set. The spectacular display did nothing to lighten her mood.

Where was Wyatt right now? By this time, that guy he used to ride with should have arrived in town. What was the man's name? It started with a vowel. Irving? Ed? No and no. Earl. That was it. The two of them would share a few drinks, Wyatt buying them both shots of whiskey to lull Earl into revealing what he and the others were up to.

Was Wyatt thinking of her at all? Could he even remember who she was now that he was caught up in his own life again? Was it selfish of her to not want to be the only one who hurt this much? Probably.

With that cheery thought, she went back inside. She curled up on the couch, looking around for some kind of distraction. Nothing in Ray's movie collection held any appeal, and she couldn't focus well enough to follow the plot in the mystery she'd been reading.

Finally, she reached for Ray's journal. Maybe now would be the right time to finish reading it. Her heart hurt over the loss of her uncle, but she suspected that pain would pale in comparison to how she'd feel losing Wyatt, as well.

At first her tears blurred the words on the page, but she blinked hard until Ray's writing came back into focus.

My time on the mountain is growing short. The doc says my heart is worn out, and I can't say that I'm surprised. He tried to get me to move closer to town, but I've found it peaceful up here on the mountain and see no reason to change things this late in the game. I could probably live down below now, but maybe not. I know my sister has never understood my love for this place, but that's all right. She never once felt the power of the mountain and the people that it claims as its own.

I only catch the occasional glimpse of them passing through the woods, mostly in the summer as the time grows near for tragedy to play out again. I've gone years without watching it all happen, but I did climb to the belfry one final time last summer. I felt I owed Wyatt McCain that much for keeping me company for all these years. Granted, I didn't talk to him much, but that was just me.

Despite or maybe because of how the gunfight turned out, I've always felt a certain kinship for the man who put his own life on the line to protect the others in Blessing. I know all too well the cost of being a warrior in this world. Eventually, my heart will simply stop, and I will finally rejoin my unit.

Rayanne, if you're reading this, know that I loved you, and I'm so damned proud of the woman you've become. It's my greatest hope that you'll find a way to

lay Blessing's past to rest once and for all. That last
summer you visited, you not only saw Wyatt McCain,
but he heard and saw you. Your warning didn't change
the final outcome, but it did change a few things.

I tried for years afterward to do the same, but with
no luck. I have to think that somehow you managed
to forge a special connection between you and Wyatt.
Not sure how or why. Maybe because you still had the
innocence of a child.

One thing I do know is that a man's soul can't find
peace until he forgives himself for the things that he's
done in his life. Once I managed to do that, the ghosts
of my past finally faded away.

But enough of this. Embrace the mountain, Ray-
anne, because it has chosen to share its secrets with
you.

Uncle Ray

She reread the last few paragraphs, their truth reso-
nating with what she believed. Wyatt needed to forgive
himself because no one else who mattered held him
responsible for Billy's death. Amanda certainly hadn't
blamed him, and Rayanne knew the price he'd paid for
his mistake. A hundred-plus years of Wyatt reliving
his own personal hell was punishment enough. She
could only hope that her love and her promise to try to
save Billy would finally help Wyatt let go of his pain.

An hour later she crawled into bed, breathing deeply
of his scent on her pillow. It eased her heart almost as
if he'd been there to hold her close all night long.

But only almost.

* * *

By the time she awoke the next morning, the sun had already cleared the horizon. Realizing how late it was, she lurched out of bed and grabbed some random clothes and ran for the bathroom.

How could she have slept so late on such an important occasion? She'd meant to be in town before sunrise, hoping to watch it all unfold. What if she'd already missed her chance to affect the outcome of the day's events?

She ran a brush through her hair and charged down the steps to the kitchen. Pausing only long enough to grab a couple of bottles of water and a box of granola bars to shove in her pack, she headed out the door.

To her horror, she wasn't alone. This time it wasn't the ghostly remnants of Blessing standing in the meadow outside of the cabin. No, the three people climbing out of the car were far scarier. Her parents were bad enough, but it was the third member of the group that left her mouth as dry as cotton.

She walked down the steps, her heart in her throat. Rather than try to talk when she wasn't even sure she could swallow, she stopped to take a swig of water first. It didn't help much. "Mom, Dad, Dr. Long, what an unpleasant surprise. I'm assuming you'll be leaving soon."

Judging from the looks and nods they exchanged, that wasn't the smartest approach she could've taken. Her father stepped forward, clearly planning on being the spokesperson for their group.

"Rayanne, I'm sorry we came unannounced, but we

all know you would have told us to stay away. Your mother has been very worried about you."

Oh, brother. Her own worry for Wyatt lit her already short fuse.

"Why? Because I inherited Uncle Ray's estate instead of her? Or because I didn't leap at the chance to sleep with Shawn when she sent him up here, hoping I'd do just that? Hell, the only thing that he was missing was a big red bow with an 'Open me next' tag on his shirt."

Her mother gasped in outrage. "Rayanne! I did no such thing."

"Then how did he find his way up here, Mom? I sure didn't tell him where to find me. That alone should have told you that there was nothing serious between the two of us." At least not on her part.

Her father shot his ex-wife a dark look. "Is that true, Lana? Did you send him up here without asking Rayanne how she felt about him first?"

"Well, she never even gave the man a decent chance. While she spends all of her time caught up in research, life is passing her by."

Then her mother did an end run around her father to get right in Rayanne's face. "Shawn is perfect for you. I thought if the two of you spent some time together away from the college and away from this place," she snarled, pointing at the cabin, "that maybe, just maybe, you'd come to your senses. Obviously, that didn't work."

Rayanne rolled her eyes. "No, it didn't. Three points

for the melodramatics, though. Now, if you'll excuse me, I have work to do."

When she started past them, her father blocked her path. "I'm sorry, sweetheart, but even if your mother made a mistake with this Shawn guy, that doesn't mean she isn't right about the fixation you've developed for this place. It's not healthy for you. Just ask Dr. Long."

For the first time, the psychiatrist spoke up. "Rayanne, it is my opinion that the death of your uncle may have caused you to have a relapse. With prompt treatment, we should be able to keep this episode from becoming as severe as the one fifteen years ago. I've already blocked out two appointments a week for the next month for you."

She could only laugh. "Nice that you can make a diagnosis without ever speaking to the patient, Doc. Well, sorry, but you can take those appointments and pills and…"

Rayanne paused to rethink what she was about say. Calm was far better than hostile. "And cancel them. Please."

Her mom started in again. "Rayanne, I will not watch you go through that hell again. I'll have you forced into care if that's what it takes."

Her words cut like shards of glass, sending Rayanne staggering back several steps. "Mother!"

The shock on her father's face was too genuine to be faked. "Lana! Now you've gone too far."

It was all too much. Maybe they'd be able to mend fences later, but right now there were more important matters that needed Rayanne's immediate attention.

Before she walked away, though, she laid it out plain and simple for all of them. It took every bit of willpower she could muster, but she kept her voice even, her manner nonthreatening, when what she really wanted to do was shake some sense into the lot of them.

"Dad, I'm very sorry you made the trip up here because of Mom's hysteria. I understand that Uncle Ray's death hit her hard, and that has intensified her worry about me being up here. But truly, I've been working hard to complete my research on the town before the end of the summer. Go home. I'll call you when I get a chance."

What could she say to her mother that wouldn't permanently damage their relationship?

"Mother, this is my home, and you are no longer welcome here. Don't come and don't call. If necessary, I will get a restraining order. I'd rather not involve my attorneys, but I will if you force my hand. I know you have issues with this place, but that's not my problem. It's yours, plain and simple. Don't push me on this. You won't like what happens."

Her mother flinched as if Rayanne had actually struck her. It was tempting to relent, but right now it was more important that the three intruders leave.

Finally, she turned to the final member of this little party. "Dr. Long, thank you for your concern, but let me make something clear. I'm a historian, and studying a place like Blessing is what I do for a living."

She glanced back at her mother before once again meeting Dr. Long's gaze head-on. "If you're planning on billing somebody for this little trip up the mountain, it better not be me. After all, I have not been your patient for fifteen years.

"Now, if you all will excuse me, I'm going to return to my research. I will be eternally grateful if you are gone by the time I get back."

Then she turned her back and walked away.

That calm lasted less than half the distance to Blessing. As she walked, she scrubbed at her face with the hem of her shirt to wipe away her acid-hot tears. If only she could do the same with her memories. Right now, she needed all of her wits about her just to get through the rest of the day.

She'd just reached the edge of the slope leading down to the town when the sound of running footsteps brought her to an abrupt halt. They coasted to a stop a short distance behind her. She forced herself to turn around.

"Dad—"

He held up his hands to cut her off. "I just wanted to make sure you're all right. You know, after that debacle back there. Your mom knows you don't want to see her right now, but she wanted me to tell you that she's sorry. Hell, even Dr. Long seemed impressed about how well you handled the situation."

His mouth quirked up in a half smile. "He also said to tell you that he wouldn't dream of billing anyone for a nice drive in the mountains."

Okay, that helped.

"Thanks, Dad. Tell Mom…" She paused while she tried to find the right words. She settled for, "Tell her I'll call when I'm back in town."

"Do that, honey. I know you like to putter around in places like Blessing, but it's hard not to worry about you being up here all alone in those derelict buildings."

Then he frowned as he stared past her toward the town. "That's odd. I know it's been years since I've been up here, but I don't remember there being that many buildings still standing."

Oh, God. Rayanne had been too caught up in her pain to even notice. The last thing she needed right now was for her father to get curious. All her efforts to convince him and the others that she was fine would go to hell in a handcart if she pointed out that her ghost town was currently full of ghosts—real ones.

"I think maybe Uncle Ray had done some restoration work since you were last up here."

That wasn't even a lie. He'd replaced those steps in the church. That counted.

Her father smiled at her. "Maybe sometime you'll take me through the town. I'd like to see it through your eyes."

As peace offerings went, it was a good one.

"I'd love that, Dad. Now you'd better get back to Mom."

He gave her a quick hug and hustled back the way he'd come. She waited impatiently until he disappeared behind a bend in the trail to take off running for Blessing, praying she wasn't too late.

* * *

Bert, the saloon owner, poured Wyatt a shot of whiskey from a bottle he normally kept under lock and key. He thanked the man and savored the burn on its way down his throat. He didn't often get to enjoy the good stuff. When Wyatt tossed a couple of coins on the counter, Bert shoved it right back toward him.

"Your money's no good here today, Wyatt." He picked up the bottle. "Want another one?"

It was tempting, but Amanda was already mad at him for smelling like cheap liquor when he went back to her cabin last night. He didn't figure on surviving the day. But on the chance he was wrong about that, he didn't want to provoke her temper unnecessarily.

She'd already torn a strip off his hide with that sharp tongue of hers for what he was about to do. The woman had strong opinions on many subjects, one of the reasons he liked her, and evidently him facing off against his old gang was one of them. He'd tried to explain that the thieving bastards would keep coming and coming if someone didn't put a stop to it. She didn't understand why Wyatt had to be that someone.

In truth, he didn't want to be, but he was the only one in town with any chance of reasoning with Earl and the rest. If words failed to convince them to leave, he was also the only one with the ability to state his case with bullets.

Outside, he could hear the townspeople talking, a rising note of panic in their voices. He nodded to the bartender and headed for the door where Tennessee Sue blocked his way.

"What?"

"Be careful out there." Then she kissed him full on the mouth.

He brushed a lock of her hair back behind her ear. "I'll try."

Before stepping out onto the sidewalk, he paused when a shiver of fear waltzed up and down his spine. Not for him, although that was there, too.

No, he was worried about Billy. He'd made Amanda promise to stay home and to keep the boy with her. No matter how this all turned out, he'd needed to know they were safe. That was all that mattered to him. They'd find out soon enough if he lived through this.

If he didn't, well, neither she nor Billy needed to see that. He'd do his best for the town, but he had a bad feeling about how things were going to turn out. He could almost see it in his head, as if it were a play and they were all following the script.

For some reason, the first place he looked was across the street at the church. Why was that? Despite Amanda's urging, he'd never set foot in the place. It was a little late for a man like him to find religion. Even so, there was something about the belfry that drew his eye. A memory danced just out of reach, something he couldn't make sense of. Then the image of a woman's face flashed through his mind. Who was she? She looked a bit like Amanda, but different enough to know that it wasn't her.

Whoever she was, simply thinking about her calmed his mind. The cards were already on the table. Only time would tell if he'd been dealt a winning hand.

He took one more step forward, hoping he looked a hell of a lot more calm than he actually was. He took a deep draw off his cigarette and blew out a cloud of smoke. Something else Amanda wouldn't like, but a man deserved a few vices in life. Despite his brief relapse into drinking and smoking, he hoped Amanda knew he'd been a better man because of her.

Someone from down at the mercantile shouted, "They're coming!"

The remaining few people on the street scattered like quail. Doors slammed. Windows closed. The only sounds now were the pounding of hooves in counterpoint to his heartbeat. He tossed the cigarette down and ground it out with his boot heel.

He shifted his rifle to his right hand and shoved the front edges of his duster back so he'd have easy access to his pistols.

Earl and the others were in sight now, riding hard toward Blessing. At the edge of town, they slowed to a walk. He noted that the riders checked all the doorways and windows they passed for any sign that he had backup in place. He smiled. If they were that nervous, maybe they'd make a mistake.

They slowed to a stop at the far edge of shooting distance. He stood his ground, preferring they come to him.

Evidently, Earl wasn't only their scout but also their spokesman. "Wyatt, and here I thought we was friends, especially after all those drinks you kindly bought me last night. Hell, all these boys were jealous when I told them how generous you were."

"That was last night. This is today." Wyatt made sure his smile couldn't be mistaken for friendly. "Earl, I have to admit I'm disappointed that you've ignored my advice to avoid Blessing. Things are about to get dangerous. I'd hate to see you get shot."

"I ain't too worried, Wyatt." Earl leaned forward, resting his shotgun across the front of his saddle. "See, there's just one of you and a whole bunch of us."

"Well, that's true enough. To be honest, I'd just as soon buy another round of whiskey for you boys if you'd promise to ride on out of town without causing any trouble."

Earl exchanged a knowing grin with his friends. "We'll take you up on that offer as soon as you turn over the gold from the mining office. Stealing is thirsty work and a few drinks will taste mighty good."

They were already laughing. He didn't give a damn. He'd known all along it would come to this.

"Well, Earl, that's not going to happen, and we both know it. And you're right about there being more of you. I'm better with guns than any of you, but I'm not good enough to take out all of you before someone gets off a lucky shot. But there's one thing you can count on, Earl."

"Yeah, what's that?"

"That you'll be the first I shoot."

Then Wyatt pulled the trigger and the dying began.

Chapter 20

Past experience had made it clear that shouting a warning wouldn't save Wyatt. Despite it being midmorning, a time when the town would normally be at its busiest, there was nothing but a heavy silence hanging over the town.

It was as if the entire world held its breath, waiting for a storm of blood and pain to be unleashed on the people of Blessing. Rayanne couldn't stop events that had unfolded over a century before. But maybe, just maybe, she could save one person. One innocent. Billy. That's all Wyatt had asked of her.

Neither of them knew if she could pull it off, but she would try. The selfish part of her argued that if she could rescue only one of the players in this tragedy, it should be Wyatt. Surely he'd earned a reprieve after all these decades of suffering through this alone. But in her heart, she knew the man she loved would never forgive her if she didn't try to save the boy.

So rather than heading toward the belfry as she did the last time she'd lived through this horror, Rayanne ran to the spot where Amanda's cabin used to stand. What would she do if the woman and her son weren't even there?

She approached the cabin cautiously, not sure what would happen if she entered a building that didn't really exist in her own time. The door was certainly solid enough when she rapped her knuckles on it.

"Amanda! Billy! Are you in there?"

No answer.

She pushed the door open and looked around. The interior looked much as she'd imagined it would. In fact, if she wasn't mistaken, that exact same vase now sat on the mantel over the fireplace in her mother's living room. The small connection with the great-great-grandmother she'd never had a chance to meet had Rayanne smiling. If only she could tell her mother about it.

Yeah, like that would ever happen.

She checked the second room and the loft, each as empty and silent as the next. Back outside, she ran around the house to see if there was a cellar they could be hiding in. No such luck. She passed the rick of wood that Wyatt had chopped for them. For a man who thought so little of himself, he'd done some awfully nice things for people, including sacrificing himself to keep them safe.

But right now, her fear for Amanda and her son had ramped up to new levels. She'd never forgive herself if she failed to find them in time. As long as Billy kept dying, then Wyatt would, as well.

She pelted back down the way she'd come, skittering to a halt when she reached the back of the church. Time for some caution on her part. Fifteen years ago, Wyatt's bullet had been real enough to kill that man in the belfry. More than one of the townspeople had been hit by stray shots that day. She didn't want to add herself to their number.

The silence was broken by panicky voices. The riders were on their way into town, the gunfight only seconds from starting now. She wouldn't accomplish anything cowering here behind the building. Entering the church from the back door, she made her way through to the front. She dropped to all fours and scrambled across to the small window by the front door.

Rising up, she saw a scene right out of her past and a whole lot of nightmares after that. Wyatt walked out of the saloon. If memory served her right, he'd pause there to finish his cigarette. Next, he'd step out in the street and die.

She'd never seen that part, but that didn't matter. Except for the one year when she'd interfered, he'd taken a shot in the shoulder from the guy on the belfry and seven more before it was over.

Even then, Wyatt had lived long enough to realize that he'd killed Billy. Maybe if he hadn't been so stubborn about dying, he would never have realized what he'd done. Would he have found peace then?

A movement at the opposite end of town caught her attention. It was Billy making his way along one of the buildings that had reappeared overnight. He was moving slowly, no doubt doing his best to sneak close enough to watch without being caught. At the moment, the boy couldn't be seen by Wyatt or any of the riders who rode right past the boy as they headed toward the center of town. She had to get to Billy before that changed.

Rayanne bolted out the back of the church at a dead run, knowing she had only a minute, maybe two before the firing started. She rounded the corner and charged toward where Billy was inching forward again. By now he was holding on to the side of the building, his feet dragging as he walked.

When she yelled his name, he froze and glanced back in her direction. At the same time, Rayanne spotted his mother across the street, looking horrified that her son had disobeyed her orders to remain at the cabin.

"Miss Rayanne, I need my ma," Billy called as he reached out toward her, his words a harsh whisper.

Before she could answer, the bullets started flying. She charged forward and tackled Billy, dragging both of them down to the ground.

A bullet hit the wall right over their heads, showering them both with splinters. She raised her head long enough to see what was going on. Wyatt looked straight at her, recognition dawning in those pale blue eyes.

"Rayanne! Stay down!"

She didn't need to be told twice. Maybe it was cowardly of her, but she couldn't bring herself to watch the man she loved die. Eventually, the shots died away; the only thing left was the fog of blue smoke drifting on the summer breeze. A riderless horse wandered by, its reins dragging in the dust.

"Miss Rayanne, help me."

Had Billy been hit, anyway? She sat up, checking him for any sign of blood. Nothing.

"What's wrong, Billy? Are you hurt?"

"I was playing by the woodpile. Got snake bit twice."

He held out his arm to show her twin sets of punctures. The fear in his eyes broke her heart. Without prompt treatment, the venom would likely prove fatal. The thought made her sick.

By then, Amanda had reached them.

"Who are you?"

Now wasn't the time for introductions. Rayanne pointed toward the wound. "Your son's been bitten by a snake."

Amanda blanched. "Billy! I told you to stay inside!"

The boy was in obvious pain, his eyes glassy and feverish. His voice was so weak as he whispered, "I'm sorry, Ma. I'll listen next time."

Amanda met Rayanne's gaze, her dawning horror painfully clear. Without a word, she stepped past Rayanne to scoop Billy up off the ground and ran toward the mercantile where so many of the townspeople had taken refuge.

There was nothing Rayanne could do for the boy, and her presence would only be a distraction. Leaving Amanda to see to her son, Rayanne whispered a prayer for them all as she ran to where Wyatt lay sprawled in the street, the surrounding dust splattered with his blood.

Oh, God, the reality was so much worse than anything she could have imagined. His breath rattled in his chest, and blood bubbled and pulsed out of too many holes to count. He blinked up at her, looking confused at first, but then clarity returned. She lifted his head onto her lap, trying not to hurt him any further even knowing nothing she did would save him.

"Billy?" Even that one word was a struggle for him.

"He's with Amanda."

That much was true, but there was no way to know if he'd survive. Maybe as she'd told Wyatt before, it was simply the boy's time.

The tension in Wyatt's face eased, and his smile was so sweet. "Thank you for that."

Tears poured down her cheeks. "I wanted to save you, instead. God, Wyatt, I love you so much."

"Love you, too…with you always."

He said those last words with strength, conviction and his last breath. He shuddered slightly, then he was gone.

Literally.

A powerful wave of energy washed through Blessing and caught Rayanne up in its maelstrom. She was buffeted with dust and gravel, and even the sun overhead blinked out of sight, trapping her in total darkness. She screamed for Wyatt, and she screamed for help.

The wave was gone as quickly as it had come, but it left Rayanne dizzy and sick. Rather than fight it, she let the darkness sweep away her pain and grief and simply slept.

When consciousness returned, Rayanne had no idea how long she'd been passed out in front of the saloon, but the sun was already low in the western sky. She sat up slowly, fighting dizziness and nausea. Realizing that this was the exact spot where Wyatt had died sent her scrambling up to her feet. She took a cautious look around.

Everything was back to normal; the only buildings surrounding her were the ones that had survived the past century. The others had faded back out of existence again. The past was back where it belonged, the only question being if it would stay there this time.

She needed to get back to the cabin before nightfall, inside thick walls. Once inside, she'd take a long, hot bath and try not to think about how it had been to share that tub with Wyatt. She'd curl up in Uncle Ray's old robe with a cup of tea laced with brandy and then cry herself sick.

In the morning, she'd…what? At this point she didn't know. Tomorrow would have to take care of itself. For now, she had a plan of action that would get her through the next few hours. Anything to keep her moving forward.

Her bones ached as if she'd aged forty years. Who knew that grief carried so much weight? It was all she could do to stand upright. One step at a time, she made her way through the trees to the meadow that surrounded the cabin.

It was full night by the time she let herself in the cabin and locked the door. Safe at last from ghosts and family alike. What a shame she couldn't leave her memories out on the porch to deal with later when she found the strength. With that happy thought, she headed upstairs to that bath. She sank down in the hot water up to her chin, gave up all pretense of control and let the tears come.

Chapter 21

"You look like hell, young lady. Haven't you been taking care of yourself?"

Phil glowered at her from the other side of the counter. He added a third scoop of ice cream to the banana split he'd insisted on making for her. She watched as he smothered it with chocolate sauce, whipped cream and chopped nuts. He plopped a spoon down in front of her.

"I asked for a single scoop of chocolate, Phil. That's more ice cream than I normally eat in a month."

He just huffed at her. "There's nothing normal about this week of August up here on the mountain, and you know it."

Okay, what did he know about what went on in Blessing? How much had Uncle Ray told him over the years? Rather than respond immediately, she took a big bite of chocolaty goodness to buy herself some time.

Her friend crossed his arms over his chest and leaned back against the cooler behind him. Clearly, he didn't plan on going anywhere until he got some answers. When he arched a single eyebrow, he might as well have shouted, "I'm waiting."

"Yesterday was the twenty-third." She set the spoon down and waited to see how he'd respond.

His shoulders slumped down, but whether it was because he was relieved or worried was impossible to tell. "Damn it, Rayanne, did you watch from the belfry again?"

Evidently, he knew quite a bit.

"No. I didn't see the actual gunfight. I was down the street between two of the buildings."

"And those scratches on your back and shoulders?"

She took another small bite before answering. "A bullet tore into the wood right above us."

This time both eyebrows slammed down over his eyes. "Us? Who was up there with you? Tell me it wasn't that ditzy mother of yours. Wasn't that her car I saw go by early yesterday morning?"

She had to laugh. "It was, but I sent her and my dad packing before I headed into Blessing."

Her smile faded as she went on. "I tried to save the boy who got hit with a stray shot. His name was Billy, and he was my great-uncle. Or would've been if he hadn't died that day."

"Did it work? Saving Billy, that is."

She shrugged as she stared down at her ice cream.

"I don't know. Fifteen years ago, I changed one link in the chain of events when I yelled out a warning about the shooter in the church belfry. It didn't change the ultimate outcome of the gunfight. Wyatt McCain still died that day, and so did Billy."

She looked up at Phil. "So I don't know if anything is different. Billy didn't get shot this time, but he was in town looking for his mother because he'd been bitten by a snake. If he survived, wouldn't my family already know? I mean, if he lived past that day, it would've been in my great-great-grandmother's journal. By the way, that's what was in the box you gave me from Uncle Ray."

Phil tossed her a couple of napkins as if she'd spilled something, but then she realized they were for her tears. "I'm sorry. I can't seem to stop crying. It's all so awful."

"So Ray was right."

Phil dragged another stool over to the counter and sat down beside her, his heavy hand on her shoulder. "Your uncle knew what was going on in Blessing every year. Some old-timers around here always claim they've heard the gunshots or maybe caught a glimpse of someone in the woods. Hell, one year Ray and I were out hiking together and we saw some riders heading in that direction."

He smiled. "Scared the hell out of me when they rode by in absolute silence and then disappeared a second later. That's when Ray told me the whole story."

It was good to know that she wasn't alone in this. "What do you think he was right about?"

"That the gift for seeing the truth of Blessing was growing stronger from generation to generation. Ray knew what went on in town on the twenty-third, but most years he only got glimpses of the action. Sometimes he'd see people and at other times he'd only hear sounds."

Phil let his hand drop back down to his knee. "But that year you were up on the mountain, you saw everything. He felt real bad about that."

She'd never blamed him for anything. "Uncle Ray had no way of knowing what would happen."

"Feeling guilty and being guilty don't always walk hand in hand, Rayanne."

Phil gave her ice cream a pointed look. She picked up the spoon and started eating again.

"He thought maybe you were the one who could fix what was broken up there. End it for everybody and let those folks rest in peace."

"I hope it worked. I can't go through that again."

"You're stronger than you think, Rayanne. Most folks would have come screaming down the mountain at the first sight of a ghost. You hung in there right up to the last."

She swallowed her ice cream and wished she could swallow her pain as easily. "It's not that. I promised Wyatt McCain I wouldn't spend my life up there on the mountain trying to change things for him."

"You spoke with him?"

She blushed furiously. They'd done a whole lot more than talk, but she wasn't about to share that bit of news with her elderly friend.

"We spent a lot of time together. He helped me map out the whole town the way it used to be."

"What was he like, this McCain fellow?"

What could she say that wouldn't give too much away? Even if Phil did believe that there were ghosts on the mountain, that didn't mean he wouldn't think she was crazy for falling in love with one. She settled on the simplest truth.

"He was a good man, Phil. A real good man who sacrificed himself for that town. He knew full well he was outmanned and outgunned, but he did his best to protect the people of Blessing. He died for them."

She smiled, letting herself remember some of their special moments, starting with his blue eyes staring down into hers as he made love to her. How funny he'd been when she told him modern women would think he was hot with his sleeves rolled up or if they saw him in his duster. How he'd made her feel complete, special and loved.

"I'm not going to ask what's going through your mind right now, but I'm guessing you have some strong feelings for McCain. Call me an old softy, honey, but I think you being up there wasn't some accident. It was meant to be."

Another customer came in. Phil stood up and patted her on the shoulder again. "Finish your ice cream. Something tells me you're going to need all your strength."

She almost choked when his words echoed what Wyatt had said to her the night he'd made her finish her sandwich before he'd let her take him upstairs to make love. Right now the memories were too raw to dwell on for long, but it was nice to know she could still smile.

Back up on the mountain, she sat on the front porch and stared up at the sky while the sun came up. Another day had passed with no sign of Wyatt. She still needed to go back into Blessing to retrieve the last of her papers and to finish the last of her sketches and measurements. The only building left was the old church.

She'd put it off until last, although she didn't know why, exactly. Maybe because that was where all of this had started for her fifteen years ago. It seemed fitting that the church be the last place she added to her portfolio.

Now that it was light enough to see where she was going, she set her coffee cup aside and rose to her feet. She hadn't yet decided whether to return to the college or if she'd winter over here in the cabin. Right now, she was taking each day one at a time.

The birds were busy in the trees, their chittering a welcome sign that she was alone. She paused at the edge of the trees to stare at Blessing. The morning sun was kind to the faded wood, reminding her how different the place had looked when the buildings were all new.

She took that first step on her return to Blessing and found that it wasn't as hard as she'd feared. Wyatt had told her that once the gunfight was over, sometimes it was late fall before it all started again. She wanted to finish her work now while there was no chance of running into him.

She couldn't stand the thought of Wyatt getting caught up in the same old pain again. In town, she gathered up all of her work in the saloon and packed it away. With that finished, she drew a slow breath and headed across the street to the church.

Inside, she stopped to look around. Of all the buildings in town, this one had withstood the passage of time the best. Maybe the people who had built it had done so with more care. Although she didn't attend church herself, she savored the profound sense of peace that seemed to have soaked into the walls of the building.

For a few seconds, she bowed her head and offered up a silent prayer that the man she loved and that boy he cared so much about had finally found peace on the mountain. Hoping somebody up there had been listening, she set her stuff down and got busy. It didn't take her long to measure everything. Then she took a few minutes to sketch in the few details she remembered from the short time she'd been inside the building as it had been in its prime.

Finally, she reluctantly headed up the stairs to the belfry. This time, the memories from fifteen years ago stayed firmly in her past. Instead, she concentrated on the present as she stepped through the door onto the platform outside. The sun warmed her skin as she walked over to the railing to look down. The view from the roof gave her a new perspective of the town. She opened her pad to a new page and started drawing as fast as her pencil would move.

Slowly, the town took shape. When the buildings

were all in place, she added the people—miners, store-keepers, ladies running their errands, children kicking a rock down the street. She could see it all so clearly in her mind.

And one lone man wearing a dark red shirt with his hat pulled down low over his face stood down on the sidewalk, staring across at the saloon. She closed her eyes and then looked again. He was still there.

The point on her pencil snapped, and her pad slipped out of her fingers.

"Wyatt?" she whispered.

From this angle, she couldn't see his face. That shirt was different, and he wasn't wearing a duster. Even so, there was something about him that looked so familiar.

Spots danced in her eyes and there was a loud roaring in her head. She tried to hold on to the railing, but her fingers wouldn't cooperate. When her knees refused to support her, she sat down before she fell down.

What had she just seen? She braced herself for the worst and peered through the railing toward the street below. Just as she feared, it was empty. Perhaps by drawing the town as she wanted to remember it, her imagination had filled in the few details she'd most wanted to see. Maybe it had been too soon to come back.

She was done for the day. Maybe for good. She started to gather up her sketches. Where had she left her pack? She spotted it a few feet away, but before she could make a move in that direction, she heard the familiar creak of the door to the belfry opening.

Okay, the last time someone had shown up on the

belfry when she was there, it hadn't turned out all that great for her or Wyatt. Rather than face a potential threat sitting down, she rose to her feet and grabbed her pack to use as a weapon if it became necessary.

The man she'd seen down on the street stepped out onto the roof. His hat now tipped back off his face, and the sun gleamed off his blacker-than-night hair. A pair of sky-blue eyes stared right at her.

The boards beneath his feet creaked in protest as he took a cautious step toward her. She stared at his feet in amazement. He had weight. Substance.

This time she shouted his name. "Wyatt!"

His answering smile was everything she could have hoped for. "I should've known I'd find you up here."

He held out his arms and she ran straight into them. "Wyatt, what are you doing here? You said you'd disappear until fall. I didn't break my promise to stay away."

The rush of words came out in a single breath. Instead of answering her, Wyatt picked her up in his arms and swung her around and around.

"I'm back, but not like before. I'm real again, Rayanne. For good this time. I don't know how I know that, but I do."

When he set her back down on her feet, she was breathless. "Really real? How can that be?"

"I don't know." Then he looked down at the street below, his expression haunted. "Why isn't Billy here with me?"

She had to tell him the truth. It wasn't going to be easy. "I'm sorry, but Billy didn't sneak into town to watch the gunfight, Wyatt. He stayed home like he was supposed to, but he was bitten by a snake near the woodpile. He was in town looking for Amanda, not you."

"Damn it, so he died that day, anyway, didn't he?" Wyatt tightened his hold on her.

"I have to think so. Amanda's journal said she lost Billy that day, but not how he died. I'm so sorry, Wyatt."

"Me, too, but maybe you were right, and it was just his time. Nothing we did changed a thing."

She hugged him back. "But it did. Now you know that it wasn't your fault that Billy came to town, no matter how he died. I told you Amanda never blamed you for her son's death. You shouldn't, either."

She caressed his face with her fingertips. "My uncle, a surprisingly wise man, said that a man had to forgive himself for the things in his past before his soul can find peace. Now that you know Billy's death wasn't all your fault, maybe you can make peace with what happened."

Wyatt closed his eyes and took a deep breath and then another one. When he finally opened them, she saw nothing but a calm acceptance in their depths.

"Maybe your prayers were answered, and I am getting a second chance to live my life right. But it's going to take a powerful lot of adjustment to this new world, and I'm going to need some help with that."

Wyatt tightened his hold on her. "Know anybody who would be willing to take on the job? It would take a special woman to love an ex-gunslinger."

The last vestige of pain in her chest melted away.

"That all depends. Think that ex-gunslinger could put up with a woman who likes to spend her time wandering in ghost towns and reading dusty, old books?"

Wyatt stared down at her with a world of love in his smile. "She sounds perfect, the kind of woman worth waiting more than a century for. The kind a man would be right proud to call his wife."

Rayanne retreated a step. "Is that a proposal?"

He took his hat off and crumpled the brim in a tight grip. "I reckon it is."

"Then I accept."

For the second time, Wyatt grabbed her up and swung her around and around and then kissed her to seal the deal. For the first time, she didn't worry that it was too much, that he'd blink out of existence if she demanded more than he had to give. It was amazing, a gift she'd never take for granted.

When he set her back down, his expression turned solemn. "It won't be easy, Rayanne, explaining me to your folks and friends. And I'm not sure what I can do to earn a living, either. Things have changed so much since I died."

She understood why he was worried, but at least he was looking forward, no longer trapped in his past.

"Not to worry. I have a friend who owns a small store near here who could use some help. I suspect he'd be thrilled to meet you. Besides, Uncle Ray left me both this land and the cabin free and clear along with enough money to ensure neither of us has to work. But even if he hadn't, we can handle anything as long as we're together."

Then she tugged Wyatt toward the door back down to the church. "But we'll worry about all of that later. Right now, let's head back to the cabin. I think we both could use a long soak in the tub."

Wyatt's blue eyes sparkled with heated intent. "Lady, I like the way you think."

After he stepped through the door, she realized she'd left her sketch pad and pack behind. "I forgot something, but I'll catch up in a second."

With her artwork tucked under her arm, she paused to take in the view below. Everything looked the same and yet there was a different feeling in the air. Something calm and soothing. And then she knew. For the first time in over a century, the streets of Blessing were at peace.

* * * * *

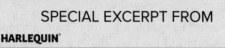
DEMON WOLF
by Bonnie Vanak

The moon hung like a silver nickel in the sky.

Hovering in the woods, Keira waited for lieutenant commander Dale Curtis to arrive home.

Other houses on the street showed signs of life. Lights
flicked on. Children ran in the backyard and then ran inside
as their mothers called them in for supper.

Or their mothers threatened to zap them inside. It was a
paranormal neighborhood, after all.

Hiding in the shadows, she felt a pinch of deep melancholy.
She'd adjusted to loneliness during the infrequent intervals
when the demons gave her brief freedom so she could find
new men for them to torture. Keira had beaten the demons
by refusing to associate with anyone, refusing to give them
new victims.

They'd found one, anyway. This last session had sliced off a
piece of her heart. Dale Curtis had taken her spirit and turned
it inside out. She'd almost killed him. And then, a miracle had
happened.

The commander's friend had arrived in the house where
Curtis was being held prisoner and chanted a cleansing spell

to vanquish evil. The spell had sent the demons temporarily to the netherworld and freed her. But in a few weeks, as they always did, the Centurions would use their bolt hole to this world and break free.

Then the real fun would start. They'd find her, find Curtis and force her to torture the SEAL once more, maybe until he died. The demons would steal all his strength and courage and become solid entities, tasting the pleasures of the flesh once more.

Keira touched the valise containing the silver armband, which enslaved her to the Centurions. When the demons had vanished unexpectedly, the bracelet had unlocked, freeing her from their spell. Only by enslaving herself to another could she escape them.

And lieutenant commander Dale Curtis was the only living person with enough power and courage to destroy the Centurions.

Crouching down, Keira watched the commander's house. Beneath the light of the nearly full moon, she waited and hoped, and wondered if this brave man would be the one to kill her captors and finally set her free.

**Don't miss the exciting conclusion to
DEMON WOLF by Bonnie Vanak,
available only from Harlequin® Nocturne™
in June 2014.**

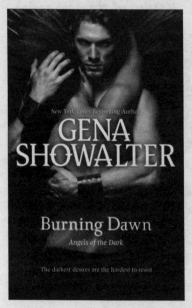